THE GOOD THIEF'S GUIDE TO BERLIN

ALSO BY CHRIS EWAN

THE GOOD THIEF'S GUIDE TO BERLIN

CHRIS EWAN

MINOTAUR BOOKS ☙ NEW YORK

THE GOOD THIEF'S GUIDE TO BERLIN. Copyright © 2013 by Chris Ewan. All rights reserved. Printed in the United States of America. For information, address St. Martin's Press, 175 Fifth Avenue, New York, N.Y. 10010.

www.minotaurbooks.com

Library of Congress Cataloging-in-Publication Data

Ewan, Chris, 1976–
    The good thief's guide to Berlin / Chris Ewan.
        Pages   cm
    ISBN 978-1-250-00297-6 (hardcover)
    ISBN 978-1-250-03113-6 (e-book)
1. Howard, Charlie (Fictitious character)—Fiction.   2. Novelists, English—Fiction.   3. British—Germany—Fiction.   4. Thieves—Fiction.   5. Secret service—Fiction.   I. Title.
    PR6105.W36G67 2013
    823'.92—dc23

                                                                2013009829

Minotaur books may be purchased for educational, business, or promotional use. For information on bulk purchases, please contact Macmillan Corporate and Premium Sales Department at 1-800-221-7945 extension 5442 or write specialmarkets@ macmillan.com.

First Edition: August 2013

10   9   8   7   6   5   4   3   2   1

Dedicated to the memory of Eric Howard, my grandfather
(1918–2004)

THE GOOD THIEF'S GUIDE TO BERLIN

ONE

Rules. They can be a tricky proposition for a thief like me. It's not often I find myself on the right side of the law, and the truth is, I enjoy breaking most rules almost as much as I relish breaking into a stranger's home. But there are certain rules I try very hard to obey. Naturally, the rules I'm talking about are ones I've devised for myself. Over the years, the list has grown pretty long, though it all developed from one simple principle:

Don't get caught.

Want to hear a selection? Well, let's see. I never break into a property that's occupied, unless I absolutely have to. I use my picks wherever possible, because I don't enjoy destroying somebody's door. I don't ransack or leave a mess. If I'm working for myself, I target folks who can afford it, and I rarely steal anything of sentimental value. If I'm hired on commission, I only work for people I can trust or individuals who pay me enough to overcome my concerns. I always wear gloves. I always knock before I enter. I always lock up before I leave.

And, as of right now, I have a new rule to add to my list.

Don't admire the view.

The view was of a rain-drenched street in the Tiergarten. The Tiergarten was in Berlin. And so, for the time being, was I.

To be precise, I was in the third-floor apartment of one of my compatriots, an Englishman by the name of Daniel Wood. Now, I'd never met Mr. Wood, and I didn't plan on making his acquaintance any time soon, but I'd have to compliment him on his housekeeping if I ever did.

The apartment was modern and spotlessly clean. There were two bedrooms, a well-appointed bathroom, a compact kitchen, and a spacious living room. The place had all the telltale signs of a rental home. The walls were painted an inoffensive shade of cream. The furniture was cheap and functional. There were no framed family photographs or ornaments or personal touches whatsoever.

And alas, there was no sign of the very item I'd been hired to steal.

Well, I say "the very item," but the truth is that I had absolutely no idea what I was searching for. My client had neglected to tell me. To be perfectly frank, my client had *refused* to tell me. All of which had made locating my elusive swag a good deal harder than it had any right to be.

"You're really not going to explain?" I'd asked my client, with a noise in the back of my throat that can best be described as a scoff.

"Can't," he said. He was English and comfortably overweight. His speech was well mannered and he had the bearing of a fellow who'd been privately educated at considerable expense. "Top secret, I'm afraid."

"Then how do you expect me to find this mysterious object?"

"You'll recognize it when you see it."

"Will I? How am I supposed to recognize something when I don't know what I'm looking for?"

"Believe me, you'll know. You'll understand the second you set eyes on it. I wouldn't hire you if I didn't think you could work it out."

"Save me the trouble, why don't you? Give me a clue."

"No clues."

"This is insane." And I circled my finger by my temple, just to emphasize how loony he was being. "Seriously. What are we talking about here? Photographs? Jewels? Cash?"

He shook his bloated head.

"Tell me its size, at least?"

He shook his head some more.

"Weight? Color?"

"I told you." He showed me his cushioned palms. "I can't."

"Animal, mineral, vegetable?"

"Listen," he said, "what are you worried about? You get your fee whether or not you find what we're looking for."

"Not the bonus."

He paused. "That's true. Not the bonus. But if you don't find what we're looking for, it'll be after you've broken into all four apartments. And the fee for all four apartments is pretty generous, wouldn't you say?"

I would say. Which explains why I was currently inside the first apartment on my client's list. And his refusal to tell me what exactly I was seeking explained why I was staring out the window in frustration.

I'd been inside the apartment for exactly twenty-nine minutes, making the time 8:08 P.M. precisely when I glanced outside. The place had been oh-so-simple to access. There was an underground car park beneath the apartment complex, and I'd waited until Daniel Wood had driven away in a mid-range sedan before ducking underneath the garage door that was automatically lowering itself behind him. From there, I'd made my way between the lines of abandoned cars, through the scent of cold rubber and diesel, and across the echoing concrete floor to the elevator. The elevator required a swipe card to be operated. But it was also fitted with an override system that accepted a plain, old-fashioned key. And since anything that accepts a key also accepts my picks, it wasn't long before I had the elevator moving, and it took but a trifle longer for me to trick my way through the dead bolt lock on the door to the apartment itself.

Not knowing what I was searching for meant that I'd had to look everywhere I could think of. I didn't know if the loot was flat or round, big or small, light or heavy. But after twenty-nine excruciating minutes, I did know it wasn't in the apartment. I'd hunted inside cupboards. Behind cupboards. Above and under furniture. I'd rifled through drawers. I'd rooted through the freezer. I'd delved around inside the washing machine. In short, I'd used all my experience and applied every single trick I could think of and found absolutely nothing of consequence.

So I was feeling thoroughly vexed, and normally when I get that way, I like to smoke as I stare out a window. I do it a lot when I'm writing one of my mystery novels if I happen to be blocked on a problem scene or stumped by a tangled plot thread (which happens more often than I'd care to admit). But one of my rules was never to smoke inside an apartment I'd broken into for fear of giving myself away, so tonight I was reduced to staring out the living room window without a cigarette to ease my nerves.

It was dark outside and I could see my reflection in the rain-splattered glass. The rain was falling in sheets. It was blowing sideways in the stiff gusts of wind funneling down Kirchstrasse from the swollen river Spree toward the red-brick church at the opposite end of the street. It was bouncing off the lines of parked cars, the limbs of the evenly spaced plane trees, and the canvas canopies above the pavement cafés and bars. It was catching the glare from the street lamps. Hammering against the leaf-blown tarmac. Gurgling in the drains.

I asked myself if it would thunder and I honestly couldn't tell. But it was going to be a long, wet night. A miserable, fruitless night, if the weather and my mood were anything to go by. And to my considerable dismay, it was about to get an awful lot worse.

Because as I scanned the windows of the apartment building facing my own, I saw something I really wished I hadn't. And it left me with a dilemma I honestly could have done without.

TWO

There was a Venetian blind in the window I was looking at. The blind was all the way down but the slats were open and there was a light on inside the apartment. If only the blind had been closed, it would have saved me a whole heap of trouble. But it wasn't, and though my view was impeded by the darkness and the rain and the horizontal wooden slats, I could see what was going on quite clearly.

The first thing I saw was a woman. It was her silhouette that snagged my attention. She had what you might call an hourglass figure. If the circumstances had been different, I would have liked to have spent an hour appreciating it. She had plenty of curves, and all of them good. They were emphasized by the tight white sweater and black skirt she had on. Her hair was blond and pulled into a ponytail. The ponytail exposed her neck and her delicate throat. I could tell her neck was delicate because somebody was in the process of crushing it.

The somebody with the inappropriate grip had their back to me, but he was clearly a man. He was wearing a black jacket or coat, and the sleeves had ridden up on his forearms from where he'd thrust out his hands. He was very tall. The woman wasn't short but the man towered over her. He had neat, dark hair and prominent ears. His shoulders were wide. The muscles in his back and arms were bunched and shaking. He was putting a lot of effort into throttling the girl.

I pressed my face and gloved hand against the window and craned my neck to look down into the street. Wasn't anyone else seeing this?

It didn't seem so. One young couple was hurrying along beneath an umbrella, but they were huddled together with their eyes fixed on the pavement, dodging puddles and drifts of autumn leaves. A cream Mercedes taxi crawled toward me from the direction of the church. The driver was peering out through his windscreen wipers at the doorways on my side of the street. He was facing the wrong way.

I forced myself to look back at the blonde. I could barely glimpse her face from behind her attacker, but it was clear that she was fighting hard. Her hands were a fast blur, pummeling the man's arms and torso. It wasn't doing her much good. He was a determined character, and he seemed intent on squeezing the life from her. She clawed at his hands and tried to pry them away.

I reached for the phone.

The phone was fixed to the wall beside the kitchen. It had a spiral, extendable cord. I lifted it down from the hook and returned to the window and hesitated for just a fraction of a second.

Reprehensible, I know, but I didn't want to get involved. But then, what choice did I have?

I thought about opening the window and yelling across the street, but I doubted the man would hear me through the wind and the rain and the glazing, and I wasn't crazy about drawing attention to myself in the middle of a break-in.

I could try and intervene directly, I supposed. But it would take

7

me time. I'd have to cross the street and pick my way inside the building and find the right apartment. And even if I hammered on the door, there was no telling if the guy would take a break from the murder he was engaged in to come and answer my knock. And all right, I could use my picks to let myself in, but did I really want to confront a murderer?

Nope. Not a chance.

So that left me with the phone, but it wasn't a perfect solution, either. If I'd been in the UK, I could have punched 141 before I dialed, in the hope the police couldn't trace the call. If I was in the U.S., I could have tried *67. But I didn't know the equivalent code in Germany, and I doubted it would work with the police in any event.

I stared at the phone. I stared at the girl.

I shook my head and cursed myself for looking out through the window in the first place, and then I jabbed 110 with my finger and raised the receiver to my ear. A burr. A click. A long, flat note. Then the sharp, clipped voice of a woman repeating an efficient, well rehearsed phrase.

Now, my German's not bad, but it's a long way from proficient, and this wasn't the time to dither over the vocabulary for "stran-gled" or to mangle my directions. So I babbled at her in English and I kept babbling until it seemed that she'd understood me, and then I slammed down the receiver, hung the phone back on the wall, and peeked outside one last time.

The girl was on her knees, her back arched, her head shaking loosely in the man's fierce grip. The man was crouching over her. His arms were slanted down at an angle, elbows locked. I could see the side of his face but not in any detail. The slatted blind and the rain distorted his features. He was Caucasian. He was clean-shaven. Apart from his considerable height and his protruding ears, he was just about as unremarkable as it's possible to get.

It was time for me to leave. I hadn't found what I didn't know I was looking for, and I don't tend to hang around when the police have been called, least of all when I've summoned them myself.

Turning my back on the window, I paced across to the door and pressed my ear to the wood. I listened for any sounds above the pounding of the rain and the desperate yammering of my damn stupid conscience, and then I turned the handle and poked my head into the corridor. It was deserted and the elevator doors were beckoning to me. I locked the apartment behind myself and left the elevator doors to beckon to somebody else, and then I followed the corridor as far as the main stairwell, hurried down to the glass door at the front of the apartment building, turned up the collar of my mackintosh and stepped out into the rain.

Cold water beat against my head and trickled through my hair and inside my ears and down my neck. It danced on the pavement and wet my shoes and socks and trousers. I clenched my coat tight around me and glanced up at the offending window. It had been one floor below me. Now it was two floors above. The light was still on but the blind had been closed. I couldn't see inside anymore, and I thought I knew why. The tall guy must have finished his nasty work. He was beginning to think about cleaning up after himself and he didn't want anyone spying on him while he did it.

I yanked off the plastic disposable gloves I was wearing, stuffed my hands inside my pockets, hunched my shoulders and walked away up the street. And all the time I was asking myself, why me? Why did I have to look out the window? Why had I taken on this crazy assignment in the first place? And what else could possibly go wrong?

THREE

The crazy assignment had come my way two days before, on a Sunday evening. I'd been minding my own business, inside my own apartment, when my telephone had started to ring. I'd jumped up from my writing desk and answered right away.

That was my first mistake.

"Ah, *très bien*," said a voice on the end of the line. "Charlie, you are home. *Ça va?*"

I had no difficulty recognizing my caller. It was my fence, Pierre, telephoning me from Paris. Pierre's not his real name, by the way—I have no idea what his real name happens to be—but since he revels in clichéd French dialogue, it's always struck me as a perfectly appropriate thing to call him.

"I'm good, Pierre. And you?"

"Formidable," he said. *"Mais,* I am calling for business. There is a man who wishes to meet with you."

"I see."

"He wishes to meet with you right away."

Small mercies, I guess, that he hadn't said, *"tout de suite."*

10

I shot a guilty look toward my writing desk. My laptop and my thesaurus and my notebooks were there, arranged beneath my charred and battered first edition of Dashiell Hammett's *The Maltese Falcon*. I kept the *Falcon* stored inside an airtight picture frame, and it was supposed to inspire my writing and drive me on. It always had in the past, and as a result, it had assumed a special importance to me. But following a recent fiery mishap in Venice, it seemed to have lost some of its magic. Or rather, I'd lost some of my momentum. Because the awful truth was that I hadn't made much progress with my latest mystery novel, and the worst part of all was that I had only myself to blame.

You see, since coming to Berlin, I'd been engaged in a veritable spree of larceny and misappropriation. It had been a mighty busy and a mighty rewarding spell. But it hadn't been at all good for my word count and it had been even worse for my deadline. The book was supposed to be finished inside eight weeks. I already knew that couldn't possibly happen, and I had a suspicion that Pierre's call was only going to make things worse.

"What do you mean by right away?" I asked.

"I mean this very minute. There is a park outside your building, *oui*?"

It wasn't exactly a park, but I knew what he meant. I lived in the former eastern district of Prenzlauer Berg, in a second-floor apartment in a converted town house that overlooked a leafy recreational ground known as Kollwitzplatz.

Kollwitzplatz had been at the heart of the gentrification that swept the neighborhood in the decades since the Berlin Wall came down. The grand terraced buildings that surrounded the triangular wedge of grassland were painted in appealing pastel shades, and since the first wave of artists and poets and alternative-lifestyle types had moved on, most of the inhabitants were young professionals with well-paying jobs. Rent was high, which was one reason for my recent run of lucrative burglaries. There were other reasons, too. Greed. Thrill-seeking. The intellectual and physical challenge of breaking in somewhere that was difficult to access. Oh, and of course, going out on the prowl was a terrific way to avoid tussling with my new book.

"There is a man waiting for you at the Ping-Pong table," Pierre said. "Do you see him?"

I set the phone down and moved across to my window and peered out at the darkened view below. There were two table-tennis tables next to a children's play area in the point of the triangle nearest to my apartment. True to Pierre's words, a man was loitering beside them in the hazy light of a period street lamp.

The man was somewhat short and somewhat tubby. He had a head of thick, curly hair, brownish-blond in color, and a rounded face with swollen cheeks. He wore a houndstooth overcoat, dark trousers, and polished brogues. He was holding a red table-tennis paddle in each hand and swinging his arms around aimlessly, as if signaling for a kamikaze pilot to come in to land.

I returned to the telephone. "I see him," I said. "What does he want?"

"He wishes to hire you."

"Can I trust him?"

"But of course. This is why I am calling. You will recognize him, perhaps? He is the brother of a mutual friend of ours."

"He is? Who?"

"Charlie, I will let him explain. It is a surprise, *oui*? But before I say *au revoir*, may I ask if the beautiful Victoria is with you now?"

I thought about pressing Pierre for an explanation. I don't like surprises. Never have. Especially where clients are concerned. But then again, I don't enjoy staring at the flickering screen of my laptop for hours on end, fretting about words and ideas that stubbornly refuse to come. And since a diversion from my current funk wasn't entirely unwelcome, I decided to answer his question instead of insisting on a response to my own.

"Victoria arrived back from Frankfurt yesterday," I said.

"Ah, *mon cher*. I told this man she may come with you. You'll kiss her from me?"

"Absolutely," I told him.

But that would have been my second mistake. And I wasn't about to make it anytime soon.

After hanging up the phone, I walked along the corridor and knocked on the door to my spare bedroom. There was no answer. I knocked again, then nudged the door open and counted to five before poking my head inside.

"Hey, Charlie. What's up?"

Victoria was talking very loudly. She was talking that way because she was wearing a pair of earphones and listening to some music on her mobile phone. She was sprawled on the bed in the middle of the room and a ring binder was open on her lap. The binder was jammed with papers and she was scribbling on them with a Biro.

I winced and patted the air, and she plucked the earphones from her ears and conjured a wonky grin.

Wham. I wished she hadn't done it. That particular grin, combined with the way she was looking up at me from beneath half-lidded eyes, her nut-brown hair falling across her face just so, had lately developed the power to throw me completely off balance.

"Sorry," she said. "What's up?"

"Have to go out," I mumbled.

"Out?" She consulted her wristwatch. "But I thought we had dinner plans?"

"We do. Pierre was just on the phone. He wants me to meet someone and I thought you might like to come along with me first."

13

She tipped her head onto her shoulder and squinted at me. "Does this someone want you to steal something?"

"Looks that way."

"Well then . . ." She beamed. "Why didn't you just say so?"

Victoria's my literary agent. She's also my closest friend. Outside of Pierre and a few shady characters I've had the dubious pleasure of meeting over the years, she's the only person who knows about my hush-hush sideline as a professional thief. Perhaps a little worryingly, she tends to find my exploits as a burglar a good deal more interesting than my novels. At least, that had always been the case, until around six months ago, when I'd completed a manuscript that had turned my entire world upside down.

The Venetian Cat was something of a departure for me. It was still a crime novel and it was still about a burglar, but it was my first book that didn't feature the character of Michael Faulks. This time around, my protagonist had been based on a stunning female cat burglar I'd had the misfortune to meet in Venice. The book was a calculated attempt to be more commercial. It was filled with over-the-top scenes, high-stakes action, and larger-than-life characters. None of the sentences had more than eight words in them. None of the words had more than three syllables. There was plenty of violence, oodles of sex, and countless implausible plot lines. In short, it was trash, but it was trash that had developed a real buzz of excitement since a major UK publisher had signed me up to write a three-book trilogy with quite an eye-watering advance.

The book and the buzz were the reason Victoria was visiting me in Berlin. For one thing, she wanted to know how the second book in the series was coming along (it wasn't). And for another, she'd dropped by on her way back from the Frankfurt Book Fair, where she'd been attempting to drum up some international interest in my work. Perhaps the most unsettling thing of all was that she appeared to have succeeded.

My sudden success, after years of mediocre sales and snide reviews, had come as a surprise to us both. But it was nowhere near as shocking as my recent discovery that I was finding Victoria oddly alluring. Worse still, I had it on good authority (namely, her father, Alfred) that she felt the same way about me. I was beginning to fear that these strange new emotions I was experiencing were more than a passing fad. And whenever my pulse raced in her company or her wonky smile caused me to lose all sense of balance, I could hear a small, childish voice inside my head, taunting me with the ridiculous notion that I *lurved* her.

So these were dangerous times, and as fortune would have it, I could think of few better distractions than a clandestine meeting with a complete stranger at an outdoor Ping-Pong table in the middle of old Berlin.

The stranger grinned boyishly as he saw us approaching from the shadows, then wafted a table-tennis paddle through the air with a fast swish.

"Good, good," he said. "Knew you'd come. Nathan told me you wouldn't let me down."

"Nathan?"

"Nathan Farmer. My elder brother."

And suddenly I understood Pierre's connection to this man. "Our mutual friend," as Pierre had so mischievously referred to Nathan, was a guy capable of forcing Pierre to do pretty much anything he desired, including, apparently, obliging me to meet with his younger sibling to discuss a potential assignment. Nathan's hold over Pierre was the result of an unfortunate set of circumstances that had involved us both in Paris some years ago now. I was beginning to fear that I might have cause to regret it.

My temples started to tingle. My pulse was up and I was aware of a peculiar buzzing in my ears. I possess a kind of sixth sense where danger is concerned, and right now an alarm was ringing inside my head with all the subtlety of a fire bell.

"He sends his regards from Paris," the man added. "Here, I'm Freddy."

He switched both paddles to his left hand and extended his right to shake. Aside from his attitude and his accent, which were a little pompous and fairly reeked of the British upper class, he didn't look at all like his brother. He was short, not tall. Dumpy, not thin. Unkempt and a little knocked about the edges, instead of being immaculately tailored and impeccably groomed. He was younger, too, by at least ten years, and he lacked his brother's air of calm authority. He seemed unsure of himself. Awkward and fidgety. Almost as if he was embarrassed by the comparisons he must have known we were making.

"Charlie Howard," I said, and shook his hand.

His grip was sudden and eager. So was the way he transferred his attention to my companion. "And am I right in thinking this delightful creature is your friend Victoria?" Freddy straightened his shoulders and puffed out his ample chest.

I swallowed my irritation and explained that my agent was indeed the creature in question.

"Jolly good. Nathan assures me I can trust both of you." Ah, if only the feeling was mutual, I thought to myself, as Freddy summoned a dinky bow for Victoria's benefit. "But my goodness," he said, "only a few hours ago I never would have believed that burglars have agents. Especially such delightful ones."

Victoria did her best to look demure. Or perhaps she was genuinely flattered. She offered him her hand. The goof ducked his head and kissed it.

"One has to move with the times, Mr. Farmer," Victoria said. Her hand was still gripped in Freddy's. He took his own sweet time releasing it. "How is your brother?"

"He's incredibly well."

I didn't doubt it. Nathan Farmer was one of the shrewdest customers I'd ever crossed picks with. His job description and his remit were somewhat fluid, but I tended to think of him as a fixer. He was somebody that well-heeled clients and discerning institutions across Europe could call on for help if they ever found themselves in the kind of trouble where police involvement might be, shall we say, *undesirable*. Above all else, he was a results man, and for his more law-abiding clients, some of his methods were best left unmentioned. I was beginning to suspect his brother was in the same racket.

"What is it you want to talk to me about, Mr. Farmer?"

"Freddy, please," he said. "And here, do take a paddle." He forced a table-tennis bat on me, then cast a suspicious glance over his shoulder toward a patch of gloopy blackness. "Would you care for a game? I think it might afford us a useful cover."

"A cover?"

He began to remove his overcoat. "Oh, I don't think it would do for us to be seen talking like this without some kind of explanation. Though I fear I must warn you, I've become quite the Ping-Pong fiend since I've lived in Berlin."

FOUR

Freddy wasn't kidding. He laid down his coat on a nearby bench, rolled up his shirtsleeves, and treated me to a lesson in sporting humiliation. He danced and he jinked and he huddled intensely around his end of the table, his brow knotted in fierce concentration, his stubby arm describing a precise, efficient arc that sent the little white ball pinging and ponging toward me at an array of alarming angles and speeds. My only solace was that we weren't keeping score.

"Been honing my game for eighteen months now," Freddy told me, between points. His breath was clouding in the cool night air and his face was flushed. "There are hundreds of these tables throughout the eastern side of the city. It's something we have the good old GDR to thank for."

It wasn't hard to believe. The table we were playing on was sturdy and functional in design, and like a lot of the Soviet-era architecture, it was formed out of concrete. The legs were concrete. The tabletop was concrete. The net, for variety, was made from a gridded strip of metal that glinted in the electric lamplight. Oh, and the whole thing was covered in a colorful array of graffiti. Layer upon layer of names and slogans and profanities and symbols, almost as if we were playing on a horizontal slab of the Berlin Wall.

Graffiti could be found most places in Berlin, and there was plenty of the stuff surrounding us now. It had been sprayed on tree trunks, on litter bins, on benches, and on the green metal pissoir just outside the perimeter railings of the *Platz*. It covered every square inch of the spare table-tennis table where Victoria was perched, her chin tucked down inside the collar of her red down jacket, her hands buried in her pockets and her legs dangling in the murky shadows beneath. She seemed to be enjoying the way Freddy was thrashing me. I was pretty sure she was smirking every time I had to turn my back and wander off to collect the silly little ball from whichever area of unlit pea gravel Freddy had dispatched it to.

"So," I said, on one of my many treks back to the table, "do you think we might talk now?"

I swatted the ball toward him and Freddy looped it back, high and gentle. I almost lost it in the sodium glare.

"Let's talk *and* play," he said. "We'll rally."

"Don't you think that might be a bit distracting?" I asked, blinking hard and returning the ball on a similar, if less certain, trajectory. I'm not very good at Ping-Pong. Having two arthritic fingers on my right hand makes holding the bat a real challenge.

"Not at all. I daresay we can build up a good rhythm."

Oh, we had a rhythm, all right. The ball papped and popped between us. It blipped and it bopped. And as it arced to and fro, Freddy finally began to explain himself.

"I work for a company," he said, dispatching a sliced forehand. "Here in Berlin. And in the last few days, something was stolen from the office of our head man."

I mirrored his shot with a sliced forehand of my own. It was a mistake. The arthritic knuckles on my middle and fourth fingers

19

felt like they might pop. "What was stolen?" I asked, through gritted teeth.

"We'll come to that." His eyes were wide open in concentration. His mouth was a gaping void. I would have loved to smash the ball deep inside it. "The important thing is that we've narrowed down the suspects to four employees. They all had access to the office in question during the time the theft must have occurred."

"Just four?" Victoria asked, her head swiveling from side to side as she tracked the ball's movement.

"That's the good news," Freddy said. He was panting like a dog by now. Steam was rising from his body and he was perspiring heavily. His shirt was marked by two dark half-moons of sweat beneath his armpits.

"And the bad news?" I asked.

"The bad news is that we need the item retrieved. Quite urgently." He moved sideways to use his backhand. "But confidentiality concerns mean we don't wish to involve the police, and we can't risk alerting the culprit that we're on to him—a factor that prevents us from seeking a solution via the internal procedures or more predictable options available to us. Our problem has arisen from *inside* our organization. We need help from *outside*. Specialized help. Unconventional help."

"Which is where I come in, I presume."

"Quite so. We'd like you to reclaim the item and identify the guilty party."

"Reclaim it?"

"By searching the homes of each of the four suspects."

"Hmm," I said, and patted the ball back to him. "How do you know that whoever took this thing is still holding on to it?"

His feet scuffled in the dirt as he adjusted his stance to reach my somewhat wayward shot. "As I said, it's sensitive. If the item had passed into the wrong hands, we'd have heard about it by now."

20

"You're certain that it's been stolen? It couldn't have been borrowed, say?"

"No. Nobody had any right to take this item. And it definitely couldn't have been misplaced."

"What makes you think the thief is keeping it in his home?"

"It's an assumption, though you may find evidence to suggest otherwise."

"I'm not a big fan of assumptions."

"I can understand that," Freddy told me. "But I think you may appreciate how our proposal is structured."

He hung his tongue out of his mouth as he sent an ambitious shot curving way out over the side of the table. The ball started to curve back in, but not nearly enough. It cannoned off the table edge and skittered away beyond the cone of lamplight to settle among the blackened roots of the graffiti-riddled tree.

I went and hunted for the ball, grumbling sourly to myself, and when I finally found it, I wrapped it in my fist. I was through with his silly game—both of them. I leaned forward over the table, arms straight, my bat in one hand, the ball in the other. The graffiti-smeared concrete was cold against my knuckles.

"Enough fooling around," I said. "What exactly is your proposal?"

Freddy pouted, very much like a kid who wanted his ball back from a dreaded neighbor but was too afraid to ask.

"Very well," he said. "There's a company function this coming Tuesday night. Our chief exec is receiving an important dignitary at nine o'clock, and all four employees will be on duty at our headquarters from eight P.M. to help with preparations and, in some cases, to attend as guests. We want you to search each of their homes, in the order of our choosing. We'll pay you for every place you search until you find the item we're looking for."

I glanced across at Victoria. She was chewing her lip in thought.

"How much?" she asked. "For each place, I mean."

"Two thousand euros."

I felt myself rock back a little. It sounded like a pretty good deal to me. A potential fee of eight thousand euros was a handsome return for one night's work. But there was a downside, too.

"What if I find this secret object in the first apartment?" I asked. "I'll only receive one installment."

"Thought you'd spot that," Freddy said. "So we're offering you a bonus—a finder's fee, if you will. Five thousand euros for retrieving the package. It's a generous deal, I think you'll agree."

I was certainly inclined to—despite my earlier misgivings, money tends to have a soothing effect on me—but Victoria spoke up before I had the opportunity.

"I'm not comfortable with this," she said, wagging a finger at Freddy. "Think about it. With every theft Charlie carries out for you, his chances of being caught increase. One burglary in a night might be okay. But four separate burglaries—particularly when he doesn't know the locations involved and you haven't said just yet what he's meant to be searching for—well, that's a different scenario entirely. So a fair deal, in my opinion, would include a sliding fee."

"A sliding fee?" Freddy repeated.

"That's right," Victoria said. "But nothing too exploitative. Let's say an extra five hundred euros for each subsequent burglary Charlie carries out after he knocks over location one. So that's two thousand for the first place, like you suggested. Then two thousand five hundred, three thousand, and three thousand five hundred for locations two, three, and four."

Freddy paused. His chubby face clouded over. I daresay I was wearing a similar expression. I was tussling with the math in my head. Unless I was very much mistaken, Victoria's suggestion would give me a total of eleven thousand euros for all four burglaries. An increase of three thousand on what I'd originally been offered. Stack that together with the bonus Freddy had mentioned and I'd have a very respectable sum indeed.

I was still checking my calculations when Freddy surprised me by shuffling toward Victoria and offering her his hand.

"Deal," he said.

They shook on it, and then Victoria winked at me and smiled her wonky smile.

I tried not to let it distract me. I needed to concentrate. Arithmetic has never been my greatest talent, and it took me a long moment to appreciate why Victoria appeared quite so smug. Then I got it. Our agent-author agreement gives her twenty percent of any foreign deals she negotiates on my behalf, and I had the distinct impression she intended to claim her share of this particular transaction. Twenty percent of eleven thousand was, oh, just over two thousand euros. And that would put my own fee almost back to where it had started.

I raised my hand and scratched the side of my face with the pitted rubber of my table-tennis bat. I was holding the bat in a modified pencil grip and my fingers were spread in a conspicuous *V*. Victoria seemed to grasp my point.

"Don't be too hasty," I said to Freddy. He'd collected his overcoat from the bench and was threading his stubby arms through the sleeves. "You still haven't told me yet what it is you'd like me to steal."

And that was when Freddy sucked air through his teeth, and looked at me apologetically, and, well, you'll recall just how unsatisfactorily that part of our conversation had evolved.

"Please try to understand," he said, once he'd finished explaining why he couldn't possibly tell me what it was he was hoping I'd find. "This situation is very troubling for our company. For our chief exec in particular. If for any reason you fail in your assignment, we couldn't possibly afford to have the information get into the public domain."

"Charming," I said. "You don't trust me."

He smiled awkwardly. "Forgive me, Charlie, but we're hiring you precisely because you're a thief. Surely you can understand a little hesitancy on our part?"

He dropped his table-tennis paddle into one coat pocket and removed a mobile telephone from another.

"Give me your number," he said, "and I'll pass on all the information you'll require as and when you'll need it. I'll start by texting you the first address and the identity of suspect number one."

"No you won't," I told him. "I don't have a mobile."

Freddy reared backward, as if I was certifiable.

"No mobile? But how can you possibly—"

"Don't exhaust yourself," Victoria said, and hopped off the table-tennis table. "I've nagged him about this enough times to know he's not going to change."

"They're dreadful contraptions," I explained. "One never knows when they might go off."

"One could always switch them to silent." Victoria fished around in the back of her jeans and removed her own phone. "Here, I'll give you my number," she told Freddy. "You can text the information to me and I'll pass it along."

Freddy seemed more than pleased with her suggestion. He rushed to input Victoria's number into his mobile, and I shifted my weight between my feet as the dinky gadget blipped and beeped and shone brightly in the darkness. Then he jabbed it with his thumb and wafted it in Victoria's general direction, and a moment later Victoria's phone lit up and issued a beep of its own.

"Got it," she said.

"Excellent. And you'll text me once Charlie has searched the first apartment?"

"Whether or not he finds the item," she confirmed.

"Marvelous." Freddy beamed at Victoria and dug his hand inside

24

the chest pocket of his overcoat. I heard the telltale rustle of stiff paper and watched him pass Victoria a thick white envelope. "Here's two thousand to start you off. As a gesture of our goodwill." He began to back away with a deft little bow, like a besotted courtier in some sappy costume drama. "It's been an absolute delight meeting you."

"Lovely to meet you, too," Victoria replied, in a voice that sounded worryingly sincere.

"Er, there is something else before you go," I told Freddy, raising my voice to snap him out of the spell he seemed to be under. "Who exactly *is* your employer, if you don't mind my asking? Or is that something you can't trust me with, either?"

"Oh, I can tell you now, I suppose." He ambled toward me and I returned his bat and ball to him. "The truth, Charlie, is that I work for the British embassy in Berlin."

A gust of air escaped my lips. "The British embassy? But wouldn't that make your chief exec—"

"The ambassador? Yes, Charlie, I'm rather afraid it would."

FIVE

So I was stealing on behalf of Her Majesty's Government. And I was royally screwed. The first apartment on Freddy's list had been worse than a dud. It had offered me a choice view of a murder. A murder I'd been drawn into. And so far as bad omens went, I didn't think they could get much worse.

The atmosphere in the nearby café-bar where Victoria was waiting for me certainly didn't help. The place was as quiet as a morgue. I guessed the rain had kept people away. Either that or the young guy behind the bar needed a radical new business plan. He was talking in a relaxed, companionable way to his only other customer—a woman who was sitting on a high stool at the counter. The way she was leaning forward and interacting with the guy made me think they were a couple.

The guy looked up and frowned as I stood dripping in the doorway, the wind and the rain sweeping in from behind me. I closed the door against the breeze, then inclined my head toward Victoria, and he curled his lip and returned to his conversation.

Victoria was sitting at a table beside the rain-lashed window, staring at the lighted screen of her mobile phone. She had two drinks in front of her. A red *Berliner Weisse mit Schuss* for her—a kind of light beer with raspberry syrup, served in a shallow glass with two straws—and a sparkling mineral water for me. I peeled off my sodden mackintosh and hung it on a nearby stand, being careful to make sure my collection of picks and probes didn't fall out onto the floor. Then I smoothed my wet hair away from my forehead, dried my hands on my trouser legs, and dropped into a chair across from Victoria.

"You're an idiot," she said, without looking up at me.

She was right. I *was* an idiot. I should have been long gone by now. Far away from the neighborhood. But I got the impression she was talking about something altogether different, and I didn't have the energy for it.

I glanced outside through the sign that had been etched into the window glass. It had to be almost five minutes since I'd called the emergency services. Where were they?

I fumbled in my jeans pocket for my cigarette pack and flipped back the soggy lid with shaking hands. I stabbed a cigarette into the corner of my mouth, struck a flame from the book of matches in the ashtray on our table, and sucked hard.

"Did you hear me?" Victoria asked, still focused on her mobile. "I said that you're an idiot."

"I heard you," I told her, and vented a weary lungful of smoke. "And believe me, I'm not in a position to argue."

I took a sip from my water. Another rule. *Don't drink when you're on the job.* But the rule didn't account for my nerves being on edge, so I scooped Victoria's beer toward me.

"Hey!"

I slurped on one of the straws. Then I pulled a face. The beer was sour and the raspberry syrup was sweet. It wasn't a combination that worked for me.

I nudged the glass away, drew raggedly on my cigarette, and looked out above the limbs of a nearby tree toward the offending apartment window. The closed blind was still illuminated from behind. I drummed my nails on the scarred wooden tabletop. It didn't help in the slightest.

"Don't you want to know why you're an idiot?" Victoria asked me.

I checked my watch. Time was ticking on.

"Charlie." Victoria kicked my shin under the table. "Will you pay attention to me?"

I coaxed some more fumes from my cigarette and scowled at her over the lit embers. I was still scowling when I heard the first distant strains of a siren. I pricked up my ears and returned my attention to the dark and rainy street. The siren grew louder. It drew closer. I could feel Victoria looking pointedly at me. I raised my clammy palm, hushing her before she began. There was more than one siren. I was sure of it now. The keening was dissonant and out of time. It merged into one long wail.

Victoria lowered her phone. She turned in her seat and stared out through the window, tracking my gaze.

"What's happening?" she asked, white-faced. "Did somebody see you?"

"More like the other way around," I told her. "And keep your voice down, can't you?"

The young guy behind the counter and the woman had stopped talking. They'd turned their heads in the direction of the sirens.

Victoria huddled over the table toward me. "Are they coming here for you?" she asked, in a strained voice.

"Nope," I whispered back. "I'm the one who called them."

"You? Are you mad?"

I shrugged. "Like you said, I'm an idiot."

I stubbed out my cigarette as the vehicles the sirens were attached to careened around the corner at the end of the street. The

28

shrieking din made me shudder. Occupational hazard. Emergency sirens always have that effect on me.

There were two cars and a van. The cars were silver hatchbacks with green flashes along the side and blue lights on top. The word *Polizei* was branded on them. The van was bright orange, with tinted windows. It was an ambulance. Blue bulbs popped and flashed and twirled on its roof.

The vehicles slewed to a halt in the middle of the slickened road. Doors opened. Men and women emerged into the rain. The police were wearing blue uniforms and peaked caps, their trousers tucked into heavy black boots. The ambulance crew sported red jumpsuits with reflective strips. There were two of them and they ran around to the rear of the van and hauled open the cargo doors. They removed a stretcher on collapsible legs and wheels, and hurried away through the puddles in the direction of the apartment building.

But I wasn't focused on them. I was looking up through the rain and the pulsing blue lights at the second-floor window. The light behind the blind had gone out. The guy must have heard the sirens approaching. He must have guessed they were coming for him.

"Will you please tell me what's going on?" Victoria hissed.

I hesitated. The guy from the bar and his companion had moved across to stand by the door. They were paying close attention to events out on the street, but I was pretty sure the noise of the wind and the rain would mask anything I might say.

I watched the police and the ambulance crew hurry inside the building, and then I spoke to Victoria from the corner of my mouth, my voice hushed, eyes fixed on the darkened apartment window. I gave her the short version. It was enough to bring her up to speed.

"My God," she cried, when I was finished. "Do you really think she's dead?"

"I don't know, Vic. I hope not."

But really, I didn't believe that she had a chance. How long could it take to strangle a person? Two, maybe three minutes? Perhaps a lot less. The guy had gotten started before I'd even spotted them. And then there was the delay while I made the call. The wait for the emergency services to arrive.

"You did the right thing," Victoria assured me.

I didn't say anything to that. Part of me wished that I was a better person. That I'd intervened directly. And part of me wished that I was a lot more ruthless. By contacting the police, I'd compromised myself *and* my assignment.

"Did you find what Freddy was looking for?" Victoria asked.

I shook my head and fired up another cigarette. I would have felt a lot better if I'd found the mysterious item. Yes, it would have meant less money for me, but less trouble, too. If the police traced my call, they'd be likely to contact Daniel Wood, because they'd assume that he was their witness. And if I'd only discovered the damn secret object in his apartment, then he might have guessed why somebody had been inside and there was an outside chance that he'd elect to keep his mouth shut about my visit. Now, though, there was nothing to stop him from talking to them. There was a risk that the police would begin to question who could have made the call. Witnesses might come forward. It could be that someone had seen me loitering near the building. It could be that my description would be circulated.

I didn't like it. It was messy. And messy was never good, particularly when it came at the beginning of what had the potential to be a long night of larceny.

My cigarette wasn't helping. I wasn't sure what would. Part of me wanted to leave the bar and get moving to the next target on Freddy's list. But I also wanted to know if the woman was alive or dead. I wanted to know that her attacker had been caught. And I didn't imagine it would be wise to leave the bar right away. The young guy and his companion might become suspicious of me.

"What do we do?" Victoria asked.

30

"We wait," I told her. "And meantime, you can text Freddy. Ask him for the next address."

We didn't wait long. After a couple of minutes, the light came on behind the blind in the apartment. Five minutes after that, the light went off again and the first police officer emerged onto the street. She was joined by a short, balding chap in a brown jumpsuit. The guy was twirling a set of keys in his hand. I guessed he was some kind of live-in janitor and that he must have helped the police access the apartment.

I ground my cigarette into the ashtray as the ambulance crew appeared. But something was wrong. The two paramedics weren't carrying a loaded stretcher. And they weren't in a hurry. They exchanged words with the police officer and the janitor. There was a lot of shrugging and eye-rolling and pouting. They all looked a little disconsolate. A little resigned and world-weary. Then the ambulance crew waved a jaded farewell and ducked their heads and ran out through the rain to return the empty stretcher to the back of the ambulance. They shut the cargo doors and climbed up into the cab and killed the blue emergency lights. The driver swung the van around and drove away up the road at a leisurely pace.

"I don't get it," Victoria said.

"Me, either."

The rest of the police officers emerged from the building and congregated with the janitor in a knot by the front door, sheltering from the rain. The rain hadn't let up at all. It was pounding down hard, hammering on the police cars and the drenched tarmac, blasting against the plate glass of the bar window.

"Charlie, there are four police officers in that doorway."

"I can count, Vic."

"Only four showed up."

"I know."

"So who's up there with the killer? Who's with the victim?"

31

Nobody, apparently. And things were about to get even worse. Three of the officers split away and ran through the rain to the police cars. They cut the emergency lights, and one of the units drove off in the same direction as the ambulance. The other car pulled into a parking space farther up the street. Meanwhile, the lone female officer in the doorway of the apartment building was using the radio clipped to her uniform, her mouth lowered to the speaker. The janitor twirled his keys alongside her. Then he gestured with his thumb and disappeared into the apartment building.

Inside the bar, the young guy and the woman returned to the counter.

"They didn't find her," I said, as if I couldn't quite believe my eyes. "They can't have."

"Maybe they went to the wrong apartment?"

"No." I shook my head. "The light went on in the right window."

I looked at the darkened window once more. It gave nothing away. No hint of understanding. I didn't like it. Not even a little bit. A sick, grievous feeling was coiling inside my gut. It was the sensation of knowing that something bad had happened and being powerless to do anything about it.

I could feel an itch in my fingers. The itch was telling me to go and check for myself. To walk confidently across the street and breeze right inside the apartment building, past the sheltering police officer. I wanted to satisfy my curiosity. Perhaps even right a terrible wrong.

Victoria's mobile emitted a high-pitched beep. She consulted the screen, then showed it to me.

"Message from Freddy," she said. "The next address and the name of suspect two."

I read the information for myself. Absorbed it. Nodded to Victoria. Neither of us mentioned how Freddy had added a couple of kisses to the end of his text.

"Get your stuff together," I said. "We're leaving."

SIX

Back into my cold, wet mackintosh. Back into the slanted rain and the driving wind. Heavy raindrops tapped me on my head and shoulders, like a hundred tiny fingers trying to get my attention. My attention was elsewhere. It was focused on the unlit window. It was penetrating the glass and prying open the closed Venetian slats and taking a good look around inside the murder apartment.

I could picture the blonde. She was just as shapely as before, but she was lying on her side on the floor of a small back bedroom. She looked like she'd been dropped there from a great height. Her legs and arms were splayed, her hands were unfurled, and her throat was badly swollen. Her skin was discolored, mottled with bruising and the livid imprints of hands and fingers and thumbs. Her mouth was wide open, her lips peeled back over gums and teeth.

Behind her, the tall, faceless killer had his ear pressed to the closed door of the bedroom. He was listening very hard for any sign that the police might return. Would he try to get away? Did he plan to dispose of the body? Would he turn himself in?

". . . listening to me. *Hey!*" Victoria's elbow jabbed me in the

33

side. I grunted and snapped out of my reverie. "I *said,* which way are we going?"

I hooked my hand through her arm and hauled her roughly off the pavement into the road. She had an umbrella open above us. The wind caught it and I grabbed her wrist and helped her to tilt the umbrella into the breeze. The canvas shook and trembled and buckled. I listened to the splash of my footsteps on the soggy tarmac. The click of Victoria's heels in the dampness.

We were getting close to the apartment building. Close to the female police officer.

It was maddening. I wanted badly to go inside. I wanted nothing more than to burst into the apartment and turn the whole place upside down until I found the corpse and the killer.

And what then, hero?

I heard a burble of static. The noise of the policewoman's radio. She inclined her ear toward the speaker. I listened as best I could. I didn't catch it all, but I got enough to understand that she was being given an address. It was an address I was familiar with. I'd been inside the same apartment not so very long ago.

The policewoman stepped out of the doorway in front of us and lowered her head and darted across the street through the rain. The door she'd vacated was starting to close. It was swinging through a slow, steady arc, controlled by a pneumatic hinge. I watched it closing and I tried to decide what to do. I was torn. I was confused. The door had almost sealed when I veered to one side and reached for it.

But Victoria pulled against me. A short, sharp tug. My fingers stretched for the handle. They missed.

"What are you doing?" she hissed. "Don't you see where that policewoman's going? We have to get out of here, Charlie. We have to move."

We crossed the river Spree and boarded an S-Bahn train at the Bellevue station. Our carriage was close to empty. A couple of young men were standing toward the rear with backpacks on their shoulders. They had on glistening rain macs, and their rucksacks were protected by plastic covers. Toward the front, a thin, elderly woman with a drawn face and tightly permed hair was sitting on a long bench with a drenched terrier sprawled on the floor beneath her legs.

The dog had settled in front of the vents that were blowing heated air into the brightly lit carriage. The vinyl benches were lilac in color and covered in hundreds of white logos of the Brandenburg Gate. Transfers of the same logo were repeated on all the windows and doors in a haphazard pattern. I could see a nightscape of Berlin through the glass, hunkered down and lit brightly against the dreary rain.

"Are you nuts?" Victoria asked me, as we sat opposite each other in the middle of the carriage. She shook the rain from her umbrella. "Have you gone completely loco?"

"Huh?"

"For a minute there, I honestly thought you were going to go inside that building."

I shrugged. "What if I was?"

"Well, for starters, that policewoman might have seen you."

"So? That could have been a good thing."

"How?" Victoria wiped rainwater from her face. She glared at me. "You have your picks and your burglary tools on you. You have a scrap of paper with the name and address of Freddy's number-one suspect in your pocket. The address is for the apartment the police were called from. And they were called by an Englishman sounding very much like you."

"I saw a woman being killed, Vic." I glanced down at our wet footprints on the rubber floor. The cuffs of my jeans were soaked. "I can hardly ignore it."

I wasn't worried about our conversation being overheard. I was pretty sure anything we said would be drowned out by the chatter and rumble of wheels on track, the screech of brakes and rails, the banging and rattling of the carriage.

Victoria shook her head. "No, Charlie. That's what you *thought* you saw. But you must have made a mistake."

I looked up at her. Held her eyes. I could smell the dampness of my clothes. "I didn't," I said.

"But the police checked, Charlie. We saw the light go on in the apartment. They went inside."

"Then the killer must have hidden the body."

"In five minutes? Come on. And don't you think the police would have taken a good look around? They're not idiots, you know. They obviously treated your call seriously. And they wouldn't have left without a reasonable explanation."

"The only explanation I can think of is that they screwed up."

The train was slowing and pulling into the glass and steel expanse of the giant Hauptbahnhof station. It stopped at a platform where a knot of passengers were waiting. The doors on an S-Bahn train don't open automatically. You have to press a lighted button if you want to get on or off. But so many people were intending to board that all the doors in our carriage shuffled apart. The two backpackers stepped out, to be replaced by many more passengers. The doors shuffled closed. A recorded announcement informed us that the next stop would be Friedrichstrasse.

"I can think of plenty of other explanations," Victoria told me, as the train began to pull away and a man in a tan raincoat settled down close to her. The man was reading a paperback book. I checked the cover. Force of habit. But it wasn't one of mine.

"Such as?" I asked.

"Such as perhaps they were rehearsing for a play."

"A play? Are you kidding me?"

36

"Or perhaps it was"—Victoria shifted forward in her seat and leaned toward me over the aisle—"*sexual*. Maybe that's why they closed the blind. Maybe it was getting too heated."

I pressed the heel of my hand against my forehead. "I can't believe I'm hearing this."

"I know it sounds weird, but some people are into that kind of thing."

"They were fully clothed, Vic. The guy was in a jacket or an overcoat. The woman was in a sweater and a skirt. Oh, and she was fighting for her life."

The man next to Victoria snatched a look at us over the top of his paperback. I got the impression he was finding our conversation a lot more interesting than his book.

"But think about it, Charlie." Victoria's body was rocking with the movement of the train. The vibrations were modulating her voice. "You were looking at a distant window at night, in the rain, through a slatted blind. You have to admit that's not a perfect view. There's plenty of scope for things to get scrambled up."

I jerked my chin toward the doors nearest to us. The train was braking and juddering to a halt. I got to my feet, grabbing hold of a rubber strap to keep my balance.

"This is our stop."

We didn't have far to go. Just a short stroll and a few flights of stairs to a platform on another level. We waited beside a stall selling newspapers and magazines and snacks. Victoria was clutching her folded umbrella in one hand and her transport ticket in the other. I never bother with a ticket myself. There are no barriers or turnstiles to contend with in the S-Bahn and U-Bahn stations. The whole Berlin network operates via an honor system, and as you might imagine, it doesn't exactly play to my strengths.

Victoria was different. She couldn't stand the idea of being caught and embarrassed by an undercover ticket inspector. I'd tried to convince her that the odds of that happening were really quite slim. After all, it's been my misfortune in life to have stumbled across a number of corpses. But ticket inspectors? Never happened.

I glanced up at the electronic information board above our heads. "One minute until our train," I said. "Want to wow me with any more explanations?"

"Would you listen to them?"

"Probably not. I know what I saw. And to be perfectly honest, I'm having a hard time forgetting about it."

"Then perhaps it'll help if I give you something else to ponder. Like, for instance, why you're an idiot."

"Excuse me?"

"You don't remember?" She sighed. "Charlie, when you came into that bar, I told you that you were an idiot."

"You're always telling me things like that." I kicked the sodden toe of my baseball trainer into the ground. The water had soaked through to my socks. "And I *was* a little distracted, Vic."

"Well, me, too. I'd just used my phone to check my e-mail. And I hadn't liked what I'd seen."

Before she could continue, I felt a blast of gritty air against my face and hands. I turned to see our train approaching. We stepped aboard. There were seats available but not many, and we opted to stand and share a handrail. Our bodies shifted rhythmically with the carriage as it began to pull away.

Victoria raised her mouth to my ear so that I could hear her over the noise of the train and the rattling of the doors. "I had three new messages in my inbox."

"Only three?"

"Just three that should concern you."

"Me?"

"That's right. They were all from editors at different German publishing houses. When I was in Frankfurt, I pitched *The Venetian Cat* to five German editors."

"Right. And is this your way of telling me that three of them have turned me down?"

"Actually, no." She stared hard at me. Her face was drawn, her skin pulled tight. "Quite the opposite, in fact. All three have expressed an interest in buying the German rights. Two have even made pretty generous offers."

I flashed her a grin. "But that's great news, Vic."

"No, it's bloody not."

"Oh. And why's that?"

"Because they all felt encouraged to make an offer due to a strange coincidence." She stepped a little closer. Spoke a little lower. "Obviously, it goes without saying that they liked the book—or rather, they could see its commercial potential. But all of them, quite separately from the others, mentioned that something had happened to them that made it seem like fate."

"Really," I said, trying to lighten the tone. "And what might that be?"

Victoria stabbed the point of her umbrella into my toe. "As if you don't bloody know."

"Ow." I leaped out of her range and clenched my foot in my hand. Bad idea. Now my hand was covered in rainwater and soggy dirt. "I'm afraid you've lost me," I said, massaging my toe with my thumb.

"Oh, really." She waved the umbrella in my face, like an old lady cursing me with a walking stick. "Well, Charlie, allow me to enlighten you. The fact is that all three editors live in Berlin. And it seems that every one of them was burgled while they were out of town at the Frankfurt Book Fair."

The train eased to a stop at Unter den Linden. Victoria lowered the umbrella. A young, skinny man with a bicycle boarded our carriage. He was wearing leggings, a luminous jacket, and a cycling helmet. The doors closed and the train started up again.

"My, that *is* a coincidence," I said.

"It's not a sodding coincidence. I can see it in your face. You ripped them off!"

"Moi?" I batted my eyelids. Pressed my hand to my heart. "I think you must have me confused with somebody else."

"Oh? And did that somebody else have access to my business folder before I went to Frankfurt? Were they able to check the names of the three Berlin-based editors I'd be meeting? Honestly, Charlie, you used that information without my permission. You *used* me."

"Actually," I said, holding up a finger, "your information was kind of patchy. It didn't include their home addresses. I had to find those for myself."

"You *moron*." Vic tried to stab me in my other toe. I jumped clear, parting my legs, and in that instant, I could see that she was tempted to swipe the brolly up and inflict a far more grievous injury. I backed away, waving my hands. The cyclist seemed to find it very amusing.

Victoria's eyes narrowed, and she lifted her umbrella until the point was aimed toward my belly button.

"Now, now," I said.

"But using me wasn't even the worst of it," she told me, stiff-jawed. "Publishing is a small world, Charlie. At some point, these editors are going to talk to one another. Maybe not tomorrow. Maybe not in the next few days. But trust me, sometime, someplace, they're going to get around to chatting about how much one of them paid for your stupid manuscript. And then they're going to mention the strange coincidence that led them to try and buy the thing in the first place. And do you know what they're going to discover?"

"That they missed out on a surefire hit?"

"No," she hissed. "They're going to discover that all three of them were burgled while they were in Frankfurt. And then they're going to put two and two together."

"Or even three and three?"

"And then they'll send the police after you. And how funny will you find that? Hmm?"

"Oh, relax," I told her. "You worry too much."

Victoria glowered at me as the train pulled into Potsdamer Platz. She kept glowering in silence all the way to Anhalter Bahnhof. I pressed the button to open our doors and ushered Vic off onto the platform, catching the eye of the smirking cyclist as we left.

"Good luck, comrade," he muttered to me in German, and I responded with a casual salute as the doors closed behind us and the train began to glide away.

"What did he say?" Victoria snapped.

"No idea," I told her. "But I know what *I* want to say."

"And is that sorry, by any chance?"

I shook my head. "Actually, I wanted to ask if I could borrow your phone."

SEVEN

The rain had stopped by the time we emerged from below ground. Water dripped from the trees and the streetlights and the green lollipop sign for the S-Bahn station. It ticked off the metal bollards and the parked cars and the many bicycles that were locked to the nearby racks and railings. The gray concrete office building of *Der Tagesspiegel,* the German broadsheet, towered above us. To our left, a shabby Turkish restaurant marked the corner of Schöneberger Strasse.

We took in the scene without speaking. There was a very good reason for that. Victoria was giving me the silent treatment. Actually, she was giving me a variation of the silent treatment. She was huffing a lot, and clucking her tongue a lot, and making a sort of dry rasping noise in the back of her throat whenever I tried to communicate with her. In short, she was leaving me in absolutely no doubt that she was miffed. But there was nothing wrong with her hearing, and when I asked again if I could borrow her phone, she dumped it in my hand.

I knew Victoria expected me to apologize for breaking into the homes of the three German editors. But really, I wasn't sure why. Yes, I'd done it. But that shouldn't have come as a surprise. I was a burglar. Stealing things was what I did. Victoria had known that for a very long time. And though I don't mean to shock you, I wasn't the least bit sorry.

Listen, I'm not a guy who believes in making things difficult for himself. In an ideal world, I like to case a joint before I break in to it, and if I happen to learn that a venue is likely to be vacant for a couple of days, I'm only too happy to exploit the situation and avoid unnecessary risks.

Victoria's information file had given me a great head start. True, it had been buried in the bottom of her suitcase—a suitcase I'd been expressly forbidden to snoop through—but, hey, telling a professional thief not to take a tour through your things is like telling a compulsive eater not to peek in your fridge. It doesn't work. The temptation is too much. And I'm a sucker for temptation.

I'm also a sucker for handsome belongings, and during my time in the editors' homes, I'd found plenty to tickle my fancy. I'd picked up a selection of expensive silk ties, and I'd had my choice of e-readers. I'd located a reasonable amount of hard cash and an intriguing sculpture from an up-and-coming German artist. I'd even taken a peek at the new manuscript from a best-selling crime author I happened to admire.

So all things considered, Victoria's tiff really wasn't a terribly high price to pay for such a golden opportunity, let alone three of them, and I wasn't about to apologize for being who I was and doing what I did, no matter how annoyed she might be.

Instead, I led her around the corner and along the street toward the destination Freddy had included in his text. To my mind, we were now in the extreme northwest corner of the Turkish district of Kreuzberg. Others would disagree. To the city's young and hip, the neighborhood was little more than a tourist zone, oozing out from

Mitte and the redeveloped Potsdamer Platz, with its skyscrapers and multliscreen cinemas and shopping malls and food courts. For them, the *real* Kreuzberg was farther east, where bohemians, punks, and anarchists had squatted following the collapse of the Wall, and where musicians, artists, and creatives had settled, in the years since.

I don't suppose it mattered all that much. It certainly didn't concern me. The only thing weighing on my mind just then (apart, of course, from Victoria's sulk and the unfortunate murder I'd happened to witness) was the way time appeared to be racing on. Freddy had told me that the function the embassy's staff were attending would conclude at midnight. It was nudging toward ten o'clock already, and I still had as many as three properties to tick off my list. And we all know what happens when the big hand and the little hand hit the magic number twelve. That's right, princesses turn back into servant girls, carriages into pumpkins, and burglars into sitting ducks.

The Mövenpick Hotel had a multicolored light canopy hanging above its entrance. I guided Victoria inside and to our left, where I deposited her at the hotel bar. The bar was very dark, lit only by a series of colored neon tubes and an image of a crackling fire that was being projected onto the far wall. It was moderately busy. The clientele seemed to be a mixture of businesspeople and tourists. I heard a variety of accents and languages. Some Dutch. Some French. A good deal of German. And a smattering of English.

I accompanied Victoria to a red leather stool at the bar. "Order me a mineral water," I told her. "And anything you'd like to eat or drink. Anything at all. I'll settle the bill when I get back."

"Generous," she muttered.

"Listen, can we be friends again?"

She glared at me so savagely that I felt compelled to pat myself down and check for injuries.

"How about acquaintances?"

"Just go, Charlie. Give me some space."

I could tell there wasn't much point saying anything more, so I quit while I was very definitely behind, and left the bar. On my way out, I raised Victoria's mobile to my ear and embarked on a tedious conversation with a colleague back in London. The colleague didn't exist, and neither, for that matter, did the phone call, but the act was enough to get me past the staff in reception without my presence being questioned, and from there I stepped inside an elevator and traveled up to the first floor.

A sign inside the carriage had informed me that the hotel occupied the site of the former Siemens factory, and the interior design retained a number of nods to the building's industrial past. There was an old chunk of machinery in a glass case outside the elevator doors. The cast-iron radiators in the hallway were painted a metallic brown and reminded me of the heating system in my old boarding school. The corridor windows were giant sash units with multiple panes, and the stairways were workmanlike structures with concrete treads.

But the overall impression was strikingly modern. The carpet was a deep purple in color, inlaid with bold floral patterns. The walls were painted off-white and decorated with long German phrases in a flowing black script. The doors to the hotel rooms were made of sleek, dark wood, with aluminum fittings. And the information signs and room numbers were etched onto squares of jauntily colored plastic, backlit by electric bulbs.

Room 134 was at the far end of the corridor. According to Freddy's text, it was the temporary home of a lady by the name of Jane Parker, who was in residence at the hotel during a short-term posting in Berlin. Freddy's message had concluded with the information that she was a security consultant, on assignment from London. The idea that a security specialist could have stolen something of value from the office of the British ambassador seemed a bit iffy to

45

me, but since Freddy was the guy calling the shots (not to mention paying for them), and since he'd insisted that the mystery item had been stolen, I was going to have to go ahead and search her belongings.

First, though, I knocked.

It was a pretty timid knock. I wanted it to be just loud enough to be heard from the inside but not so loud as to draw the attention of a guest in an adjoining room.

There was no response, but that was hardly conclusive, so I held my breath for a moment and knocked again. I even cleared my throat and spoke in a low, fast voice.

"Room service."

On reflection, it was just about the dumbest thing I could have said. If there *was* somebody inside and they answered the door, it was going to strike them as pretty odd if they hadn't ordered any room service. And it was going to seem even stranger if they opened their door to find me standing there in my soggy raincoat, drenched jeans, and scummy baseball trainers, without a food cart or a serving tray.

Lucky, then, that my knock went unanswered, and after a short pause to recover my senses and remind myself that now really wasn't the time to be a total moron, I turned my attention to the next obstacle in my way—the key card entry system.

It goes without saying that there are several ways to defeat a magnetic card reader, and naturally enough, the best way of all is to have the right key. Failing that, you can try and bluff the folks in reception by claiming that you've mislaid your card. But since the room was booked in the name of a female guest who happened to be staying alone, and since Victoria wasn't in the most amenable frame of mind to assist me just at the moment, I didn't believe I'd try that particular technique. But I wasn't about to cry into my sleeve, either. Because just like the garage elevator in the Tiergarten, the system employed a manual backup—there was a trusty keyhole fitted in the very center of the door handle.

I was just about to drop to my knees and give it the once-over when I heard hushed conversation from behind me. Turning around, I saw a middle-aged couple wheeling suitcases along the corridor. I rolled my eyes and patted my coat pockets like I was searching for my key card. Nope, couldn't find it. I rolled my eyes some more. I even added a shoulder shrug, just to test my acting range, and then I curled my hand into a fist and rapped lightly on the door.

"Darling," I cooed. "Sweet pea. I seem to have lost my key."

The man and the woman smiled awkwardly at me, then huddled around their own door and fitted their card in the slot. The lock disengaged with a clunk and the man held the door open for his partner.

"Honey," I persisted. "Are you in the bathroom?"

The man dragged his suitcase inside and allowed the door to close behind him.

As soon as the corridor was empty again, I searched inside my coat and removed my gloves and the spectacles case that contains my burglary tools. There was every chance I wouldn't need my gloves. After all, this was a hotel room, and it was likely to be lay-ered in many thousands of fingerprints. But hell, wearing gloves was one of my key rules, and given how my night had started out, now didn't seem like the time to take chances.

My gloves were cheap, disposable numbers, made of a very fine, opaque plastic. They were also customized. Some months ago now, I'd spent a very dull evening snipping away the middle and fourth fingers on an entire box of gloves to accommodate the warped digits on my right hand. I'll admit it's not a perfect solution, since it makes the gloves a little more delicate than I might prefer, but I was compensating by carrying another two sets in case this pair disintegrated, and I'd wrapped surgical tape around my exposed fingertips to be certain I didn't leave any prints.

With my gloves secured, I popped open my spectacles case and removed an aluminum raking tool and a medium torsion wrench. I'd been so active just recently that I'd treated myself to a whole new set of tools from a locksmith supply company on the Internet, and they made short work of the locking mechanism.

After only a few tweaks and twists, I heard a reassuring click, followed by another, and one more, and finally a very welcome clunk. Moving as swiftly as possible, I stepped inside the darkened room and hung the DO NOT DISTURB sign on the outside of the door. Then I sighed, and rubbed my hands together, and allowed myself to relish, just for a moment, the sudden rush of endorphins that coursed through my body. I was all atingle. Another forbidden space. Another violation of privacy. Sick, I grant you, but I can't pretend it didn't feel *good*.

EIGHT

The room lights could only be triggered by slipping a key card into a slot on the wall, and since there was no override (or rather, no override that I could be troubled to find), I clicked on my pocket torch.

My penlight is tiny, but it's powerful, and I cast the beam around to get my bearings. I found that I was standing in a short hallway with coat hooks on my left and a series of fitted cabinets and a bathroom on my right. Ahead of me, the ceiling height doubled above a living-sleeping area that ended in floor-to-ceiling windows shrouded by net curtains.

My first move was to cross the room and close the heavy fabric curtains in front of the nets. Couple of reasons for that. One, the hotel was arranged around a central courtyard, where the hotel restaurant was located beneath a glass atrium, and I didn't want any inquisitive guests or staff to spot my torch beam bouncing around. And two, I was determined to stick to my new rule and make sure I didn't glance out the window and spot some dastardly crime.

Once the curtains were drawn, I took a second glance around the room. My torch beam bounced back at me on a whole spectrum of crazy angles. The light was being refracted by a wall of thick glass tiles positioned between the sleeping area and the en suite bathroom. Clearly, this wasn't the place to stay if you or your partner happened to be a prude.

I have to say I liked it. I liked the high ceiling and the high window. I liked the yellow, modernist armchair. I liked the bold writing desk, fashioned from some kind of lush olivewood, and I liked how the bed frame and headboard had been manufactured from the same timber. I was a little confused by the way the king-sized bed had been made up. The linen was a startling white and high quality, but there were two duvets, and they'd been formed into rolls at the bottom of each side of the mattress. One for each guest, I assumed, unless like Jane Parker you were staying on your own.

But enough about the décor. I had a task to complete and not a vast amount of time to do it in. There weren't many likely hiding places for whatever it was I was supposed to find, but I knew where I planned to start.

I returned to the hallway and opened a low cupboard down by my knee. The minibar. Not what I'd had in mind, but I scanned it all the same. There was nothing I wouldn't have expected to see. Alcoholic miniatures. Tiny cans of soft drinks. A couple of chocolate bars and some mixed nuts and potato crisps.

I tried the tall cupboard door on my right. This was more like it. A selection of jackets, blouses, trousers, and skirts were suspended from a metal rail. I patted the clothing down, for form's sake if nothing else, and then I dropped to my knees and aimed my torch at what I was really interested in.

No, not the laundry service bag. The room safe.

It was a dinky little thing, and the way it was squatting there, acting all tough, was sort of like a kitten pretending it was a jungle cat. There was a ten-digit electronic keypad and a short list of helpful user instructions printed on the plastic fascia. The safe itself was fashioned from reinforced steel, with concealed hinges, and it was about as secure as a wet paper bag. Seriously. I know of at least eight ways to defeat one of these suckers without breaking a sweat. Some of them are simple, and some of them are ingenious, but most of them require a fair amount of time.

Which is why I was going for the fastest option.

Removing Victoria's smartphone from my pocket, I connected to the Internet. Alas, Web access wasn't complimentary inside the hotel, so this was going to hurt just a smidgen when Victoria eventually saw her roaming charges.

I typed in the Web address for the blog I was after. The site is administered by a guy in Poland who has an interest in hacking a wide variety of security devices. His real passion is complex intruder systems, but he started out small, and if you search through his archive, you're nearly guaranteed to find what it is that you're after.

I found the name of the manufacturer of this particular safe smack in the middle of a handy alphabetical list. I clicked on the name, then waited for the relevant page to load, and once I had it, I held the screen up next to the keypad and started to type.

What was I doing? Well, it's really quite simple. With any appliance that's designed to be used by human beings, tolerances have to be built in for the mistakes that will inevitably occur. Take a hotel room safe. There'll be times when a guest forgets the code they've selected. On other occasions, a guest might check out of a hotel and travel home without remembering to empty their things. And in both scenarios, and many others besides, the hotel staff need to be able to open the safe.

They can do this by using a reset code. Every safe manufacturer has them, and they usually issue them on cards to the person who purchases their equipment. But if you know where to look, you can find the code for pretty much any cheap brand on the market.

The code for the safe in front of me was fairly average, in that it was twelve characters long. It consisted of numbers and asterisks and hash symbols. I punched in the sequence and the safe whirred and hummed and had a good think about what I'd done. Then the locking mechanism buzzed and retracted and the door bounced open.

The good folks at the safe factory had thought of everything, and a handy lamp came on to aid my search. Alas, there wasn't much to look at. Just three items, in fact. The first was a bundle of cash, held together with a bulldog clip. I took the bundle out and counted it. Just short of five hundred euros. The second item was a charm bracelet made of solid silver, and the third was a pair of pearl earrings in a tiny velvet-lined box. The earrings were a time-less choice, and the bracelet was desirable in a quirky kind of way, but I didn't think they were what Freddy had hired me to find. *You'll know it when you see it* simply didn't seem to apply.

I suppose I could have swiped the jewelry for myself, but I'm a softy at heart, and I guessed the charm bracelet, in particular, might hold some special significance for Ms. Parker.

Naturally, I took the cash. I might be a good thief, but I'm not *that* good, and the money was likely to come in handy.

I closed the safe back up and locked it with a code of my own devising, and then I shut the cupboard door and had a think about what to try next.

Next was Jane Parker's luggage. There was a suitcase down on the floor between the bed and the wall of glass tiles. Soft brown leather. Quality stitching. Not too big. Not too small. Distinctive enough to be recognizable on an airport luggage carousel but not so distinctive as to be gaudy.

I got down on my knees and flipped back the lid and shined my torch inside. There were clothes, a pair of training shoes, a paper-back novel—again, not one of mine—and a three-pin adaptor plug.

There were a couple of additional zipped compartments. One of them contained a glossy magazine, but the rest were empty. I poked, pinched, and prodded the lining, just to be sure there were no secret hiding spots, and then I put the suitcase back just as I'd found it and turned my attention to the bed.

I unrolled the duvets and rolled them back up again. I felt beneath the pillows and inside the pillowcases. I lifted the mattress and shined my torch underneath.

I tried the drawers of the bedside cabinets. One of them contained a Bible. The other was empty.

Hmm.

Location two really wasn't looking very promising, and that was before I moved into the bathroom. I didn't stay there for long. The floors and the walls were covered in yellow mosaic tiles. There was a shower over the bath, a toilet, and a sink. There was a stack of fluffy white towels, a modest collection of hotel toiletries, and a handy disposable kit for cleaning your shoes. The only sign of habitation was a toothbrush and a tube of toothpaste that were resting in a glass tumbler, a hairbrush, a scattering of makeup, and a wash-bag hanging very neatly from a hook beside the mirror. I checked the wash-bag and found nothing out of the ordinary.

There really wasn't much left to search. That's the good thing about hotel rooms. You can be in and out of them within minutes if you know what you're doing. I cast my torch around the room, checking for anything I might have missed. There was just one thing.

The desk.

I rolled aside the leather chair in front of it and opened the central drawer. The drawer contained a few sheets of hotel stationery, a pen branded with the hotel's name, and the odd speck of dirt and fluff. I went down on my knees and craned my neck, shining my torch around the underside of the desk. I found a wire for connecting a laptop to the Internet. Big deal.

I crawled back out and straightened up and turned my attention to the leather folder in the middle of the desk. It contained a whole lot of information about the hotel. There was a welcome letter from the manager, an index of guest services, and a menu card for the hotel restaurant.

And there was also something else entirely. The instant I saw it, I understood exactly what Freddy had meant. I reached for it, and I lifted it before my eyes, and I didn't have the slightest doubt that I'd found precisely what I'd been hired to retrieve. My assignment was over. Jane Parker was the guilty culprit. And I was one very smug thief.

NINE

Victoria was sipping from a glass of chilled white wine and twirling a black napkin around on the counter when I returned to the bar. Her wineglass was very large. It was very full. And I had a feeling it wasn't her first.

A lone guy was warming up to approach her, sipping a little courage from a long-necked bottle of lager. He was an athletic, handsome type, dressed in a black turtleneck sweater and black jeans. His dark hair was slicked down with gel and combed very neatly to one side. He could have been a poet or a graphic designer. He could have been a threat.

I swept in and dropped onto the cushioned stool next to Victoria, showing my back to the guy. He checked himself, then swerved away, and I slid Victoria's phone along the bar. She considered my empty hands, frowning quizzically. Her eyes were a little swimmy. But a little less hostile, too.

"No luck?" she asked, and I caught the hint of a drawl.

"Plenty of luck," I told her, propping my elbow on the counter and my chin on my fist. "I found it."

She straightened. She blinked. "Seriously? Then where is it?"

"It's on my person," I said, and wiggled my eyebrows.

There was a glass of sparkling water in front of me and a dish of cashew nuts between us. I didn't eat any of the nuts. I'd already helped myself to a packet of crisps from the minibar in room 134 on my way out.

"In that case, it must be small," Victoria said.

"Not all that small."

"Flexible?"

"You're getting warmer."

"Something you could roll up and fit down your sleeve?"

She reached across and pinched her way along my arm, through the material of my raincoat. When she didn't find anything, she leaned back on her stool, pressed a finger to her lips, and gazed at my ankles.

I could feel the handsome guy watching us from across the room. I fought the temptation to wave.

"Now you're getting colder," I said.

Her eyes narrowed. Her lips puckered up. "I'm also getting bored. And my patience with you was pretty low to begin with."

"So I'll give you a clue. It's flat."

She backed away on her stool and studied me some more. She took a contemplative sip of her wine.

"Is it inside your coat?"

"Not exactly."

"What is it?"

"A document folder."

"Go on."

I paused and checked over my shoulder. There was nobody close. The guy in the turtleneck sweater was busy hitting on a red-head in a side booth. I leaned toward Victoria and lowered my voice. "It's a buff cardboard folder. It has a stamp on the front of it. Two words. Red ink."

"And what are the words?"

"Top . . . secret."

Victoria jabbed her finger at me. "Read my mood, Charlie. I swear, if you don't tell me soon, I'm going to cause you a lot of pain."

"No," I said. "Those were the words on the file. 'Top secret.'"

"Oh," she said, and leaned a good deal closer. I could smell the wine on her breath.

"Do people really do that?" she whispered. "Write 'top secret' on stuff?"

"It appears so."

A lazy grin curled her lip. "So now we know why Freddy was so sure you'd recognize what you were looking for."

"Uh-huh. He even gave me a clue. Remember, when I tried to push him on what I'd be looking for, he said, 'Top secret, I'm afraid.' Clever, really."

"Top secret," Victoria repeated, as if she was trying the phrase out for size. Her words were a touch more slurred than she might have liked. "But didn't Freddy's text say that the woman staying here is a security specialist? Maybe she has permission to be keeping the file."

"Not according to Freddy."

"Huh. And did you . . . you know?"

"What?"

"Take a peek?"

I placed my hand on my heart. "I can't believe you'd even ask me that."

"You looked," she said, and wagged her finger at me. "You're *you*, after all."

I squared my shoulders. "Vic, I'm working on Her Majesty's Service, here. I'm practically a Knight of the Realm."

"You *so* looked. I know you did."

"I'm genuinely hurt by your accusation."

"Yeah, right. So what did it say?"

I signaled to the girl behind the bar. She was busy stocking a low fridge with bottles, but she came across to us right away, wiping her hands on her apron. I requested the bill in German and told her that my colleague would like to charge it to her room. The girl nodded and moved away to the till.

Victoria kicked me in the shin. "Cheapskate. Do you think I don't know what you just did? You expect me to pretend to be this Parker woman."

"Vic, come on, I'd never underestimate you," I said. "And anyway, I'm glad you're up to speed. Because she'll need you to sign off on the charge."

The girl returned and placed a small leather folder and a pen down on the counter in front of Victoria. Then she bid us good night and returned to her work.

Victoria flipped open the folder. She stared at the printed bill and the spaces where she could write Jane Parker's name and room number. She chewed her lip. Then she exhaled sharply and reached for her handbag and removed her purse, counting off a handful of euro notes.

"You're mad," I told her.

"No, just honest. There's a difference."

I didn't say anything to that, but I was sorely tempted. Speaking personally, I'd done pretty well out of the evening, at least in cash terms. I'd be able to keep Freddy's two thousand euros for the first apartment and charge him a further two thousand five hundred for the hotel room. I had the money I'd found in the safe, and when I added all that to my finder's fee, my earnings would be just shy of ten thousand euros. But there was no doubt in my mind they'd be a little more shy by the time Victoria had climbed down off her high horse (not to mention her bar stool) to claim her cut.

"Here," I said, and closed her hand around her money. "Allow me."

I peeled off the necessary notes from the bundle I'd found in the safe. The bundle didn't escape Victoria's notice.

"How very kind," she said. "Stop at a cash point, did we?"

I offered her my arm and helped her down from her seat. We walked toward the exit, and I couldn't help casting a smug glance toward the pickup artist.

"Am I forgiven?" I asked. "For ripping off those German editors, I mean?"

"Nope." She shook her head. "Not even close."

"There must be a way I can make it up to you."

"You can start by telling me what's inside the folder you've found."

"I'll do better than that," I told her. "I'll show you, once we get back to my apartment. And we'll take a taxi. My shout."

We stepped out from the hotel onto the street, and I signaled to a nearby cab.

Victoria scrutinized me, as if she didn't entirely trust her hearing. "Really?"

"Really. And in return you can do me one tiny favor."

She opened her mouth to complain, but I placed my hand on her lips and shushed her.

"All I'm asking is for you to send Freddy a text to let him know that we've found what he's looking for. Tell him the guilty culprit was suspect number two, and that we'll meet him tomorrow morning to return his precious package. Oh, and add some kisses from me."

"That's it?"

"See?" I said, and opened the taxi door. "This burglary lark is a lot simpler than you realize."

But not for the first time that night, I turned out to be wrong. The situation I was involved in wasn't the least bit simple. Not even close.

TEN

The lights in my hallway and living room came on before I'd even reached for the switch. I'd like to be able to tell you that they were triggered by some kind of sensor, but the truth was a lot more basic. They were flicked on in the old-fashioned way, by a guy using the muzzle of a gun.

He was stocky and bullnecked. His hair was shaved close to the scalp and the stubble on his face looked abrasive enough to sand wood. Naturally, he had a scar on his cheek. He wouldn't have been much of a thug without one. The scar was long and jagged and stretched from close to his right ear to the corner of his mouth. The way the skin had healed and tightened meant that his mouth was tugged down on one side, as if he was suffering from Bell's palsy. I waited for him to speak, half expecting him to slur his words. But it was the second stranger in my apartment, the guy sitting over in my desk chair, who did the talking.

"Come forward into the room. Put your hands in the air."

"Impressive," I told the first guy, acting as if I hadn't noticed his

61

talkative buddy. "Learn to do that while you're drinking a pint of beer and you could make a lot of money."

"I said, hands up. High."

"Amazing. And in English, too. Though I do believe I detect a strong Russian accent."

The mute thug looked perplexed for a moment. Then he did that thing crooks do when they want to emphasize a point. He looked mean and he cocked the trigger on his gun and pointed it at my head. They do that for a reason. It does tend to grab one's attention.

The gun really wasn't all that big. It looked sort of cute in the tough guy's hand—like a toy water pistol. But I was pretty sure it was real. Sure enough to do as I'd been told.

I reached for the ceiling and Victoria did likewise. She was lurking behind me, treating me a lot like a human shield. I couldn't really complain. If she'd been the first one inside the room, I might have done the same thing.

"Both of you step forward." The guy in my chair was growing less patient every moment. "Away from the door."

"Glad to," I said. "There's a nasty draft coming in."

"Enough with your jokes. You will turn and look at me now."

I shuffled to my right and finally faced the guy issuing the instructions. His pose was relaxed, with one leg crossed over his knee, and he was much younger and slimmer than the thug with the gun. They say you should dress to impress and he'd certainly done that. His shoes were highly polished brown leather brogues and his tan trousers had stiff pleats ironed into them. His woolen overcoat was neatly tailored and unbuttoned to reveal a navy cashmere sweater over a crisp white shirt. There was a fawn-colored scarf knotted rakishly about his neck and he wore his dark hair in a no-nonsense crew cut. To complete his outfit, he sported a pair of black leather gloves on his hands.

I didn't like the gloves. Oh, they were beautifully stitched and made from what appeared to be a supple, high-grade hide, but they conjured some unfortunate associations in my mind. Associations that had to do with violence and pain and suffering. With the breaking of bones and the application of pressure and the clean, efficient sort of killing that spoke of a certain kind of professional.

I didn't like what he was touching with his gloves very much, either. He was holding my badly burned copy of *The Maltese Falcon,* a single gloved finger resting between the splayed pages. He must have removed the book from the picture frame. I was only too aware of how fragile it had become in recent months and I really didn't want it to suffer any more damage.

"Who are you?" Victoria asked from behind me. "What are you doing here?"

The man looked up from the book with a pained expression on his face, as if we'd rudely interrupted his reading. "Who I am is none of your concern, Miss Newbury." His Russian accent was becoming more pronounced. So was the unease he was causing me. "But who *you* are interests me very much. I have learned a great deal about you in only two days. You also, Mr. Howard. Forgive me, but you interest me in particular."

"You're forgiven," I said. "I do have a pretty engaging personality. Perhaps we could meet for a drink sometime? Somewhere other than my apartment late at night?"

He smiled thinly. The light from the ceiling bulb bounced off the lenses of his glasses.

"Your book," he said, in a clipped voice, and lifted it in his hands. "It is burned, yes?"

"An accident," I told him.

"Ah, yes. Accidents can be so . . . unfortunate. Especially where fire is concerned."

The temperature in the room seemed to have heated up all of a sudden. The stocky guy was still pointing his gun at the side of my head, holding it in a two-handed grip. My skin was prickling beneath his aim.

I wet my lips and did my best to keep my voice even. "That's a threat, right?" I said. "I only ask because I like to be sure about these things. It's kind of embarrassing to misread a social situation. I mean, it could be you've let yourself into my apartment with your rent-a-goon, here, for some sort of spontaneous book club. A quaint little chat about Sam Spade and Dashiell Hammett."

He closed my book and tossed it carelessly onto the surface of my desk. Then he clasped his gloved hands together and rested them on his knee.

"Did you find what you were looking for?" he asked.

"Excuse me?"

"The item," the man said, and plucked an imaginary shred of lint from his trousers. "The one Mr. Farmer was so keen for you to fetch."

I swallowed. Heavily. I didn't like the way things were shaping up. I didn't like how much he seemed to know.

"Listen," I said, "how about you let Victoria wait outside for a while? At least until we've finished talking. She really has nothing to do with any of this."

"So chivalrous, Mr. Howard." There was a studied cadence to his speech, the minor delay of the translation going on in his mind. "But I am sorry, I cannot grant your request."

"I won't call the police," Victoria told him. "I promise."

"Oh, but there is no need for your promise, Miss Newbury. Of course you will not call the police. You've been helping a burglar. You negotiated a fee on his behalf. Calling the police would be a very dangerous thing for you to do."

I shuffled my feet. It felt like I was balancing on a high wire. And I really didn't want to stumble and fall.

"Can we put our arms down, at least?" I asked.

"No, you can answer my question. Did you find the item?"

I could feel Victoria staring at me. Urging me to provide the answer the man wanted.

"I'm afraid not," I said.

"Then I'm afraid, too, Mr. Howard. I'm afraid that you are lying to me."

He reached one gloved hand inside his overcoat and removed it again very quickly. Now he was holding a pistol of his own. It had a suppressor screwed onto the barrel.

I might not have the sharpest of minds, but even I could tell the situation was deteriorating.

"I will ask you again," the man said. "And if you lie to me, I will shoot you in the leg."

"Which leg?"

"Five seconds, Mr. Howard."

"You're kidding me."

"Five."

I shook my head. "I honestly can't believe you're giving me a countdown."

"Four."

"You struck me as such a sophisticated guy. But now you're engaging in the worst sort of cliché."

"Three."

"Charlie," Victoria hissed. "Be serious. Please."

"Two."

"The common hoodlum I could live with," I told him, with a nod toward his scarred friend. "But a countdown. It's just so . . . predictable."

"One."

He tightened his finger on the trigger and released a faint sigh, as if he was disappointed by my attitude but not unduly troubled by its consequences. I realized then that he was serious.

"Okay, wait," I yelled, waving my hands.

He relaxed a fraction and raised his head above his gun.

"Just so I'm clear. Are you shooting on zero, or are you saying zero, and then shooting?"

He clamped his lips together and shook his head. Then he unfolded his legs, planted both feet on the floor, and leaned forward in the chair. He squinted along the gun barrel, drawing a bead on me.

"This will be a very painful joke, Mr. Howard. I will shoot your right leg, I think. Just below the knee. There is a lot of bone there. Not so much flesh. It is likely to be excruciating."

"All right," I told him, and this time I meant it. I spread my fingers, as if to signal the shift in my attitude. "You've made your point."

"The item, then."

"I have it," I said. "But it's stuffed down the back of my trousers. If you'll just let me lower my hands, I'll pass it to you."

"That will not be necessary."

He issued a series of commands in rapid-fire Russian to the scarred Neanderthal. The stocky guy stuffed his gun inside the leather jacket he had on and paced over to me with his knuckles scraping on the floor. He lifted the tails of my soggy raincoat and roughly tugged my shirt out of the waistband of my jeans. He snatched at the folder and delivered it to his boss.

Then he turned back to face me again. He stepped close and raised himself up on his toes so he was breathing right in my face. His breath was foul. I could feel the heat coming off him. He was sweating inside his leather jacket and he fairly reeked of testosterone. I daresay that if I'd lit a match, he'd have ignited like he was dowsed in petrol.

I tried to hold his gaze but not all that hard. It may surprise you to hear that I'm not such a manly chap. I've never been very skilled at lifting weights or flexing my muscles, mainly because I don't have many muscles to flex.

He drew back his right hand and faked a punch to my jaw. I

flinched and jerked backward and accidentally clipped Victoria in the temple with the back of my head. The guy enjoyed my reaction very much. He enjoyed the way Victoria yelped even more. He chuckled and split his slanted lips and grinned at me. His teeth were awful. They were yellowed and gapped, and he was missing his upper-right incisor altogether. The missing tooth really shouldn't have surprised me. After all, you can't call yourself a true bovine thug unless you have a missing tooth to go along with your disfiguring scar.

Talking of surprises, the guy delivered another one. He punched me with his left fist, hard into my stomach. I'd like to be able to tell you that I have a washboard gut, honed by many hours at the gym and countless thousands of sit-ups. I'd love to be able to say that my abs are so well defined that the guy hurt his knuckles more than he hurt me. But the last time I'd visited a gym was after-hours when I was checking to see if there was any cash in the till. And my waistline had definitely softened with all the dense German food I'd been enjoying just recently. Regular plates of currywurst and mashed potato had a lot to answer for.

So the moment he hit me, I crumpled and dropped onto my side on the floor. I clutched my hands to my stomach. My gut was in spasm. I gasped for air. I did a lot of moaning and some uncontrollable drooling.

Victoria shrieked but not for long. The guy stamped his foot, like a Big Unfriendly Giant who was coming to get her, and she choked her scream down and dropped to her knees beside me. She was muttering a lot. She was swearing repeatedly.

I made some more noises, mostly of the groaning and moaning variety. I stayed down. I did a lot of teeth clenching and fast breathing.

Scarface didn't seem impressed. He snorted in disgust and bent down to prod my cheek with a big, dirty finger.

"Get up," he said, in slow, measured English, delivered with a thick Russian tongue.

"Can't," I said.

"Up," he commanded, and then he grabbed me by the collar of my jacket and hauled me to my feet. "Up."

My legs were rubber. But Victoria hooked her hands under my armpits and fought to keep me on my feet.

The thug smiled nastily, his scar tweaking his expression into a snarl.

"This is all that you found?"

The question came from the man in my desk chair. He didn't seem the least bit interested in my suffering. He had the buff cardboard file open on his knees and he was sorting through the loose pages inside. He was still holding the silenced pistol in his hand, but he wasn't aiming it as studiously as before.

"I swear," I said, panting. "You can search me if you like. There's nothing else."

"No, Mr. Howard." He closed the file. Pushed himself up out of the chair. "This will not be necessary. I believe you."

"Glad to hear it," I managed, and swallowed a gob of hot saliva.

"Myself, also." He pulled a face, like he was disgusted by my pitiful state. "I do not like hurting people. It can be so . . . *messy.* But please believe me when I say that if you are lying to me—if I find out that you have lied in any way at all—then I *will* kill you. And Miss Newbury, too. I make you a promise of this."

I felt Victoria's grip tense.

"You look like a man who keeps his promises, Mr. . . . ."

"You may call me Pavel," he said. "And this is my colleague, Vladislav."

"Pavel and Vladislav. And are those your real names?"

"Nyet." He shook his head. "But you do not wish to know them. If I tell you our real names, it suggests we must meet again. And

68

you do not want this, believe me." Pavel tucked his pistol away inside his overcoat. "Thank you for this," he said, lifting the folder in the air.

"Pleasure," I told him.

He circled around us to the door and his stocky pal followed, shifting sideways like a crab. He faked one final punch, jinking his right shoulder forward, and if Victoria hadn't been holding me up, it would have been enough to floor me. He grinned his crooked grin and showed me his missing tooth. He seemed proud of it. I guess he felt like he'd earned the right to be proud of most things.

They left my apartment and I listened to their footsteps on the stairs. They were steady. Unhurried. Then I heard the front door to my building open and close.

"Holy crap," Victoria said. "What do we do now?"

"Well, I don't know about you, but I'm likely to faint."

I broke free of Victoria's grip and staggered across the room, doubled over with one hand clutched to my stomach. I made it as far as the window and looked out at the street below. A sleek black town car was parked alongside the railings of Kollwitzplatz. Pavel climbed into the rear and his henchman with the fast knuckles got into the driver's seat. A few moments later, the headlights came on and the car pulled away from the curb and sped off along the rain-soaked street.

"Are they gone?" Victoria asked.

"They're gone," I told her, collapsing onto the windowsill.

But long after they'd left, their presence still lingered. Two strange men had broken into my home. They'd paced my rooms and pawed my things. Threatened my security. Scared me half to death and pummeled me halfway to the hospital. And yeah, I know, I'm a fine one to talk, but the truth is, I didn't like it in the slightest.

ELEVEN

Victoria collapsed into my desk chair and gripped her head in her hands. Her shoulders were shaking. I wasn't sure what to do. I could hobble over and hold her, I supposed. That would be the gentlemanly response. But it was fraught with danger.

"There, there, Vic," I said, from over by the window. "Try to relax."

"Relax? Are you serious?"

"They got what they came for. They won't be back."

"But why on earth did they come in the first place? Who were they? And how did they find out about you?"

"*Us,*" I said, and immediately regretted it. Victoria lowered her hands. She was gaunt and slack-jawed. "Shall I get you some water?" I asked.

"I don't want any water. I want to know what's going on."

I shrugged off my mackintosh and lifted up my shirt to inspect my stomach. It was enflamed and tender. A lot of blood vessels had burst beneath my skin. I prodded and poked myself, gauging my pain. I imagined it was possible that I was bleeding internally, and I supposed it was the sort of thing one should see a doctor about. But a doctor would require an explanation.

Apparently, they weren't the only one.

"Charlie," Victoria said, "what *is* happening?"

"We were robbed, Vic. At gunpoint." I dropped my shirt and pressed my hand to my side. My stomach pulsed angrily. "It's pretty ironic when you think about it."

"Ironic?"

"Yes. The robbers, getting robbed. We go out and do all the hard work, and they just wait here for us to get back and snatch what we've found."

Victoria sucked in a deep breath. "I am *not* a robber."

"I hear you." I raised my free hand. "I hate the term, too. 'Robbery' always suggests some level of violence. It's a grubby form of theft. No art to it. No craft."

"Not what I meant," she said. "As well you know. And can we please dispense with the breezy attitude? Who were those men?"

I glanced out the window again, as if they might still be there. They weren't. The street was deserted. Even the table-tennis tables were abandoned.

"Well, I don't know for certain, Vic. You have to understand that I've never seen them before tonight. But I think they really were Russian. And their car was fitted with diplomatic plates."

Victoria gripped tightly to the arms of the chair. "You're saying those men were working for the Russian state?"

"It would make sense, I suppose. Freddy has us working for the British embassy, and he wanted that folder recovered very badly. He was afraid of it falling into the wrong hands. I guess those were some of the hands he was concerned by."

"And what was in the folder?"

I turned to face her, resting my legs against the radiator beneath the window. It was warm. It was pleasant. I hoped it might begin to dry my jeans.

"I don't know."

"But you said you looked," Victoria protested.

"And I did. But the information inside the folder was in code."

"Code?"

"Four pages of it. Densely scrawled in cramped handwriting. The paper was yellowed with age and the ink had faded."

"You mean like spy code?"

"I mean like code, code. The type you can't read without the key."

"Are you sure? Perhaps it was in Cyrillic. Maybe that's why the Russians want it."

"No," I told her. "The letters were from the Roman alphabet. But they were scrambled up. Consonants and vowels all over the place. It was like no kind of language I've ever seen."

"Was there anything else? Any pictures? Names?"

"Nope."

"Drawings? Diagrams?"

I sighed. "There was just the code, Vic."

"Huh. And do you think the Russians have the key to the code?"

"I don't know. And if I'm honest, I really don't care."

My legs were getting toasty. I bent down to gather my raincoat from the floor, then stumbled across the living room with my hand clutching my gut to inspect the open door to my apartment.

There were three locks on the door. Good ones, too. I'd fitted them myself when I'd first moved in. It's a habit I've fallen into over the years. Being a thief does tend to give you an appreciation of your own potential vulnerability.

The locks had been engaged when we'd got home—I'd had to use my keys on all three of them. And they showed no obvious signs of tampering.

I hung my coat on a hook fixed to the wall, then removed my penlight and crouched down to study the locks more closely. I started with the unit at the top and worked my way to the bottom. I looked very carefully. Very thoroughly. But I couldn't see any nicks or scratches.

I found that interesting. I knew for a fact that picking the locks would require a high degree of skill. I'd find them challenging myself, and I'm a pro with just the right tools and exactly the right knowledge. Now, it was possible that one of my visitors had a similar skill base, but setting all modesty aside for a moment, I thought it was highly unlikely they'd be as good as me, let alone better. Sure, the stocky guy with the scar was capable of getting through my door, though he'd most likely have used his head for a key. And his boss, Pavel, didn't seem the type to spend time teasing away at pins and tumblers when one of my neighbors might have spotted him.

I closed my door and turned the locks from the inside, and the clunk—thunk—clunk was like a set of ideas falling into place in my mind. I headed along the corridor and poked my head inside Victoria's room, flicking on the light, and when I didn't see anything out of the ordinary, I checked my own bedroom at the rear of the apartment.

The temperature inside my room was several degrees colder than out in the corridor. The window was a sash and one of the panes had been broken. A chill, damp breeze was funneling inside. Fragments of broken glass were spread across the carpet next to my bed, and they crunched under my feet as I approached the window.

The metal catch between the two sashes was undone. It wasn't the most sophisticated of security devices to begin with, I grant you, but there was no way I would have left it like that. I heaved up the bottom sash and stuck my head outside, shining my torch into the black. An aluminum ladder was propped against the wall, its rubberized feet resting in the narrow, unlit alley running behind my building.

So that was how they'd got inside. Not the most dignified of approaches, but undeniably effective.

"You should really close that window," Victoria said from behind me. "It's freezing in here."

She was leaning against my doorway, hugging her arms about herself. She'd shed her padded jacket and was wearing a long green cardigan over damp blue jeans. Her mobile was in her hand.

I pointed to the broken windowpane.

"Oh," she said. Then she shivered. Partly the cold, I guessed. Partly the shock of coming home to find two strange men lying in wait for us, with threats and guns and violence.

Ducking my head, I got a firm grip on the ladder and pushed it sideways, so that it fell away from my window and crashed against the ground. Not a complete solution, by any means, but the alleyway was dark and the likelihood of an opportunistic thief spotting the ladder and my broken window didn't seem very high. I yanked down the sash. Engaged the catch. Short of taping a piece of cardboard over the broken pane, it was the best I could do for now.

"Freddy just sent me a text," Victoria said, and showed me the lit screen of her phone from across the room. "He wants to meet tomorrow morning at ten o'clock. Should I tell him what's happened?"

"No, not yet. Just say that we'll be there."

"But we don't have the file anymore."

"You can leave me to worry about that."

Victoria didn't look convinced. She chewed on her lip and considered Freddy's message. How many xs this time? I wondered.

"Don't you think we should let him know that the Russians have the secret file?" she asked.

"We will, Vic. Tomorrow."

74

"It might be too late by then."

"Not our problem."

She twisted her lips in thought. "You do realize we won't get paid our bonus now you can't give him the file?"

I smiled. Notice how that telltale "we" and "our" had crept in there?

"You can leave me to worry about that, too," I said.

"But what about those men? What if they come back?"

"They won't."

"For God's sake, Charlie." She thumped her fist into the door frame. "I'm scared."

She looked it, too. She was pale and she was trembling. Her teeth were clamped together and her eyes were half shut, like she was bracing for some kind of impact. Perhaps she was seeing haunting visions of Vladislav and Pavel returning when we least expected it. Sneaking through my apartment in the dead of night. Pouncing on us. Attacking us.

Hell, now I was getting a little scared, too.

"Hug me, can't you?" she said.

Could I? I guessed I was going to have to. I mean, it's not the kind of request you can very well decline without causing offense.

I dumped my torch on my bed and edged across the room, like I was moving toward a very high and treacherous precipice. I spread my arms very wide, like a kid playing airplane, and gently closed my arms around her.

"Christ, Charlie, that's not a hug. *This* is a hug."

She squeezed me hard and held me close, her head just below my chin. Her hair scratched my neck and I could smell the scent of her shampoo. It was fragrant and sweet and undeniably pleasant. So was holding her. She was warm and soft and shapely. And, well, we just seemed to *fit*.

I relaxed. My shoulders dropped. I smoothed my hands up and

down her back, stroking the material of her knitted cardigan. I lowered my lips to the crown of her head. I could feel the beat of her heart. It was beating very fast.

"Your heart is racing," she said.

"Adrenaline," I muttered. "Been an eventful night."

She stirred and backed away from me, resting the flat of her hand against my chest. I lowered my arms, cradling her waist. I looked deep into her eyes.

"You know, I almost forgot about what happened at that first apartment," she said.

"Lucky you. I've been trying my best to forget it altogether."

"I wonder if the police are still there."

I wondered that, too. I didn't think it was likely. They hadn't found the blonde, and it wouldn't have taken long for the female officer to discover that the guy who'd called them to report the incident wasn't at home. They'd probably concluded that my report was a hoax.

"Nothing we can do now," I told her. "Feeling better?"

"A little."

She smiled timidly and we released each other. I stuffed my hands inside my pockets and shifted my weight between my feet. Victoria pushed her hair behind her ear.

"Do you think we should stay in a hotel tonight, Charlie?"

"There's really no need. They won't return. I promise. And even if they did, they couldn't get in. The locks on my door were too much for them the first time around. And if they tried to crawl through my window again, I'd hear them right away."

She looked down at the floor. She nodded and she sniffed.

"I'm still a little scared," she said. "And it's so cold in here, Charlie. With the broken window and all." She raised her eyes, and they were wet and glimmering and shifting around with a fidgety uncertainty. "And I don't want this to be weird or to freak you out at all, but I'd really appreciate it if you might sleep in my room tonight." She paused, monitoring my reaction. "On the floor," she added hurriedly. "Next to my bed. I think it would really help me to know that you're close."

My mouth had gone dry. I swallowed. It felt like something was lodged in my throat. My heart, perhaps.

"I can do that," I managed.

"I just have a bad feeling, you know?"

Oh, I knew all about bad feelings. I had plenty of them myself. Sleeping in Victoria's room seemed like a terrible idea to me. There were countless pitfalls. Any number of traps. But one thought alone filled me with more dread than anything else. If I was so aware of the perils, then why hadn't I said no?

TWELVE

Victoria snores in her sleep. There, I've said it. But she snores ever so sweetly. She makes a halting kind of whimper as she inhales. And when she exhales, she half sighs, as if each and every breath is a minor obstacle she's overcome.

At first, it's endearing. But trust me, it rapidly loses its appeal. Pretty soon, the faltering whimper and the faint sigh become loud and insistent. You start to dread them each and every time they come around. I dreaded them for sure. And it wasn't long before I wanted to thump her.

My desire to thump Victoria explains why I was digging my fingernails hard into my thighs. But it wasn't the only reason. I was also trying to distract myself from the thoughts that were preoccupying me. My mind wouldn't settle, and that meant I couldn't settle, and once you add in the discomfort my bruised stomach was causing me, perhaps you'll begin to understand why I was still awake at closing in on two in the morning.

I really didn't believe the Russians would be back. I hadn't simply said it to ease Victoria's nerves. Why would they return? What possible reason could they have? They already had the file. And they'd taken a risk by breaking into my home the first time around.

It was my suspicion that Pavel held a certain oblique position in a highly secretive branch of the Russian government that came with a particular degree of power. He was an educated and cultured type. He was accustomed to riding in the back of luxury town cars, and perhaps he even enjoyed some level of diplomatic immunity. But it wouldn't have done him much good to be caught breaking in to an apartment. The police might have become involved. The justice system. The press. And he wouldn't be eager to flirt with that kind of notoriety a second time around.

But he'd flirted with it once. He'd dirtied his hands. Climbed up a ladder and in through a window. Pointed a gun at a defenseless man and woman. Robbed them and threatened them. Overseen a shabby beating.

He'd gone to what even I, as a self-confessed crook, would tend to view as extremes. And to get there had required a high level of motivation. It suggested that whatever was in the file I'd taken from Jane Parker's hotel room was of real importance. I knew that already, of course, because Freddy had hired me to retrieve it. He'd offered me a very generous fee, and he'd told me it was vital that the information not fall into the wrong hands.

It seemed to me that his fears had now been realized. But the situation was worse than that. I'd been targeted precisely because Pavel knew that I was involved. He knew that Freddy had hired me and that Victoria had helped to negotiate my fee. That kind of knowledge implied that Freddy's security had been breached at a fundamental level. Sure, it was possible that someone had eavesdropped on our Ping-Pong game in some way. Perhaps the Russians had even used some variety of sophisticated listening device. But it was also possible that Freddy had a leak inside his own department. It could be he suspected that already. After all, he'd gone outside the embassy and approached me to help locate the stolen file. But he can't have imagined that his own solution would have been used against him.

Would he blame me? Possibly. Would he suspect me of touting the information around and drawing attention to myself? No, I didn't believe so. I wouldn't have known who to approach in the first place, and I'd had very little time since he'd hired me to think about arranging an auction.

Victoria, then? Maybe someone who didn't know her could suspect her of something along those lines. But Freddy's own brother had worked with us in Paris. He'd vouched for her. And it was quite clear that Freddy had been susceptible to Victoria's charms, so I couldn't imagine him pointing the finger her way.

Was the loss of the file a really severe problem? I didn't see it. An embarrassment, maybe. A concern, for sure. But if this was a matter of genuine national security, then nothing could convince me that Freddy would have come to me for help. He'd have appealed to the British secret service. He'd have held all four people suspected of the theft in detention until Jane Parker admitted her crime and returned the pages of code. So I did feel bad. I was concerned for Freddy and the implications that losing the file might hold for him and the embassy. But I didn't believe I could be involved in a true emergency.

That's not to say I wasn't pretty steamed up about the whole thing. Finding the secret object was never going to be easy, but I'd surprised myself by managing to complete my assignment, and it bugged me that my triumph had been snatched away so cruelly. Hell, if you want the truth, the part that *really* rankled was that there was no elegance about the way I'd been ripped off. If it had been me, I'd have been embarrassed about scampering up a ladder and clambering in through a window. It was so . . . *degrading*. And it was irritating to think that someone who was prepared to stoop so low could have got the drop on me.

But it wasn't just me I was thinking about. I was also thinking about poor Jane Parker. I was asking myself how she'd react when she returned to her hotel room and discovered that the file had been snatched. Because she'd check. I felt sure of it. If it was me, it'd be the first thing I'd do. And she was going to feel awfully sick when she flipped back that leather folder and found that the file was missing.

Would she telephone reception and report a theft? No, I didn't think so. First, she'd check her room thoroughly, trying to convince herself that perhaps the file had been moved elsewhere by a hotel maid. Then she'd probably drop onto her bed and clutch her head in her hands and wonder what on earth she should do. Call the embassy? Confess to what she'd done? Or carry on as normal, hoping the theft of the file would never come to light and her involvement would never be discovered?

Yes, she'd been in the wrong. Betrayed her country, even. But who knew what her personal circumstances were or what had driven her to do it? She might be under all kinds of pressures. She could be in some sort of personal danger. And besides all that, I could empathize with how galling it felt to have the file taken away from you after going to all the trouble of stealing it in the first place.

So I felt pretty guilty about the turmoil she might be experiencing right now. But in truth, that was nothing compared to my fears for the girl I'd seen throttled.

I couldn't get her out of my mind. Oh, I'd tried. I'd done my best to banish her from my thoughts altogether. But the image of her gasping for air, pleading with her eyes, while the faceless brute in the dark jacket squeezed the life from her was something I couldn't escape. I was pretty sure it would be stuck in my mind for a long time to come. I've seen people who've been killed before. Far too many of them for my liking. But never had I been forced to watch, completely helpless, as someone was murdered in a terrible, relentless way in front of my eyes.

Helpless. That was a big part of what was bothering me. Was it really true? Was there something more I could have done? Maybe I should have opened the window and shouted, after all. Or perhaps I could have approached the police and prevented them from leaving the building until they found the girl. And what had stopped me? Self-preservation. Selfishness. I hadn't wanted to draw attention to myself. I hadn't wanted to scupper the mission I was on. But, as it turned out, the mission had been scuppered anyway. I no longer had Freddy's precious file. And the girl was still dead.

At least, I *thought* she was dead. I was practically certain she had to be. But somehow the police hadn't believed it. And Victoria had her doubts, too. Now, true, she hadn't seen what I'd seen. She hadn't watched it play out before her eyes. But I did value her opinion. I did trust her judgment. And hey, I confess, I have been known to make mistakes in the past. Was it really possible that I'd got it wrong? Why hadn't the police found anything suspicious inside the apartment? Where was the girl now?

My thighs were really stinging. My fingernails were in danger of drawing blood. I tore my hands away and laced them together behind my head, adjusting my spine against the floorboards. Then I winced and moaned. I'd forgotten about my tender stomach. I lay very still and waited for the ache to fade. I couldn't help thinking I'd have been a lot more comfortable lying in my own bed. On a soft mattress. Or even better, lying in Victoria's.

It hadn't escaped my notice that there was a convenient space right next to her. A neat little hollow beneath the duvet. If I lifted the covers ever so gently and sneaked my way underneath, I could probably fall asleep much easier.

Yeah, right.

Lying next to Victoria. In the same bed.

Who was I kidding?

I couldn't stop thinking about her, either. And not just because of her snoring. Because of plenty of other things, besides. Her wonky smile. The scent of her hair. The way she'd felt when I was holding her in my arms.

She really had seemed to fit perfectly. *We* seemed to fit. And I was starting to wonder if I'd been fooling myself for all these years. I wasn't getting any younger. I led a life that was governed by chance and by risk. I was only ever one bad job or one dumb move away from a spell behind bars, or perhaps a fate even worse. And meanwhile, my writing was finally taking off. Quite out of the blue, I had the opportunity that I'd been working toward for all these years. And instead of concentrating on the sequel I needed to finish, I'd done just about everything I could think of to blow my big break.

There'd been far too many random thefts just recently. Far too little writing. And I had to wonder if I was trying to sabotage myself. If I was trying to push Victoria to a point where she'd walk away from me so that I didn't have to take that terrifying step toward her. And I wasn't sleeping because of it. Least of all tonight.

I growled and threw back my covers. What to do? Turn on the light and wake her? Talk about what was on my mind?

Or should I get up and go sit in my writing chair? Hammer out a few pages and get my sequel moving again?

Or, and hear me out here, would it be altogether better for me to leave the apartment entirely and set out on some foolhardy errand, one that had the potential to place me in far more jeopardy than I was possibly equipped to handle, but that might just distract me for a few more precious hours?

Hell, put it like that, and what possible choice did I have?

THIRTEEN

It was raining again by the time my taxi dropped me back in the Tiergarten. It felt like it had never stopped. Water was battering the windscreens and the hoods of the cars parked along Kirchstrasse. It was pooling and babbling in the leaf-choked gutters. I bid my driver farewell and sheltered beneath a drooping lime tree. The tree didn't offer a lot of protection. Its half-stripped limbs were weighed down by the falling water, and the rain was blasting sideways, soaking me fast.

I hunched my shoulders and pressed my back against the slickened trunk. My hands were deep inside the pockets of my raincoat and I was clutching my torch and my spectacles case, but neither of them was going to do me much good. The police were long gone. There was no sign of them at all. But the front door to the apartment building was secured by a modern electronic lock that could only be released by waving a signal card in front of a sensor plate. There was nothing mechanical for me to pick and no easy way of tackling the electronic equipment from outside the door.

It was half past two in the morning. The street was wet and deserted. My odds of following a resident inside, or of waiting for someone to emerge from the underground car park, were slimmer than my chances of zigzagging through the slanted rain without being hit by a single drop.

I raised my head and water sluiced down my forehead into my eyes. The second-floor window was still unlit. The blind was still closed. I had no way of knowing what I might find up there and no safe way to satisfy my curiosity. The sensible thing would have been to go home. To put it all down as a bad experience and try to move on. But I wasn't good at sensible. Never have been. And I was determined to get inside.

There were a couple of options available to me. There always are. The simplest thing would be to smash one of the glass panels in the door. A couple of swift blows with the heel of my shoe would do the job. But it would be noisy. It could draw unwanted attention. And it was undeniably crass.

My other option was crass, too. It was hardly the most covert of approaches. But it had worked for me in the past, and I was confident it would work again tonight.

I pushed away from the tree and approached the entrance. It was set back in a well-lit alcove, and I was pleased to step in out of the rain. I was less pleased when I saw the security camera that was pointing at me from behind the glass doors. I turned sideways and raised my arm to cover my face. Too late to do much good, but better than holding up my ID and shouting my address.

An intercom panel was set flush into the wall. There was a camera there, too, fitted behind a small square of thickened glass. I placed my hand over the lens and buzzed a random apartment.

The buzz was loud out on the street. I guessed it would be a good deal louder inside a silent apartment in the middle of the night. Loud enough to disrupt somebody's sleep. And irritating enough to draw them out of bed if I kept buzzing. Which I did. Insistently. Relentlessly. For more than a minute.

I took a break. The break lasted a couple of seconds. Then I pressed the buzzer again.

I held it for a long time. Long enough for my finger to begin to quiver. Maybe the apartment was empty. Or maybe I'd picked a really heavy sleeper.

I decided to play a tune, just to be sure. A tune could be truly annoying. If I did it right, even the most stubborn person would be bound to come and investigate. The tune itself didn't really matter. I could have gone with anything, I suppose. But I chose the British national anthem. "God Save the Queen." I'd been working on Her Majesty's behalf earlier in the evening, so I guessed it was only appropriate.

I was just finishing "Happy and glorious" and was about to embark upon "Long to reign over us" when I finally got a response. It sounded more like a bark.

"Wer ist da?" asked a short-tempered male voice.

"Martin, it's Johnny," I slurred. "Lost my key card. Very drunk."

There was a pause. A strained wait.

"Martin, it's Johnny," I mumbled again. "Lemme in. *Drunk*."

A sharp exhalation crackled through the speaker. "You have the wrong apartment."

And with that, the speaker fell silent.

But I didn't.

I pressed the buzzer again. No need for a tune this time. Just a series of short, intermittent bursts would do the trick.

The response came in less than five seconds. There was no speaking. No communication. Just another kind of buzz. A long, flat droning. And a sudden clunk. It was the very noise I'd been waiting for. The sound of the lock disengaging.

86

"Thanks, Marty," I drawled. "You're a legend."

I snatched at the door, swaying for the sake of appearances, and staggered toward the elevator. Once I was sure I was beyond the scope of any camera lenses, I veered toward the stairs, wiping the rain from my face with my coat sleeve and reaching inside my pocket for my customized plastic gloves.

The plastic clung to my damp skin, which made slipping the gloves on harder than it had any right to be as I climbed the stairs to the second floor of the building. The stairs were clean and functional and very brightly lit. I could hear the hum of electricity coming from the lights above my head and the echo of my soggy footsteps in the cavernous stairwell. But I couldn't hear anything else. There was nobody close. No other sounds whatsoever.

The corridor I entered was long and silent. The walls were painted a stark white, and the flooring was some kind of hard-wearing carpet, dark blue in color. There were a lot of doors at evenly spaced intervals. They all looked identical, manufactured from some kind of sleek laminate. There were spy holes and snap locks and dead bolt locks of an unremarkable design. There were sequential numbers screwed to the wall beside each door.

The noise of my breathing seemed loud and obtrusive inside the corridor. So did my footsteps as I squelched along the carpet. I've trained myself over the years to tread as lightly as possible, but in the small hours of the morning, you can tiptoe in thick woolen socks and still convince yourself you're making a racket.

I was concentrating hard on working out which door I needed. This would be a very bad time to make a mistake. The window where I'd seen the woman being strangled had been two along from the front entrance. Judging by the distance between the doors and the quality feel of the building, I got the impression the apartments would be spacious. So I didn't have far to walk. No more than twenty paces. But I took my time. I was about to do something that was really quite stupid. And I wanted to give myself a chance to come to my senses and back away.

Nope. I didn't seem to be quitting. I was still moving. Slowly but resolutely. The door I'd set my eyes on was drawing closer. It was becoming ever more sinister. And sure, partly that was because I was about to break in, and no matter how experienced I've become, I don't think I'll ever shake the heady swirl of fear and excitement that takes hold of me whenever I face up to cracking a lock and sneaking inside a stranger's home. But it was also because I was about to break something else. Two of my golden rules, in fact.

I never break into a property that's occupied unless I absolutely have to.

Hmm, well, let's see, there was a very good chance that this apartment would be occupied. First, by a corpse. And second, by a murderer. And there was no way I could convince myself that I absolutely *had* to break in. I certainly wanted to. I was curious. I was concerned. But I wasn't compelled to do this. It was my choice. An act of free will. And no doubt, a pretty foolish one.

I always knock before I enter.

Er, not this time. Forgive me for sounding like a wuss, but if I was going to drop in on a cold-blooded killer in the middle of the night, I didn't intend to let him know a whole lot about it. It would be rude, for one thing. Oh, and a trifle dangerous. Because if the guy had killed once, he might be inclined to do it again, and I wasn't keen to play the role of his second victim.

So I was going to be quiet. I was going to be stealthy. I was going to be all those things that a really great burglar is supposed to be.

Except smart, perhaps.

Rainwater dripped from my overcoat and tapped out an irregular rhythm on the floor. The tempo was much slower and less erratic than the beat of my heart. I sucked in a deep breath. I wished I was sucking on a cigarette instead. I popped open my spectacles case, removed the necessary tools, and stooped down toward the dead bolt lock in the middle of the door.

Believe me, it takes a lot of practice to really excel at picking locks. Most of the time, you can't possibly see what you're doing, so you have to learn to feel for the slightest variation in the tension being transmitted through your torsion wrench. A tiny drop in resistance from the locking cylinder lets you know you're on the right track. Unfortunately for me, the arthritis in my fingers had deadened my sensitivity to a small degree. The change was only fractional—perhaps not something a doctor could quantify—but I'd become increasingly frustrated by it during the past few months.

As a result, I'd started to rely a little more on my hearing. I'd taught myself to listen intently for the tiny, giveaway click of a lock pin shuffling into position. I was listening harder than ever tonight. I was hearing click after click after click, and for once, I didn't welcome the sound. Maybe it was my nerves. Maybe it was the silence in the corridor. But I could swear that every time a tiny brass pin jinked up and hunkered down exactly where I wanted it to, it sounded about as loud as a man clapping his hands right next to my ear.

I told myself to calm down. Inside the apartment there'd be all kinds of ambient noise. The hum of electrical appliances. The settling of water in pipes. The percussion of the rain against the windows. And, perhaps, the soft, even breathing of the killer I was hoping to avoid.

At last, the final pin fell into position. I wedged the dead bolt lock open, turning my attention to the snap lock. It was cheap and highly susceptible to being shimmed.

In the movies, actors often use a credit card for this trick. It's not something I recommend. For one thing, it never works—the type of plastic used to make credit cards isn't flexible enough to do the job—and for another, it risks destroying your credit card. The better option is to invest in a proper shimming device from a decent locksmith supply company. I'd done exactly that, which explains why I had a set of five sheets made from a particular type of plastic known as Super Mica. The sheets are approximately the size of a playing card and are graded according to varying degrees of strength and pliability, but there was no need for me to experiment on this occasion. The first sheet eased the latch back readily enough, and as soon as it retracted, I prodded the door open with my foot.

There was no response from inside. No shouts of protest. No slamming of doors or sudden attacks. No light, even. The interior was in darkness. I planned to keep it that way.

Very carefully, I swung the door open just wide enough to be able to slip through, then I retrieved my burglary tools and moved inside.

I stayed very still, waiting for my eyes to adjust to the gloom. I didn't want to bump into anything—least of all a corpse. So I kept waiting. I stayed patient. And before very long I could see pretty clearly.

And what I saw rocked me to my very core.

FOURTEEN

I found myself in a large, open space. I guessed it was what would pass for the living room. But there was no living going on. No furniture. No belongings. Nothing at all.

The air was chill and tasted stale. I got the impression the apartment hadn't been lived in for a long time. But of course, it was only an impression, and I wasn't about to risk my neck on it. True, the room was completely bare, but maybe whoever lived here was a fan of extreme minimalism. I was going to have to check the rest of the apartment to be sure. I was going to have to wade into the darkness, my hands in front of my face, my body braced to react in case somebody jumped out at me. I couldn't use my torch. Shining my penlight would be like painting a target on myself. And I already felt very exposed. I had nothing to hide behind. Nowhere to shelter.

And no time to lose.

I left the front door ajar. It wasn't what I'd normally do, but this whole situation was a long way from normal, and if I needed to flee in a hurry, I didn't want anything to get in my way.

I sneaked across the timber flooring to an open doorway in the facing wall. I poked my head inside. This room was even darker. But it was still and silent. And when I squinted and peered very hard, I couldn't make out a thing.

It was the same with the next room along.

The same again with the room after that.

The apartment appeared to be unoccupied. I began to relax. There was a switch on the wall near my shoulder, and I flipped it down and nearly flipped completely out. The switch was for a bathroom, and when the lights came on, an extractor fan came with them. The noise was sudden and unexpected and very loud. It damn near gave me a heart attack. But my panic was short-lived. The bathroom was as vacant as everywhere else. Just a toilet and a sink and a bath. No towels. No toiletries.

Quickly now, I paced back across the living room, closed the front door and powered up the main ceiling lights. The room seemed bigger in the glare of the recessed bulbs. I returned to the bedrooms and found a built-in closet in one of them. I slid the doors open. Empty. There was one more room to explore. It was on the opposite side of the apartment. I turned the light on in there, too, and discovered an unused kitchen. There was a fine layer of dust on the countertops. Enough to suggest the place had been empty for a couple of months, minimum.

The barren state of the apartment didn't surprise me a great deal. Berliners take *everything* with them when they move out of a place. I'd even heard one expat complain that he'd rented an apartment without taps and power sockets. So it was perhaps a little unusual that the ceiling bulbs were still here, along with the Venetian blind in the living room window. The blind was closed. And it looked awfully familiar.

I moved across just to be sure. There was a plastic rod on one side, and I twirled it until the slats rotated into a horizontal position.

I parted them with my fingers and peered outside into the darkness and the rain.

I scanned the blurred apartment building opposite, tracking upward from the main entrance until I found the window to Daniel Wood's apartment. I checked my bearings. There was no mistake. I was standing where I'd seen the blond woman strangled.

But there was nothing to suggest a murder had taken place here. No signs of a struggle. I suppose it would have been difficult to leave any evidence behind. There was no furniture to topple over and no ornaments to upset. And strangulation was a pretty tidy way of killing someone. No awkward bloodstains. No wayward bullet holes. If the place had looked this abandoned when the police had arrived, then it was little wonder they'd left so soon.

Had they dismissed my call for good reason? Could I really have made a mistake? I'd been in a high-stress situation when I'd looked out the window. I'd built up a lot of frustration. A lot of nervous energy. And I was a guy with a pretty creative mind. A mystery writer, no less. Someone who spent his days describing heinous crimes and his nights committing them. Had I let my imagination run away with me?

I closed the blind and turned to consider the room. Why would a murder occur in an empty apartment? What would bring two people here?

I was still asking myself that question—still shaking my head at the senselessness of it all—when I happened to spot something down on the floor. A simple thing. Utterly unremarkable, in fact. But I experienced a tingle when I saw it. A trembling in my throat. I dropped to my knees and lifted the item between my gloved finger and thumb. It was a long, curling strand of blond hair. There were more strands on the honey-toned floorboards. Five or six, at least. And they were collected together in the exact spot where I'd seen the woman being throttled.

I took a moment to collect myself. Then I popped the strand of hair inside my spectacles case. I don't know why exactly. It proved something to me, but it wouldn't prove a great deal to anyone else, and I wasn't about to go to the police and demand that they analyze it for DNA.

One thing seemed obvious to me now. The killer must have moved the blonde's body. He must have done it right away, clearing out of the apartment before the police arrived and hiding somewhere until they left. Then he'd made his escape.

With the body? I wasn't sure. The girl I'd seen had struck me as kind of slim. Petite, even. And sure, the guy who'd attacked her was taller than average, but moving any kind of body was no easy task. And even supposing he was physically equipped for it, a lifeless corpse wasn't the kind of thing you could take on the S-Bahn with you. Did that mean he'd brought along a car? A van? Maybe. Or maybe he'd stashed the body somewhere close by, ready to return for it later. Or never.

I decided to check a few obvious places on my way out of the building, but there weren't many available to me. I walked the second-floor corridor and I didn't find any utility cupboards or laundry rooms. Every door led to an apartment. That only left the elevator and the stairwell. I called the elevator, just to be sure, and I waited impatiently for the doors to part on an empty compartment. I waited for them to shuffle closed again and then I returned to the stairs. I went up a level and checked the corridor above. It was exactly the same. Then I headed down to the ground floor and scouted around in the entrance vestibule. There was a blank door on the far side of the elevator. The camera that had filmed me coming in was pointing in the opposite direction, toward the main entrance. There was no other security that I could see.

I scurried across to the door, fumbling in my coat pocket for my spectacles case. But I had no need for my picks. The door was unlocked. An overhead light flickered on, and light bounced off bare cinder-block walls and a set of metal shelving units. A line of communal washer-dryers were butted against the wall, alongside a wall-mounted ice dispenser with a metal bucket beneath it. The bucket was half filled with melting ice. There was a large chest freezer in one corner. A couple of bicycles propped against the wall. A few boxes scattered around.

There was no dead blonde.

I lifted the lid on the chest freezer and a haze of frosty air escaped. I wafted it aside and peered in at a world of ice and frozen groceries labeled with conspicuous nametags. No frozen corpse.

I dropped the lid and checked my watch. It was 3:30 A.M. At least half an hour until the first S-Bahn and U-Bahn trains would start up again. I wasn't in the mood to wait. One of the bicycles was a man's mountain bike. It was very nicely engineered. The front forks were fitted with some kind of suspension system, there were at least twenty-one gears, and when I lifted it to turn it around and wheel it toward the door, I found that it weighed just a little more than a feather.

I allowed the door to fall closed behind me and then I scanned the vestibule one last time. There were no other possible hiding places, but a bank of metal mailboxes were set into the wall facing me, and seeing them made me think of something else. A small point but important perhaps. I let myself out into the rain and walked my new bike across the drenched road to the apartment building on the other side of the street.

The foyer design was pretty similar. There was an alcove entrance door, an elevator, a stairwell, and a set of mailboxes. But there was no security camera and no electronic locking system. I picked the door lock without a great deal of trouble—I'd had a lot of practice during the past few hours—and I snuck inside and paced across to the mailboxes. There were no names attached to them. Just numbers. But I knew the number of Daniel Wood's apartment, and defeating the cheap lock on his mailbox was simplicity itself.

There were a couple of glossy flyers inside, but only one item that interested me. It was a folded piece of notepaper, and when I straightened it out, I found that it was branded with the crest of the Berlin police. Someone had scrawled a Biro note in a neat, slanted script. I had a pretty fair idea who the message was from, and my German was good enough to confirm my suspicions. It had been written by a "POK'in Fuchs." "POK" was short for the rank of *Polizeioberkommissar* and adding *in* denoted a female officer. The message had been penned by the policewoman who'd followed up my emergency call and it asked Mr. Wood to contact her regarding the serious incident he'd reported by telephone.

I wasn't surprised that the note hadn't been picked up just yet. Wood had gone out for the embassy function in his car. He would have returned the same way, gaining access to his apartment via the parking garage and the elevator. He would have had no reason to check his post because he wouldn't have been expecting any new mail until the morning.

I scrunched the note up and popped it into my coat pocket. Then I stepped out into the rain, fired up a cigarette and jammed it in the corner of my mouth. I straddled my new bike and puffed contentedly as I pedaled away in the direction of the river. It was raining persistently. I was going to get very wet. But I didn't altogether mind. Cycling always reminds me a little of my time in Amsterdam. It would be a pleasant enough way to amble home through the sodden, lonely streets, and it was a wonderful way to think.

And boy, did I have a lot of thinking to do.

FIFTEEN

I was cold and thoroughly soaked by the time I got home. My hair was plastered to my head and my clothes were pasted to my body.

I leaned my bike against the metal railings outside my building and gave the saddle a friendly pat, as if I was thanking a loyal steed for good service. I didn't expect it to still be there the next time I stepped outside. I had no lock and chain to secure it, and to be perfectly honest, I was beginning to suspect there were one or two untrustworthy types living in Berlin.

I trudged toward my front door, and then I turned and scanned Kollwitzplatz. The middle of the square was dark and unlit, but there were plenty of street lamps around the edges, and I didn't spot any town cars with diplomatic plates or any shady types watching me from the shadows. I guess I should have felt relieved, but as I swiveled back around and fitted my key in the lock on the front door, I couldn't ignore the way my shoulders tensed and my scalp tingled. Something felt wrong. I spun quickly and checked behind me once again. Nobody there. Just darkness and stillness and the steady, pelting rain. Weird. Perhaps my preoccupation with fictional hoods and crooks was coming home to roost, turning me into a nervous wreck.

Or perhaps not.

Because as I pushed open the door and stepped inside the foyer, I found that I wasn't alone. A man was slouched at the bottom of the stairs, his head resting against the half-tiled wall. He was holding a paperback novel in his hand, the pages rolled back over the spine. He had on a black leather jacket over a black turtleneck sweater and black jeans. His dark hair was studiously gelled and combed to one side.

I recognized him. How could I not?

Oh, I suppose I should have been surprised, but I was running a little low on surprises, as it happened.

"You as well?" I said, and threw up my hands. "But you're the guy from the hotel bar."

He worked a sly grin. "You remember me? I am flattered, Monsieur Howard."

There was a braying, husky quality to his voice, and an unmistakable Gallic accent. He sounded French. He looked French. Hell, in a minute I was going to go out on a limb and assume he actually *was* French.

The weak yellow light in the hallway cast ghoulish shadows across his face. He seemed to relish the effect.

"I like your book very much," he told me, though he leered as he showed me the jacket design. It was a French edition. A translation of my fourth Michael Faulks mystery, *The Thief on the Run*. Not my finest work, perhaps, though every sale helps. "I find it very interesting, this thief you write of. You are convincing, yes? Experienced, perhaps?"

"Save it," I told him. "I've heard this routine before. Why don't you just skip to the part where you tell me who you are and what you want?"

He tapped the book with his fingernail and smiled crookedly. "But this is something your burglar would say, don't you think?"

I glanced past him, up the stairs. I was trying very hard not to let him unbalance me, but fear was beginning to prickle all over my skin, like a rash.

"You worry for your friend." He shook his head and clucked his tongue, as if I'd insulted him badly. "She is very beautiful, I admit, but she is quite safe. My name is Henri. I wish only to talk."

"So talk," I said, pinching the rainwater from my eyes. "What are you? Some kind of spy?"

He laughed. A show laugh. But the guy was no actor. At least not a good one.

"Listen, can we get this over with?" I asked. "I'm tired. I want to sleep. And in return, I assume you want the secret object. The one the British embassy hired me to find."

His smile grew a little. It was in danger of becoming genuine.

"Then prepare to be disappointed," I told him. "I don't have it. You're too late. Some other guys already beat you to the punch. Literally." I unbuttoned my soggy raincoat and lifted up my shirt. I showed him the bruising and the welts that had bloomed around my stomach. "They were Russian, if that helps."

He took a moment to absorb what I'd said. He was having trouble accepting it. The muscles in his face were getting a terrific workout. His square jaw was clenching and unclenching, the skin around his eyes tightening and relaxing. "When was this?"

"A few hours ago. While you were trawling the bar. You should have stopped me when you had your chance."

"And the item?"

"It's a file," I said, weary now. "That's all I know. There were coded pages inside. I don't know what the information relates to. And I honestly don't care." I straightened my clothes and dropped my hands by my sides. "Now, can I get to bed? I'm cold and I'm wet, and to be brutally frank, I'm a little fed up with dealing with strange men wanting to run a half-baked shakedown on me."

I moved as if to pass him on the stairs, but he gripped the tail of my coat and yanked me around. He pushed me hard against the wall, flattening my face against the crackled tiles. He patted me down roughly. He found my torch. He found my spectacles case and my burglary tools. He found the crumpled note from Officer Fuchs of the Berlin constabulary. But he didn't find the file or anything else that particularly interested him.

"If you lie to me," he warned, then left the consequences unspoken and pressed my belongings into my chest.

"Yes?"

He leaned close to my ear. Dug his fingers into my bruised stomach and squeezed hard. "I will watch you, Monsieur Howard. Know this. Remember it."

He grunted and shoved me sideways. I fell and grazed my knee on a stair edge.

"How could I forget?" I said, pressing my hand to my gut. "But hey, knock yourself out. At least you have a good book to keep you company."

He was out the door and gone before I turned my head, but he'd had a final insult up his sleeve. He'd dropped my novel on the floor behind him and stamped on it for good measure. The pages were splayed and ripped, and I could see the muddy imprint of his shoe treads on the jacket.

Terrific, I thought. *Another satisfied reader.*

I sucked down a lot of oxygen on my way upstairs with my woebegone book. It helped to calm my nerves but it didn't do a lot for my throat. I'd smoked too many cigarettes during my bike ride home, and when I inhaled deeply, it felt like I'd swallowed a cheese grater.

My trousers clung to my thighs. My fingers were pale and bloated and stiff. The cold and the wet were a terrible combination so far as my arthritis was concerned. I held out my hand, palm down. It was shaking badly. So was the rest of me.

Hell, was I getting too old for this game? Maybe it was time to rethink my lifestyle and adjust to a safe, law-abiding existence. Maybe now was the moment to settle down in my writing chair and put my life of real crime behind me.

Or maybe I just needed a good rest.

I slowed my footsteps as I approached my apartment. The locks were still engaged, and there was no sign of forced entry. I used my keys and slipped through the door as quietly as possible, placing the French edition of my book inside a rarely used drawer in the hallway cabinet, peeling my coat from my shoulders and plucking my shoes from my feet. I sneaked into my bathroom, where I lay on the floor and heaved my trousers off my legs as if I was struggling out of a wet suit. Then I toweled myself down and crept along the hallway toward Victoria's bedroom in just my boxer shorts and my damp shirt.

Victoria wasn't snoring anymore, but I could hear her breathing, soft and regular. I checked my watch. Four-thirteen A.M. We weren't due to meet Freddy until ten. If I was lucky, I could snatch a few hours' sleep.

Victoria was facing away from me, wrapped tightly in her duvet. I could see the covers rising and falling in the blue-black light. I went down on my hands and knees and crawled across the floor to the blankets I'd abandoned just a few hours before. I pulled them over me. I stretched. I yawned. I uttered a small sigh of contentment.

And then the telephone started to ring.

It was shrill and it was jarring.

Victoria gasped and reared up in bed like she'd been punched in the gut.

"Whaaa?" she mumbled, and looked around wildly. Her mouth was wide open, her eyes a swollen, glittery black.

"Easy," I told her. "It's just the phone."

She raised her hand to her head. Her hair was sticking out at all kinds of crazy angles, like she'd been sleeping with her arms wrapped around a Van de Graaff generator.

"What time is it?" she asked.

I told her. I was able to be very exact.

The phone kept ringing in my living room. The ringing seemed to be getting louder. I could almost picture the phone shaking itself loose from the wall and skittering along the hallway toward me. I swear, it was the only way I was going to answer it.

"Aren't you going to get that?" Victoria asked.

"Nope," I said, yawning.

"But it could be important."

"Then I'm sure they'll call back later."

"What about your neighbors?"

"Don't worry about them. They have their own phones to answer."

The phone kept ringing in the darkness. It sounded as loud as a fire alarm. As urgent as an air-raid siren.

I lifted my blankets over my head and clamped my palms over my ears.

"Charlie," Victoria said, "I really think you should answer the phone."

I groaned. "I know you do, Vic. But trust me. They'll give up soon enough."

And they did. Right then. Almost as if I'd willed it to happen.

There was a pause of at least five seconds.

Then the phone started to ring again.

"It doesn't seem like they're going to stop," Victoria said. She was helpful like that.

I growled at my misfortune, then yanked back my covers,

hauled open the door, and stormed down the hallway. I snatched the phone off the hook.

"What?" I snapped.

There was a long beat of silence. Just the faintest trace of breathing on the end of the line.

"Who is this?" I demanded.

More silence. More breathing.

Then, finally, a voice.

"Herr Howard? Herr Charlie Howard?" The voice was male. My caller's English was good, but I'd spent time with enough locals in the past few months to recognize a German accent when I heard it.

"Do I know you?" I asked. And meantime, what I was actually thinking was, *Do I want to know you?*

"No, you do not know me. But you will know me soon, I am thinking. I fear you may trust me on this."

I opened my mouth to say more, but just then I heard a click, followed by a long, flat note. The guy had hung up. I wasn't sure his call had been worth answering. It certainly didn't make me feel any better.

I turned to find Victoria shuffling into the room, clenching her duvet around her shoulders.

"Who was it?" she asked.

"Wrong number."

"Oh," she said, and stifled a yawn. "That's a pain."

I grunted, then placed the phone on the cradle and staggered past her along the hallway.

"Where are you going?" she asked.

"Bed," I told her. "My own, this time."

It was cold inside my room. The wet breeze through the broken window had cooled the temperature considerably. But I didn't care. I collapsed on my mattress and dived beneath my covers and tucked myself into a tight ball. Then I closed my eyes and willed myself to sleep. I wanted to drop off straightaway, to plunge into absolute nothingness.

But in that, as with so much else that day, I didn't have the best of luck.

SIXTEEN

I didn't sleep. I barely dozed. And as I thrashed around in bed, growing grumpier and more resentful all the while, my drowsy brain fired questions at me that I couldn't begin to answer. The questions multiplied. So did my concerns. It didn't do a lot to improve my mood. But it was a wonderful way of becoming agitated.

I gave up on sleeping before eight, hauled on my dressing gown and stomped through to my living room. I collapsed onto my writing chair, lit a cigarette, and sucked on it hard, trying to kindle some kind of mental spark. It didn't work. It just hurt my ravaged throat. I scowled at the telephone on my wall. I scowled at my laptop. I scowled at my sorry copy of *The Maltese Falcon,* with its charred jacket and flaking pages. Then I groaned and twirled around in my chair and scrambled to my feet and gazed out my window at the scene below.

The rain had finally stopped and the sky was beginning to lighten from wet slate to dry asphalt. Office workers were climbing inside their Volkswagens and BMWs, throwing their legs over old bicycles, or walking stiffly with briefcases clasped tight. A woman wheeled a child in a stroller toward the soaked and leaf-scattered playground beside the table-tennis tables. I didn't see any kids shuffling to school. No doubt they'd already be in class by now, thinking clearly and precisely about the problems that had been set for them. Unlike yours truly.

I coaxed more smoke into my lungs. The soreness in my throat wasn't easing at all, but I wasn't about to stub my cigarette out. This was what I did when I was blocked on a novel. I could be a stubborn fellow when I set my mind to it. I could smoke and stare out my window for hours until I understood my next move. And all I had to do now was apply the same technique to the situation I'd found myself in. If I marshaled all the information I had to hand, if I ordered it and analyzed it, probed it and poked at it, there was no reason why I couldn't develop a better understanding of what was going on.

Except it wasn't working.

I didn't know where to start. I couldn't figure out which problem to tackle first. Was it the blonde I'd seen murdered, in what appeared to be an abandoned apartment? Was it the peculiar assignment Freddy had handed me and the way it had gone spectacularly right, only to go spectacularly wrong when the coded file was taken from me under duress? Was it my surprise visit from Henri, the bibliophile spy, or the abrupt and unsettling phone call I'd received in the dead of night?

Hell. That was the problem with trying to think your way forward in somebody else's plot. I hated the feeling of having a story imposed on me. It was a terrible way to work. Over the years, there'd been times when Victoria had tried to sell me on the idea of ghosting some mystery novels for more famous writers, but I'd always turned the opportunity down flat. Figuring out my own puzzles was tough enough. Trying to construct a book from somebody else's premise was no kind of fun.

My cigarette was just about finished. So was my patience. I stabbed my smoke out, then went and took a fast shower and dressed in an old pair of jeans and a hooded top. By the time I entered my kitchen, Victoria was pouring boiling water from a kettle into a pair of mugs branded with the slogan WORLD'S BEST BOSS. There aren't many perks to being self-employed, so you have to entertain yourself where you can.

"Coffee?" she asked.

"It looks to be."

"Do you want some?"

"Sure. But make it black. And strong."

She sucked air through her teeth. "I'm sorry, Charlie. Did you have a lot of trouble dropping off last night?"

"You might say."

"Then I apologize. You were right. Those men didn't come back. I was overreacting."

Oh, if only you knew, I thought.

Victoria added an extra spoonful of granules to my mug and passed it to me. She had on a navy V-neck sweater and gray cargo trousers. The pockets and pouches on her trousers were weighed down and bulging, and I dreaded to think what might be stashed in them. When she'd stayed with me in Venice, she'd taken the precaution of equipping herself with a worrisome collection of self-defense weapons in case I got us involved in yet another dangerous scrape. It wouldn't have surprised me to learn that she'd upgraded her arsenal for Berlin.

"So," she said, before I could voice my suspicions, "what do you want to do about Freddy?"

"I can tell you what I *don't* want to do. I don't want to meet him by those damn Ping-Pong tables."

"Afraid he'll humiliate you again?"

"No-o," I said. "It's not safe, is all. Too close to this apartment.

Too much risk of being overheard or of people following us back here."

"So what do you suggest?"

"Text him," I said. "Tell him we'll come to the embassy."

Victoria reached a hand inside one of her many trouser pockets and removed her mobile. She thumbed the screen and slurped her coffee. "Done," she said, after a short pause.

"Marvelous."

I swallowed some coffee myself. It was strong, all right. And bitter. But I wasn't convinced it would compensate for a sleepless night.

"You really do look awful," Victoria told me.

"Thanks."

"Completely exhausted. You have bags under your eyes and your skin is all blotchy."

"Charming."

"And your eyes have this crazy, unfocused look. It's like you're drunk and hungover all at the same time."

"This is a big help, Vic. Truly."

Her phone blipped. She shrugged and lowered her face to the screen. Then she shrugged some more.

"Freddy says he won't meet us at the embassy. It has to be somewhere else."

"Fine," I told her. "I have just the place."

The place was the Brandenburg Gate. It was located only a five-minute stroll from the British embassy, and it would have been hard to think of a more dramatic setting. The vast triumphal arch had been conceived as a monumental gateway to the city, but during the Cold War it had been situated just east of the Wall. Not so much a thoroughfare as a dead end. I hoped that wasn't an omen.

Nowadays, the gate overlooked the glitzy public space of Pariser Platz, a generous square fashioned from polished flagstones, where street artists posed for photographs in a bizarre selection of costumes that included chicken suits and Darth Vader outfits. Famous buildings surrounded the space, from the Kennedy Museum and the glass-faced Academy of Arts, to the imposing U.S. Embassy and the exclusive Adlon Hotel, now infamous as the place where Michael Jackson had once dangled his baby out of a window to the baying fans below.

Looking beyond the square, I could see along the dramatic boulevard of Unter den Linden, with its boxed lime trees, to the Fernsehturm, the golf-ball-on-a-tee television tower that's visible from most areas of Berlin. Over to my left was the sparkling glass cupola that topped the Reichstag, the dark-stoned German parliament building.

But really, I hadn't chosen the spot for its location, its history, or its mesmerizing view. I'd selected it because of the number of spy novels and espionage movies that had featured the Brandenburg Gate as a backdrop to the action. The place spoke to me of daring adventure and double-dealing and intrigue. And hell, if I was going to be caught up in a world of gun-toting hoodlums and threatening phone calls, mysterious government assignments and barfly French agents, then, blow me, I was going to exploit the opportunity for all it was worth.

Mind you, the weak autumn sunshine and the colorful tourist crowds weren't exactly what I'd had in mind when I'd visualized the scene. In my head, I'd rehearsed my meeting with Freddy in the flickering black-and-white of an old movie reel. We'd all been terribly English. I'd been dashed courageous and commendably stoic. Freddy had been a little world-weary and knocked about the edges. Victoria had been prim and skittish, with an admirable dose of pluck. Mighty odds had been against us, great misfortunes had beset us, but together we'd somehow pulled through and the fate of the world had been safe in our hands for just a few hours at least.

It was a pleasant little fantasy. Diverting, for sure. But as so often seems to be the case for me, reality had other ideas.

"We can't talk here," Freddy barked, as he paced through the colonnaded archway toward me. "Far too public."

At least he was wearing a trench coat. It was tan in color and buttoned close to his chin, with a matching belt that struggled to contain his tubby waist. If only I could have got him to turn up the collar and invest in a trilby, he wouldn't have been so far off the Freddy I'd imagined.

"Nobody's listening," I told him. "Everyone here is a tourist. We'll be fine."

He glowered at me, then flashed Victoria a conciliatory smile and reached across to stroke her arm.

"Hello, my dear. You look very well. The red of your coat really becomes you." He checked over his shoulder and leaned toward me. "I may have been followed."

I suppose I should have told him to get a grip, but I quite liked the way his behavior was getting toward the kind of thing I'd idly fantasized about.

"So what is it you suggest?"

Freddy's eyes slid one way, then the other.

"Do you have the package?" he asked, from the corner of his mouth.

It was all I could do not to pull the guy close and plant a big sloppy kiss on his cheek. I can't tell you how many years I've spent in this racket, waiting for someone to ask me that very question.

"We have the package," I told him, in my best matinee drawl.

Victoria jabbed me with her elbow.

"Ouch!" I doubled up and clutched my stomach. She'd hit me smack where I'd been punched the previous night. Freddy didn't know that, of course, and he looked at me as if I was a very poor excuse for a man.

"Tell Freddy the truth," Victoria said, standing over me.

"Fine," I managed, through gritted teeth. "The truth is we *sort* of have it."

"I beg your pardon?" Freddy backed away from me. "What exactly does that mean?"

Victoria jabbed me in the stomach a second time. "That's not the truth."

"It is," I groaned. "And if you'll just stop hitting me for a moment, we can find somewhere safe for me to explain."

SEVENTEEN

The somewhere safe was my idea. I'll admit that Freddy wasn't wholly convinced, and Victoria was downright skeptical, but I thought it was a masterstroke.

The bus was a green double-decker and it was a long way from new. There were patches of rust around the wheel arches, and the idling engine was gruff and clamorous. The side of the bus was branded with a colorful mural featuring Berlin's landmark sites and the words HOP-ON, HOP-OFF CITY TOUR were plastered on every available surface. A clutch of bewildered tourists stared out from behind the scratched windows like a herd of sheep who'd been rounded up and penned inside without any real understanding of what they were doing there.

Freddy began to protest, but I ignored him and approached a ticket seller who was wearing a bulky green coat that matched the color of the bus exactly. He was chatting with a woman in a garish yellow parka and a man in a bright red fleece. The red and yellow tour buses hadn't arrived just yet.

The guy in green offered me a bored rendition of some practiced spiel, but I cut him off by handing him enough cash for three tickets. Then I beckoned Freddy and Victoria to follow me on board and up the cramped, twisting staircase to the top deck.

Most of the tourists were seated near the front of the bus, so I ducked my head and shuffled toward the rear. There was a giant canvas roof above our heads that could be rolled back during the summer months. It smelled of damp and mildew, and it didn't offer a great deal of insulation. To compensate, hot air was being pumped hard through perforated vents running along beneath the seats. The system was loud and the interior stuffy. It was just about the least pleasant way of touring a city that I could think of.

I took a cramped window seat and folded my knees up by my ears. Victoria settled alongside me, and Freddy collapsed on the bench in front. He turned around to face us, his forearm resting on the metal rail running along the top of his bench. I got the impression he was a bit miffed that Victoria wasn't sitting next to him.

"I don't like this," he said. "We're too enclosed."

"What are you talking about? This couldn't be better. If anyone follows us on here, they'll find it impossible to blend in. I mean, look at this crowd."

I pointed with my chin toward the front of the bus. Most of the tourists seemed to be expecting it to rain again. They were sporting waterproof coats and crinkled PAC-a-MACs. Several were consulting guide books. Many were holding cameras. None appeared to be German.

I could hear two lads talking in loud American accents and three girls conversing in rapid-fire French. There were a scattering of Japanese youngsters, a middle-aged couple eating sandwiches who couldn't have looked more English if they'd wrapped themselves in Union Jacks, and one Asian man who was fast asleep.

"The *crowd* is what bothers me," Freddy said. "What we'll be discussing here is highly sensitive."

"So we'll keep our voices down. And besides, the real beauty of being on this thing is that nobody is going to be eavesdropping. They'll be too busy listening to the commentary."

All of the passengers were wearing earphones. We had some, too. They were hanging from the railings in front of our seats, connected by coiled wires to little black boxes that no doubt provided a tediously dull narrative in a variety of languages.

"I don't know," Freddy said. The vibrations from the idling bus engine made his voice waver, so that he sounded even more uncertain.

"Well, I do," I told him. "Believe me, it's a hell of a lot safer than your ruse with the Ping-Pong table."

He looked confused. "How do you mean?"

"I'll tell you," I said.

And as I began to explain about the two Russians who'd been waiting for me in my apartment the night before, not to mention the French guy who'd visited me in the early hours of the morning, the bus pulled away with a throaty diesel roar and an unfortunate grinding of gears.

Before long, we passed in front of the main entrance to the Reichstag, and the heads of our fellow passengers swiveled to the right. Some of them raised cameras and took photographs. I focused on Freddy and gave him the rest of the story. The bus had pulled over outside the glass and steel structure of the Hauptbahnhof station by the time I was done.

He didn't say anything for a long moment. I wasn't sure why. I glanced at Victoria. Victoria glared at me.

"You didn't tell me anything about a Frenchman," she said.

I shrugged. "He knocked on the front door just before four A.M. and hauled me out into the corridor when I answered. You slept right through it, and I didn't see the sense in waking you, or worrying you unnecessarily."

She looked skeptical. I wasn't surprised, but I wasn't about to tell her about my late-night excursion if I could help it.

Freddy was still preoccupied. I gave his arm a shake, and he blinked and shook his head like he had a bug in his ear.

"These men, the Russians, they took the file, you say?"

"I'm afraid so."

"And you found this file in Jane's hotel room?"

"That's right. But don't worry. All is not lost."

"It's not?"

"Nope." I winked at Victoria. "Be a sweetheart and pass me your phone, will you?"

She gave me a level stare. "Ever feel that you're pushing your luck?"

"Chop-chop," I said.

She sighed and reached inside one of the pockets on her cargo trousers, removing her mobile. Then she got cagey. "Who do you want to call?" she asked.

"Nobody," I said, and made a *gimme* gesture.

Victoria rolled her eyes and dumped her phone into my palm as the bus pulled away again. We circled in front of a collection of modern government office buildings before crossing the river Spree and looping back toward the Reichstag. Just as I was beginning to think we'd been vastly overcharged for a seriously repetitive city tour, we swung right and headed out through the flat parkland of the Tiergarten, along John-Foster-Dulles-Allee.

I pressed a few buttons on Victoria's phone and accessed her camera. Then I switched to her library of photos.

"There," I said, and showed Freddy and Victoria the screen.

I cycled through the pictures I'd taken. They were all neatly focused and carefully composed. The first shot was of the buff-colored file with the words TOP SECRET printed on it. The file was resting on the plain white duvet on the bed in Jane Parker's hotel room. I'd taken the pictures as insurance before I'd left. There were five images altogether. One for the cover, and another four for each of the pages of handwritten code I'd found inside.

I beamed at Victoria and Freddy. Then I raised my arthritic fingers and tapped my temple.

"Not too shabby, right?"

"Not bad," Victoria conceded, a little begrudgingly.

"You should be able to blow these images up," I told Freddy. "Victoria will text them to you. So you'll still have the code."

He was staring intently at the last image on the phone. Some of the color seemed to have leached from his face.

I glanced out my window. We were just swinging left and coming alongside the Schloss Bellevue, the stark white residence of the German president.

"Listen," I said to Freddy, "I know it's bad news that we had the file taken from us. And I'm sorry about that. But you slipped up somehow. You led those Russians to us. The French guy, too. And I think you'll agree that I made the best of a bad situation." Still nothing. I clicked my fingers before his eyes. "Er, Freddy?"

I'd like to say he snapped out of his reverie, but his eyes remained watery and unfocused. I was starting to believe his brother had got all the brains in the family.

"I'm assuming I will still be paid," I told him. "The fee for searching location two, plus the bonus for finding the file. After all, I did what you hired me to do. The situation with the Russians is unfortunate for you, I admit, but they were never part of our bargain."

Freddy shook his head vaguely.

"Now, hold on," I told him. "A deal's a deal. Agreed?"

He squeezed his eyes tightly closed and pinched the bridge of his noise, like a man suffering a bad migraine. When he did finally speak, his voice was strained.

"The package isn't a file," he said.

"Come again?"

"It's not a file," he barked.

The bus slowed abruptly, almost as if the driver had been startled by Freddy's outburst. I checked behind him. The tourists were craning their necks and gazing up out of their windows, trying to catch sight of the Siegessäule, the imposing Victory Column that had been installed in the center of the Grosser Stern roundabout. A gilded statue of a winged lady was fixed to the top. I couldn't see it from my position at the back of the bus. Kind of fitting, I guess. I seemed a long way from victory just at that particular moment.

"Not a file?" I repeated. "How do you mean exactly?"

Freddy gripped so hard to the railing on his seat that he looked like he was clutching the safety bar on a roller coaster.

"I didn't hire you to steal a file," he said. "The *package* is not a file. It never was. It never could be. Whatever you stole, whatever it is that you've taken, has absolutely nothing to do with what I hired you to find. Understand?"

I didn't understand. Not even close. Oh, I got what he meant, all right. I'm not a complete dunce. But it didn't make a whole lot of sense.

"But hang on," I said. And from the way he was clasping the seating rail, he seemed to be doing exactly that. "If you didn't want me to find that file, then why did the Russians take it from me? They knew all about my assignment. The French guy, too."

"I can't explain that. I don't know who those men were."

"The Russians had a car with diplomatic plates. The French guy struck me as some kind of spy."

He looked at me blankly.

"The lead Russian was smartly dressed. He was neatly groomed and he spoke perfect English. The guy who was with him had a scar. A big, jagged one, running down his cheek."

"A scar?" Freddy said, and I got the impression he was starting to doubt me.

117

"I'm not making this up."

"It's true," Victoria told him. "I was there, too, remember? It was scary, I can tell you."

He smiled fleetingly at her. "And you say they knew that I'd hired you?"

"Yes," I told him. "They asked me if I'd found the item you'd hired me to find. They knew about Victoria's involvement, too. I got the impression they'd listened in on our conversation with you."

"Impossible."

"Then what about the French guy?"

"Hmm," was all Freddy would say, and then he snatched Victoria's phone from me and cycled back through the photographs I'd taken.

The bus was accelerating again. We were driving out of the park, passing joggers and dog walkers and a group of guys kicking a football around. We were cruising along the main boulevard of the Strasse des 17 Juni, and according to the little map above my seat, the next stop on our itinerary was the Schloss Charlottenburg. I can't say I was enjoying the trip all that much. I was feeling a little queasy. It wasn't travel sickness, so much. It was confusion and fear.

I remembered very well what Pavel had said to me. He'd asked if the file was all that I'd found. He'd made me assure him that there was nothing else. And then he'd told me that if he discovered that I was lying to him, he'd kill me. And not just me, but Victoria, too.

Now, I hadn't deceived him deliberately. I'd allowed his pet goon to take the file from me, and at the time I'd honestly believed it was exactly what Freddy had hired me to steal. But if Pavel suspected that I'd tricked him on purpose, then it could be a very costly mistake.

I felt a sharp pressure on my leg. Victoria was squeezing my thigh. She was squeezing pretty tight. I got the impression she'd been following the exact same thought process and that she liked where it had taken her almost as much as I did.

"What was I supposed to find?" I asked Freddy. "What was I meant to be looking for?"

Freddy handed the phone back to Victoria. It seemed like the code and the top secret file didn't interest him very much. "You know I can't tell you that."

"But you still need it, right?"

He nodded.

"And it has to be in location three or four."

"Does it?"

"Logic dictates so," I said, talking fast now. "I searched the first two places and the only thing I found was the file."

"Assuming you didn't miss something. You've made one rather big mistake already."

I paused. I counted to five. Now really wasn't the time to lose my rag.

"I wouldn't have *made* a mistake if you'd simply trusted me enough to tell me the full facts."

"So what are you suggesting? You wish to search the other two locations?"

It wasn't so much that I wished to do it. It was more that I *needed* to.

"You'd be working on the same basis as before," Freddy told me. "You'd be searching in the dark."

"Then the job just got even crazier than it was the first time around."

"Those are my terms. You either accept them or the deal is off."

I would have liked to have walked away. I would have loved for it to be the simplest solution all round. But I had a feeling I'd have to walk a very long distance for a very long time. And that I'd be checking over my shoulder incessantly.

"Fine," I told Freddy, "give me the next address."

But even as I said it, I could feel a fast pounding in my ears. My blood pressure was up. My nerves were tingling. The assignment had been risky enough the first time around. Four separate burglaries. Four distinct opportunities to be caught. But right now, it seemed a whole lot more hazardous.

EIGHTEEN

Freddy bid us farewell, bowing his head to kiss Victoria's hand before stepping off the bus at Checkpoint Charlie. I suppose there was a kind of harmony in that. My spy fantasy had begun with a rendezvous at the Brandenburg Gate, and now it had concluded at perhaps the most famous Cold War location of them all. But if I was looking for encouraging patterns or a neat way of bookending my daydream, then I was plumb out of luck. The outcome of our meeting with Freddy had been a pale imitation of what I'd hoped it might be. Then again, the same could be said for Checkpoint Charlie.

The area around the old Allied border control was a mess of fast food franchises and souvenir stores selling enough 'genuine' itty-bitty chunks of the Berlin Wall to divide the city four times over. There were beggars and drug dealers. There were pickpockets and con artists. There were more tourists to go round than opportunities to exploit them. And right at the very heart of it all was the modest border hut that everyone had come to see.

The hut was no bigger than your average garden shed. It had a pitched roof and white wooden cladding. There were floodlights attached to it, along with a sign reading U.S. ARMY CHECKPOINT, and it was surrounded by banked sandbags.

Oh, and it was utterly fake. A complete fabrication.

So were the two guys standing in front of it, wearing shabby American army uniforms. They were holding a pole with a tattered Stars and Stripes flag on the end of it, and if you tipped them a couple of euros, they'd pose for a photo. Tip them an extra couple of euros and they'd stamp your passport with a fake border pass that would go a long way to invalidating it. Catch them later the same day, and you could tip them a few euros more to shed all their clothes. Think I'm kidding? I wish that were so. But the guys doing the posing were part of a troupe of male strippers who took it in turns to don knockoff army costumes during the day and considerably less during the night.

I hated the place for the tacky theme park it had become. I can't say I felt a great deal better about the bus we were on, but there was an undeniable appeal to staying put. For one thing, I didn't want us to get off at the same location as Freddy, just in case someone really was following him. And for another, I was feeling listless and melancholy. Part of it was how little sleep I'd managed the night before. Part of it was the cloying heat on the bus. And part of it was not being sure what my next move should be.

After a good deal of cajoling and reassurance, Freddy had finally given me the address and a description of the third location on his list. It was an apartment on Karl-Marx-Allee that belonged to a cleaning lady who was responsible for tidying the ambassador's office and who'd been on duty to assist with cleaning during the embassy function. By Freddy's reckoning, her access to the ambassador's office had given her an opportunity to swipe whatever it was that had been stolen. But as to why she might have taken the blasted *package* or what exactly it might be, Freddy had had nothing useful to add.

The bus lurched on toward its next stop. I propped my head against the vibrating window glass and folded my arms across my chest. I blew air through my lips and pouted at Victoria. She was in the process of texting Freddy the photographs I'd taken. I waited until she was finished, then batted my eyelids and huffed loudly.

"Am I to take it that you're frustrated?" she asked, pocketing her phone.

"Very."

"Well, join the club. I can't believe you didn't tell me about the French guy."

Yeah, and my German telephone friend, I thought.

"And you were really quite rude to Freddy," she added.

"Was I? Chalk it up to jealousy, I suppose. I don't know why you're the only one who gets to be pawed by him."

Victoria thumped me on the arm. "That's really all you have to say?"

"Not quite," I told her. "I'd also love it if you could tell me what the hell I'm supposed to be looking for."

"Can't help you there."

"Then maybe you can think of some way of explaining things to our Russian friends that won't make it seem like I deliberately duped them."

Victoria smiled flatly. "You think they'll realize the file wasn't what Freddy hired you to find?"

"Sooner or later."

"How soon?"

"Judging by the way things are going, I'm guessing it's going to be sooner than either of us would prefer."

"So what can we do?"

"I wish I knew. I suppose the best we can hope for is that I find something marked 'Property of the British Ambassador' in this cleaner's apartment."

"You think that's likely?"

"I honestly don't know. And the annoying part is that we won't be able to find out until she starts work."

Freddy had told us that the cleaner would begin her evening shift at six o'clock and that she'd be on duty at the embassy until eight P.M.. I'd asked him if she cleaned for anyone else and if her apartment might be empty during the afternoon, but he hadn't been able to say. I'd also asked him if she lived alone or if there was a risk of anyone else being home when I broke in, but he hadn't been able to tell me that, either. All things considered, Freddy wasn't exactly the most informed client I'd ever had.

"What do you plan to do in the meantime?" Victoria asked me.

"Think," I told her. "And sulk."

"In that order?"

"Probably not."

I wasn't lying. I sulked about the situation I'd found myself in a lot more than I thought about it, and although it didn't get me very far, it did occupy my mind until the bus delivered us as far as Alexanderplatz.

"Come on," I said, nudging Victoria. "Let's get off this thing."

"Why here?"

"Follow me and I'll show you."

"There," I said. "Right *there.*"

"Where?" Victoria asked. "I don't see it."

"Right where my finger's pointing."

"Your finger's pointing at a piece of glass, Charlie."

"Yeessss," I conceded. "But look *through* the glass. Line your eyes up with my finger and you'll see the building I'm pointing toward."

"Fine." Victoria sighed. "I'll try again."

I got the impression it wasn't fine. In fact, I got the impression Victoria was more than a smidgen frustrated. But she propped her chin on my shoulder all the same, and then she squinted along my arm toward the very end of my pinkie finger.

The pad of my finger was squished up against a sheet of double-thick glass. The glass was sloping away from us at a shallow angle. Below it was two hundred and three meters of nothing but vaporous gray air. I gripped a little harder to the metal railing that was fitted down by my waist. I've never been a great fan of heights, but the circular viewing platform inside the Fernsehturm was making my palms sweat.

Well, all right, that wasn't the only reason. Victoria was awfully close. I could feel her hair brushing my face. I could smell her perfume.

"See it now?" I asked, doing my best to conceal the quiver in my voice.

"I *think* so."

"Either you do or you don't, Vic. There's no 'think so' about it."

"How do you even know that's the right building?"

"Because it stands right out," I said. "Because it's one of the only Bauhaus properties left in the area. Everything else looks like it's straight out of Moscow in the 1980s. It's practically the only thing that isn't gray or green."

The building I was pointing toward was a pale pinkish red. To me, it was as clear as a ship's distress flare. I could have mentioned the color to Victoria, but the truth is I already had. Twice. And if she wasn't seeing it now, I didn't believe she ever would.

We were facing the wide concrete band of Karl-Marx-Allee. The imposing boulevard speared out from Alexanderplatz toward the giant circular crossroads at Frankfurter Tor. I knew the Allee was a couple of kilometers in length, but I couldn't escape the feeling that if the Fernsehturm were to come loose from its foundations and topple forward right now, it would fit perfectly into the space, like a tall dessert spoon in a chest of silverware.

The Allee was lined on either side by vast, boxy apartment complexes. There were many more blocks and towers all over the eastern side of the city. Looking down on them, I was struck by how ordered it all appeared. Everything was a straight line or a rectangle or a square, reminding me of a giant Airfix model. If I just pressed my thumb against the glass, it seemed as though I might be able to pry the individual pieces out of their giant plastic frame, ready to build a new model city somewhere in the Cold War depths of the USSR.

The boulevard was streaming with traffic. Cars and vans and buses, mostly. The vehicles looked like die-cast toys on a huge patterned rug. Belowground, U-Bahn trains would be shuttling fast along concealed railway lines. Thousands of people heading to destinations unknown, for reasons unclear. Most of those reasons would be law-abiding, though in a city the size of Berlin, I doubted I was the only one planning a crime. Mind you, I don't suppose there were many thieves casing their target from a mile away in one direction and several hundred feet up in the air.

"Is this helpful at all?" Victoria asked.

"Not in the slightest," I told her. "I just thought you might like the view."

She stepped away from me and rested her hand on a floor-mounted telescope. I thought about feeding a couple of euros into it and inviting her to study the cleaner's building through the magnified lens. But what if she didn't see it then?

"Come on," I said. "Let's take a look at the rest of the city."

We strolled around the precarious sphere, watching the world revolve slowly below us. The gray blocks and gridded streets of the east gave way to a more organic layout as we moved west. Color seeped in. Red roofing tiles. The blackened river Spree. The dirty

126

brown of railway tracks. The egg-yolk yellow and new-sneaker white of a street tram.

"So I take it you're not planning to spend the entire afternoon up here," Victoria said.

"I thought we'd go home," I told her. "Take a few hours to ourselves. You'll be pleased to hear I have some writing to catch up on. And I need to gather some equipment."

"For later?"

I nodded.

"So, I've been thinking," Victoria said. "I'd really like to come with you this evening."

"Thought you might," I told her, and smiled despite myself. "But as it happens, I'm afraid you can't. Truth is, Vic, I have something *much* more important for you to do."

NINETEEN

I'm ashamed to say that I didn't work when we got back to my place. I shut myself in my chilly bedroom and slept for a couple of hours instead. Naturally, I told Victoria that I was writing, and I even carried my laptop and my notes into my bedroom to try to create the right impression. Somehow, though, I doubt it worked. Victoria's a long way from stupid, and she would have spotted that she couldn't hear the tippety-tap of my fingers on my laptop keys, let alone the frustrated pacing or hopeless playacting I tend to engage in when I'm battling a new scene.

I didn't care. Right then—book or no book—I needed to rest. True, I was capable of making mistakes at the best of times, but even I knew that it would be a really bad idea to try to break in to a highly exposed apartment building in the early evening when I was barely half awake.

Of course, if by some unexpected fluke Victoria really had believed that I was hard at it, then the urgent bleat of my alarm clock would almost certainly have given the game away. And my subterfuge was hardly helped by the fuzzy-eyed stagger I made past the open doorway to her bedroom on my way to the bathroom, or the distinct pillow imprint I happened to find in the side of my face when I squinted into the mirror above the sink.

No matter. I washed my face and wet my hair and tidied my clothes, and then I breezed into the living room and snatched up my telephone. My landlord's number was scrawled on a pad right beside it, and I punched in the digits and waited a few moments for him to answer. Our conversation didn't take long, and it was every bit as productive as I'd hoped it would be. Once it was concluded, I returned to my bedroom and gathered together the equipment I'd be likely to need on my latest felonious escapade, and then I went and talked to Victoria as I fitted my arms through the sleeves of my raincoat.

Whether Victoria was impressed by my multitasking, I couldn't say, but she left me in absolutely no doubt that she didn't appreciate the special mission I'd assigned her. I can't pretend I was surprised. Nobody enjoys waiting around for a tradesman to arrive. But hey, my bedroom window wasn't going to fix itself, and *somebody* was going to have to deal with the glazier.

Some forty minutes later, I emerged from the Weberwiese U-Bahn station onto Karl-Marx-Allee. I'd ridden up on a slow-moving escalator without paying attention to my bearings, only to discover that I was on the wrong side of the street. Not normally an issue, I grant you, but when the street in question is strikingly wide and happens to be divided by multiple lanes of fast-flowing traffic, it becomes more of a challenge.

I set off in search of a crossing point. The pavement was about the size of your average motorway, but part of it had been torn up for maintenance work. I weaved around the construction site and between a line of plane trees, all of them stripped of their leaves by the October winds and rain. It wasn't fully dark just yet, but the evening sky had faded to a dusky half-light, and the vehicles streaming by had their headlights and brake lights flaring.

The building on my left was a monumental apartment block that had the appearance of a huge office complex. It was so long and so high that I felt as though I was shrinking as I paced alongside it. Shops, bars, and businesses were located right along the ground floor, facing the street.

Running just above them was a bright pink industrial waste pipe. I'd seen the pipes elsewhere in Berlin, and it was a sight I was still struggling to adjust to. The pipe was held together by no-nonsense rivets and supported on metal columns, painted in the same garish pink. It stretched as far as the end of the apartment complex before hooking to the right, snaking up in the air and crossing over the lines of speeding traffic to the opposite pavement, where it continued into the far distance.

There was a pedestrian crossing nearby, and I pressed the button and waited for the lights to change. This wasn't the kind of place you wanted to make a run for it, especially since jaywalking is seriously frowned upon in Berlin. I can't tell you the number of times that elderly German women have appeared, as if from nowhere, simply to berate me for setting a bad example to the city's children. It's happened so often now that I honestly believe they'd be more understanding if they disturbed me while I was in the process of stealing from their homes in the dead of night.

Eventually, the green Ampelmännchen appeared, halting the traffic. This jaunty little fellow used to be confined solely to the eastern sectors of Berlin, but these days he pops up most places in the city, and not just at pedestrian crossings. With his wide-brimmed hat, swinging arm, and confident stride, you'll find him on all manner of souvenir merchandise. In popularity, he ranks right up there alongside the Fernsehturm, which it just so happened

I could see as I glanced to my right while crossing the street. The tapering concrete tower was lit vividly from below, lending the panorama globe the appearance of a hovering spaceship.

I hopped up onto the pavement and followed the pink spaghetti pipe work as far as the apartment building I was interested in. It was five stories high, with a peach and white façade. There were balconied corridors all along the front, and two main entrances with glass doors, where the central stairwells were located. There was a newsagent and a general store to the right, and a line of ground-floor apartments to the left.

I vaulted the low brick wall in front of the ground-floor apartments without breaking my stride, grumbled at the painful twinge in my bruised stomach, then walked to the door at the end of the line. I tugged a scrap of paper from my pocket and made sure I had the right place. Then I glanced around quickly and ducked below the wall.

Resting on my haunches, with my back against the stippled plaster, I eased my customized plastic gloves onto my hands and took a closer look at what I was up against.

Despite the jolly peach plaster, the apartment was quite drab. There was a single window on the right of the door and a double window on the left. The door was dark gray, fitted with a security peephole in the center and a standard dead bolt lock at the side.

I didn't anticipate the lock posing a problem, and since I was down on the floor already, I was able to get a good look at it before selecting an appropriate pick and a likely torsion wrench from my spectacles case. That only left one unanswered question. Was anybody home?

TWENTY

Part of me was reluctant to knock. I didn't want any of the neighbors to hear me, and I most especially didn't want anyone to answer my call. But I couldn't see a way of avoiding it. I had to know what I was, quite literally, letting myself in for. And although there were no lights shining from behind the chintzy net curtains in the windows, that didn't mean there wasn't somebody occupying a room in the rear.

I waited until a delivery lorry was thundering by before standing and banging my fist on the door. Then I fought my natural instincts and made sure that my head was perfectly aligned with the peephole. Sure, my feet were pointing in the opposite direction, toward the street and my likely getaway, but I was doing my best to hold the position. I counted to ten. I continued to twenty. When I reached thirty, my knees went from under me and I dropped back down to my cover.

Short of lurking there until I evolved some kind of X-ray vision, I knew as much as I possibly could, and it was time to go in.

You want to know the truth? This is the part I like most of all.

First, there's the charge of excitement that comes with the anticipation of doing something that's expressly forbidden. But it's more than that. It's also the satisfaction I get from doing the job right. It took me years to master the craft of picking locks. It's taken me years since to develop my skills as a burglar. It's not an easy profession—trust me, it requires a lot of nerve and a lot of careful thought, and even then an awful lot can go wrong—but just now I was about as good as I was ever going to get. I knew most locks inside out, and until the day that the arthritis in my fingers seized my knuckles for good, I was every bit as dextrous as I needed to be. I'd refined and reworked my approach to searching a place, so that I was as methodical and as error-free as possible. I was still young, and despite my lingering addiction to nicotine, I was passably athletic. I was still ambitious. I was still greedy. And I still craved the buzz that came from stepping over a stranger's threshold and discovering something that I could never have expected to find.

I cracked the lock in question easily enough. Almost too easily to take genuine satisfaction from it. Then I reached up and poked the door open ever so gently. There was nobody on the other side. No obstruction whatsoever. I pocketed my tools, reached for my torch, and eased the door open until the gap was just wide enough for me to slip through.

I pulled the door closed behind me without the slightest sound. Then I straightened and stretched the aching muscles in my legs and back. I felt a smile creep across my face and I sucked a deep breath in through my nostrils.

And then I sneezed. Hard and fast and loud.

The sneeze came out of nowhere. An involuntary reaction. There'd been an itch and a tingle in my nose, and then there'd been the sneeze. Nothing in between. No warning at all. I hadn't even raised my hand.

I raised my hand now, as if to ward off a blow or to take the whole thing back. I was standing very still. Not even my heart was beating. I stared in horror toward the end of the hallway. There was movement across the far wall. A wavering shadow. Someone *was* here, lurking behind a doorway. And thanks to my damn sinuses, they'd definitely heard me.

My limbs felt leaden. My reactions slow. So much for the wonders of youth and adrenaline. Forget fight or flight. I felt about as nimble as a statue.

The shadow moved again. It was low down on the wall, but it was growing in size. The person behind the doorway was edging closer. He was going to confront me.

My lungs were burning. I needed to breathe. But I was scared to inhale.

I tried to resist, but I couldn't hold out for very long. I felt myself weaken and I began to draw air through my nose. I opened my mouth wide and squeezed my eyes tight shut. But it didn't help. The moment the breeze whistled through my nostrils, I knew I was doomed. There was a very particular scent in the hallway. A pungent, musty aroma. The air was thick with it. It was something familiar. Something unpalatable. I was trying to place it. Trying very hard. And all the while I could feel the tingling and the agitation getting worse. I was definitely going to sneeze. There was no way around it.

I cracked my eyes open just a fraction, grimacing against the traitorous urge that had taken over my sinuses.

And that's when I saw him step out into the hallway.

The lurker was a cat. A ginger tom. I'm allergic to cats at the best of times, but in a confined space like an apartment, my sensitivity is at its worst.

The sneeze detonated in my nostrils, jerking my head forward.

The cat arched his back and bared his fangs. His eyes were green. They were piercing. And they were mean. This was one hostile feline.

And he wasn't alone. Two more cats followed from behind the doorway. One gray and one black with white flashes. They crowded together, claws extended, hackles raised. They had all the attitude of a team of thugs craving a knife fight in a slum alley.

My eyes were beginning to water, and my nose was starting to run. I wiped a gloved finger across my top lip and fought the impulse to sniff. I pinched my nostrils hard and breathed through my mouth. It was probably just my imagination, but it felt as if my tongue was beginning to swell.

There was a galley kitchen on my right. I dived for the sink and turned on the cold tap and ducked my head beneath the flow. I splashed my face and my streaming eyes. Then I blinked and glanced to my left, and saw another cat curled up on the windowsill. It had a tortoiseshell coat and its backside was pointed toward me.

I reached for a stained dishcloth and soaked it in the water until it was very wet. I pressed it under my nose like a gas mask. It smelled foul, but I turned off the tap and found myself grinning.

This was the fourth cat I'd seen so far, and there were a varied collection of dishes and water bowls down on the linoleum floor. Some of the dishes contained meat paste. Some contained a biscuit mixture. But one thing was clear. The ambassador's office cleaner was a woman who loved cats. She was a lady who was content for her home to smell like a cattery. She allowed her pets to roam freely and to lounge around on her kitchen surfaces. And that made me certain of one thing.

She lived by herself.

Yes, it's a cliché, but hey, I'm a mystery novelist and I trade in them. I felt confident that I was right and I began to relax. Because if the cleaner was a spinster, then I had until she finished her shift to search her home. That gave me ninety minutes, minimum. And ninety minutes would be more than enough.

TWENTY-ONE

I was finished in under an hour. The apartment wasn't large. There were two compact bedrooms, an even more compact bathroom, and a modest living room to add to the kitchen and hallway. I found plenty of evidence to suggest that the cleaner lived by herself and no sign whatsoever of a companion or a lodger. I counted six cats in all, but as the damn things kept moving around, I suppose it's possible that my math shouldn't be trusted.

There wasn't much of value. The television was dated, the VCR was practically an antique, and it might have been more accurate to call the radio a wireless. I uncovered a modest stash of money in a shoe box in the wardrobe, and despite my better instincts, I left it untouched. There was a set of porcelain bear figurines in the spare room that might have fetched a small sum if I'd been inclined to swipe them. But I hadn't been inclined. I'd been depressed and dejected. I was feeling that way because I hadn't found any sign of an object that could conceivably have belonged to the British ambassador.

I was congested, too. My allergies had really come up trumps.

My eyes were stinging and rheumy. My nostrils were sore beyond the point of itching and my lungs felt like they were filled with wire wool. All things considered, it had been a miserable trip.

Like a doctor giving up on a prolonged but ill-fated resuscitation, I called off my search at the fifty-five-minute mark. There was no denying the ambassador's cleaner could use some extra money, but there wasn't any indication that she'd resorted to theft. I had the feeling she lived an entirely respectable, entirely solitary life, and for the first time in a long while I felt more than a little sordid about having poked my nose into it.

Before I left, I hunted through the kitchen cupboards to find a replacement dishcloth to set out on the side that wouldn't be impregnated with my germs, and then I took one final tour to make sure I hadn't left any trace of my presence. I couldn't spot any mistakes. I'd done a thoroughly professional, thoroughly unproductive job, and now I could be on my way.

The peephole revealed an unthreatening slice of the Allee when I set my eye to it, so I hauled back the front door and locked it securely behind me with my picks. Then I checked both ways, whipped my gloves off my hands, hurdled the low balcony wall, and marched away toward the U-Bahn station.

My march didn't last long. It was interrupted before I'd taken more than a handful of strides. I was passing a row of parked vehicles at the side of the road when a door opened in front of me. The door was black. So was the town car it belonged to. So was the man who stepped out onto the curb.

The man was very large, in a weighty, very wide sort of way, and the town car rose up on its suspension once he'd vacated it. He had the type of neck that begins at the shoulders and ends at the chin with nothing very much in between, and his thick, dark hair was clipped close to his scalp. He was wearing a badly crumpled black suit over a white shirt and black tie, and a pair of wraparound sunglasses with a dark tint that matched the windows of the car exactly.

"Get in," he said, and opened a door at the rear of the vehicle. He had a deep voice, loaded with gravel, and a bass American accent. East Coast, maybe. New Jersey, perhaps.

"Crikey," I said. "It's awfully kind of you to offer me a lift, but I'm fine walking."

"I ain't offering. I'm telling. Now *get* in the car."

He tightened his grip on the door, as if it was a telephone directory he planned to rip in a show of strength.

"Listen, I'm flattered," I told him. "But you're really not my type. And if I might offer you a friendly word of advice, this is a very odd way to pick up men."

He glared at me over the top of his shades. "Just get in the damn car," he said. "I hate hurting English guys. They squeal too much."

I gave some thought to the idea of legging it, but I wasn't sure what good it would do. People in Berlin seemed to find it alarmingly easy to track me down, and I didn't relish the idea of being made to squeal.

"Where do you plan on taking me?"

"Your place. Come on, man. Be cool. I'm a safe driver."

I didn't doubt it. You'd have to be a complete moron to crash into this guy.

"Fine," I said, "but if you're hoping I'll invite you inside for coffee, you should brace yourself for a major disappointment."

The inside of the town car was only a touch smaller than the apartment I'd just vacated, but it was a lot more beige. Beige leather seat upholstery and door panels. Beige upholstery in the roof. Beige carpets.

I dropped onto a rear-facing seat and was nearly swallowed whole by the supple leather. My generously proportioned friend in the chauffeur outfit slammed the door behind me, and the tinted windows dyed the world outside in sepia tones. The soundproofing was impressive, and the heavy traffic sped by in a muted blur. It felt like my ears had popped.

A small, slim woman in business attire, age about fifty, was perched in the seat opposite my own. Her hair was styled into a no-nonsense bob, the color nut brown with streaks of gray. Her skin was heavily pouched and wrinkled, reminding me of dried fruit. The navy blue suit she had on had been tailored in a masculine style, and her shoes were as flat and as unremarkable as her chest.

A zipped document wallet lay open on her lap, and she gripped a bulbous fountain pen in her clawlike hand. She didn't look up from her papers at me. She didn't even bother to speak until our driver had lumbered inside and swung the car into the flow of vehicles with all the patience and grace of a guy riding the bumper cars at a carnival.

"So you're Charlie Howard," she said, in an offhand American drawl.

"Terrific," I replied. "Another complete stranger who knows my name."

"Tell me. Did you find what you were hired to steal?"

"Oh, and my business. Whatever happened to a person's right to privacy?"

Her eyes flicked up from her documents. Her expression was neutral, even bored. I got the impression I was only a very minor entry on the busy agenda she was working through that day.

"My team tells me you're not without talent." There was a monotone quality to her voice. I got the impression she didn't have a lot of time for intonation.

"Your team?"

She grimaced, as if I'd failed to understand my role in our impromptu meeting. Evidently, I wasn't supposed to pose questions.

"I'm informed that your IQ rates above average. Though we deducted a few percentiles for your profession."

"Burglar?"

"Mystery writer."

She returned her attention to her papers, and I gazed out the tinted window, trying to act nonchalant as we swerved between a moped and a delivery van on a trajectory that looked certain to end at the emergency room. I closed my eyes, and when I opened them again, we were swinging onto a side road at such velocity that I feared my retinas might become detached. A hapless pedestrian jumped out of the way like a man diving backward into a swimming pool, and I decided to focus my attention back inside the car.

The woman was scrawling a note on the bottom of a page. I tried to read her writing but she turned the paper before I had a chance.

I sniffed, and my nostrils twitched. I dug inside my pocket for the wet dishcloth I'd taken from the apartment and clamped it beneath my nose.

The woman shot me a wary look. "You're sick?"

"Allergies," I told her. "Cats don't agree with me."

She relaxed a fraction. "So how come you didn't pop a pill before you entered the apartment?"

"I wasn't warned."

"My, my." She shook her head. "Poor Freddy. Talk is he only got the role because of his brother's connections."

"And what is his role, exactly?"

She smiled. It took some concentration. Not a group of muscles she used very often, I didn't think. The effect was reminiscent of a death rictus.

"I guess you might say that he's a protector."

"Come again?"

"His job is to make sure your ambassador doesn't embarrass

140

himself or the UK. But if something goes wrong, Freddy needs to fix it. And fast."

"That's it?"

"It's not as easy as it sounds." She shrugged. "For Freddy, anyhow. Poor guy is too easily distracted by his libido. Won't be long until some backwater state snares him in a honey trap."

It surprised me that I didn't appreciate the way she was talking about Freddy. Was it possible that I was experiencing some misplaced sense of loyalty to him?

"And you?" I asked. "What's your involvement in this? What's your interest in me?'

"Well, now. Why don't you apply some of your rumored intellect and figure it out for yourself?"

I didn't particularly want to play her game. I've never enjoyed dancing to other people's tunes. But I didn't feel like I had a lot of alternatives.

"Fine," I mumbled, reaching for my tap shoes. "You're American, obviously. You know Freddy and you're keen to create the impression that you know what he hired me to do. You're in a black town car, and although I didn't happen to spot the plates before your rent-a-heavy obliged me to join you, I'd guess they'd suggest that you're a diplomat or possibly even an intelligence officer of some kind. And I imagine you want me to give you what Freddy hired me to find."

"I'm impressed."

"Don't be. I had a Russian crew pull this routine on me last night. They beat you to the drop."

"Oh, I don't believe so. You wouldn't still be searching, if that was the deal."

I paused, then wiggled my finger toward her papers. "You know, you're not so intimidating. Your Russian competitors pulled a gun on me. They roughed me up a little, too."

"You want me to do the same?"

"No need. Your driver already threatened to make me squeal."

"He's real good at it, too. Believe me."

I avoided her eyes and checked outside to judge our progress. We were speeding by the green expanse of the Volkspark Fried-richshain. A few minutes more, and we'd be outside my front door.

"So what happens when we get to my place?" I asked.

"That kinda depends. Did you find the item?"

I shook my head.

"That's a little disappointing, don't you think? Three apart-ments. Three blanks."

"You don't believe me?"

"Sure I believe you. Why would you lie?"

I puffed out my chest. "Well, I *am* British. I'm working on be-half of my government."

"Quaint. But my people tell me you're really no more than a common thief."

I bristled at that. "Maybe not so common. A lot of people seem to be interested in what I've been hired to find. You included."

"Me, in particular."

"Oh? And why's that?"

She closed her file. Stabbed the leather folio with her pen. "The truth? Curiosity, mostly. The diplomatic world is kinda small in Berlin. We all live in each other's pockets. We all hear rumors and tall tales. Most of it doesn't mean squat. But Freddy? Well, he's made a real scene about this theft from your ambassador's office."

"He has?"

"Unintentionally, I guess. But sometimes that's all it takes. And like it or not—and personally, I truly don't—we're allies with you guys. If your ambassador embarrasses himself, it could impact on the U.S. Plus, when I heard that Freddy had approached you for help, it sounded so wackadoo that I figured it had to be worth finding out more."

"You're not alone in that."

"Your Russian friends?"

"Plus more besides."

I found myself telling her about my visit from Henri, the Frenchman, and my mysterious phone call of the previous night.

"Your German caller sounds mighty intriguing."

"You could say."

"He hasn't approached you yet?"

"Not directly."

"Well, don't worry. He will."

Wonderful.

"Am I in danger?" I asked.

"What else did you expect?"

I shrugged. "A harmless bit of burglary? A nice, uncontroversial way to make a little money?"

She pouted and shook her head, as if she doubted anyone could be quite so naive. "How little?" she asked.

I told her that, too. I couldn't see the harm in it.

"And tell me, how profound is your sense of patriotism?"

"Excuse me?"

She smiled again. The pearly rictus was every bit as forced and untrustworthy as before. "Let me make this as simple as I can. Find what's been stolen from the ambassador, bring it to me, and I'll double your fee."

I stared at her. "You're serious?"

"Do I look like I engage in jokes?"

Hmm. Not good ones, in any event. I rubbed my chin, thinking it over.

"Listen, there's no pretending that your offer isn't a lot more attractive than the one the Russian crew presented me with. But suppose I accept. They won't like it. And neither will Freddy."

"Go on."

"Can you offer me protection? Would I have to defect?"

"Writers." She tutted. "Always so dramatic. I can give you a window of protection. That's all."

"Huh. And how big is this window?"

"Twenty-four hours."

"And after that?"

"You'll need to leave Berlin."

"Right." The car came to a sudden halt outside my building. So sudden that I nearly ended up in my impromptu date's lap. "And if I refuse your offer?"

"Then maybe I'll start thinking how our Russian friends took the better approach. Maybe Duane'll help you to change your mind."

Oh, boy.

"Then we have a deal," I said, and extended my hand rather hastily. "Would you care to tell me your name, at least?"

"My name is Nancy Symons," she said, studiously ignoring my offer of a handshake. "Duane will pass you a card with a number to call. Contact us as soon as you have the package."

"Fine," I said, lowering my hand and reaching for the door lever. "No problem."

But not even I was thick enough to believe that was really the case.

TWENTY-TWO

I had to force myself not to glance back as I climbed the steps to the front door of my building. The last thing I wanted was for Nancy to see how intimidated I was feeling.

I kept my eyes fixed stubbornly ahead as I fitted my key in the lock. Then I darted inside and kicked the door closed behind me and let go of a long sigh when I discovered that there was no artfully disheveled Frenchman waiting for me there. I bent double and clutched my knees in my hands. I counted to five. I swiveled and poked open the letterbox and gazed out at the street.

Dumb move.

Nancy was looking straight at me. Her tinted window was down, and she smirked and nodded to herself, like a craftswoman who was very pleased with her handiwork. Then she issued a command to Duane, and he gunned the engine and the car sped off along the street.

Marvelous.

I dropped the flap on the letterbox and trudged up the stairs to my apartment, cursing myself with every step I took. I could have done with my thesaurus because I was beginning to repeat myself by the time I reached the second floor, but I wasn't all that concerned. One thing I've learned about writing over the years is that repetition can be a good thing—a useful way of building a rhythm or emphasizing a point. And besides, I felt sure that when I told Victoria about my latest setback, she'd offer me a wealth of new insults to add to my list.

I did some more repetition when I reached my front door because it was hanging ajar. Victoria must have forgotten to lock up after the glazier had left. It annoyed me, but worse than that, it frustrated me. I'd reminded Victoria on countless occasions just how costly a slip like this could be. As a thief, you never switch off. You're always aware of every little opportunity that comes your way. And if I'd happened upon an open apartment door like this one, I'd have found it seriously tempting to nip inside and see what I could snatch.

In fact, I found it so tempting that I decided to teach Victoria a lesson. Ghosting through the doorway, I moved with exaggerated care into the well-lit living room. Victoria wasn't there, but my laptop was, and so was my charred, though still very precious copy of *The Maltese Falcon*. I scooped them into my arms, and I was just about to make my exit when I happened to notice something out of the corner of my eye. Victoria's wristwatch was resting on one of the sofa cushions.

The watch was fashioned from platinum with a pink pearlescent dial and a tiny pink diamond embedded in each hand. It had a chain-link strap and a short inscription etched into the back. *To Sugar Plum, Love, Daddy.*

It wasn't the first time I'd seen the inscription. Some months ago now, Victoria had passed me the timepiece and asked me to give her a rough appraisal of its value. She was worried about wearing it, and having met her father, I could appreciate her concern.

Alfred was a man I admired greatly, but since he also happened to be a professional casino cheat who'd purchased the watch following a successful excursion to Atlantic City, Victoria was afraid that he'd blown a ridiculous amount of cash on the thing.

Fortunately, I was able to set Victoria's mind at rest and tell her that although the watch was very handsome, the diamonds were low-grade and the whole thing was worth a couple of hundred pounds, at best.

I'd lied, of course. It was worth a small fortune. But I knew she'd never wear it if I told her as much, and I knew its true value wouldn't change how much it meant to her. She was always toying with the thing, always touching it to reassure herself it was still there, and she'd be heartbroken if it was ever stolen.

Well, it was going to get stolen right now. Theoretically, at least. I added it to my laptop and Hammett's novel, and then I marched down the corridor toward Victoria's bedroom.

"You left the bloody door open," I said. "Look at this, Vic. Look how easily it could have all been pinched."

But she wasn't in her bedroom. Her light was on. Her ring binder of notes was open on her bed. But she was nowhere to be seen.

Frowning, I crossed the hall into my bedroom, and when I switched on the ceiling light, my confusion and panic ramped up a level. Victoria wasn't there, either. But my window was still broken. The wintry night breeze was gusting through the shattered pane.

I walked in a dazed fashion back along the hallway, passing the darkened bathroom. I prodded the front door shut, then returned to the living room. The silence was booming and absolute. It left me with only my thoughts, and my thoughts weren't very welcome.

My first concern was that Victoria had been far angrier with me than I'd realized. It had been rude of me to expect her to wait for the handyman to come and fix my window, and perhaps I'd underestimated how miffed she really was. It could be that she'd stormed out of the apartment after I'd gone, without caring enough to turn off the lights or to close the door behind her. It could be she'd tramped around the block before finding a bar to hole up in for a while and sulk about my behavior.

I dumped my laptop and Hammett's novel on my desk and tightened my fist around Victoria's watch. Then a new notion occurred to me. If she'd left because she was mad, perhaps she'd wanted company. And there were only a handful of people she knew in Berlin. I didn't imagine she'd contact any of the editors who'd bid on my new book. If she'd left because I'd upset her, she wouldn't want to put herself in a position where she'd have to talk about my writing. And that only left one other person I could think of. Freddy. A man who'd made it very clear that he was attracted to Victoria.

I growled to myself and snatched my phone down from the wall. But I couldn't call Freddy. I didn't have his number. It was logged in Victoria's mobile.

Victoria's mobile.

Of course! Why hadn't I thought of that before? I'd call her, and I'd apologize, and after she'd made me grovel for a time, we could be back on an even keel again.

I punched in her number. I listened to the static on the line. But I didn't hear a ringing tone. I heard a piercing beep followed by the clear enunciation of a recorded German voice. The voice was female. It was telling me that my call couldn't be connected because Victoria's phone was switched off.

I swore under my breath. More repetition. Then I cut the connection and dialed the number for my landlord. He wasn't at all pleased to hear from me. It seemed the glazier he'd contacted had turned up over an hour ago, but there'd been no answer when he'd buzzed my apartment. He'd been forced to leave without carrying out the job he'd been hired for, but he was still planning to charge a call-out fee, and my landlord was intending to add it to my monthly rent.

I apologized and told him that was fine, and once he'd left me in no doubt that I was now expected to arrange my own repairman at my own expense, he ended our conversation and returned me to silence again.

I didn't like the way things were shaping up. It really wasn't like Victoria to leave her precious watch lying around or to go out without scrawling me a note. She'd know that I'd fret about her, especially after the events of the past few days.

I hung up the phone and opened my palm and gazed down at the timepiece. And that was when I finally noticed something odd. The strap was broken. The platinum buckle was securely fastened, but the chain-link band had been ripped clean apart.

I didn't believe it could have been an accident. The watch was beautifully manufactured and built to last. Breaking the strap would have required a lot of strength. Some kind of fast, violent tugging motion.

My head was beginning to swirl. The room was swirling with it. I groped for the wall and gazed across at the sofa. One of the seating cushions was out of place, as if it had been dragged forward. And there was a deep impression in the padding of the backrest that looked as if someone had tried to flatten themselves against it. Had Victoria wedged herself there? Had she been yanked off the sofa against her will?

I was slipping down the wall. Melting to the ground.

Then the telephone started to ring. It squealed in my ears but I was struggling to react.

The telephone trilled some more. In the brief pause between rings, my apartment felt even emptier than before.

I reached above my head and knocked the receiver from the hook, then scrambled to raise it to my ear.

"Herr Howard?"

The voice sounded distorted. Warped and ponderous. But I

recognized it all the same. It was my mystery caller. The guy with the German accent.

"Where is she?" I asked, and as I said the words, I screwed my eyes tight shut and ground my fist into the side of my head.

"She is safe. For now."

Awful, awful words. I didn't believe them. Not for a minute. I hated hearing them. I felt sick and weak and juddery.

"I want her back," I said, and I couldn't hide the desperation in my voice.

"Then you must find the package. You must exchange it for her."

"But I don't have the stupid package. I don't know where the damn thing is. I don't even know *what* it is."

"You must find it. Your girlfriend is in danger."

"She's not my—"

But the guy had already hung up. Leaving me to my cavernous apartment. The droning note of the telephone. The terrible silence all around.

TWENTY-THREE

I didn't move for a long time. I stayed down on the floor, feeling powerless and confused, weak and disoriented. I was numb. I was angry. And I was scared.

I was so scared that I was afraid to think. If I started to think about the situation Victoria was in, where she was being held, how she was being treated, it would become real. It would exist. So I shied away from it, like a guy trying hard not to gaze into a bright white light that was being shined directly into his eyes.

But it was impossible to do. Completely unavoidable. The light was making my eyes water. I was crying. I was a wreck.

My imagination was the problem. I could visualize Victoria's plight because I'd written the exact same scene many times before. Most every hack out there penning mystery novels has. Nearly all of us follow the same broad template. Nearly all of us use italics.

It starts with a barren, cheerless room, described with a handful of keystrokes. Bare walls, concrete floor, no windows, little furniture. Maybe there's a soiled mattress or a single ladder-back chair. Maybe there's a bare bulb flickering in the middle of the ceiling.

Our victim is huddled in the corner. Chances are she's shackled. She may be injured in some way. Perhaps her wound was sustained during a foiled escape attempt, or perhaps it was inflicted by her captor as a sign of worse to come.

The poor, sniffling heroine is unkempt and distressed. Her clothes are badly torn or discarded altogether. But she's just beginning to gather her strength. She's summoning her wits. She's starting to search for the one tantalizing flaw in her jailor's plan, the single weakness in her dungeon.

Footsteps approach. Keys rattle in a lock and a bolt is thrown. The evil sadist steps into the room, face shadowed, to issue threats and warnings. Maybe he describes the variety of pain and torture the victim can expect to endure. Maybe he explains exactly why the hero won't be able to save her this time. Oh, and just for good measure, the moment he's about to leave, he happens to spot that one potential weakness our heroine has been relying upon . . .

Enough.

I rolled onto my side, pushed up from my knees, and staggered into my bathroom. I ran the cold tap over the sink and bathed my face and the back of my neck. I gazed at myself in the mirror, water dripping from my brow. I looked like I'd shed about a stone in weight. My cheeks were scooped out, my eyes red and wild and protruding from my face.

They protruded a little more.

In the corner of the mirror, I'd spotted something down on the floor behind me. I turned and crouched beside the bath and lifted the pigskin document wallet in my hands. Victoria's weapons kit. It was unzipped, and its contents tumbled out and bounced on the tiled floor.

The items now scattered around me could be divided into two categories. First, there was a selection of spy gear: covert listening devices, drugged cigarettes, a sedative pen, concealed cameras and the like. Then there was the self-defense weaponry: a stun gun and a Taser, a switchblade and a telescopic billy club, a pepper spray and a quite bewildering array of cuffs and restraints.

I didn't like how I'd found the wallet abandoned on the floor like this. It made me think that Victoria had heard her abductors coming in and had tried to hide in the bathroom to arm herself. I didn't suppose it had worked out too well.

I gripped the wallet tightly. I gnashed my teeth. I cursed. I raced back to my telephone and dialed Victoria's mobile again and again, never getting through.

Then I got hold of myself, and I went and gazed out my living room window until I had the fragile beginnings of a plan.

I was standing across from the British embassy by seven-thirty in the morning. The sky was beginning to lighten from full black to indigo gray, and a damp, drizzly breeze was swirling around me, lifting my hair and wetting my face and hands. I could have used a pair of mittens. My arthritic fingers were starting to bloat and tingle and stiffen. I wrapped them around the takeaway coffee cup I was holding and transferred my cigarette to my left hand.

I was leaning against the brickwork of the building opposite the embassy entrance, one leg bent at the knee, my foot resting against the wall. The embassy was located on Wilhelmstrasse, alongside the rear of the Hotel Adlon and just round the corner from the Brandenburg Gate. The road was closed to most traffic. There were bollards at either end of the street that could be lowered for authorized vehicles, and a lighted security booth manned by two guys in Kevlar vests and baseball caps, with assault rifles hanging from straps on their shoulders.

The embassy had a striking exterior. Faced in sandstone, it had the appearance of a modern office building except for two peculiar shapes that protruded from a horizontal slash in the middle. One was a triangular glass structure that jutted out at an angle and was cantilevered so that it appeared to hover in midair. The other was a giant cylinder in royal purple. Between the two structures, a sloping flagpole extended outward and a Union Jack fluttered limply in the breeze.

Despite the quirky architectural touches, I couldn't help focusing on the security measures that were in place. They were substantial. The windows were thin, vertical notches that seemed designed to deter anyone from trying to peek inside or out. The main entrance was protected by two retractable metal gates, an internal guardhouse, and an airport-style security scanner. There were at least eight closed-circuit cameras that I could see and probably more that I couldn't. All things considered, it wasn't a property that encouraged unexpected visitors, and it would be all but impossible to sneak into.

Difficult to get out of, too. I'd walked the entire block, and I couldn't spot an alternative exit. The only option was to be funneled out past the guardhouse and the scanning machine and the metal gates and the surveillance cameras. Anybody leaving would be highly visible. So would anything they happened to be carrying. And that made me think some more about the mysterious package that had been swiped from the ambassador's office. The thief would have had to come out this way. They would have had to pass through close scrutiny. There was always the risk of a routine search. And if they were carrying anything unusual or suspicious, there was every chance they'd be challenged. Did that mean the item was small? Easily concealed? And if so, how small were we talking? Because if it was tiny, then perhaps I really had overlooked it in the three locations I'd already searched.

I sipped my coffee. I smoked my cigarette. I gave it a good deal more thought.

As eight o'clock approached, more and more embassy staff arrived. Some came by bicycle, wearing glistening raincoats and waterproof trousers. Others arrived on foot, carrying black umbrellas above their heads and briefcases by their sides. The rest came by car. I counted six vehicles in all. It was the same routine every time.

A black town car with tinted glass and diplomatic plates would approach the security booth at the end of the street. The driver would power down his window. One of the armed guards would lean out of the lighted hut into the gauzy drizzle and inspect the driver's credentials. Then the bollards would be lowered and the car would ease along the street, windscreen wipers sweeping lazily from side to side, and turn toward the double gates at the front of the embassy building. The gates would shuffle apart. Then the car would glide inside and the gates would narrow behind it, leaving just enough space for a cyclist or a pedestrian to enter.

Watching the cars gave me another idea. I guessed it was only the most senior staff who were provided with vehicles and allowed to park inside the embassy building. And their cars had tinted windows. They had spacious trunks and countless little cubbyholes. They would be ideal for concealing a stolen item. Perfect for shuttling that item out through the embassy gates and along the street and away.

I was still considering the possibilities a short while later when I saw movement from the inner guardhouse. A door opened and a man stepped out. He passed through the metal gates and hustled toward me.

He was a short, stocky guy, dressed in a tight-fitting blue suit with a white shirt and dark tie. His graying hair was trimmed army-style and I could see a flesh-colored wire extending from his shirt collar to his right ear. His left hand was pressed flat against his chest, holding his tie in place against the wet, blustery wind.

His right was down by his waist, tucking the tails of his jacket behind a gun holster with a pistol in it.

I slurped my coffee and tapped some ash from my cigarette, then plugged it back into the corner of my mouth.

"Sir," the man said. He was approaching me in a crablike stance, sideways on. "Can we help you?"

"Help me?" I asked, venting smoke off to one side.

"Sir, this is the British embassy. You've been standing here for close to an hour."

I nodded over his shoulder, toward the fascia of the building. A British Government crest, fashioned from metal, was fixed to the wall. The words BRITISH EMBASSY were etched into the sandstone beside it.

"I kind of figured."

The man fitted his hand around his pistol. He adjusted his grip. "Sir, you can't just stand here."

"Why not? It's a public street." I gestured along it with my cigarette. "People are walking through here all the time."

"Sir, if I have reason to believe you pose a security risk to the embassy, I can ask you to move along."

"So ask. But I'm not a security risk. What are you afraid of—that I might flick my cigarette at a window?"

He removed his free hand from his tie and held it in the air, palm out. "Sir, I'm going to ask you to stay very still. I don't want you to move."

He lowered his mouth toward his shirt collar. Mumbled something incoherent.

"Make up your mind," I told him. "First you want me to leave. Now you want me to stay still."

"Sir, this is no joke. What we have here is a situation."

"You don't have a situation." I gestured at him with my cigarette, holding it between my finger and thumb, like a dart. "You have a request. A deadly serious one."

"Sir?"

"I need to speak with Freddy Farmer. I need to speak to him inside his office, inside your precious embassy. I need that to happen within five minutes from now."

"I don't understand."

"Sure you do," I told him, taking a lingering draw on my cigarette. "Freddy sent you out here, didn't he? I'm guessing he turned up in one of those blacked-out town cars I've seen driving into the building. Then I'm guessing he phoned down to your guard booth and told you to make sure I was sent on my way. But that's not going to happen. At least, not how Freddy has in mind. Now," I added, evacuating smoke through my nostrils, "I want you to go back inside and dial his extension. I want you to tell him that unless he agrees to have me escorted inside your building and up to his office, I'm going to walk round the corner into the middle of Pariser Platz, and I'm going to start shouting in my loudest voice about the very things he doesn't want me to mention. Got that?"

The man peered at me for a moment, then glanced over his shoulder toward the embassy entrance. I could tell he was conflicted. He was feeling that way because I'd guessed right about Freddy. And that gave me some legitimacy in his eyes.

"I won't move a muscle," I told him. "I won't even inhale. But if you don't do as I say, you're going to regret it. You'll probably be fired. Chances are, you won't be working here tomorrow."

The man fixed on my eyes for a moment longer, then scuttled backward. I watched him enter his guardhouse. I saw him pick up a phone. Less than a minute later, he beckoned me over to him.

I took a final draw on my cigarette, flicked the butt away, and swirled the cooling coffee around in the bottom of my cup. I passed through the metal gates. The security guard was joined by his colleague. He was dressed the same. Built the same. He even spoke the same.

"Sir, come toward me through the scanner."

I did as he requested. The scanner beeped as I passed through. I wasn't surprised. They hadn't asked me to empty my pockets. I was pretty sure it was deliberate. I guessed they were trying to intimidate me.

"Sir, raise your arms."

I lifted them from my waist, parallel to my shoulders, my coffee cup in my right hand. The guy approached me. He patted me down thoroughly. He started at my wrists, then worked along my arms, down through my chest, my waist, my legs, my feet.

"Remove your shoes."

"If you ask me," I told him, "I reckon the beeping noise came from what's inside my pockets."

"Your shoes, sir."

I sighed. Kicked off my scuffed baseball trainers. They were empty. The guy ducked behind the scanner and returned with a small plastic tray.

"Empty your pockets."

"Now why didn't I think of that?"

I dumped my coffee cup in the tray, then rummaged inside my trouser pockets and added my wallet and my house keys, my cigarettes and my lighter.

"Anything inside your coat?" he asked.

"Other than me?" He didn't even smile. "Here," I said, and dropped my penlight and my spectacles case inside his tray.

He checked everything in turn. He parted the compartments of my wallet and shuffled through my cards, verifying my name. He took a peek at my cigarettes, even raising the pack to his nostrils and sniffing the filters. He flashed my torch off and on. Then he pried open my spectacles case and did a swift double take.

"What's all this?"

"My tool kit," I told him. "I'm a handyman."

It was true. In a fashion. But he didn't believe a word of it. He turned to his colleague, the one who'd crossed the street to speak with me. He showed him my collection of picks and probes. My shims and torsion wrenches. The nine-volt battery, the coiled lengths of electrical wire, the razor blade, the micro screwdrivers, the fountain pen with the lid removed.

"What's all this?" his colleague asked.

"Amazing acoustics you have here," I told the first guy. "It took almost a minute for your echo to come back to me."

"You can't bring these inside."

"Fine. I'll collect them on my way out."

"And you can leave the torch, too. And the cigarettes. This is a no-smoking building."

I stuffed my wallet and my keys and my lighter back inside my trouser pockets. I put on my shoes. Then I reached for my coffee cup and toasted the guy who'd conducted my search.

"Follow me," said the guy who'd crossed the street. "Stick close."

"Like glue."

He led me across an open-air courtyard. The embassy building surrounded us on all sides. There was a lot of glass and gray granite and exposed metal. It was very contemporary. Achingly so. In the center of the courtyard was a single English oak. It looked a little lonely. A little sad. I felt like I could relate.

I was marched around the tree and through a set of revolving glass doors to a reception counter where I was made to sign a register and take a security pass. Then I was accompanied up a flight of stairs and across another large courtyard enclosed beneath an expansive glass atrium. I clocked an impressive collection of modern art. Coiling sandstone sculptures, a large wall painting, a pair of light boxes, and a circular, mirrored sculpture by Anish Kapoor.

"This way," the guy said. "Keep up."

There was nobody else around. Our footfall was loud and ominous in the cavernous space. We climbed more stairs to a galleried balcony, where a guy in a blue uniform was pushing a mail trolley along. Then we turned a couple of corners and strolled along a couple of corridors until the guard paused outside a door with Freddy's name tacked to it.

He squared his shoulders. He rolled his neck. He coughed into one fist and raised the other as if to knock. He hesitated.

"Oh, for goodness' sake," I said, and opened the door and breezed right in.

Freddy was sitting on an inflatable turquoise posture ball behind a very large wooden desk, with his head in his hands. His tie was loosened and the collar of his white shirt was unbuttoned. There were stains under his armpits and a day's worth of stubble on his chin. His eyes were red-rimmed and glassy. His tightly curled hair was greasy and sticking out all over his head, like a bunch of loose springs.

"Good news," I said, and raised my takeaway cup in the air. "I've brought you some coffee."

TWENTY-FOUR

Freddy didn't seem impressed by the coffee. He was even less impressed when he pried the plastic lid off and saw the cold dregs in the bottom. He turned up his nose and tossed the takeaway cup into a metal bin beneath his desk. Then he teetered to one side on his giant inflatable ball and peered behind me, as if he suspected that I might be concealing something from him.

"Did you find the item?" he asked.

"Afraid not."

Freddy seemed to crumple in on himself, bouncing gently on his ball. "Then what is it you want?" he asked, in a voice that was high on whining and low on patience.

"Charming. Is that how you greet all your guests?"

"I don't have time for manners, Charlie. Or for silly games."

He could have fooled me. There might not have been a Ping-Pong table in his office, but there were plenty of other toys and distractions. A nearby shelving unit was filled with Airfix models of classic RAF fighter planes. Framed prints of steam locomotives and vintage sports cars lined the walls. A fun-sized basketball hoop was fitted to the back of his office door. He even had a windup tin robot on his desk.

I grabbed the robot and took it for a stroll to the window in the facing wall, winding back the mechanism as I gazed out over the top of the glass atrium. Rainwater had pooled on the glazed roof, forming warped reflections of the bleak gray sky.

"Be careful that you don't overwind that, will you?" Freddy said. "He's an original."

I kept winding. I could feel the tension starting to build. The mechanism creaked and strained.

"Did you manage to search the cleaner's home, at least?" Freddy asked. "You never replied to my texts."

"Oh, I searched it."

I released the dinky metal handle and the robot's feet flailed helplessly.

"And?" Freddy prompted.

"And nothing," I said, as the robot's movements slowed to a few final, fitful kicks. "I didn't find anything. At least, nothing that looked like something you'd want me to find."

Freddy groaned, and the rubber posture ball squeaked as he adjusted his weight. "Then you shouldn't have come here," he said. "You're wasting time. And you certainly shouldn't have threatened me with the disclosure of our arrangement."

I glanced across at him, weighing the robot in my hand. "I needed to talk to you."

"Then you should have had Victoria send me a text."

"Couldn't."

"Why not?"

I smiled, showing a lot of teeth. It was better than snarling, I supposed. I paced across and slapped the robot down onto his desk with a clang.

"What's eating you, Freddy? You don't look too good."

162

"I'm under pressure. You know that."

"Work stress? Poor guy."

"We need the package back. We need it today."

"Yeah? Says who?"

He folded his arms across his chest. Bounced on the ball. "The ambassador. He's really steamed about the whole thing. He's even talking about involving the police."

"The police? Heavens."

"It would be a disaster. We'd lose all credibility."

I titled my head to one side and absorbed the image of him sitting there on his daft turquoise ball. "Well, from what I hear, you're running pretty dry on that account already."

"Who told you that?"

"Americans. People in your line of business. One lady in particular."

I removed my wallet from my back pocket and fished out the card Duane had given me with Nancy Symons's name and telephone number on it. I passed the card to Freddy.

"Oh," he said, face falling. "Her."

"Makes quite an impression, doesn't she?"

Freddy flexed and bent the card between his stubby fingers. "When did she get to you?"

"She picked me up from outside the cleaner's apartment. She was waiting for me there. She knew all about our arrangement. Same as the Russian crew. Same as the French heartbreaker who confronted me in my hallway. Same, for that matter, as a cryptic German guy who telephoned me in the middle of the night with an idle threat that lately doesn't seem so idle." I speared my index finger into his desk. "So it's not *my* discretion you need to worry about. Everyone I meet seems to know your business. And trust me, I'm not the source. I don't appreciate having these people harass me."

My finger was shaking by now. Pain was flaring in my arthritic knuckle.

Freddy paused. He pressed the corner of Nancy's card into the pad of his thumb. "What did you tell her exactly?"

"The truth. That I didn't know what I was looking for. That I hadn't found it yet."

"And?"

"And she offered me more money to pass the item to her." I eased off on my bad finger. "Assuming I ever find it, that is."

Freddy shook his head. "Damn cheek."

"It was a little crass, I admit."

"It's plain rude."

"Oh, I know. When you hire a burglar to break into a bunch of homes for you, the least you'd expect is a little good grace and decorum."

Freddy laid Nancy's card down on his desk. "You're mocking me."

"I'm trying hard not to. Believe me. I'm focusing just about everything I have right now on making sure that I have your full cooperation. I need you to explain what it is that I'm looking for, Freddy. I can't afford any more mistakes."

He shook his head, jiggling on his ball. "We've been through this. I told you, it's sensitive."

"But you said yourself that the ambassador is talking about contacting the police. You'll have to tell *them* what was stolen."

Freddy glanced over his shoulder, toward an innocuous-looking door set into the wall behind his desk. "That's not going to happen."

"So you say."

"He's just blowing off steam. He's frustrated."

"We're all frustrated." I cast my hand to one side, toppling the metal robot over onto its back. "Me, most of all."

"I've told you, you'll recognize what you're looking for if and when you see it."

"That's not good enough anymore."

"I fail to see why."

"Then allow me to enlighten you." I leaned right across his desk, knuckles clenched, the head of the tin robot poking into my gut. "They have Victoria."

Freddy reared back so far that he had to flail his arms to prevent himself tumbling off the ball. "Come again?"

It was all I could do not to come *at* him.

"That's why you didn't receive a reply to your texts last night. She was abducted. Snatched from my apartment while I was out on the fool's errand you'd sent me on."

"Snatched? Are you quite sure?"

"Of course I'm sure. I received a telephone call. A threat, from my coy German friend. He told me Victoria was in danger unless I found and exchanged the package."

"But that's awful. It's preposterous. It's—"

"Real," I said. "It's happening. So enough fooling around. I need you to tell me what I'm looking for. I need to make sure that I find it."

Freddy blinked and ran his fingers through his tangled hair. Then he squeezed his head between his hands, as if he was struggling to contain everything that was going on inside his brain. I took the opportunity to palm Nancy's business card while he was distracted.

"Tell me what was stolen. Help me to resolve this thing."

"I *can't.*"

I jabbed my finger at him. "You want to be the one to tell that to Victoria? I imagine she'd be really keen to hear it right now. Think about it. She's alone. She's scared. I daresay the location where they're keeping her is isolated. It gives them a whole lot of scope to hurt her, doesn't it?"

"You think I like this?" he spluttered. "If anything happened to that delightful girl . . ." He left the sentence unfinished and glanced over his shoulder again.

"Why do you keep looking at that door, Freddy? Who's through there?"

"The ambassador," he said, then covered his mouth with his hand, as if he'd let slip a terrible secret.

"I see." I moved around his desk. "Then I think I'll go and talk to the organ-grinder."

"No." He scrambled to his feet, almost tripping over the ball, and moved in front of me. He was surprisingly fast for a big guy. "You mustn't."

"Oh, come now. I'm sure he'll want to resolve this situation."

"But he's the ambassador."

"Blimey. When your argument's as complex as that, how can I possibly disagree?"

I advanced toward the door, but Freddy spread his arms and legs as wide as they would go, barring my access.

"Don't be daft, Freddy. He hired me. He's bound to want to meet me, at least."

"I can't allow it."

"You don't have a lot of choice."

I took another step forward. Freddy tensed and flattened himself against the door. He took a lot of flattening.

"Look," he said, "he doesn't know who you are."

"Then I'll introduce myself."

"No." Beads of sweat had popped out all over his brow and nose. "You don't understand. He doesn't know you exist. He doesn't know anything about our arrangement. I handled it all myself."

"Excuse me?"

166

"He mustn't know. In case it goes wrong. He needs plausible deniability."

I hesitated and took a step backward. "But you said—"

"I know what I said. But the truth is, this was all my stupid scheme. The ambassador doesn't know the first thing about you."

I can't pretend Freddy's little revelation didn't sting just a touch. Nobody likes to be the forgotten man in a clandestine situation. Let alone yours truly.

"But hang on," I said. "If he doesn't know about me, then how does he think he's going to get his precious package back?"

"I told him I'd take care of it. That's my job. That's what I'm supposed to do around here. He knows enough to realize it's not in his interest to ask awkward questions. But he's getting impatient all the same."

"He *is* covering my fee, I assume."

Freddy squirmed. He lowered his voice. "The fee will come from the embassy's budget. You'll be hidden as an expense. Office equipment. Stationery. Something like that."

Boy, I thought. And wouldn't the British taxpayer be thrilled to hear it.

"So is this why you're so stressed?" I asked. "Your little experiment with me, your off-the-books solution to the ambassador's predicament, you're scared of being found out?"

He looked down at the floor. I'd like to say he was staring at his toes, but I had a feeling it was a long time since he'd been able to see them. "That's part of it, I suppose."

"And the rest?"

He glanced up. "Oh, do take a seat," he said. "I fear you'll need to."

TWENTY-FIVE

I didn't sit down. I was too wired. But I did step away from the door and cross back to the window. The wind and the drizzle hadn't let up at all. It didn't look as if they were going to anytime soon.

Freddy lowered his arms and fussed with his shirtsleeves. He wiped his forehead with the palm of his hand. I've seen people with severe allergic reactions look more relaxed.

"There's something else," he said. "Something I haven't told you just yet."

Oh, joy. Words I really didn't need to hear.

"It's about Jane Parker. You remember her?"

"I tend to recall most people whose underwear I've riffled through."

"Well," he said, "she's disappeared."

I raised an eyebrow.

"Completely vanished, I mean. She never turned up at the embassy function on the night you broke into her hotel room. The ambassador received the mayor of Berlin at nine o'clock, but there was no sign of Jane. She hasn't shown up for work. She's not answering her phone."

I frowned. It wasn't something I'd expected to hear. But it wasn't altogether surprising, either.

"It's no big deal," I said. "She had a top secret file stolen from her. She probably thinks she's in trouble."

"But she doesn't *know* it was stolen."

"Of course she does. As soon as she got back to her hotel room she'd have discovered that the file had been swiped. She probably panicked and went on the run."

"You're not listening to me. She never returned to the hotel. We checked. I had men positioned there as soon as I received the text Victoria sent me. Their job was to detain her. They didn't know why. They were working for me on a strict need-to-know basis. But she never showed. And we interviewed the hotel staff. Nobody saw her anywhere close. Not in the lobby, or the bar, or the restaurant."

Freddy rested his hands on the edge of his desk, elbows locked, as if he was bracing for an impact.

"Listen," he said, "when you first got in touch to say you'd found the stolen item among her things, it seemed to fit with her no-show at the function. But now we know you hadn't really found what we were looking for, her disappearance makes no sense at all."

I hummed. I hawed. I even plucked at my lower lip.

"Sounds fishy," I said.

Freddy threw up his hands.

"But I wouldn't put too much faith in what the hotel staff tell you. They're not the most observant group of people. Have you asked to review the footage from their security cameras?"

"We can't."

"Why ever not?"

"Because the CCTV might show *you* breaking into her room. And that's the last thing I need."

"Oh. I hadn't thought of that."

"Well, I have. I've barely stopped thinking about it. It's not going to look very good if the police become involved."

More words I didn't like the sound of. Freddy was becoming a regular scaremonger. "The police? Why would they care?"

"Because the hotel management are aware that she's missing now. I gave our men permission to speak to them and request access to her room. I told them to search for anything that might tell us where she is. If she doesn't turn up soon, the hotel will have to empty her things so her room can be made available to other guests. And all her belongings are still there. Her passport, even."

I recoiled a little. "I didn't come across her passport."

"It was taped to the underside of one of the bedside drawers."

The significance of our exchange didn't escape me. I'm pretty sure it didn't escape Freddy, either. I hadn't checked the underside of the drawers, and I really should have. Truth be told, I daresay I could have taken my search more seriously. The problem had been my incentive. It hadn't been big enough. Yes, I always take a certain pride in my work, but on this occasion I'd known I was being paid regardless of whether I found the secret item or not. And I'd been frustrated that Freddy hadn't told me what I was looking for. My only consolation was that I couldn't have missed the mystery object, too. Freddy had told me it would stand out. By the sounds of it, Freddy's men had searched her room thoroughly enough to have spotted it, even if their primary mission had been to find clues to Jane's whereabouts.

"Anyway," Freddy said, "the hotel will have to report it to the police eventually."

"Right," I said. "And I'm guessing that if they do that, the police are going to want to know why the embassy didn't get in touch with them direct. After all, you have an employee missing. Even if she was only meant to be in Berlin temporarily."

170

"Quite."

"Well, that's a conundrum."

Freddy was looking at me as if I was a touch simple. Perhaps I was.

"What was in the file?" I asked him.

"You know that already," he snapped. "You're the one who found it and photographed its contents."

"Yes, but everything was in code. I'm asking you what the code said. Has it been deciphered?"

"I can't tell you that."

I had a sudden urge to lash out and slap Freddy across the chops. It was all I could do to restrain myself. My arm was practically vibrating.

"Honestly, Freddy, if only you could tell me all the things you can't tell me, I reckon I could help you to clear this mess up in no time at all."

He shook his head roughly. "I can't tell you because I don't know myself. The code went to our security people. They've not been in touch with any results. I asked, of course. Naturally I did. But there's been no response. And in my opinion, that can mean only one thing."

"They couldn't crack it?"

"Goodness, no. Of course they could. They have some of the world's finest brains available to them. They have advanced computer systems you and I can't even begin to imagine. No, they'll have cracked it all right. Their silence just means the information relates to something above my pay grade."

"Your pay grade, maybe. But what about Jane Parker's?"

"Hers, too, I imagine. Look I'm sorry, I'm in the dark here every bit as much as you are."

"I seriously doubt that. It seems to me there are a whole cast of people running around who know a hell of a lot more about what's going on than I do."

"You mean the Americans?"

"And the Russians. Them in particular. Think about it. They seem to have been content enough with the pages of code they took from me. Otherwise, I think I can pretty much guarantee I'd have heard about it by now. So perhaps they might be able to help you with the whereabouts of your missing employee. They might even have had a hand in her disappearance."

Freddy gawped at me. "You don't really think so, do you?"

"Why not? Victoria's already being held as bait."

"By this German character, you say? What do we know about him?"

"I was hoping you might tell me, though I sense that's not going to happen. Still, it seems perfectly possible that Jane Parker could be being held as well. But then, what do I know? I only have a few scraps of information. You're the guy in possession of all the facts."

"Hardly."

"Sure you are. You just don't know how to use them. Take the job you hired me for. You came up with a list of four possible culprits and four locations. But I bet with a little careful thinking, you could have narrowed the suspects down even further."

"I fail to see how."

"Then allow me to show you. I'll bet the embassy keeps personnel files on all their employees. Let me take a look at them for you."

"I can't—"

"Save it," I said, and raised my hand to stop him before he got into his stride. "Stop telling me what you can't do and start telling me what you can. You need to take control of this situation. It's no good festering here in your own funk. Chin up, Freddy. Both of them. It's time to start solving this puzzle."

I wasn't confident that my little speech would have the desired effect. I've never been very good at chivvying people along. Hell, I'm slack enough myself at the best of times. One glance at my current manuscript, and my rapidly encroaching deadline, was proof of that. But either I sounded a lot more confident than I felt, or Freddy was a good deal more desperate than I realized, because after a long moment's reflection, he gathered up his telephone and punched a single button.

His call was answered right away, and he requested the four personnel files as a matter of urgency.

"On their way," he said.

"Marvelous."

"Would you like more coffee? I can arrange it."

"I'm fine," I said. "But I do have a question. How many of your suspects come to work at the embassy by car?"

"What does that have to do with anything?"

I told him about the thinking I'd done out on the street. About the security on the exit from the embassy and how a car might be a great way to smuggle a stolen object out of the building.

Freddy moved his mouth around, chewing over the idea. "I'd have to check," he said.

"So check."

He picked up his phone again. Punched the same button. Spoke in the same gruff tone. Then he hung up and told me the results.

"Everyone commutes by car."

"Crap."

"I'm not finished. Only two of them are allowed to park inside the embassy gates. That's Daniel Wood, my first suspect, and Andrew Stirling, suspect number four."

"What about Jane Parker?"

"A taxi from her hotel. It's a firm we have an account with. But they're not allowed inside the gates."

"And the cleaner?"

"We employ a cleaning firm. They provide a minibus for their staff."

"So it's a possibility."

Freddy pulled a face. "I don't think so. Not with other cleaners on the minibus. They'd have spotted something."

"I see," I said. "So the item's not small, then?"

Freddy winced, but before I was able to quiz him further, there was a sharp rap on the door to his office and a young woman stepped inside. She was smartly dressed in a dark pencil skirt and a black silk blouse, and she was clutching a stack of buff document files in her hands.

"Excellent," Freddy said. "Set them down on my desk."

She did as he asked, then turned on her heel and vacated the room. I watched her leave. I would have watched her walk most places.

"Now then," Freddy said, once the door was closed. "What are we looking for here?"

He scooped the stack of files toward him, but I reached out and claimed them for myself, carrying them over to the window and resting my backside on the ledge.

"Tell you when I've found it."

I didn't find it. Not even close. And truth be told, I hadn't really expected to. But I had wanted to take a look at the files and learn a bit more about the people Freddy suspected of stealing from the ambassador.

First up, I discovered that Daniel Wood was a junior diplomat. From the information in his file, I could see that he'd worked in Berlin for just over a year, and there was a batch of tedious paperwork relating to his impeccable employment history. A portrait photograph was clipped to the inside cover of the file, showing a neat, squared-away guy in a shirt and tie.

Jane Parker was only in Berlin on a short posting, and her file contained nothing but a brief letter confirming her appointment, a color snapshot, a personnel form that included her home address in Crouch End, London, her date of birth, and her seniority grade.

The cleaner's file also contained a headshot image, as well as a security clearance, initialed by the embassy's head of security, and a letter in German from her employer. The letter informed the embassy that she'd worked for the cleaning firm for a period of twelve years, that she had an exemplary service record, and that they would have no hesitation in recommending her as an entirely trustworthy individual.

The remaining file belonged to Freddy's fourth and final suspect. It was thick with paper. Andrew Stirling's portrait shot revealed a man in his late fifties with dark, neatly trimmed hair styled in a side parting, and a drawn, haggard-looking face. He was a senior diplomat and his record included stints in embassy outposts and consulates all across the world, from Washington, D.C., to Sierra Leone. He'd been working in Berlin for almost six months and had another eight to go until his retirement. I got the impression the Berlin posting was the culmination of a long and distinguished career.

"Anything?" Freddy asked. He'd settled back down on his posture ball and was watching me keenly from across his desk. His palms were pressed together, fingers steepled, as if in prayer.

"Not much," I told him. "They all might have done it. And from what you say, they all had the opportunity. But if you want my honest opinion, I think we can exclude the cleaner. I'd say she's the least likely of all your suspects."

"Agreed."

"Then why on earth did you have me search her home before this chap's?"

I tossed the file belonging to suspect number four onto Freddy's desk, spinning it round so that the information was pointing toward him. I tapped the guy's face.

"It's . . . a sensitive situation."

"You mean he could have your job if he found out you suspected him?"

Freddy held my gaze. "I'm as interested in self-preservation as the next man."

"Right," I said. "And you wanted to see how I did on the other locations first. You wanted to be sure I didn't screw up before you set me on this guy's apartment."

"I'm not sure I'd put it quite like that."

"But you like him for it, don't you?"

Freddy exhaled. " 'Like' is not the word for it." He clasped his hands to his face, then pulled them downward, tugging at the pouched skin beneath his eyes and doing a fair impression of a bloodhound. "Believe me, I'd rather it was just about anyone else."

"But he's the guy you always felt could have done it. The moment you heard about the theft, he's the first one who sprung to mind, isn't he?"

Freddy shuddered. "There is a certain logic to it."

"On account of he's nearing retirement? He might be looking to make some extra cash. He might be willing to take a risk?"

"There's that," Freddy allowed. "But there's also his attitude. There's a . . . tension between us. Always has been. He's made it clear to the ambassador on more than one occasion that he believes I'm underqualified for my role. He practically told me I have my brother to thank for my job. He could be right, of course. Look at me now. You probably think the same thing. But I'm here to protect the ambassador. So, naturally, when he challenged my capabilities—"

"You began to question his motives."

"Precisely. And there have been times when I've seen him . . . well, loitering outside the ambassador's office."

"All right," I said, and nodded. "That's what your instinct tells you, then your instinct can't be completely off. I'm willing to buy it. He's our guy. Tell me, is he working today? In this building?"

Freddy nodded.

"Good. Then I'll head to his place right away. I'll get inside and

I'll search it and I'll check everywhere until I find what we're looking for."

I turned the file back to face me. The personnel form stapled to the inside cover listed Andrew Stirling's address as an apartment in the Hackescher Markt.

Freddy released a burst of air. "You will be careful, won't you?"

"I'm always careful. He'll never know I've been there. But there is one thing I'll need from you."

"What's that?"

"Your trust. You have to tell me what the secret object is. This whole situation has gone too far. There's too much at stake. Victoria's in danger. You can't afford for me to make a mistake, and neither can she. And frankly, I'm not prepared to break into this guy's home until you spill the beans on what I'm hunting for. I'm done wasting time, Freddy. Either you tell me, or we forget the whole thing."

He reared back like I'd punched him in the face. "That was never the agreement."

"Forget the agreement. Things have changed."

"How do I know you won't betray me? How do I know you won't exchange the object with this German chap for Victoria?"

"You'll just have to take a chance on that. I want Victoria back. No question. But if you tell me what we're dealing with here, there may be a way I can satisfy us both. And besides, what else are you going to do? If you had another viable option, you'd be using it already." I placed my hands on my hips. "So what's it to be?" I asked. "Will you tell me?"

"Very well," he said, shoulders slumping. "I'll tell you."

And so he did. And though I was braced for the worst, what he said was far more fanciful than I could possibly have imagined.

TWENTY-SIX

When I got back to the security booth, my two friends with the attentive hands patted me down thoroughly to make sure I hadn't pinched any paper clips. Then they returned my cigarettes, my penlight, and my spectacles case to me. I popped open the case and went through the routine of checking its contents. I didn't really believe they'd have swiped anything—there was nothing of any obvious value inside—but hey, they'd treated me like a common thief, and the petty part of my psyche wanted to return the favor.

Once I was finished laboring my point, I bid them so long and walked away up the street, turning left onto Behrenstrasse and pausing beside a litter bin. Now that I was out of sight of the embassy gates, I opened my spectacles case and selected what appeared to be a fountain pen with the lid removed. I say appeared to be, because when I unscrewed the nib, it revealed an earphone socket.

I ducked down and reached a hand beneath the litter bin. There was a plastic sandwich bag taped to the underside that I'd stashed earlier. Inside the bag was a set of earphones. I fitted the little foam buds inside my ears and plugged the jack into the socket in the pen.

There was a lot of static on the line. There was a fair bit of whistling, too. It was pretty much what I'd expected to hear. The system was only good for perhaps five hundred meters, and I was standing on the outer limits of its range. Plus, there was a lot of concrete and glass and steel between me and the bug I'd planted.

The bug and the listening device had formed part of Victoria's spy kit. The transmitter was in the lid of the pen, and the lid was currently swathed in the plastic from another sandwich bag. Oh, and the plastic was adhered to the bottom of the takeaway cup I'd carried into Freddy's office, submerged beneath the thin layer of cold coffee.

I'd tested the device back at my apartment before I'd set out for the embassy, and I'd been pleasantly surprised by the way the transmitter had been able to pick up the tunes playing on my kitchen radio through the plastic bag and the liquid I'd poured over it. Now, though, the signal kept being interrupted by short bursts of white noise, and whenever it came back online, the low-level whistling was constant.

It wasn't something I could stand for long, so it was just as well that I didn't have to. Within minutes, I could hear Freddy speaking on the phone.

"Nathan? It's Freddy. I'm calling about this situation with the embassy again. Your man's just . . ." A swirl of whistling static killed the feedback for a long five seconds. ". . . sent him to the fourth apartment. It's in Hackescher Markt. I'm feeling uncomfortable about it. I'm not sure . . ." More whistling. More interference. ". . . you would do? I'm concerned that . . ."

The signal cut out again. This time the whistling was so intense that I removed the stereo buds and covered my ears with the flats of my hands.

I could have tried listening for longer, I suppose, but I didn't see the point. The bug had already told me what I needed to know.

Obviously, this wasn't the first time Freddy had called his brother for guidance about the job he'd hired me to do. It was just as Nancy Symons had said: Freddy was out of his depth. And while I imagined it would be fairly tough for a foreign agency to bug a telephone line into the British embassy, I guessed it would be a lot easier for them to tap into Nathan Farmer's phone in Paris.

I was pretty sure that was how the Russians and the Americans, not to mention the French guy and my German caller, had come to know about my involvement in this shambles. It explained how they always seemed to know my whereabouts and my next move. Speaking of which, I was going to have to hurry. Freddy had just spilled the information on the fourth location, and there wasn't a moment to lose.

I lost too many. It took me twenty minutes to get across to the Hackescher Markt on the U-Bahn and the S-Bahn network, and by the time I hurried down the stairs inside the red-brick train station, I walked straight into the waiting arms of the Russian crew.

Not that their arms were spread wide in an embrace. Pavel, the dapper guy with the tailored overcoat, was leaning against the graffiti-covered brickwork with his arms folded across his chest, like a well-dressed model in an urban photo shoot. Vladislav had his hands in the pockets of his leather jacket. His right pocket was bulging. Now true, he exhibited all the basic characteristics of a primate, but I didn't think he was gripping a banana.

Nope, definitely a pistol. He eased the butt out to show me and smiled his lopsided grin just as I was contemplating turning on my heel and running back upstairs to the train platform.

"Mr. Howard." Pavel pushed off from the brick wall and paced toward me through the crowds. His coat collar was up around his neck. No scarf today. "May we speak with you?"

"I don't suppose you'd believe me if I said I was too busy right now."

He inclined his head toward the exit. "You will follow with me."

"And if I don't?"

His pal with the scar circled behind me until he was standing very close, then jabbed his gun into my side. I gasped in pain. He'd drilled the muzzle right into the center of my bruising. I can't pretend I wasn't impressed. I hadn't credited him with the kind of brain power to remember where he'd punched me.

"Well," I said, through gritted teeth, "since you asked so nicely, I suppose it would be rude of me to refuse."

Pavel led us out through a brick archway onto a cobbled square. There were sidewalk cafés to my left, and plenty of patrons were huddled in plastic chairs, sipping steaming coffees and hot chocolates. A group of tourists were standing nearby, waiting impatiently for a young guy with a satchel slung over his shoulder to begin a city walking tour. Hot dog vendors prowled among them, wearing portable griddles around their waists with gas canisters strapped to their backs like jet packs. I could see a delivery van and a couple of cars parked close by. One of them was the Russians' black town car.

I was ushered away from the square and beneath a domed brick tunnel that doubled back under the train station, where a network of tram tracks crisscrossed the ground. A row of metal Dumpsters were pushed up against one wall. The Dumpsters were almost camouflaged against the brickwork behind them by the graffiti that had been sprayed over the area. There was a smell of damp and urine. There was an echoing silence. It was a suitably lonely spot.

I was forced up against one of the Dumpsters. Pavel checked both ways to be sure nobody was watching us, then nodded to his pet thug, and Vladislav surged forward and buried his fist in my side.

It was the kidney opposite the one he'd pummeled before. I didn't know if that was a good thing or bad. I guessed it would give me a matching pair of contusions to admire in my bathroom mirror, but to be perfectly honest, I'd have preferred it if he hadn't hit me at all.

I went down on one knee and clutched my arm to my side. Vladislav pinched my chin between a grubby finger and thumb and tilted my head so that I was gazing up at him. To an outsider, I might have looked like I was proposing. He would have made some fiancé. His ugly face was slanted by the tug of the scar and drool was pooling in the corner of his mouth.

He bunched his spare hand into a fist and frowned at his knuckles. They were scuffed and scarred from years of hurting people. I was certain they were coming my way.

But before he could treat me to a backstreet nose job, Pavel stepped up and placed a hand on his cocked shoulder. He peered down at me with all the compassion of a guy staring at roadkill.

"The code is incomplete," he said.

"Excuse me?" My voice was soft and high and wavering.

"The code," he repeated, "is incomplete."

"No, I heard you. I just don't understand you."

"What is not to understand? There is code missing. A page, at least. Tell me where it is."

"I have no idea. Truly."

Next thing I knew, my skull had bounced off the Dumpster behind me. It took me some moments to realize that Vladislav had boxed me on the ear. A sound wave expanded in my head very fast, like a bubble of compressed air. It popped with a percussive whoosh that felt as if a balloon had burst inside my brain—one filled with sharp tacks and acid.

Something trickled out of my ear. I pressed my fingertips to it. They came away wet with blood.

My hearing wasn't good, but my balance was terrible.

Vladislav bent low and snatched me by the hair and hauled me to my knees again.

The world tilted sideways and then flipped right over. I didn't flip with it. The brute wouldn't let go of my hair. I thought I might pass out. There was hot liquid in the back of my throat. Saliva or blood or bile. I couldn't tell which.

"Where is the code?"

Pavel had hitched up his tailored trousers and ducked down in front of me. He was resting his forearms on his knees, hands clasped loosely together.

"Where . . . is . . . the . . . code?"

Saying it slower didn't help at all. It just made the distortion of his words even worse, like a record that was being played at the wrong speed.

I tried to focus on his hands, but they were spinning like disks. My eyes were spinning with them. I felt like I was being hypnotized.

I blinked and shook my head, and regretted it immediately. The pain was still there. It was an evolving beast, growing worse all the while. My ear throbbed. It was filled with a swirling, droning, piercing buzz.

Then there was a different noise. Something clipped. Precise. It echoed off the brick archway above us.

A woman in heeled shoes was hurrying by. She glanced at me furtively, then away again. She fixed her attention on the ground. Picked up her pace.

"I don't have your stupid page of code," I said, spitting the words out along with some blood. It seemed I'd bitten down on my lip when I was punched. "You took everything I had."

Vladislav yanked at the roots of my hair. I yowled and raised my arms in front of my face, scrabbling at his wrists.

183

"We know why you are here," Pavel said. "We want the package."

I dropped my arms a fraction and squinted at him. "But I thought you wanted the code?"

"We want both."

Greedy, I thought. But I didn't say it. This wasn't a time for smart talk. This was a time for survival.

"What is this package?" Pavel asked.

"No idea," I lied. But his question was interesting. It didn't sound as if Freddy had given the *entire* game away on his phone call to his brother. "But I'll get it for you," I said. "I'll break in right now and I'll figure out what the package is and I'll bring it to you. You can wait here for me."

"Nyet."

"Help me out here, will you? Either you want the package or you don't."

"We want it. But we will come with you."

I didn't speak for a good few seconds. I didn't care for his suggestion. Not even a little bit.

"No can do," I told him, tasting the blood on my tongue. "I work alone."

Vladislav tugged at my hair so hard I feared my scalp might tear.

"I have a proven method," I said, talking fast now. "A set of rules. I don't work in groups. It's too dangerous. We'll draw attention. If you'll only wait here, I'll—"

Vladislav seized a fistful of my coat and shunted me backward against the Dumpster.

"We will come with you," Pavel repeated.

"Well, if you put it like that . . ." I said, and gently probed the back of my head, steering clear of my thick ear. "But you have to do everything I say. You have to listen to me and pay attention."

Vladislav grunted and finally released me. It was all I could do not to collapse to the ground.

"You will not fail us," Pavel said. "Now, get up. We must not waste time."

"You're right," I told him, dusting myself down. "I apologize. I should never have thrown myself against your man's fist in the first place."

TWENTY-SEVEN

So this was a novel dilemma. I finally knew what I was looking for, but I wasn't on my own anymore. I had company. Unwanted, unpredictable company, and I didn't like to imagine how the Russians would react if the not-so-secret package wasn't inside the apartment Freddy had dispatched me to. But likewise, I had no idea what I was going to do if I *did* find the object. There was no way I could let the Russians have it because I needed to exchange it with my cryptic German caller for Victoria. And yet I was pretty sure they'd have a problem with that.

Talking of problems, I couldn't see a way to get inside the apartment building without appearing suspicious. The glass entrance door I was interested in was located between a pharmacy and a shoe shop, opposite the station cafés and just along from where the Russians had parked. It was about as conspicuous as you could get. So were the Russians. They looked like dangerous men. They radiated a tangible threat. And having them crowd around me as I got busy with my picks would be a long way from subtle.

Then again, I was beginning to believe that discretion was

overrated. Take the woman who'd hurried by as they'd beat me up. She hadn't intervened. She hadn't stopped to ask what they were up to. And I doubted that anyone else would be dumb enough to take a different approach.

We walked toward the door in a tight group. I was leaning to one side, clasping my hand to my aching gut. Vladislav was to my left, Pavel on my right. They both slipped on black leather gloves as we approached.

I tried the door. It was locked. No surprises there.

The lock was a simple spring latch. No dead bolt. No guard plate.

The Russians arranged themselves around me, facing the street, like a human shield or a security cordon. I tried not to let it go to my head.

Humming a distracting little ditty to myself, I pried open my spectacles case, moved my tools aside, and removed my plastic shims. I selected one at random and swiped it down past the latch. Then I hauled the door open and breezed inside the foyer.

The two Russians still hadn't moved. They were waiting on the wrong side of the door.

"Ahem," I said.

They glanced over their shoulders, then did a fast double take.

"What can I say? I'm a professional."

They exchanged a look that suggested they were beginning to revise their opinion of me.

"Here," I said, and passed one of the shims to Pavel. "You might want to hold on to this. It could save you the trouble of breaking somebody's window, maybe."

I released the door and Vladislav stiff-armed it open for his boss. They followed me across the foyer. The foyer was little more than a short corridor with an elevator dead ahead and a fire door on the right. The fire door would open onto a stairwell, and normally it was the route I would have selected. But Freddy had told me that Andrew Stirling lived in a penthouse apartment on the seventh floor of the building, and I didn't feel capable of climbing that far.

I was still a little nauseated and plenty dizzy. My ear was hot and tingling, and my hearing was yet to clear. It was buzzing and whistling, a bit like listening to the dodgy bug transmission from Freddy's office. And my stomach was churning and gurgling and cramping. I was stooped over like I had a hernia. Maybe now I did.

I prodded the call button. There was a muted ding followed by the instant parting of the elevator doors. I stepped inside and waited for my new colleagues to join me. The carriage bounced under our weight. The compartment was tight and cramped, and I was pressed flat against the mirror on the back wall.

"Penthouse, please," I said.

Pavel sighed and pressed the button marked *P*. But the elevator failed to move. He jabbed it again. Still nothing. The Neanderthal looked across. He grunted and smacked the button with the heel of his hand. Oddly enough, that didn't work, either.

I squirmed between their shoulders and switched positions with Pavel. Bending down, I spotted a socket for a key beside the button for the penthouse suite. It was the same system I'd encountered in Daniel Wood's apartment building.

I created some wiggle room with my elbows, then removed a raking tool and a torsion wrench from my spectacles case and got to work on the keyhole. I had the thing rotating in just under a minute, and then I leaned forward and prodded the *P* with the tip of my nose. The button lit up. The elevator doors shuffled closed. The carriage started to ascend.

It was about time for me to slip on some gloves of my own. I tucked my spectacles case away and set about easing one of my customized gloves over the taped fingers of my right hand.

"Your fingers, they are broken?" Vladislav asked, in labored English.

"Hey," I said. "It speaks."

"What happened?"

"Shark bite." I raised my taped fingers. "Hell of a thing."

The guy grunted. Conversation over.

The elevator continued climbing and we fell into silence. I might have said it was awkward, but embarking on a break-in with these guys was never going to be a relaxing jaunt. I didn't relish being in any space with them, let alone a confined one.

Eventually, the carriage slowed to a halt on the seventh floor. I was weightless for a tiny fraction of time, then there was a muted ding and the doors slid apart, opening directly into Andrew Stirling's apartment.

So much for security. One snap lock on the front door. One flimsy pin tumbler inside the elevator, and here we were.

"Top floor," I said. "Household goods, kitchenware, bed linen."

The Russians ignored me. They bundled out of the elevator and stood admiring the apartment.

I have to say it was magnificent. The floors were laid with a dark, highly buffed parquet that seemed to go on forever. The walls were a startling white that sloped inward toward a flat area of ceiling in the middle of the apartment, mimicking the mansard roof on the outside. There were ample windows. A lot of glass. The whole place was flooded with light and had a generous, airy feel.

The elevator doors shuffled closed behind me, and I ambled to my right, into an open-plan kitchen. The kitchen was sleek and minimalist. The units were bright orange, the countertops white granite.

"Where is the package?" Pavel asked, and his voice seemed to echo around the cavernous space.

"I don't know," I told him. "We'll have to search for it."

I ran my gloved fingers along the kitchen counter and sauntered into a dining area. Six clear plastic chairs were arranged around a glass dining table. To my left, in the very middle of the room, a central fireplace had been fitted flush inside a narrow partition wall. On the other side of the fireplace I could see a generous L-shaped couch and a leather recliner.

The windows beside me offered a wonderful view over the raised iron train tracks below and the rooftops beyond. I looked left and the Fernsehturm slid into view, the silvery observation dome glinting like a tacky Christmas tree bauble.

"You waste time," the Russian said.

"Patience," I told him. "I'm just getting a feel for the place."

"You must search for the package."

"*We* must," I corrected him. "And we will. In just a moment."

There was a low white cabinet below the window and resting on top of it was a table lamp and a dome-shaped object draped in a heavy black cloth. A pungent odor permeated the cloth. A stale, musty, gassy scent. I lifted the cloth away.

And that's when the racket started up.

There was a sudden caw. A piercing screech. An urgent flapping.

It was followed by some fast twittering and chirruping. Some modulated whistling.

Then the plump little bird turned around on its perch, cocked its head, and screeched, *"What's your name? What's your name?"*

The bird was jet black with an orange beak and yellow flashes on the side of its face. A band of yellow curved around the base of its neck and there were streaks of white on its wingtips. It was bigger than a starling, smaller than a crow. It was housed inside a large metal cage. There were three perches, a tray of feed, and a water dish clipped to the bars. Plenty of wood shavings and newspaper lined the base.

"My name's Buster. What's your name? What's your name?"

I laughed. Couldn't help it. Then I ducked down and poked a finger through the cage. Buster considered me with his glittering black eyes. He blinked. Then he turned his back on me, acting coy. I swiveled the cage until he was facing me again.

"What's your name?" he asked.

"Charlie," I told him.

He raised his beak in the air and blinked some more. Something seemed to build up from inside him and bubble in his gullet. He issued a long, croaking, creaking noise. *"Cheeky boy,"* he squawked.

I turned to the Russians. "Can you believe this?" I asked. "A talking bird."

"You waste time," Pavel said. "We must find the package."

"But it's a bird that talks!"

Pavel shook his head, as if exasperated. Vladislav fiddled with his gun, flicking the safety on and off.

"Oh, my goodness," Buster twittered. *"What* are *you doing?"*

"Gotta go," I told him, and wiggled my finger inside his cage. "It was nice meeting you."

"What are *you doing?"*

"Good question." I straightened and rested my hands on my waist. I considered the room. Considered the Russians. "We should split up," I told them. "This is a big place. It could take some searching."

"Big place," Buster said. *"Big place."*

"See?" I told Pavel. "Even the bird agrees."

"Then what is it you suggest?"

"One of us starts in here. Another one tackles the bedrooms. The last guy takes the bathrooms."

"The bathrooms?"

"Absolutely. There are a whole bunch of hiding places inside your average bathroom."

191

"Bathroom," Buster said. *"Bathroom. BathROOOOM."*

"I hate this bird," Pavel said.

"So I'll search in here."

"Nyet." He shook his head. "You waste time with the bird already. You will search the bathrooms."

"Fine. What about you two?"

"I will search the bedrooms." He glanced at his companion with the scar. "Vladislav will search in here." He jutted his chin toward the cage. "Kill the bird if it talks too much."

"Hey!"

Vladislav showed me his bad dental work. I could almost picture him swallowing the poor creature, like Sylvester the Cat eating Tweety Pie.

"You leave Buster alone. He's not *that* annoying."

Buster flapped his wings and issued a fast cackle. *"My name's Buster. What's your name? What's your name?"*

"Okay," I admitted. "So he's a little annoying."

"Cheeky boy!"

I raised my palms, like I was calling a truce. Then I bent low and gathered up the black cloth and draped it over Buster's cage again.

"Uh-oh," Buster said. *"Good night, all. Good night, all."*

He chirruped. He flapped his wings. He fell silent.

"See?" I whispered. "Problem solved."

"Then let us search. And if you find something, do not try to hide it from us, or you will be killed. Understand?"

"Perfectly."

"Then we must begin."

TWENTY-EIGHT

There was a corridor to the side of the kitchen, with two doors off to the right, one for a bedroom and one for a bathroom. There was a third door at the very end.

I led Pavel toward it and discovered a spacious bedroom with an en suite bathroom. I flipped on the bathroom light and an extractor fan whirred into life. Pavel didn't like it. He clucked his tongue.

"Hey," I said, "I need to see what I'm doing."

I left him alone in the bedroom and started to work through my search routine. I began with the toilet cistern. It was clean. Nothing inside. Then I checked the toilet bowl, scanning for any lengths of cotton or string, just in case an item had been sealed inside a plastic bag and flushed to the other side of the U-bend. I ducked down and felt around behind the toilet. Then I moved on to the sink.

As I worked, I could hear Pavel opening drawers and fumbling through clothes. It was a sensible enough starting point. If he made his way through the room slowly and methodically, it could take him anything up to twenty minutes to conclude his task. If he was

193

less patient, it could be as little as ten. I guessed that gave me eight minutes, minimum.

The sink was clean. So was the medicine cabinet. So was the shower compartment.

I dried my gloves on a towel and removed my spectacles case from my coat pocket. Then I selected one of my micro screwdrivers, ducked out of the bathroom door, and flipped the light switch off.

Pavel glanced up. I showed him my screwdriver.

"Going to check the extractor fan," I said. "Don't want my hand to get chewed up."

"You do not need to tell me everything you do."

"Just keeping you informed."

I climbed up onto the toilet seat and stretched toward the fan. I undid the screws holding the plastic cover in place and poked around inside, finding nothing but dust and lint and hair. I replaced the cover and stepped out of the en suite.

"This one's clean," I said. "How are you getting on?"

Pavel was down on the floor, scrabbling around beneath the bed. His backside was pointed toward me.

"I find nothing so far," he said, his voice muffled.

"Well, keep looking. I'm going to tackle the other bathroom."

"Please. Just do it."

I scanned the bedroom quickly. There were plenty of places still to search. He hadn't tackled the wardrobe or the laundry bin or the bookshelf against the wall. I figured I had at least five minutes.

I headed along the corridor with my screwdriver, trying not to appear as if I was hurrying. I couldn't see Vladislav ahead of me, but I could hear the clang of pots and pans being rearranged in the kitchen.

I swung the bathroom door inward and assessed the lock. It was just what I'd been hoping to find. A simple push-button mechanism. Not the sturdiest security system in the world, but probably sufficient for what I had in mind.

I flipped on the light and the extractor fan and got busy with my screwdriver again. There were two screws holding the door handles in place on either side of the door. They were long and they took some undoing. I had to be careful. The droning of the fan would mask some noise, but I couldn't afford for anything to fall and clatter against the tiled floor.

Once I had the screws free, I gripped them between my lips and eased both handles away from the door. Then I switched the handles around and reinserted the screws and fastened them until they were tight.

The bathroom suite was luxurious. There was a walk-in shower cubicle, a whirlpool bath, a sink, a toilet, and a bidet. The walls were decorated with white, brick-shaped tiles. The floor was laid in a checkerboard style.

The bath was situated in the far corner of the room and it was large enough for something to be plausibly hidden beneath it. There was a curved side panel that would need to be removed first, so I stooped and got to grips with it.

I was halfway through when Pavel walked by and entered the second bedroom. As soon as I could hear him opening drawers, I resumed my work until I was able to pry the panel free. It came away with a screech of plastic, trailing a length of silicone sealant. I set it to one side, then placed my hands flat on the floor and peered underneath the bath. It was dark and dry and dusty. It was just about ideal.

I slipped my screwdriver away inside my spectacles case. Then I wiped the sweat from my brow with the back of my hand and found my feet and crept across to the door. Slowly now, I compressed the push-button lock until it engaged with the barest click.

Then I checked my reflection in the mirror over the sink, gave myself a look that said, *Here goes nothing,* cleared my throat, and started to yell.

"Hey, I've found something. Guys! There's something in here. You should come take a look."

Pavel was the first to emerge. He seemed rattled by my outburst, as if he couldn't comprehend how unprofessional I was being. I shrugged and peered over his shoulder to see Vladislav stomping toward me from the living room.

"What is it?" Pavel demanded.

"I don't know for sure. It's trapped beneath the bath, right up against the wall."

He gazed in at the bath and the gaping hole where the panel had been. Then he turned to Vladislav and issued a set of orders in quick-fire Russian. Vladislav shoved me aside and paced across the tiled floor and got down on all fours. He craned his neck.

"It's right in the corner," I told him.

He rolled onto his back and shuffled under the bath, like a mechanic scuttling beneath a car.

"See it?"

He didn't answer. He just stretched his arm and fumbled around. His T-shirt rode up above the waistband of his jeans, exposing his hairy belly.

"His arm's not long enough," I told Pavel. "Maybe I should do it."

"Nyet." He pushed the flat of his hand against my chest. "Not you."

He stepped inside the bathroom and kicked at the feet of his colleague, barking more Russian commands. Vladislav squirmed out from beneath the bath and his boss dropped to his knees.

I didn't wait any longer. I snatched at the bathroom door and hauled it shut. It closed with a thud. The lock engaged. I sprinted for the living room.

I could hear the door handle rattling behind me. They were yanking it and twisting it, but the lock wouldn't budge. There was the slap of a hand against wood. The drumming of a fist.

"Open this door. Release us. Open this door."

Not likely. I was away on my toes, blitzing past the kitchen. I was running so hard that I couldn't stop in time for the glass dining table. I tried to swerve, but my swerve came too late, and my thigh slammed into the table edge. I stumbled and nearly went down, but I stuck my hands out in front of me and gripped hold of the low side unit and pushed myself up and grabbed for the bird cage.

It was surprisingly heavy. It was cumbersome.

It was the secret object I'd been hunting for all this time.

To be exact, Buster was the mysterious package. He was a mynah bird from the Indian subcontinent. According to Freddy, Buster had been presented to the ambassador many years ago, at the end of a posting to the British High Commission in Sri Lanka, and he'd accompanied him around the world ever since.

In case there was any doubt, I'd spotted a small brass plaque on the front of the cage. *Presented to His Excellency, the Right Honourable Donald Chambers, with warmth and appreciation from the people of Sri Lanka.* The plaque was the reason I'd spun the cage around at the earliest opportunity that had come my way. It was also why I'd been so willing to cover the cage back up with the black cloth.

I have to say I was impressed. It couldn't have been easy for Stirling to snatch Buster and smuggle the cage out of the embassy. Mind you, getting it out of Stirling's apartment was no walk in the park, either.

I swung the cage around in a hurry and knocked the ceramic table lamp onto the floor. The lamp base smashed. The momentum carried the cage on, spilling Buster's feed and his water. The cage clattered into a chair. The chair toppled over.

197

Bam.

I glanced back toward the bathroom door. A wooden panel had splintered, and a black boot had burst through the timber. Vladislav's lower leg was attached to the boot. It thrashed against the torn wood.

I dodged the table and rushed across to the elevator. I pressed the call button. The button lit up. The doors didn't open.

Bam.

Vladislav was kicking the door again. Obliterating it, maybe.

I pressed my ear against the elevator doors. I could hear a fast whirring. A meshing of gears. Then the merciful ding of the carriage arriving.

The doors slid apart. I jumped inside and turned around with the cage in front of me. I punched the button for the ground floor. No need for my picks this time. The elevator wouldn't require a key when it was summoned from the penthouse.

Bam.

There was the wrench of wood against metal. A thud. A judder. A loud, violent curse.

I punched the button again.

Bad mistake. The doors had just started to close, and now they stopped and shuffled back open.

I hammered the button a third time.

Nothing.

I looked wildly about the room. I was just about to leap out and search for a hiding place when the doors started to close once more.

My breath caught in my throat. Vladislav careered around the corner and barreled into the glass table. The table shunted sideways. He spotted me and reached for his jacket pocket. He snatched at his gun.

The doors were closing far too slowly for my liking. They still had a ways to go.

Vladislav pushed himself up from the table. He raised his gun. His wrist danced and I ducked and the mirror behind me exploded into a billion itty-bitty pieces.

The doors sealed. The elevator was still for a moment. Then it began to descend.

I felt a tugging sensation. Something was pulling against my hands.

I raised my head and squinted out through half-closed eyes as the heavy black cloth was lifted clear off Buster's cage. The more the carriage went down, the more the cloth went up. It was trapped between the elevator doors. I didn't see it for long before it was sucked clean out of the carriage.

Buster was crouched on his middle perch. His head was buried beneath his wing. He glanced up tentatively and blinked, and I did much the same thing.

Little shards of mirror glass fell from my shoulders. I brushed them out of my hair and off my raincoat. They tinkled against the ground and crunched beneath my shoes. The elevator zoomed downward. Floor four, floor three . . .

"Oh, my goodness," Buster said. Then he whistled. His whistle started high and went low. He sounded like a broken kazoo.

"Close call," I said.

"Close call," he agreed.

"Are you okay?"

He elongated his neck and ruffled his wings. He twittered and whistled.

"I'll take that as a yes," I told him.

The elevator reached the ground floor. The doors parted.

A woman was standing in front of me. She was wearing an immaculate white cashmere coat and carrying a collection of shopping bags from the KaDeWa department store. Her jaw fell when she saw the devastation inside the elevator.

I didn't linger to try and explain myself. The Russians would be coming fast behind me, and if they'd found an access point to the stairwell, they could be halfway down already.

I skirted the horrified woman and lugged the bird cage toward the front of the building. I shoved the door open and it slammed into someone coming the other way.

A man howled and reeled back on his heels. He waved his arms. He lost his balance and crashed onto his backside.

Now sure, I was in a hurry, but I like to think that normally I would have helped him back up. But I wasn't about to help this guy. It was Henri, the French pickup artist who'd surprised me in the foyer of my apartment building.

I lurched to my left and broke into a run, then quickly broke out of it again.

A car had screeched to a halt in front of me. It was a Trabant, pale cream in color, aside from a mismatched green hood. The driver leaned across the front seats. He thrust the passenger door open.

"Get in," he yelled. He was a stringy guy with long brown hair and a fuzzy beard.

I hesitated.

He revved the Trabbi's engine. Noxious gas spewed out of the exhaust. Onlookers craned their necks to watch us from the train station and the street cafés.

"Herr Howard," he yelled. "Please. You must trust me."

Goodness, there were an awful lot of people in Berlin who were keen for me to do that. Not one of them had earned my trust just yet. And this fellow merited it least of all. His voice sounded terribly familiar. I was all but certain that he was my late-night caller.

I looked over my shoulder. Henri was on his feet, straightening his clothes. Then he was back down again. The door to the apartment building had swung open fast and caught him full in the face.

There was blood on the glass. He clutched his hands to his nose and moaned and squirmed on the ground, and the two Russians stood in the doorway scanning the street.

What did I have to lose?

I jumped inside the Trabant with the bird cage on my knees, and my driver roared away before I'd had chance to close my door. He accelerated in the direction of the archway running under the train station, and the Russians opted not to leap in front of him. Cars weren't allowed to drive through the archway. There was a yellow tram coming from the right. Another closing in on our left. I heard the clamor of tram bells. The wail of metal brakes. I shut my eyes. There was a shriek of rubber, and I felt myself being thrown sideways toward the driver. When I opened my eyes again, my door had closed of its own accord and we were slaloming past a new obstacle.

It was a blacked-out town car. It had stopped very sharply in front of us. The front end was bearing down on its brakes. The rear end was fishtailing.

I screamed very loud and very high. We slewed to the left and just skimmed it, trading paint, and then we straightened up and zoomed alongside the ponderous river Spree. I turned my head and considered the chaos we'd left behind.

The driver of the town car was standing in the street. He had one elbow braced on the roof of his car, and he was shielding his eyes with his free hand, staring after us. Another familiar face. Duane, Nancy's driver. Well, he'd be pleased to know that he'd succeeded in making me squeal, though not in the way he'd imagined. Our near collision had made me yelp like a little girl. One who was in serious danger of upchucking.

TWENTY-NINE

"My name's Buster. What's your name? What's your name?"

Buster was one step ahead of me. I wanted to know the same thing. I stared at the guy driving the Trabbi.

"What he said," I told him, gesturing toward Buster.

He was a gangling fellow with a pale, lean face. His light brown hair, flecked with streaks of blond, was tied into a ponytail, and his beard was rangy and unkempt. His trousers and jacket were aged brown corduroy. The jacket was a little tight in the shoulders and a touch short in the sleeves. It revealed the flared cuffs of his paisley shirt. And from what I could gather so far, he wasn't a big fan of deodorant.

I leaned my head toward the open window and gulped down some air.

"My name is Gert," he said, eventually. "Gert Hackler."

"Okay, Gert, meet Buster. And you already know my name."

Gert offered up a quick salute. "Hallo, Buster."

Buster hopped onto his uppermost perch and shifted his weight between his feet. *"Wanna sing a song?"*

I ignored Buster's suggestion and fixed my attention on Gert. "So now that you two have been formally introduced, can I have my friend back?"

Gert's mouth formed a perfect O. His eyelids fluttered. He had long, dainty lashes, like those of a little girl. He stared at me in confusion for so long that I had to reach out and prod his hairy chin until he focused on the road again.

"Victoria had better be safe," I told him. "I might not look like much, but if you've hurt a hair on her head, I'll never let you forget it."

He stared across at me, even more gormless than before. "Wait. You think that I have her?" he finally asked.

"I don't *think* it. I know it. You're the guy who's been calling me in the middle of the night."

"*Ja,* I call you," he said, lifting his angular shoulders and glancing back at the road. "But I do not have your friend."

I paused. Tried to swallow my temper. "Then who does? Some accomplice of yours?"

"*Nein,* you do not understand. I call to warn you, this is all."

"You threatened me!"

"*Nein.*" He shook his head fast and his ponytail lashed around his weedy neck. "I help you."

Buster seemed to like Gert. He twittered merrily at him. "*Wanna sing a song?*" he asked again.

"No, Buster," I snapped. "Nobody wants to sing a bloody song."

"*Wanna hear Buster count?*"

I sighed loudly and glared at Gert. "I just want to know what's going on."

"Then I tell you," Gert said, and checked his rear mirror. "But not here. I take you somewhere safe, *ja*?"

"Good luck with that," I told him. 'The people I was running from are seriously connected. They have a habit of tracking me down. So you might want to ditch this car. I'm pretty sure at least one of them saw your number plate."

"No problem." He turned to me and grinned disconcertingly. "The plates, they fall off a long time ago."

Gert drove me across the city and parked alongside some wooded scrubland that was enclosed by a chain-link fence with razor wire coiled along the top. The location seemed very remote. The only noise was the clatter of the Trabbi's two-stroke engine and the rustle of the wind through the trees.

I realized I'd been reckless to get in the car in the first place, and chances were, I'd be foolish to stay. I didn't know where I was. Nobody knew I was here. And I had no way of telling if Gert was dangerous or not.

"You will come with me, please," he said.

I watched him get out of the car and approach the fence. His trousers were too tight and far too short, the cuffs hanging way above the battered white gym shoes he had on.

I looked at Buster. Buster turned his head away, burrowing under his wing.

"What do we do?" I whispered. "Buster? Should we run?"

Typical. The one time I wanted him to speak, Buster didn't make a sound.

Gert was beckoning me toward him. He'd found some kind of split in the fence and he was using his meager body weight to hold it open.

I hesitated. But did I really have a choice? The only other move I could think of was to return Buster to the embassy direct. But if I did that, I'd have nothing to exchange for Victoria. And my faith in Freddy's ability to help me had been seriously shaken. I was being pursued by at least three groups of people I knew of, and Gert *had* got me away from them.

I found myself opening my door and walking toward him. He smiled encouragingly, then gestured for me to duck my head, and I scraped through against the stiff wire, carrying Buster's cage in front of me. Gert followed, heaving the fence back into position behind him. Then he pointed in the direction of the trees, and I waded through the overgrown grass alongside him. Buster flitted around his cage, whistling and warbling.

Gert patted the air with his bony hand. "We must be quiet now."

"Oh, really. Why's that?"

He raised a finger to his lips and shushed me. "There are guards, sometimes," he whispered. "And dogs."

I stared at him. "Where the hell *are* we?" I hissed.

"Be patient. I show you."

"Are we trespassing?"

He walked on, shaking his head, his ponytail swishing across his gawky shoulders. "*Ja,* but do not worry, Mr. Burglar. You will be safe if you stay with me and you do not make too much noise."

"What about the bird?" I asked. Buster was still twittering away.

"He must stay quiet, also."

Oh, brilliant. That was all right then. I mean, any casual observer could see that in our short time together, I'd developed absolute control over when and where Buster decided to speak.

"Ssshh," I whispered. "Buster. Hush up."

I rattled his cage. He lifted his orange beak in the air. Whistled louder.

I gave up. Birdsong would be okay, I guessed. It wasn't exactly unusual in a grassy, wooded area.

Gert led me through the trees, taking long, rangy steps. I

blundered through nettles and brambles, dead branches snapping beneath my feet.

Then the trees began to thin, and we stepped out into a grassy clearing where I came face-to-face with a dinosaur. And not just any dinosaur. It was a triceratops. A very big, very bulky triceratops, with a thick gray hide, a spiky neck frill, and a spiked horn on the bridge of its nose. It was bent low, with its jaws parted, like it was chewing on the grass.

I froze.

"What the hell is this place?" I asked. "Jurassic Park?"

Gert smoothed his hand over the flank of the triceratops. "The Spreepark," he said.

"And what's that?"

"It is an old DDR amusement park. It is closed now. Abandoned."

"Apart from the guards and the dogs."

"Ja," Gert said.

"But why guard a defunct amusement park?"

"Because people still like to come here. They drink. Take drugs. They could start a fire, maybe. Or get hurt. The owners could be sued."

People getting hurt. Boy, I really didn't like the sound of that.

Ahead of us was another dinosaur, a brachiosaur, maybe. This one was toppled onto its side. It had a long, curved tail and a long, curved neck. Its rounded belly and its feet were pointing toward me. The feet were hollow, exposing the reddish color of the material the model had been cast from. Grass and weeds and thorns had grown long around it.

Beyond the dinosaur, in the middle distance above the trees, I could see a Ferris wheel. The red metal structure was corroded with rust. The green and yellow carriages swayed listlessly in the breeze.

"Is this where Victoria is being held?" I asked.

"Nein," Gert said.

"So why are we here?"

"You follow. I will show you."

He showed me plenty. The amusement park was a vast, sprawling adventureland gone badly to seed. Decrepit buildings were closed and boarded up. Signs reading BETRETEN VERBOTEN! were fixed to posts and railings and trees. The asphalt pathways were cracked and choked with weeds.

We passed a deserted teacup ride, where the carousel floor was covered in fallen leaves and litter. The teacup booths were listing on worn-down springs, puddles of brackish water in their bases. The bunting tied up above them was discolored and torn.

A nearby pirate ship was blighted by graffiti. Just beyond it was the starting point for a roller coaster. A line of grubby cars waited forlornly beyond a ticket counter. The looping track that lay ahead was choked by weeds and thorns wherever it ran close to the ground.

Gert climbed some safety railings and followed the track, striding along a rough path beaten through the long grass and bushes. I set off behind him, with Buster's cage becoming ever heavier at the end of my arm.

After a little while, the track tilted to the left and plunged into a tunnel. The opening had been designed to look like the mouth of a cat. It was a cat from my very worst nightmares. Painted in psychedelic colors, its slanted eyes were narrowed and its wide-open jaws were loaded with glistening fangs.

"So, we are here," Gert said.

"Huh?"

He pointed down the deep, dark tunnel.

"This is where I live," he told me.

"Of course it is," I muttered. "What could possibly be more normal?"

THIRTY

The tunnel was very dark and Gert refused to let me use my pen-light. He said there was a danger the light might be spotted from the mouth of the tunnel, and anyway, he knew where he was going. That was fine for Gert, but I didn't have a clue. The tunnel was growing blacker all the while and I kept banging my shin on the roller coaster track. I was allergic to cats at the best of times, but wandering into the belly of the beast seemed like a very bad idea.

"Gert?" I hissed.

"Ja," he called back softly.

"Just checking you're still there."

No response. Gert was a man of few words.

I wished I could say the same about Buster. He was relishing the acoustics inside the tunnel and he'd revealed a bunch of new tricks. So far, we'd been treated to the noise of a laser gun, a door-bell, a telephone, and a psychotic—and frankly quite scary—laugh. He was presently having fun with the phrase *"Cooeee."* Every few seconds, he'd ruffle his wings, clear his throat, and shout, *"Cooeee,"* into the black. Moments later, a weak echo could be heard. I wasn't convinced that Buster understood the concept of echoes. I was fairly sure he thought he was in the middle of a conversation. Each time his words bounced back to him, he'd flick his wings and provide a response. The response was always *"Cooeee."* It was becoming an endless refrain. I was going to hear the damn word in my head for days.

"Shouldn't you be asleep?" I hissed, under my breath. "It's dark in here. Just like that cloth you had draped over your cage."

"Cooeee," Buster said.

Oh, boy.

The air inside the tunnel was stale and it smelled of damp and mold. The temperature was chill, like we'd ventured into a cave. I was becoming less convinced about the wisdom of following Gert with every step I took, and I felt really quite daft holding Buster's cage ahead of me, as if I was carrying a sacrificial canary down a mineshaft.

After a few more minutes of stumbling and cursing, Gert came to a halt somewhere in front of me. "Do you touch the track?" he asked.

"Er, no," I said. "Why?"

I didn't get an answer. I just heard the noise of a switch being thrown and the buzz and crackle of a sudden electrical surge. There was a bright spark of light. A dry fizzing. Then the heart of the tunnel lit up like some kind of twisted Christmas grotto.

There were fairy lights and fairground lights all around me. Some were plain. Some were colorful. Some were twinkling. They were hanging from the domed ceiling and zigzagging above my head in looping strings. They were coiled on the ground and draped around the furniture.

Well, I say furniture, but it was mostly a collection of crates and boxes, plus a foldout camp bed, a metal clothes rail, and a desk of sorts that had been constructed from an old door balanced between two dented oil drums. There was junk everywhere, on every available surface. Antique radios. Boxy computers. Dated televisions. Cash registers. Countless books and magazines. Hundreds of tins and pots and buckets of who-knew-what. The whole thing looked like an underground pawnshop on the skids.

"Careful," Gert said. "You must not touch the track. The electricity, it is not so safe, *ja*?"

I glanced down in the gloaming twilight. My feet were on either side of a rail. I stepped carefully away.

"You really live here?" I asked him.

"Sometimes, *ja*."

I released a low whistle. Buster joined in. I couldn't begin to imagine what it would be like to spend a night down here.

"Why?"

"It is secret. Only Gert knows it is here."

I hoped he was right. I didn't like the idea of being followed and trapped inside the tunnel by any of the people who'd been pursuing me around Berlin.

"But wouldn't you prefer an apartment?" I asked. "Somewhere more . . . normal?"

He frowned and fiddled with a space heater on the floor. He clicked a switch and the filaments glowed a vibrant orange. It would take some time for the warmth to begin to penetrate the heavy chill.

"But normal is maybe not so safe," he said. "Think of your apartment building. Think of the men who have been inside. Your friend who is missing."

Point taken. But how did he know about my visits from Pavel, Vladislav, and Henri?

"So tell me," I said, "what's your involvement in all this? Are you after this little guy, too?" I lifted Buster's cage, then set it down on top of a nearby pallet.

"I look over you," Gert said, scratching the back of his neck. "This is all."

"You look over me? How do you mean?"

"It is a favor," he said. "For Pierre."

I peered hard at him through the soft twinkling.

"Pierre?" I said. "You mean my fence, Pierre? Pierre from Paris? Pierre whose real name isn't really Pierre?"

Gert nodded eagerly, as if this should have been a perfectly reasonable explanation.

"But how do you know him?"

He blew air through his lips and cast his lean arm around our murky surroundings. "I am a collector. Sometimes, I find things Pierre may like. I sell them to him."

"And by collector, do you mean thief?"

"*Nein*," he said, sounding scandalized. "I sell only what I find."

Hey, me too, I felt like saying. But to Gert, there was obviously some greater distinction.

"Like a scavenger, you mean?"

"If you wish."

"Okay," I told him, and walked toward a trestle table piled high with dated newspapers and magazines. A selection of vintage propaganda posters were scattered across them, featuring stylized images of Lenin and Marx. "What sort of stuff do you scavenge?"

"You will call it memorabilia, I think."

"Of?"

"The history of Berlin. The Cold War especially. The DDR. There is a big market for it. They call it *ostalgie*."

"You mean like bits of the Berlin Wall?"

"Tsk," he said, and waved a disparaging hand. "This is for tourists."

"And your stuff?"

"For enthusiasts. For experts."

211

"I see," I said, though I didn't entirely understand. "But if that's all you do, why did Pierre ask you to watch over me?"

"He was afraid. This man who hired you—"

"Freddy."

"He was afraid he could maybe bring trouble."

"Well, that's terrific," I said. "Pierre's the guy who set me up with him in the first place. He told me I could trust him."

Gert folded his arms across his chest and picked at the faded patch of corduroy covering his elbow. "But his choice was not free."

I thought about that. I remembered the hold Nathan Farmer had over Pierre. Was it possible that Nathan had been eavesdropping on Pierre's call to me?

"Because of Freddy's older brother?" I asked.

"Yes, I think so."

"But that still doesn't explain why he came to you. What did he expect you to do?"

"To watch you."

"Yes, you said that. But I still don't—"

"And to listen." He moved behind his makeshift desk and dropped onto a rickety swivel chair that was badly in need of some oil. There was a stack of electrical equipment at one end of the desk that looked like the component parts of a hi-fi system from the early 1980s. Gert punched a button and a series of dials became illuminated. He picked up a pair of stereo headphones and passed them to me. "Here," he said. "You try."

The headphones didn't look altogether clean, but I accepted them and set them over my ears. I heard nothing to begin with. Then Gert punched a few buttons and twiddled a few dials and suddenly I was listening to a guy talking in fast, hushed German. His speech was too quick for me to understand all but the occasional word.

"Who is this?" I asked.

Gert twisted the dial some more. Now I was listening to a

212

woman. She had a hoarse, scratchy voice, but she sounded every bit as serious as the man. I lifted the earphones away from my head and set them down on top of the equipment.

"You listen to people?" I asked.

"And talk." He tapped a desk-mounted microphone. "There are many of us. All over the city. We share information."

"And are all of you . . . collectors?"

His eyelids fluttered several times, waving his fair lashes. "Some of us."

"And the rest?"

"They are what you would call squatters. People who live like me."

Nobody lives like you, I thought. But maybe I was wrong. Maybe plenty of people did. Enough to pass information around? To watch over someone like me?

"So what, you have some sort of secret network here in Berlin?"

"It is not so secret. Anyone may join."

"Is it legal?"

He smiled and stroked his beard. He didn't answer that one.

"And who was telling you about me?"

"The man you listen to just now. The woman, too."

I shuddered. Couldn't help it. "Would you care to explain?"

"I asked them to do it. They live on the Kollwitzplatz."

I frowned. "There are no squats on the Kollwitzplatz."

Gert exhaled wistfully, as if I'd embarrassed myself with my naïveté. "There are many empty homes, *ja*? There are rich people who live in them for only a few weeks each year. It is simple to avoid these people."

"Yeah? Maybe you could give me their addresses. We could both make some cash."

He shook his head. "This is not what we do. We do not steal."

I wasn't so sure about that. Gert's friends were living in other people's homes. Using their things. Tapping into their utility supplies. But I didn't argue with him. There was something else I was far more interested in.

"These people watching my home," I said. "Did they see who took Victoria?"

Gert nodded.

"So who was it?"

"A black man," Gert said. "Very big. And a white woman, in a blue business suit. They put your friend in the trunk of their car."

THIRTY-ONE

It took a moment for what Gert had said to sink in. It took a little longer for the full meaning of it to become clear to me.

I thought back to how the Americans had first approached me outside the cleaner's apartment on Karl-Marx-Allee. So far as I was aware, the Russian crew hadn't been there. Neither had Henri or Gert. That suggested Freddy hadn't broadcast the location to his brother. So the Americans had to have found out some other way. From Victoria.

The timing was beginning to make sense. They must have snatched her from my apartment shortly after I'd left. Then they must have made her tell them where I was going.

With Victoria in the trunk of their town car? It seemed possible. And that would mean she'd been very close when I'd been talking with Nancy. Would she have heard me? I didn't know. The sound-proofing in the car had been impressive, and I certainly hadn't heard her. But maybe there was no chance of that anyway. Perhaps she'd been gagged. Bound.

Then a new thought occurred to me, more terrible than any I'd had so far. Duane liked to make people squeal. Had he hurt Victoria in some way? Had he forced the information out of her?

"Did your friends say how Victoria looked?" I asked Gert. "Had the Americans harmed her at all?"

"They told me she was asleep."

"Asleep?"

"*Ja.* The black man was carrying her. Over his shoulder. She was like this."

Gert let his spindly body sag, his head droop, his arms go limp. I got it now. Victoria had been unconscious. Sedated, perhaps.

"I don't get it," I said. "The American woman tried to bribe me. She offered me double what Freddy was paying me to deliver Buster to her. So why take Victoria, too?"

"A guarantee, maybe? In case this bribe was not enough."

I thought about that. There was a sad logic to Gert's suggestion. Nancy had struck me as tough and businesslike. Cold, even. She wasn't the type of woman to let something she wanted slip through her fingers. She was the type to make sure she came out the winner in whatever twisted scenario she found herself. Even if that meant rigging the odds.

But why hadn't she let me know that she was the one who'd kidnapped Victoria? To keep me off balance? To make me reluctant to trust any of the people who were trying to manipulate me, for fear that any one of them could have abducted my friend? Or was it more basic than that? Was she simply withholding the information until she judged that it would have the most telling and timely impact?

I released a long breath, then turned and pressed my face close to Buster's cage.

"*Hello,*" he said. "*Hello.*"

"I'm confused," I told him. "I'm wondering what's so special about you."

"*Bienvenue. Wilkommen.*"

"Great," I said. "You're multilingual."

"*Ciao.*"

"Any more?"

He shuffled to one side, claws skittering along his perch. He shuffled back again. Puffed out his chest.

"A dance routine. That's marvelous."

Gert said, "Maybe the bird is worth money?"

I made a dubious humming noise. I seriously doubted that Buster was worth as much as Freddy had offered to pay me, let alone what Nancy had suggested.

"*Wanna hear Buster count?*" he asked.

"Not right now." I straightened and pointed toward Gert's stereo equipment. "How about your listening network? Would anyone on there know what's going on?"

Gert stroked his beard some more. "We did not know what you were looking for. No one knew why it could be important."

I thought about that. It was probably true, but it was strange. Take the Russian crew. They hadn't been at all interested in Buster when I first found him in Andrew Stirling's apartment.

"Wait," I said. "The Russians were after the final page of a handwritten code."

"Yes?"

"So Buster is a talking bird. Maybe he knows the rest of the code."

I ducked down toward the cage and treated Buster to my best grin.

"Hey, Buster," I said.

"*Wanna sing a song?*" he asked.

"No," I said. "No songs. But what about a code? Do you know any codes?"

Buster made the sound of a laser gun. He seemed disappointed by my reaction to it. Perhaps I was supposed to play dead.

"Know any codes?" I asked again. "Does Buster have a code?"

A phone started to ring. It was ringing deep in Buster's throat.

"Marvelous," I said. "He doesn't understand."

"He is just a bird."

"Yes, but there has to be something special about him. Why else would the ambassador want him back so badly?"

"He is his pet, *ja*? This is normal."

"And is it normal for somebody to steal a bird? The guy who took Buster—Andrew Stirling—he must have done it for a reason."

"Maybe he likes Buster, too?"

I gazed at Buster. He was grooming himself. His beak was buried deep under his wing and he was pecking at his jet-black plumage. And yes, I could appreciate that he was sort of cute. I could understand how his phrases and sound effects could be diverting for a time. But, I'm sorry, he was a little irritating, too. And I'd only been in his company for a short spell. Imagine putting up with his repertoire of tricks in your home. Could a serious diplomat like Stirling really have been so enamored that he'd have snatched Buster from the ambassador? Would he really risk his career for a talking bird?

"I don't buy it," I said. "I could believe that everyone was looking for some kind of secret code. But Buster, here? I don't think so."

Buster broke off from his grooming to stare up at me. He cocked his head at an angle. He looked a tad insulted.

"What?" I asked him.

"Wanna hear Buster count?"

"NO!"

I spun away from his cage and lashed out with my foot at the nearest thing I could find. The nearest thing turned out to be the roller coaster track. My heart skipped a beat. But the fateful surge of electricity never came.

"Be careful," Gert reminded me.

"Sorry." I raised my hand.

"You were lucky."

I didn't feel altogether fortunate. Here I was, talking to a strange, paranoid guy and a pea-brained bird in the depths of an unused roller coaster tunnel that smelled a lot like a faulty fridge stocked with rotting food. My best friend was missing. I was being pursued and threatened by a bunch of devious foreigners. And my toe was throbbing like I'd struck it with a mallet. So no, right at this particular moment, lucky was about the last thing I felt.

"I suppose I should call the Americans," I said. "Tell them I have their precious package and see if I can exchange Buster for Victoria. Is there a phone near here?"

"I have some," Gert told me.

"Some?"

He wheeled his chair backward, ducked below his desk, and sorted through the contents of a wooden crate. Within a few moments, he was holding a stack of cardboard boxes in his hand, propped beneath his hairy chin. The boxes were all sealed in plastic. I took the top one and found that it contained a mobile phone.

"Something else you collected?" I asked.

"I exchange for them. They are all prepaid. No tracing. It is safe, *ja*?"

I didn't know about that, but I doubted I'd be able to find a working pay phone anywhere close. I opened the box and unpacked the phone from its plastic wrapping. Then I reached inside my pocket and removed Nancy's business card. I switched on the phone. The screen lit up and the speaker emitted a three-tone chime.

Buster opened his throat and mimicked the sound. He was note perfect.

I stared at the display on the phone, waiting for a signal, while Gert approached Buster's cage, poking a finger through the bars and wiggling it like a gnarled, pink worm.

"*Guten Tag,* my pretty friend," Gert said.

Buster made the sound of the phone switching on again. Maybe his German was a little shaky.

I started to punch Nancy's number into the mobile. I was only halfway through when I had to stop.

"Hey," I yelled at Gert. "What the hell are you doing?"

Gert froze. His hand was inside the cage. He'd opened the little metal door and he was reaching in toward Buster.

"What if Buster gets out?" I asked him. "What then?"

Apparently, Buster didn't want to escape. He leaped up onto Gert's thumb and twittered away contentedly.

"Will you leave him alone?" I said. "I don't want anything else to go wrong."

"But he is so cute."

"Oh, he's delightful. But he's also my best chance of getting my friend back safely."

"She is very beautiful, I am told."

I stared hard at the back of Gert's head. I was tempted to yank him away by his ponytail. "Excuse me?"

"My friends tell me. On the radio."

I was having trouble staying calm. It sounded as if Gert's contacts had taken their own sweet time evaluating Victoria's appearance, but they hadn't bothered to intervene when she was abducted from my home.

"Gert," I snapped. "Will you please leave Buster alone?"

Gert was feeling around the bottom of Buster's cage, shifting sawdust aside with his fingers and delving beneath it. Buster was riding his thumb and chirping gleefully, as if he was enjoying a miniature fairground ride.

"Gert," I said again.

"*Gert,*" Buster repeated.

"Hey," Gert said, "he knows my name."

"Gert," I repeated.

"Gert."

"Hey! He said it again!"

I stepped over and cracked him on the back of the head.

"Stop fooling around."

"But I do not fool," he said, rubbing his scalp with his free hand.

"Yes you do. You're disturbing things in there."

"No," Gert said. "I check the cage. For the code you mention. Did you do this already?"

Hmm. Truth was, I hadn't thought of it. I hadn't even considered the possibility. But now that Gert had mentioned the idea, there was a certain something to be said for it.

I bit down on my lip. I toed the ground.

"Er, no," I mumbled. "Why don't you go ahead."

So he did. He piled all the wood shavings up on one side of the cage, then the other. He lifted the newspaper that lined the bottom of the cage and found absolutely nothing below it.

"Oh, well," I told him. "Worth a try."

Gert shrugged and raised his thumb toward the top of the cage until Buster hopped onto the uppermost perch. Then he flattened the newspaper back down, rearranged the sawdust, and closed the little metal hatch, blowing Buster a kiss when he was done.

I concentrated on the mobile phone again and started to punch in the rest of Nancy's number. I was just about to place the call when I noticed that Gert was lifting the cage high above his head.

"I find something," he said.

"You do?" I craned my neck and took a look for myself. All I could see was the molded plastic base. "Where?"

"Look here."

I looked. Gert was pointing toward a tiny ridge in the otherwise smooth black plastic. He tugged at the base.

"It moves," he said. "Quick. Help me."

I set the phone aside and grabbed hold of the base, yanking it downward. There was a slurping, sucking noise. I tugged harder. Gert pulled on the cage. Buster whistled and flapped his wings excitedly.

The plastic base came away in my hands, leaving a matching base attached to the cage.

I looked down into the black plastic shell I was holding. There was a square of paper resting there. The paper was lined and discolored with age. It was folded in two. It looked just like the notepaper I'd found in the top secret file in Jane Parker's hotel room.

I lifted it out very carefully, then cleared a space on Gert's makeshift desk and smoothed the paper flat with my hand. The top third of the page was covered in slanted handwriting. The writing was in a familiar faded blue ink. The words were in code.

I slapped my hand to my forehead and barked out a laugh.

"You did it, Gert," I said. "You solved the puzzle. You found the rest of the code."

He grinned widely and waggled his fingers at Buster. "So this is good, I think. Would you like that I crack it, too?"

THIRTY-TWO

I confess, I thought Gert was kidding, but he was serious about cracking the code. He dropped onto his tatty swivel chair and rooted through a box beneath his desk.

"You really know how to do this?" I asked.

"It is not so difficult," he said, speaking into the box.

"Who taught you?"

"I teach myself." He straightened up with a pad of paper and a ballpoint pen in his hand. "I read how to do it in books about the Cold War. Stasi history books. Things like this."

He started by copying out the code onto a fresh sheet of paper in a hurried scrawl. It didn't take long. There were only four lines of handwriting in the original version.

"It's lucky that the message is quite short," I said.

Gert shook his head, not looking up from his work. "No, it is bad."

"Bad?"

He ripped the paper from his pad and set it down next to him. He indicated the first few letters with the nib of his pen.

"In English, you call this a cipher."

"Sure. It's a code."

"No, a cipher, it is a special type of code." He squinted at me and I got the impression his eyesight was pretty poor. Then again, I guessed living somewhere without natural light would tend to have that effect. "Each true letter is replaced by another. The replacement letters scramble the words."

"It wouldn't be much of a code if they didn't."

"But a basic cipher is quite simple. You just add a number to a letter. Say the number you choose is five. If I want to write the letter *a,* I add five letters."

As he talked, Gert printed the alphabet on a fresh sheet of paper. He arranged the letters over three lines, leaving a lot of space in between.

"Look," he said, and tapped his pen against the letter *a.* "If I choose the number five, then the letter *a* becomes *e. b* becomes *f.*"

"That's easy enough," I told him. "But how do you figure out what number the code maker used?"

"You must look for repeats. This is why it is good to have as many letters as possible. *E* is the most common letter. So I look through the code and I find the letter that appears most often. The chances are good that this is *e.*"

"And if it's not?"

"Then I begin again. I try another letter. Eventually, I solve it."

"*If* that's how this code was written."

"So let me find out. I will begin."

He lowered his face to the page and began to count letters, his ponytail coiling around his neck. He tallied his results beneath the alphabet letters he'd already set out. I got the impression he expected me to be quiet. I couldn't quite manage it.

"I have a question," I said.

He tensed and held up a scrawny finger. I waited until he'd jotted down a note.

"How do you know what language the code is in?" I asked.

He blinked and backed away from the page.

"The paper and the ink look pretty old," I explained. "And for the past hundred years or so there've been a lot of different languages floating around Berlin. You might think you're cracking it in German, but it could be a different language entirely."

Gert chewed the end of his pen. "But this should not matter."

"It shouldn't?"

"I do not think so. But anyway, I am thinking the code is in English."

"And why's that?"

"Because your ambassador had it, *ja*? In the cage."

"Only if he knew it was there."

Gert sucked his pen, then used it to lift his hairy top lip, exposing his teeth and gums. "He must know," he said, his words a touch garbled. "This is why he wishes for the cage to come back. This is why you were hired."

"And what about Buster?"

Gert shrugged. "It is as you said. He is just a bird. A very nice bird. But a bird all the same."

I shot a guilty look toward Buster. He was gazing up at a chain of fairy lights, mesmerized by their twinkling. Poor little chap. He didn't seem to be distressed by his recent adventures, but it must have been unsettling for him. I wondered if there was anything I should be doing. Fetching him water. Offering him food. But then again, I was pretty sure he'd speak up if he needed something.

Gert returned to his work. I tried to sneak a look but he crooked his arm to cover the page, like a schoolkid trying to deter an exam cheat. I took the hint and decided to distract myself with a tour of his living quarters instead.

It didn't feel like a home. It felt more like a lair. I'd never seen so many fairy lights in one place before, but as soon as I took more than a few steps beyond their glow, the blackness of the tunnel was absolute.

I returned to the light and took my fingers for a stroll along a set of metal shelving units. I found all kinds of junk. Military medals. Old army jackets. Stasi uniform patches and embroidered insignia. Interflug luggage tags. Red and yellow DDR pennants and flags. Aged canned goods. Miniature busts of Lenin. Political badges and lapel pins. Leather holsters. Oh, and guns. Lots and lots of guns.

Some were pistols. Some were rifles. Some were shotguns. All of them looked like they belonged in an antiques shop.

I reached for one of the pistols. It had a long, scarred barrel that was badly chipped and dinged. I tried the trigger. It was jammed. Or maybe the safety was on. There were boxes of cartridges on the floor by my feet. I set the pistol aside and sifted through the cartridges, letting the bronzed casings cascade through my fingers. There were crates filled with mines. There were grenades.

"Er, Gert," I said.

No response.

"Gert?" I stepped out from behind the shelves with a grenade in my hand. "None of this stuff is real, is it?"

He glanced up, then did a fast double take. "Be careful," he said.

I swallowed. "Is this ammo . . . live?"

"*Ja,* I think so."

"You *think* so?"

"I test only some of it. In the woods."

Lordy. Why had I picked up the damn grenade in the first place? And why was I spending time with this guy? He lived in a dank and dingy tunnel with a volatile and possibly quite deadly electricity supply, and he had enough live ammo and explosives to blow a crater in the middle of Berlin. I was beginning to wonder if he was the smartest ally to have on my side.

"Who does this, Gert?" I asked. "Who keeps a secret cache of guns and weapons in an unused roller coaster tunnel? Who are you really?"

"I tell you already. I am a collector."

"But you exchange this stuff. You sell it. Doesn't that make you an arms trader?"

He shrugged, a little awkwardly. "You cannot start a war with these guns. They are too old."

"And the grenades?"

For some hard-to-fathom reason, I was just witless enough to toss the grenade I was holding into the air, as if it was nothing more than a cricket ball I was fooling around with. Let me tell you, I've never taken so much care about making a catch. All my old school training drills came flooding back to me. There was no way I was letting this bad boy hit the ground.

"Please," Gert said, when I'd cradled it to my chest, "put the grenade down."

I exhaled, then did as he asked. I placed the grenade back with the others as if I was laying a fragile jewel on a silk cushion.

"Aren't you afraid there'll be an explosion?" I dusted my hands off and moved closer to Gert's desk. "I'm not sure I could sleep next to all this stuff."

"Then it is good you do not need to. Now, look."

Gert turned his pad around to face me. He'd flipped over the page he'd been working on and had printed a short message on the reverse. His handwriting was very precise and very clear. It was a shame I couldn't say the same about the message.

SO I HAVE HIDDEN IT IN THE DEVIL'S MOUNTAIN. IT WILL BE SAFE

227

THERE FOR AS LONG AS NECESSARY. I LEAVE YOU THE SEQUENCE. GOOD
LUCK, FRIEND. FAREWELL. C.

I lifted the sheet of paper. Read it over a second time.

"You think this is the coded message?" I asked.

Gert nodded. "It makes sense, *ja*?"

"Not a great deal," I told him. "What do they mean by the Devil's Mountain? It sounds like something out of *Lord of the Rings*." I hummed to myself. "Wait. Could it be one of the rides in this theme park?"

Gert smiled and shook his head. "You really do not know?"

"Know what?"

He leaned back in his creaking chair and clasped his hands together behind his head, his jagged elbows poking outward. "The Devil's Mountain is the Teufelsberg. It is a hill that overlooks Berlin."

"Spooky-sounding hill."

"It is called the Devil's Mountain because it was built after the Second World War. A lot of the rubble from the bombing of Berlin was piled there. There was so much rubble it became a hill."

"Holy cow," I said. "So if something was hidden there, it could be right at the bottom of this pile of rubble?"

Gert toyed with his ponytail, fiddling with the elastic band that held it in place. "No, I do not think so."

"You don't? How come?"

"The Teufelsberg is not just a hill. It is in the west, but it overlooks Berlin *ost*. During the Cold War, this was useful to the Americans and the British. They built a listening post there."

"Huh. And does this listening post still exist?"

"*Ja,* but now it is empty. A ruin."

"A big ruin?"

Gert nodded. There was amusement in his eyes, as if he was a teacher watching an average student finally grasp a difficult concept.

I read back over the message he'd decoded.

IT WILL BE SAFE THERE FOR AS LONG AS NECESSARY. I LEAVE YOU THE SEQUENCE.

"Gert," I said, "if something was well hidden, do you think it could still be at this listening post even now?"

"For sure, it is possible."

"And the sequence this message refers to? Any idea what that means?"

"I am sorry, no." He nudged the faded sheet of paper dejectedly. "The code does not say."

"But this is only part of the code," I reminded him. "I already found the first four pages. The Russians stole them from me. Maybe the pages the Russians now have contain the sequence. Maybe they explain what was hidden, too."

I broke off to give the matter some thought. I rested my hand on Buster's cage and glanced down at him.

"Who's a clever bird?" I asked.

"My name's Buster."

"I know, buddy."

"Wanna sing a song?"

"Not right now, pal. I'm thinking."

Buster put his head on one side and blinked at me. His movements had a jerky, mechanical quality, like the windup robot on Freddy's office desk.

From what I could gather, the code really had been what everyone was after, and the top secret file I'd found in Jane Parker's hotel room truly had been important. Did that mean Freddy had lied to me when he'd dismissed the photographs of the code that I'd shown him, or was he really in the dark, too? Had he truly believed that getting Buster back was all he'd hired me to do?

I didn't think so. Sure, he'd come across as a touch bumbling, and I'd been willing enough to buy the act. But I doubted he really believed it was reasonable to pay me upward of ten thousand euros just to recover a talking bird. He had to know there was something more going on. He had to suspect, at the very least, that Buster wasn't the end of the story.

He'd held back from me. He must have. And any sense of patriotism I might have experienced was leaving me fast. So sure, I had the option of contacting Freddy and telling him that I'd found the final page of code. I could ask him for his help to get Victoria back safely. I could even demand that he tell me the full story of what I'd become drawn into.

But I didn't want to do any of that. My priority was securing Victoria's safe release. I didn't altogether care about the code. I wasn't concerned with what was hidden up at the Devil's Mountain.

So I reached for the prepaid mobile Gert had given me and I punched in Nancy Symons's number.

THIRTY-THREE

We arranged to meet in the early evening, just inside the main entrance to the amusement park. The entrance was sadder and more sorry-looking than anything I'd seen so far. The curved sign above the gates was missing random letters and welcomed people to the *S EE ARK*. The gates themselves were buckled in the middle, as if someone had barged them with a truck, and they were threaded with coils of rusty barbed wire. Heavy-duty chains and industrial padlocks had been used to secure the gates together. To the untrained eye, they probably looked daunting, but a simple glance told me they were about as secure as a length of spider thread.

"What do those warning signs say?" I asked Gert, pointing through the sketchy dusk toward some bright yellow boards attached to the gates.

"Your entrance is forbidden."

"No, not those. The ones with the lightning bolt and the little man falling over."

"Oh, they say the gates have electricity in them."

I swallowed. "And do they?"

231

"Usually, no."

Usually. Hmm, that wasn't quite the reassurance I was seeking.

"And you're absolutely sure the guards have gone?" I asked.

"Yes. I see them leave already. They do not return."

"And the dogs?"

"One of the guards takes them, too. I promise, if they were here, you would know this. They would be hanging from your nuts, *ja*?"

Gert jabbed me with his bony elbow. His laugh was a high, wheezing number. I can't say I was feeling quite so merry.

"Fine," I said, and swallowed again. "I suppose I'd better go and pick open the padlocks."

"Yes, you do it." Gert clapped me on the back. "I will watch."

Of course he would.

I walked stiffly toward the gates and took my sweet time selecting just the right pick and the perfect torsion wrench. Then I flexed my fingers and sucked in a couple of steadying breaths and reached out a tentative hand. I paused. My fingertips were just shy of the gate. I couldn't feel any static. There was no telltale buzzing or humming. I tensed my body and squeezed my eyes tight shut and finally grasped for a padlock.

The moment I touched it, my heart thrashed around in my chest. But it was the only thing doing any thrashing. The padlock was cold and inert. It wasn't wired into the mains, and I wasn't in the process of being fried.

My stomach had turned to water. I could feel sweat in my hair. I released a long, grateful sigh, and forced myself to focus. A few minutes later, my nerves were almost back under control and I was freeing the chains from the padlocks and parting the gates.

I turned. The park didn't look any more cheery from this angle. The old ticket office was closed and boarded up. So were the fairground stalls that flanked the wide avenue of cracked and weed-choked asphalt ahead of me. Some of the booths were canted to one side, as if they were kneeling low. Their paint was faded and flaking. Drifts of litter and fallen leaves and mud and scum had collected around them. The whole place seemed utterly abandoned, like a ghost town that wasn't fit to be haunted. If something went wrong now, Gert would be my only witness. But what use was a witness if I wound up dead?

Some twenty minutes later, a pair of headlights crawled along the twilit road leading toward the park. In another half hour it would be fully dark. I was shivering. A damp breeze was gusting around me, slamming into my back. It was rocking me on my toes, and the tails of my raincoat were flapping around my legs.

I had one of Gert's ancient pistols tucked into the waistband at the back of my jeans. It was loaded, but it didn't bring me a great deal of comfort. I was no marksman, and if I needed to shoot, my chances of hitting what I was aiming at were close to zero. That was assuming the pistol even worked. I hadn't tested it. I hadn't wanted to. The thing looked like it belonged in a museum, and I was beginning to wish it was in one right now.

I could say the same about the hand grenade I'd stuffed into my coat pocket. I was holding it tight, running my thumb over the ridged exterior and being very careful not to dislodge the looped pin. I'd grown used to its weight and heft and feel. I was pretty sure I could throw it with a fair degree of accuracy. But I was absolutely certain I didn't want to. If I found myself lobbing a grenade, then things would have gone very wrong indeed, and I guessed there was a reasonable chance it would be the last thing I ever did.

In my other pocket, I fingered the aged scrap of paper with the final page of code on it. Hard to believe it was worth all this trouble. If I'd found it sooner, I would have gladly handed it over to save Victoria any distress. I just hoped she knew that. And I badly wanted to know that she was okay.

"You see them?" Gert hissed.

"I do," I said. "Stay quiet now. Don't speak again."

Gert was hunkered down in one of the decrepit fairground stalls behind me. He'd loosened a board and crawled inside through an old serving hatch, and now he was peering out through a split in the timber. He was under strict instructions to stay put and remain silent at all times. I didn't appreciate how he'd ignored my orders already. This was a perfect example of why I normally worked alone. I could trust myself to break my own rules when the occasion demanded it, but I didn't feel that way about anyone else.

Instinctively, I took a step forward and away from him. I was smoking a cigarette but taking no pleasure from it. My mouth felt dry and my lungs brittle. I flicked the cigarette onto the ground and killed it with a twist of my shoe.

The headlights drew closer, lighting up the trees and shrubs on the verge outside the gates. It was the same town car I'd seen before. Just as big. Just as menacing. It was approaching at a cautious speed, stones popping and snapping under its tires.

The gates were open, but not wide enough for the car to fit through cleanly. My plan had been to make the driver step out so that I could check my guests were the ones I was expecting. But the driver had other ideas. He eased the front end of the car against the gates and accelerated in a burst, jarring them open. The car surged through and stopped abruptly, its exhaust fumes dyed red by the brake lights.

I shifted my stance and tightened my grip on the hand grenade. It was beginning to dawn on me that I hadn't thought things through all that well. I was standing out in the open, facing up to a large, snarling black town car. They could knock me down if they chose to. They could squash me like a bug.

They blinded me instead. The driver flipped his headlights on full beam and blasted me in the face. I twisted sideways and covered my eyes with my arm, peering out from beneath my elbow. No good. I still couldn't see. I gave some thought to fighting back with my penlight, but somehow I didn't think it would have quite the same impact.

A car door opened and shoes hit the ground.

"Do you have the package?" a lone voice asked.

The voice was firm. It was American. It was female.

"Yes," I shouted back.

"Bring it to me."

Her words seemed to race on the breeze, coiling around me and chattering in my ears.

"Not yet. I want to see Victoria first."

"Once we see the package."

"No." I took a step backward. "I need to know that she's safe. And stop blinding me, will you? I'm here to cooperate. The least you can do is be civil."

I squinted into the dazzling light, tears pooling in my eyes. I listened hard. Five seconds. Ten. Then the lights finally dipped and I lowered my arm. My sight was still compromised by a lurid spectrum of floating, transparent shapes. But I could see Nancy Symons standing amid them.

She was alongside the open front passenger door of the town car, wearing a long black tailored coat. Her hands were in her pockets. I was pleased to see it. She wasn't pointing a weapon at me, and I very much doubted that she had a grenade at her disposal.

Then the driver's door swung outward and Duane emerged. He was wearing a dark suit over a gray shirt and black tie. He had his wraparound sunglasses on despite the dusky light. He looked like a bouncer with ideas above his station.

Duane tilted his glasses and peered over the dark lenses at me, as if he couldn't quite trust his eyes. I kept my composure as best I could and waited him out, then watched him stroll to the rear of the car.

He popped the trunk and heaved the lid upward. It blocked him entirely from view. For just a moment, I entertained the notion that he was about to up the stakes by pulling a bazooka from the trunk. But he removed something way more explosive instead.

A little of the tension eked out of me, then ramped back up again when I saw the vicious look Victoria was giving me. All the mental images of her imagined distress and imprisonment flooded over me again. I hated to think of the despair and punishment she must have endured, and I was afraid to ask myself how long it might take her to recover.

Duane was carrying Victoria in his arms. She thrashed her legs and pummeled Duane's chest with her fists. He endured it for a few moments, then grew irritated and plonked her down on her feet. She tried to bolt toward me but Duane reached out and yanked her hair, and she howled and dropped onto her knees.

She was wearing a cotton tracksuit and brilliant white trainers. The tracksuit was dark blue in color, with red and white flashes along the seams. It had a familiar swoosh logo on the left breast and a matching one just above the hip pocket.

"Unbelievable," I shouted. "You Yanks even have corporate sponsorship for your hostages now?"

Nobody found me funny. Nobody bothered to respond.

The icy breeze pawed at my neck and face. I hunched my shoulders. Gave the grenade a quick squeeze.

"Let her go," I said.

"The package first," Nancy replied, her voice as cool as her attitude.

"I'm not handing it over until you release Victoria."

"The package," she repeated.

Impasse. I didn't know what to do.

"For Christ's sake, Charlie," Victoria yelled, grimacing from the way Duane was now tugging at her earlobe. "Give her what she wants."

"Are you okay?" I called.

"Oh, just tickety-damn-boo. Now give her the sodding package."

Yup, this is what I'd been missing. Clear-eyed analysis. Concise instructions.

I fingered the page of code. There were perhaps twenty paces separating me from the town car. I took ten and came to a halt. I pulled the scrap of paper from my pocket and considered it for a moment. The wind almost tore it from my grasp. It flapped and rustled and crinkled.

I hopped on one leg and removed my left baseball shoe. Then I set it down on the wind-scoured asphalt and tore the paper carefully in two, right through the middle of the coded message. I stuffed one half into the warm opening where my toes had been and closed my fist around the remains.

I hobbled a few steps backward, stones biting into my heel through my sock. The ground was frosty beneath my foot.

"Come and get it," I said. "Satisfy yourself that I'm on the level. Then you can let Victoria go and you'll get the other half."

Nancy considered me with an air of detachment that wasn't altogether convincing. She shrugged her shoulders and walked carefully toward my shoe. Her steps were slow and measured. Her heels beat against the concrete like controlled gunfire.

She hunched down, holding her hair back from her eyes with one hand, and plucked the paper from my shoe. She checked my position, then carried the note back to the car. She angled the page into the beam of the headlights and read over what was written there.

She glanced at Duane. "Take her halfway," she said.

Duane let go of Victoria's ear and seized her by the arm, hustling her forward. Nancy joined them at her leisure, then bent down again and gathered up my shoe, wrinkling her nose at the aroma that escaped from it.

"So I guess we can trade," she said. "Bring me the rest of the code."

I could feel the pistol digging into the small of my back and the wind molding my coat around it. It would have been the easiest thing in the world to reach for the gun. I was tempted, too. I could feel a twitch in my fingers. But if this was going to end without the kind of escalation I might regret, I was going to have to trust them at some point.

I left the gun where it was. Left my arms at my sides. I took a deep breath, then cursed myself for having been hasty enough to chuck my cigarette away, and stepped up to them.

I met Nancy's gaze. I held it for a short time. Then I broke off and tried a smile on Victoria. She didn't smile back. Her face was gaunt. Her eyes were puffy and heavily pouched. She looked like she'd just stepped off a long-haul flight with severe turbulence and a terrible landing.

"Hey," I said. "Did they treat you okay?"

"Oh, sure, they had me in a smashing hotel. Wonderful room service. My only complaint is they wouldn't allow me to leave."

"The code," Nancy prompted.

"You know, you didn't need to snatch Victoria," I told her. "That was rude."

"You're here now, aren't you? Now, give me the code."

I held the remaining half-page out to her. She reached for it but I snatched my hand away. Childish, I know, but I wanted my shoe back first. I claimed it, then slapped the half-page of handwriting into her palm.

"This everything?" she asked.

"It's all I have. All I could find."

"Then I guess it'll have to do."

She nodded to Duane and he released Victoria. She circled around behind me, rubbing her arm.

I was feeling a little stupid tilted over to one side, with my sock getting all scummy, but I didn't want to balance on one leg to slip my shoe on just yet. It would give Duane the perfect opening to strike me, and it wouldn't leave my hands free for the gun or the grenade. So I stood there holding my shoe in my hands, as if I'd been gifted a new and curious object that had baffled me completely.

I cleared my throat. "So," I began, and tapped my shoe with my finger, "I guess we're almost done here. Apart, of course, from the small matter of my fee."

Nancy broke into a crooked smile. "Your fee?"

"Uh-huh. You offered me double what Freddy had agreed to pay me to bring you the secret object, and now I've done exactly that."

"Wow." She whistled. "You're really something else. Guess you think you're pretty slick?"

"One tries."

"Yeah, well try this. You won't be receiving your *fee*. You'll take your friend and you'll be glad to have her. And if you take my advice, the two of you will get the hell out of Berlin."

"We have a choice?"

"Hey, it's a free world."

Victoria squeezed my shoulder. She was ready to go. I wasn't there quite yet.

"You think your Russian competitors will agree with that sentiment?" I asked Nancy.

She tilted her head and said, "You know, I wouldn't rely on it."

She turned on her heel and started to pace away.

"Hey," I yelled, but she wasn't slowing down. "You offered me a period of protection, remember? Twenty-four hours."

"Gee, I don't know what to tell you," she called back. "Guess my memory must be bad."

"So that's it? You're feeding us to the wolves?"

She loitered beside the open door of the town car, then motioned Duane over to her with a heft of her chin.

"You're being overly dramatic," she said, lowering herself half into the car. "Get out of Berlin and you'll be fine. But I wouldn't leave it too long. You Brits have a habit of outstaying your welcome. And I really wouldn't like to see you make another mistake."

THIRTY-FOUR

The moment the Americans had left, I gave Victoria a hug. In truth, it was a pretty one-sided clinch. She was rigid and lifeless in my arms.

"Angry?" I mumbled, into her shoulder.

"Try livid."

"I'm sorry."

Victoria didn't reply. I guessed she blamed me entirely for her abduction. I didn't think that was altogether fair. After all, she'd been present when I'd accepted the assignment from Freddy. She'd been aware that there could be risks involved.

"I truly am sorry," I said. "I would never have left you on your own if I'd thought for one minute that anything would happen to you."

Silence. I rested my hands on Victoria's shoulders and looked her square in the eyes.

But her eyes weren't focused on me. They were cast off to one side, widening in alarm.

"Charlie, there's someone here," she hissed. "Look."

I swiveled to see Gert backing out of the old fairground stall. He'd lowered one leg but he was having trouble with the second. The cuff of his corduroy trousers had snagged on a nail. He yanked hard and left a fabric sample from his ill-fitting suit hanging in the breeze.

"Oh, *him*," I said. "Don't worry about Gert. He's harmless enough."

"Are you sure? He seems a little . . . *strange*."

I laughed. "Wait until you see where he lives. That'll really freak you out."

I wasn't wrong. Victoria didn't like the look or the feel of Gert's secret den. And from the way she wrinkled her nose and pursed her lips, I got the impression she wasn't a big fan of its particular scent, either.

"This place gives me the creeps." Victoria shivered and rolled back the left sleeve of her tracksuit to rub her wrist. There was an angry red welt on her skin. A handcuff imprint, possibly, though my guess was that it was something else.

"I found your watch," I said.

"You did?" She brightened. "Do you have it?"

"It's in my apartment," I told her. "But don't worry, I promise I'll get it back for you."

Victoria smiled glumly, not at all convinced. She was sitting on Gert's foldout camp bed. Come to think of it, "perched" might be a better way of putting it. I couldn't really blame her. Gert had a lot of junk around the place but I hadn't seen any sign of a washing machine, and I dreaded to think when his bedding had last been laundered.

I'd already treated Victoria to a quick tour of Gert's domain, not to mention his extensive stash of memorabilia and collectibles, and

242

from the way he'd blushed whenever I caught him sneaking glances at her as she followed me around, I wouldn't have been surprised to learn that she was the first female who'd ever set eyes on his secret world. He certainly wasn't at ease in her company. From the moment we'd entered the tunnel and he'd powered up the fairy lights, he'd mumbled a few words of greeting, then settled himself behind his desk, plonked his earphones over his head and plugged himself into his listening network.

"And last but not least, this is Buster," I told Victoria, setting Buster's cage down on the bed alongside her. "Believe it or not, he's what everyone was looking for. Buster's the hush-hush package. My very own Maltese falcon."

Victoria clasped her hand to her forehead. "But I thought everyone was looking for the code." The question seemed to jolt her to some new awareness and she stared at me in horror. "Oh, God, did you just trick the Americans? Charlie, I'm not sure that was such a good idea."

"No tricks," I told her. "All they wanted was that final page of code and I gave it to them. They just didn't know it used to be inside Buster's cage. And Buster is the ambassador's pet. Right, buddy?"

"Buster likes crackers."

Victoria gasped again, this time with delight. She clapped her hands and smiled in amazement. I was glad to see it. She was getting some color back in her cheeks, at last. Some animation in her face.

"Or rather," I said, "he's the not-so-hush-hush package. And trust me, you might be impressed right now, but it really won't last."

"Buster likes crackers."

"Oh," I said to Buster, "you want a reward, is that what you're telling me?"

"He's adorable," Victoria gushed.

"He'd certainly like you to think so."

243

"Oh, come on, you're smitten, I can tell."

She lowered her face to the cage and grinned in at Buster.

"My name's Buster," he squawked. *"What's your name?"*

"He's so clever," Victoria said, glancing up at me.

"Don't you believe it. He's plenty dumb."

"I'm Victoria," Vic said to Buster. "Can you say that? Can you say Victoria?"

"Buster likes crackers."

"See," I said. "One-track mind."

"Wanna sing a song?"

I groaned. "Not this again."

"Wanna hear Buster count?"

"Buster, the answer's still no," I said. "And you can take it from me, the answer'll be no until we tell you otherwise."

"That's a bit mean," Victoria said. "What does he sing, anyway?"

"No idea. And I have no intention of finding out. It's hard enough to get him to shut up at the best of times."

Victoria gave me a look that seemed to imply I was a heartless beast. "Maybe the ambassador can tell us?"

"Excuse me?"

"When we give Buster back to him. We have to return him, Charlie. He's the ambassador's special companion. He'll be missing him."

"Mmm."

"He will. Believe me."

Oh, I believed her all right. I just wasn't so sure about making contact with the ambassador or Freddy ever again. They'd got me in enough trouble as it was. Speaking of which . . .

"Do you have your mobile?" I asked.

"No." Victoria scowled. "That American cow confiscated it. She refused to give it back to me. I've lost all my contact numbers. A whole bunch of personal and business texts."

"And not just that." I groaned.

"Excuse me?"

"The code," I told her. "Your phone had the images of the first four pages stored on it."

"So?"

I nodded toward Gert, absorbed in his radio transmissions. "So Gert here cracked the cipher. He translated the final page." I snatched up the pad from Gert's desk and passed it to Victoria. I allowed her a moment to read through the message he'd translated. Then I explained about the meaning of the reference to the Devil's Mountain.

She looked up from the pad with wonder in her eyes. "You really believe something is hidden there?"

"Yup," I said. "Only we don't know what it is. Perhaps we might have done if you'd still had the images of the other pages on your phone. Gert could have deciphered them, too. We might have discovered what this mess is really all about."

"And now?"

I shrugged. "Now I don't suppose we'll ever know. It only took Gert a few minutes to figure out the cipher, so our American friends will definitely have it soon. In fact, they're probably on their way to the Devil's Mountain right now."

"You sound bitter, Charlie. Why do you care?"

"It just rankles. They shouldn't have snatched you, or backed out of paying me. And it bothers me that I don't know whether they deserve to get their hands on whatever is up there or not. For all we know, it could be of real importance to the British embassy."

"Or the Russians or the French."

"Definitely the Russians," I said. "They've had the first four pages longer than anybody. They'll have cracked them long ago, so they know what's been concealed and they're eager to get their hands on it."

Vic shook her head. "Not longer than anybody," she said. "You're forgetting, Jane Parker had those pages before that. And it's likely the ambassador knew the final page was hidden in Buster's cage. Chances are he put it there."

I thought about that. There was something bothering me. Something I couldn't quite put my finger on just yet.

"Charlie?" Victoria asked. "What is it?"

"I think you're right," I told her.

"Well, I usually am. But right about what, exactly?"

"I should have thought of it sooner. I should have seen it that way."

"What way?"

"The ambassador," I said. "Jane Parker. The code."

"You're not making any sense, Charlie. You're talking in riddles."

But they weren't riddles in my mind. I was thinking about the top secret file. I was thinking about the five pages that had been in the file when it was complete. My theory had been that all the relevant information was there. That once the code had been cracked, there'd be nothing else to know. That was the theory the Americans had been working on, too. Same for the Russians. Same for the French.

But maybe not the same for the British.

I rushed over to Gert and clicked my fingers in front of his face. He looked up, a little dazed and a touch alarmed, and I motioned for him to remove his earphones.

"Your network," I said. "You listen, right? You learn from it? That's how you knew about the threat I was facing."

Gert nodded, still unsure where I was going with this.

"But the Americans and the Russians and the French must know about your network, too. They probably know it exists."

"*Ja,* I guess."

"And they have a history of eavesdropping electronically. I mean, that's why the listening post exists on the Devil's Mountain. And there must have been a similar culture in the east, too."

Gert blinked his long lashes.

"What I'm thinking," I told him, "is that you can use your network to *broadcast* information. To pass it around. You, personally, could put something out there that people would get hold of."

He rubbed his pointed beard. "For sure, this is possible."

"Great." I lifted the pad before his eyes and tapped the deciphered message with my finger. "Then start broadcasting this. I don't want the Americans to be the only ones who have it. I want to see who else shows up."

THIRTY-FIVE

Gert broadcast the information about something of value being hidden at the Devil's Mountain listening station for a good twenty minutes, and then he set his headphones to one side and guided Victoria and me out through the park and back into the woods.

It was fully dark by now, and I kept tripping over tree roots or walking into branches, but at least Buster had fallen silent again. I couldn't be sure if it was because of the blackness, or if he was scared half out of his very small mind, but I appreciated the peace and quiet.

I was at the rear of our group, carrying Buster's cage, and Victoria was in front of me, stooped at the waist and moving stealthily through the trees. I could see her white trainers and the white flashes on her blue tracksuit quite clearly. It made her look like she was out for some kind of impromptu jog that had gone horribly wrong. But I guessed it had to be better than being held captive against her will.

We broke out of the tree cover, and Gert beckoned us toward the split in the fence. He guided us through, and then he opened the driver's door on the Trabbi for me. I dropped inside and Victoria walked around and climbed into the passenger seat. I popped Buster's cage onto her lap, then gingerly gripped the steering wheel and gazed up at Gert.

"You're sure you don't mind us borrowing this?" I asked him.

"It is no problem," he said. "Take it, please."

"You have the keys?"

He smiled and shook his head. Then he crouched down and reached a spindly arm past my legs until he was grappling with a couple of loose wires hanging from beneath the steering column. He touched the wires together. A blue spark lit up the foot-well and the feeble engine coughed and spluttered into life, rattling the lightweight chassis.

"Something else you collected?"

Gert smiled and clapped me on the shoulder. Then he reached inside his jacket and removed a pair of prepaid phones. He handed one to me and prodded some buttons on the other. A few seconds later, my phone chimed and the screen glowed yellow.

"Now, you may call me," he said, and jabbed his finger toward the number that had appeared on my screen. "Let me know if I can help."

"You mean you won't be listening in?"

He grinned. "Always, friend."

I thanked him and told him in my most sincere voice that I owed him a real debt.

"Please, it is no problem." He leaned inside and tapped the bars of Buster's cage. "Good-bye, my little one. I think I miss you already." He conjured a shy smile for Victoria, then backed out of the car. "Go now," he told me. "And drive slowly, *ja*? The brakes, they are not so good."

Gert was right—the brakes were terrible. So was the steering. Come to mention it, the lights weren't anything to boast of, either. But the rumbling, gassy engine powered us across the city toward the far western zone of Charlottenburg, where I pulled over near the base of the Devil's Mountain.

I left the Trabbi's engine idling. It wasn't as idle as I would have liked. The two-stroke unit was brash and tinny, and more than capable of drawing attention. But there was every chance we might need to leave in a hurry, and I didn't feel inclined to place my faith in the haphazard spark between a couple of aging wires.

The Teufelsberg wasn't as high as I'd imagined—certainly no mountain—but it was undeniably steep and it was covered in woodland. I popped my door and went around and opened Victoria's, then offered her my hand and helped her out. We left Buster's cage on the front seat and started to walk away.

"Wait," I said. "Do you think I should crack a window?"

"Buster's not a dog, Charlie. He'll be fine." Victoria rubbed her hands together, then zipped her tracksuit top up to her neck. "Besides, it's freezing out here."

I thought about that. I wasn't convinced. I went back and rolled down a window. Better for Buster to be chilly than dead, I figured.

I avoided Victoria's eyes as I passed by her again, then grabbed her hand and led her toward the base of the grassy mound.

Her palm was cold, but a little fizz of electricity was running up my arm. Stupid. I was behaving like a love-struck teenager. And I felt even dumber when Victoria started to speak.

"Er, Charlie. Can I have my hand back?" she asked.

"Oh," I said. "Sure."

"You were just squeezing it sort of tight."

"My mistake. I'm a bit tense."

Or a bit dim.

We climbed on, swerving around tree trunks and ducking beneath branches. It was tough going. The steep incline was slippery and I was having to concentrate on my footing. I was still looking down and panting hard when Victoria's breath caught in her throat and she tapped me on the shoulder.

"Look," she said. "Charlie, do you see?"

I did see. But I didn't quite believe it.

The listening station was ahead of us, through a break in the trees. It was a vast, derelict complex. There were walls missing from a series of low, block-shaped buildings, their concrete interiors and metal girders exposed to the elements like the inside of a dollhouse. A cylindrical tower rose up from the middle, perhaps six stories tall. It was topped by a white spherical structure, like a golf ball on a tee. The tower and the sphere were constructed from a metal exoskeleton wrapped in white tarpaulin. The tarp was torn and badly shredded, and it flapped in the strengthening wind like the sails on a storm-tossed ship. I could see more spheres positioned lower down on the flat roofs of the concrete buildings. And I could see dark figures swarming around the entire structure with flashlights in their hands.

There were fifteen, maybe twenty people, their torch beams bouncing and jerking, illuminating the white globes from within, throwing snatches of graffiti into bright relief, or lancing out into the night sky through the ruptured fabric that surrounded the tower. We were too far away to identify who they were, but I was pretty sure the Americans and the Russians and the French guy with the freshly busted nose would be up there, along with a bunch of random treasure hunters Gert had managed to rustle up.

I grabbed Victoria by the arm and hauled her down to the muddy ground.

"So what's the plan?" she asked, in a low voice, her breath misting on the air. "Do you want to join them?

251

"Not right now," I whispered back. "I wouldn't like to bump into the Americans. I doubt they'll be too happy about all this."

"It doesn't look like a very organized search. Everyone's running all over the place."

"That's what intrigues me."

"How do you mean?"

I stared at her for a moment, her face pale and her eyes wet as dark pools. "Think about it. We know the Russians and the Americans had the first four pages of code. My assumption was that when they added the information from the fifth page, they'd know precisely what they were looking for, why it was important, and exactly where to find it. But maybe I was wrong."

"Hmm. Or perhaps the Americans and the Russians have already left? Maybe one of them found whatever was stashed here right away before anyone else turned up?"

"Yeah. Maybe."

"You're not convinced?"

I sighed and leaned my weight on a tree trunk, wedging my shoulder against the knotted bark. "They'd have had to be pretty quick to get here and get away again."

"The Americans had a head start."

"Yeah, but not a big one. Thirty minutes, maximum. And if the Russians got here after them and found the hiding place empty, they'd have left by now, too. So no Americans and no Russians is the giveaway. That's why I want to stay a while."

"In case we see them?"

"Uh-huh. Think you can stand it?"

Victoria groaned and cleared a space on the ground with her toe. She settled cross-legged among the leaves, twigs, and mud, like she was practicing a yoga pose.

"You know, I wouldn't mind one of your cigarettes," she said. "I'm feeling a little sleepy. The Americans drugged me with some-

252

thing, and I think whatever they used is still floating around in my system."

"Sorry," I said, "but we can't risk it. And we should probably stop talking. The wind could carry our voices."

"Gee," she whispered. "You really know how to show a girl a good time."

"Victoria," I told her, crouching alongside her, "you don't know the half of it."

As it happened, we didn't have to wait as long as I might have feared. Some ten minutes later, just as the cold had really started to penetrate through my jeans, a figure emerged from a metal door at the base of the building and stumbled outside. He crooked an arm and pulled back his sleeve and pointed his torch beam at his watch.

The ambient glow bathed Vladislav's ugly face. I could see his scar quite clearly. It twisted his features in a ghoulish way.

Victoria tensed by my side. "The Russians are still here," she whispered.

"I see him."

"Should we approach him?"

"Are you mad?"

"Sneak up on him, then? We could surprise him."

"Vic," I said, trying to retain some degree of patience, "I could come up behind that guy on tiptoes, with a mallet in my hand, and he'd still knock me on my arse and stomp on my head before I could begin my downswing."

I didn't tell her about the old pistol I'd transferred to my coat or the grenade that was nestled in my pocket. If she knew I had a small arsenal at my disposal, I was pretty sure she'd expect me to do something with it.

"Doesn't matter," Vic said, jabbing her finger toward where Vladislav was positioned. "He's going back in."

She was right. Vladislav had turned and hauled back the heavy metal door and disappeared inside the building.

"Satisfied?" she asked.

"Let's stay for a few more minutes."

"Five, maximum. Then I'm leaving. With or without you."

But it only took three. I was gazing up toward the tower at the time, when a sudden movement caught my eye off to the right. Two figures were standing on a flat roof, close to one of the lower spheres. I couldn't see them as clearly as I would have liked, but the white tarpaulin was reflecting the light from their torches, and it was enough to be sure. The guy was very tall and very wide, with dark skin and a confident stance. The woman was smaller and slighter, but she was unquestionably in charge. She was issuing instructions, and the guy was nodding his big head along to them. She had on a black dress coat.

I rested a hand on Victoria's shoulder and directed her attention toward them. She released a low growl, fog escaping from her nostrils.

"I really hate that bitch."

It wasn't often I heard Victoria speak that way. It took me a moment to recover.

"Relax," I said. "At least they haven't found whatever it is they're looking for."

"We don't know that for certain."

"Yeah, we do. They must have been here close to an hour. If they don't have it by now, then they don't know where it is."

"Doesn't mean they won't find it eventually."

"Not tonight, they won't. That code was written on old paper. The ink was faded. If the treasure is still here, it's been hidden well enough to survive without being discovered for decades. Maybe since this place was first built. Nobody is going to just stumble across it."

"I don't know, Charlie."

"Well, I do. Come on, it's time we got out of here."

"And go where? Your apartment is hardly a safe option."

I pushed myself up from the ground and brushed the mud and leaves from my trousers and hands. Then I hauled Victoria to her feet and led her back down the hill through the trees.

"Charlie, you still haven't answered me," she hissed, from behind. "Where are we going to go?"

I hadn't answered her because I was still thinking. I was running through the options in my head. First, I thought of hotels, but hotels could be risky. Turning up without luggage might make us memorable, and there was always the chance that the Americans and the Russians and the French might circulate our descriptions. They had the resources and the manpower to do it.

So I turned my mind to some alternatives. There were the apartments of the three German editors I'd broken into recently, one of whom lived close by in Schöneberg, but I couldn't be sure if any of them would be home. Then there were the venues Freddy had hired me to break into. But they weren't any good, either. The only place that might definitely be unoccupied was Jane Parker's hotel room, but there could be other guests in it by now. I considered calling Gert and asking if he knew of a likely squat where we could crash for a time, but I didn't like the idea that somebody plugged into his radio network might live there, too, and give us away, and I didn't rate the notion of returning to the unused amusement park.

Then I thought of somewhere else. Somewhere not altogether perfect but not altogether terrible, either. And I realized it was exactly where we needed to go.

THIRTY-SIX

The apartment was exactly the same as I remembered. It was just as empty and just as silent as the last time I'd been inside. Once I'd checked all the rooms and made sure there were no surprises lurking anywhere, I headed down to the street entrance and let Victoria into the foyer. She was carrying Buster's cage in one hand and a plastic grocery bag in the other.

She lifted the bag for me to see. "Thought you might be hungry."

"Good idea."

"And I picked up some things for Buster, too."

"Really?" I only asked because I'd dropped her off outside a corner store and I didn't imagine it had been well stocked with pet supplies. "What did you get him? A magazine? A lotto scratch card?"

"Just some water and some sunflower seeds. I noticed he didn't have any food in his cage."

"You think he'll eat sunflower seeds?"

Victoria gazed down at him, balanced on the lowest perch in his cage, bobbing his head to a soundless beat. "I'm pretty sure he will.

He started whistling and hopping around when I showed him the packet."

"Huh. Not such a dumb bird, after all."

I turned from Victoria and faced the mailboxes fitted into the foyer wall. I located the box for the apartment I'd just broken in to and studied it carefully. Then I ran my eyes over all the other mailboxes.

"What are you doing?" Victoria asked.

"Working on a theory."

"Shouldn't we be going upstairs?" She hefted Buster's cage. "This is getting heavy. And what if someone comes along and sees us down here?"

"Patience."

I continued my fast scan. It wasn't long before I spotted a couple of possibilities. I stepped up close and considered them in detail. Then I fished my picking tools out of my spectacles case and approached the first mailbox.

"Charlie, now really isn't the time for some petty theft."

"Oh, this isn't petty."

I opened mailbox one, then did the same with box two. Both were empty.

"Huh," I said, stepping back.

"What?"

"Just an idea." I removed a pen from my spectacles case, rolled back the plastic glove I was wearing on my left hand and scrawled a note on my skin. "Come on. Follow me."

"You're not going to explain?"

"Oh, I'll explain," I said. "But upstairs in the apartment, over whatever delicacies you're treating me to."

The delicacies turned out to be a packet of cheese-flavored snacks, a chocolate bar, and a can of energy drink. The energy drink tasted of sugar and chemicals. I pulled a face as I swallowed.

"Yuck," I said. "That's disgusting."

"Well, I'm sorry. I thought it might keep us alert."

"Can I have some water?"

"No." She shook her head. "It's for Buster."

Victoria had filled the shallow dish clipped to the side of Buster's cage from a bottle of spring water. And yes, Buster had hopped down and imbibed greedily to begin with, but right now he seemed to be spending most of his time bathing in the stuff.

"He's not even drinking it," I complained. "He's just throwing it around with his beak."

"He's enjoying it. That's the main thing."

I could have told her it wasn't the main thing. Not by a very long way. But it wasn't likely to change her attitude.

I sighed and chugged some more of the gloopy energy syrup.

"Doesn't get any better," I gasped.

"Then have some tap water."

"There isn't any. The supply must have been cut off when the last tenant moved out."

"But the electricity still works. You put the lights on in here."

"Oh, I know," I said. "It's just one more thing in this city that doesn't make much sense."

We were sitting on the living room floor of the unoccupied and unheated apartment in the Tiergarten where I'd had the misfortune to see the blond woman being strangled. I had my back to the wall beneath the window I'd witnessed the crime through. The slatted blinds above my head were still closed, affording us some privacy. Victoria was over on the other side of the room in her tracksuit, her legs crossed, with Buster's cage alongside her.

I didn't think we'd be disturbed. The chances of the tall strangler returning to the scene of his crime seemed beyond remote. And if anyone *did* happen to hear us talking and decide to report it, the janitor or the police might well be inclined to suspect another hoax.

"What else doesn't make sense?" Victoria asked.

"This stupid code, for one," I told her.

Victoria had finished topping up Buster's water dish and now she was fighting to tear open the packet of sunflower seeds. Buster was dancing around and puffing his chest, chirruping in anticipation. "What the hell do they seal these packets with? Super Glue?"

"There's probably a tear strip."

"Nope." She bared her teeth and bit down on the packet, tugging it with her hands.

"Well, be careful, you don't want the seeds to go—"

Too late. The packet split and seeds burst into the air, raining down over Victoria, showering Buster's cage, and dancing on the wooden floor. Buster was quick to tuck in.

"Rats," Victoria said. She began collecting together the seeds that had scattered across the floor.

"As I was saying," I told her, "this code thing doesn't make sense to me. Think about it. At some point, all five pages of code were originally contained in the top secret file."

"We don't know that," Victoria said, scooping the seeds into a pile with her hands. "The first four pages might have only found their way into that file recently."

"Whatever. It doesn't really matter. The point is, sometime, somewhere, those pages were all together. Logic suggests they were being held in the British embassy. Jane Parker had access to them, because she had the file. And the ambassador had access to them, because he hid the final page in Buster's cage."

She shook her head, meanwhile plucking stray seeds from the floor and adding them to her pile. "We don't know that for sure, either. You told me you found Buster and his cage inside Andrew Stirling's apartment. So Stirling could be the one who hid the final page."

"Hmm. I suppose that's true, although it strikes me as unlikely."

"Does it change things?"

"Not really. All the pages had to have been together at some point in the past. And if we assume that whoever had them was able to crack the cipher, then they've had the information contained in the code for a fair while already. Possibly even a long time."

"Okay."

"But if we also assume that Freddy didn't just hire me because the ambassador wanted Buster back, but because he also wanted the final page returned, then I don't understand why."

A series of crinkles appeared on Victoria's forehead. "You've lost me again."

I sighed. My patience was close to threadbare by now. "That's because you're not concentrating, Vic. Enough with the seeds and the bird. Will you look at me a moment?"

"Fine." She leaned backward and rolled onto her side, propping her elbow on the floor and her head on her closed fist. "I'm all ears."

"Then look," I said, "we saw with our own eyes that the Americans and the Russians were still hunting up at the listening post. We know that the code didn't lead them to an exact spot."

"Go on."

"Well, that being the case, why was I hired? If the final page of code is enough to give people a rough idea of where something is hidden but not enough information for them to actually find it, what's the big deal?"

"Oh." Victoria frowned. "That is strange. Unless the code really was irrelevant. Perhaps the ambassador genuinely did want you to find Buster for him."

"I don't buy that. The fee Freddy agreed with us was too high. And remember, he wanted everything to be discreet. He refused to tell me what I was looking for because he said it was sensitive. But I'm not convinced that having Buster stolen would be embarrassing for the ambassador. If the news became public, he'd probably receive a lot of sympathy."

Victoria groaned and stretched out on her back, clutching her hands to her face. "We should probably just call Freddy. Ask him to explain."

"No way," I said. "Chances are he'll act clueless, even supposing he's not just acting. And I want to get a better feel for what we're caught up in here. I want to know what the stakes really are."

"You may not have that luxury."

"Maybe not. But I'm going to give it my best shot."

I drained the last of the energy drink, crushed the can in my hand, and pushed myself up from the floor. Sitting beneath the window was making me more than a tad uneasy. I was all but certain that a woman had been throttled to death nearby. I'd found the clutch of blond hairs only meters away. And I was yet to do anything about it.

"Remember the mailboxes down in the foyer?" I asked.

"Oh, yes. What was that all about?"

I turned my hand over and examined the two numbers I'd scrawled on my skin.

"Follow me," I said. "You're about to find out."

THIRTY-SEVEN

I opened the front door of the apartment, checked the corridor was clear, and beckoned for Victoria to join me. Once she was pressed up against my back, I pointed toward a door that was set into the facing wall, perhaps ten meters farther along the corridor. The number 213 was attached to it.

I showed Victoria the back of my hand. I'd scrawled down the numbers 213 and 310.

"So?" she asked, in one of her less than eloquent moments.

"I told you I saw a woman strangled in this apartment."

"I remember." She shivered. "It's not something I'd be likely to forget."

"Right. But when the police showed up and checked this place, all they found was that it was empty."

"That's the way it looked."

"So the body must have been moved somewhere else."

Victoria stared at me for a moment. "Assuming there ever *was* a body."

"There was. There had to be. And it occurred to me that the body couldn't have been moved very far. After all, the killer didn't have long between closing the blind and the police showing up. He probably heard the sirens approaching. He had to think fast."

Victoria sucked air through her teeth. "Risky," she said. "Who's going to want to drag a dead body along a corridor?"

"Not as risky as leaving the body where it was. And see? The corridor is empty right now. It could have been just as empty on the night of the murder."

Victoria's face twisted itself into a scornful knot. "But that's not something anyone could possibly predict. People could be coming and going at any moment."

"True. But if the body was only moved a short distance, there's a fair chance the killer wouldn't be spotted."

"Huh. And I assume you're suggesting that the body was moved into that apartment over there?"

I nodded.

"May I ask why?"

"Couple of reasons," I said, trying to rise above her skepticism. "First, I've already been back here once and checked a few possibilities. Storage closets. Stairwells. That kind of thing."

She reared back. "When was this?"

I waved my hand. "Not important. Point is, I didn't find anything. But then I got to thinking. Why were they even here? Why did the murderer and his victim meet in an empty apartment?"

"We don't know that."

"No, but we can guess. Let's say they wanted to meet on neutral territory. Somewhere private, but not in one another's homes."

"If you say so."

"I do. And what better place than an unoccupied apartment?"

"Hmm." Victoria folded her arms across her chest and tucked

263

her chin into the raised collar of her tracksuit. She peered toward the door to apartment 213. "So why do you think the body was dragged over there?"

"The mailboxes," I told her. "I got to thinking that if the murderer or his victim knew that there was one unoccupied apartment in this building, perhaps they also knew that there were others, too. And when I checked the mailboxes downstairs there were only three that had no nametag attached."

"Let me guess. This apartment, apartment 213, and"—Victoria lifted my hand and read the pen scrawl on the back again— "number 310."

"Bingo. And apartment 310 is up on the third floor. The murderer would have had stairs to contend with. Or an elevator. Neither of which would be very attractive."

Victoria groaned. She gestured with her chin toward the apartment door across the hall. "Why do I get the feeling you want to go and take a look inside?"

"Because you know me too well."

She groaned again. "I'm really not comfortable with this, Charlie. What if you're wrong? What if there's somebody living inside that apartment? We're meant to be hiding out here. We're meant to be keeping a *low profile*."

"Hey, don't worry. That's why I always knock before I enter."

I rested a hand on Victoria's shoulder, then ambled along the hallway and knocked on the door. I waited. There was no response.

I gave Victoria a quick thumbs-up, then slipped my customized surgical gloves back on, taking care not to tear my right-hand glove as I eased it over my taped fingers.

I went down on one knee and glanced at the security challenge I was facing. The locks were just as unremarkable as the ones on the door to the murder apartment—in fact, they were exactly the same. I removed my spectacles case and began with the dead bolt lock, probing away with a raking tool and a torsion wrench until the pins clicked into place, one after the other, like a line of cascading dominoes. Then I shimmed the snap lock with a flick of my wrist and nudged the door open.

The apartment was unheated and unlit. Not a thing to be seen. I slipped inside and was just closing the door behind me when it bounced back against my hand.

"Wait for me," Victoria said, bundling through.

"Sheesh." I covered my heart with my hand. "What are you trying to do to me?"

"I didn't want to be left on my own," she whispered. "If anything happened to you, I knew I wouldn't be able to get in here."

"And what about Buster?"

She shrugged. "I closed the door on him. He'll be fine."

I paused for a moment, waiting for my heart to start beating again. It came back online with a thump. I sucked air through my nose. Long, deep breaths. Long, slow exhalations.

"Well, what are you waiting for?" Victoria asked. "We can't just *stand* here, Charlie."

I clicked on my penlight and shone it into her eyes.

"Ow!" She squinted and raised her hands in front of her face.

"Quiet," I said.

"I'm sorry."

"Ssshhh."

Now, if there's a noise that lingers more in a darkened apartment than an urgent *ssshhh,* I'm afraid I've yet to find it.

I cringed.

I waited.

No response.

I yanked my penlight away from Victoria and cast it about the blackened room, trawling across patches of bare wall and floor as if it were a weak spotlight on a stage. There didn't appear to be any furniture. There didn't appear to be anything at all.

I reached past Victoria and flipped the switch on the wall behind her shoulder. The main ceiling bulbs buzzed into life. They revealed a mirror image of the apartment we'd just been in. Acres of exposed timber flooring. Three doors to our right. One to our left. A large window ahead of us with a slatted Venetian blind.

I tucked my penlight away, moved over to the window and peered out through the slats. I guess I'm a sucker for punishment, but I didn't see anything I'd have preferred not to. The apartment offered a view out over a central courtyard, and no one appeared to be looking our way. I closed the blinds just to be sure, and then I told Victoria to shut and lock the door behind her.

"See?" she said, her white training shoes echoing dully as she paced across the floor toward me. "It's empty. There's nobody here."

"Uh-huh."

"There's no *body* here, either."

I ignored her and approached the single door on our left. In the ambient light from the living room I could see that it opened onto a kitchen. The counters and cupboards were bare.

"Charlie, this is a waste of time." Victoria spread her arms wide in the middle of the vacant living room. "There's nothing here. I bet there'll be nothing upstairs, either. You just have to accept that you saw something you can't explain. It's a mystery you can't solve."

I lowered my head and marched across to the doors on the other side of the apartment. The first one opened into a bedroom. I flipped on the lights. There were indents in the carpet from long-gone pieces of furniture, plus a built-in closet with mirrored doors. I watched my reflection approach the wardrobe. I watched my double slide the doors to one side. I disappeared from view and found myself staring at an interior that was empty aside from a few metal hangers.

266

"Can we go back now?" Victoria asked. "I'm worried about Buster."

"In a minute. I'm not done yet."

"You are. You're just too stubborn to admit when you're wrong. And we have enough on our plates already, Charlie. We really don't need any extra hassle."

I brushed past Victoria and entered the second bedroom. It was almost identical to the first. All it lacked was the built-in wardrobe.

I stepped back out and faced up to the final door. I flipped the switch fitted to the wall outside. An extractor fan whirred to life. I'd been braced for it this time.

"Charlie, come on." Victoria tugged my arm. "This is getting ridiculous."

I shook her loose and pushed on the door, but it only budged a short distance. I pushed again. The bottom of the door scuffed against something. The something was inert.

"Uh-oh," I said.

"What now?"

I prodded the door with my gloved finger. It was definitely stuck.

"Oh, Christ," Victoria said, and raised her hands to her head. "Look, let's get out of here. Let's just leave whatever happens to be behind that door alone. This really doesn't involve us. Right, Charlie?"

I waved Victoria back and lifted my foot in the air.

"Oh, crap, no," she said. "You're not listening to me."

I kicked out hard. The door shunted backward a few inches.

"Stop it, Charlie. Please."

I screwed up my face in concentration and rammed the door with my shoulder. It juddered back some more. I leaned my weight on it and drove with my feet and forced the opening a shade wider.

Then I got down on my knees and poked my head through the gap and sneaked a look at the obstruction.

"Oh, hell," Victoria said. "What is it? Is it her? Please tell me it's not her."

"It's not her," I said, over my shoulder. "It's just a towel."

I grabbed for the towel. It was slightly damp and it had been rolled up tight and wedged against the base of the door. I yanked it free. Then I pushed the door fully open.

"Thank goodness for that," Victoria said, raising her hand to her forehead. "You had me worried. For a minute there, I really thought . . ."

But her words trailed away into nothing as she stepped up alongside me and saw precisely what I'd feared we might find. There was a woman propped up inside the bath. She was fully clothed. She was blond. And she was about as dead as it's possible to get.

"Aw, crap," Victoria said.

"You know," I told her, "sometimes it really sucks to be right."

A sweet, rotten odor filled the room. My eyes began to tear. I pressed the towel against my face and approached the blonde.

There was a shallow pool of water in the bath. It just about covered the blonde's legs and arms and backside. Beneath the water, her fitted skirt and the sleeves of her white sweater were drenched. Her flat shoes were still on her feet. Her hands and her ankles were bloated and wrinkled and pale as a fish belly. I dipped a gloved hand inside the tepid water and seized her wrist. Her wrist was stiff with rigor. Though I knew better, I checked for a pulse anyway.

"Her throat." Victoria moaned. "The poor woman. It's awful."

Her throat was badly swollen. The skin was broken and grazed. It was livid with bruising. The bruising ranged from pale mauve to deep purple where the blood had collected beneath her skin. It hadn't been a pleasant way to die. It had been about as brutal and remorseless as it gets.

I released her wrist and withdrew my hand from the still water. I stepped back and considered the tiled floor. A metal bucket was positioned next to the bath. The bucket contained a shallow pool of liquid in its base.

"Ice," I mumbled, into the towel.

"Excuse me?" Victoria said. She was covering her nose and mouth with her hand, backing away from the scene.

I toed the bucket with the tip of my shoe. "He used ice. He packed it around the body. I found an ice machine in a communal room downstairs when I came back to take a look around. There was a bucket just like this one."

"So?"

"So he must have waited in here until after the police had gone. Then he must have sneaked down to the ice machine and come back up several times. It would have taken four, maybe five trips."

"Why would he do that?"

I motioned toward the bath. "He must have reckoned it would stop the smell getting too bad. That's why he wet the towel and packed it around the door as best he could when he left. Look, the crack at the bottom is just big enough for somebody to squeeze their fingers through. He must have reached beneath and grabbed hold of the towel to pull it snug after he shut the door. He was being careful. He wanted to buy himself as much time as possible before the body was discovered."

"You really think so?"

"I really do. There's a nasty odor now. No question. But we didn't notice it until I forced my way in."

I looked again at the woman in the bath. At her arms and her legs, floating on the thin, grimy layer of water.

Victoria let go of a ragged breath. "Whoever this brute was, he must have known the building well. He knew about the ice machine. He knew about the empty apartments."

"Too right. But there's something else. Unless he happens to know how to pick locks in a hurry—and forgive me, but there aren't all that many of us about—he must have had a set of keys. Keys to the front door of this building. Keys to at least two apartments inside it."

Victoria blinked. "So what are you suggesting? You think maybe he owns these apartments? Maybe he rents them out?"

"It's possible, but I doubt it." I shook my head. "As soon as her body was discovered, he'd be the first suspect the police would speak to. And if he planned to kill her and hide her here, that would be a really stupid move."

"Perhaps it is that simple. Perhaps he's really that stupid."

I shook my head and reached inside my coat pocket. "It's not that simple," I said.

"No? How can you tell?"

I pulled two photographs from my pocket and looked at each in turn, taking my time until I was sure. Once I had the one that matched, I showed it to Victoria. She peered hard at the image, her eyes screwed tight with concentration. Then her eyes widened. She glanced between the photograph and the woman in the bath. She checked two times. Three.

"But I don't understand," she spluttered. "Where did you get her photograph?"

"From Freddy," I said, and my voice was thick with regret. "I asked to see the personnel files for the four people he suspected of stealing from the ambassador's office." I studied the photograph again. It was of a young, blonde, smiling to the camera. She looked confident and professional. Very much alive. "This poor woman is Jane Parker," I said. "Suspect number two on Freddy's list."

THIRTY-EIGHT

We closed and locked apartment 213, leaving Jane Parker's body and everything else just as we'd found it, and then we returned to the apartment where she'd been killed. Buster was pleased to see us. He whistled and twittered and flapped his wings.

"Buster says hello. My name is Buster. Buster says hello."

I didn't feel much like responding. Victoria mumbled a greeting and slumped down onto the floor next to his cage. She clutched her head in her hands.

"What a mess," she said.

I didn't think she was talking about the pile of sunflower seeds.

"Do you think Freddy knows that woman is dead?" she asked.

"Not unless he was the killer."

Victoria looked up sharply. I summoned a tired smile.

"Bad joke," I said. "The guy I saw through the window was way too thin and way too tall."

"You're sure?"

"I'm certain. But Freddy did tell me that Jane had been missing since the night I witnessed the murder. He'd held back on us before."

Victoria exhaled loudly. She rested a hand on Buster's cage. "I wonder what she was doing here? Why did she come to this apartment in the first place?"

"That's what I need to think about."

I peeled my gloves from my hands and stuffed my hands inside my pockets. I gazed up at the ceiling. I really needed to focus. To concentrate.

"Wanna sing a song?"

"Give me strength," I said.

"Wanna hear Buster count?"

"Shut up," I yelled. *"Shut up. SHUT UP."*

Buster twittered once, then fell silent, like someone had cut his power supply.

"Hey, go easy on him," Victoria complained. "None of this is his fault."

"Actually, it kind of is."

She pouted at Buster. "Poor thing. You didn't ask to be stolen, did you?"

"He might as well have, going on like that all the time. And more to the point, if he hadn't been stolen, I wouldn't be caught up in this situation. I'd be home finishing my novel."

Victoria snorted.

"What?"

She shook her head. "Who do you think you're kidding, Charlie? You're not even close."

"You reckon?"

"I know. I've been waiting for you to tell me you need an extension."

"Well." I let my shoulders drop. "I might need one now."

"And you can forget it." Victoria wiggled her fingers at Buster. "Your publishers will never agree."

Great. More bad news.

"Listen, do you want to hear why I think Jane Parker was here?" I asked Victoria.

"Oh, like you wouldn't believe."

So I told her. I spoke slowly at first, then faster as the pieces of the puzzle started to slot into place in my mind. I hadn't been sure how it was going to fit together when I began, or if it even would, but the more I explained and teased out my thoughts, the more I began to believe I could be on to something.

Jane had come here because of the code in the top secret file, I said. Yes, it was an assumption, but it was a solid one. There were plenty of people scrabbling around Berlin trying to get their filthy mitts on its contents. So she'd hidden it in her hotel room and then she'd come to this apartment to meet somebody when she was due to be preparing for an embassy function.

My guess was that she was trying to sell the file. The complete code was worth money. There was no question about it. That was why Freddy had been willing to pay me such a generous amount to find Buster. That was why Nancy Symons had offered to double my fee and had covered her options by kidnapping Victoria.

"Wait," Victoria said. "Could the Americans have killed her? Or the French guy or the Russians?"

"I don't think so. If they had, they wouldn't have been chasing around after me. The Russians wouldn't have broken into my apartment. The Americans wouldn't have snatched you. And besides, the killer didn't look like anyone I've seen so far."

"So maybe he worked for another foreign power?"

I nodded. I agreed it was possible. Then I moved on to discussing the venue for Jane's murder. I mentioned that she'd only been in Berlin for a short time, so I doubted she'd picked the location herself. My best guess was that her killer had suggested where they should meet. And since the chances were good that her killer was working on behalf of a foreign government, I thought it likely that

273

the empty apartments might belong to one of the many embassies in Berlin. After all, the Tiergarten was close to the city's diplomatic quarter, and it was common for embassies to provide accommodation for their staff in the vicinity. Take the first apartment I'd been tasked with breaking in to: Daniel Wood's home was situated just across the street.

"So," I concluded, "if we can find out which, if any, embassy owns or rents these apartments for their staff, we can tell Freddy where to look for his killer."

"And how does that help us exactly?"

Funny. Victoria always did have the knack of asking me the one question I really didn't want to contend with.

"It doesn't," I admitted. "At least not directly."

"And indirectly?"

I removed my hands from my pockets and showed her my palms. "I guess the British embassy might feel like they owe us some thanks. They might help us to get out of Berlin safely."

Victoria made a noise that suggested she wasn't altogether overwhelmed by our prospects.

"There's something else I don't get," she said.

"Go ahead. Kick a guy when he's down."

"Why was Jane trying to sell an incomplete code? She only had four pages."

I frowned and shook my head wearily. "Maybe she didn't know it was incomplete. Or maybe she didn't care. Maybe she figured she'd make some quick cash and disappear before her buyer caught on to her."

"I'm not sure about that," Victoria said. "She can't have been offered vastly more money than the Americans offered you. And that wouldn't be anywhere near enough to walk out on a successful career with the British government and start a new life somewhere else. Especially if she'd betrayed her country and risked being caught for it."

I removed the photograph of Jane from my pocket. I stared at the image. I couldn't tell how long ago it had been taken. Two or three years, perhaps? She looked untroubled, bright and alert. Back when the shot had been taken, she'd been anticipating a long and promising future.

"So she didn't know it was incomplete," I said, offhand now. "She found the file and she took a chance."

"Hell of a chance. It was positively reckless."

"Perhaps she didn't know what she was getting herself into. She could have been as clueless as we were when Freddy hired us."

"Don't count on it."

Hell, as soon as Vic uttered the C-word, I knew I was going to regret it.

"Wanna hear Buster count?"

"No," I snapped. "No one wants to hear Buster count. And no one wants to hear you sing, either."

Buster ignored me. He'd been waiting too long to demonstrate his numerical prowess. He hopped up onto his very top perch, raised his head, opened his throat, and began to chant in a rapid falsetto.

"Sixthreeeightfourtwosevenseventhreesixtwonine."

"Oh, terrific." I smacked my forehead with the heel of my hand. "You can't even do that right."

Buster seemed thrilled by his performance. He flapped his wings. Shifted his weight between his feet. Puffed out his chest.

"That's marvelous, Buster," Victoria told him.

"No it's not," I complained. "That's not counting. It's just saying a bunch of numbers in a random order."

Buster blew me a raspberry.

"Wow," I said. "So you understand criticism, at least."

"Sixthreeeeightfourtwosevenseventhreesixtwonine."

"More random numbers! Wow, that really is impressive."

Victoria was waving her hand at me. She was trying to get me to shut up. But I was on a roll.

"What next?" I asked. "Is little Buster going to scramble the alphabet? Are you going to talk backward?"

"Hush," Victoria said.

"Sixthreeeeightfourtwosevenseventhreesixtwonine."

"She said, *be quiet*," I told Buster.

"No, you idiot." Victoria jabbed a finger at me. "Listen to him. Pay attention to what he's saying."

She lowered her face to the cage. She smiled and batted her eyelids. Buster tucked his head beneath his wing and nibbled on his feathers, acting sheepish.

"Count for us, Buster," Victoria cajoled. "Be a clever boy, Buster. We wanna hear Buster count."

"No we bloody don't."

"Hush," she said again, glaring at me. She turned back to Buster and adopted a soft, coaxing tone. "Buster count. We wanna hear Buster count."

"Sixthreeeeightfourtwosevenseventhreesixtwonine."

"Ha." Victoria clapped her hands and grinned at me. Her eyes were wide with some kind of awareness I appeared to be lacking.

"What?" I snapped.

"My God, you still don't get it, do you?"

I shook my head. I really didn't.

"The numbers aren't *random*," she said. "He's repeating the same sequence. Every time."

"He is?"

"Yes."

Buster had my interest now. I crouched down and clicked my good fingers at him.

276

"Do it again," I said.

Victoria tutted. "Not like that. Ask him to count."

"I'm not going to ask a bird to count. He doesn't understand me."

"Yes he does. Buster count. Come on, Buster, sweetie, count for Charlie."

"Sixthreeeightfourtwosevenseventhreesixtwonine."

"Good boy!"

"Well, I'll be damned," I said.

"Somebody taught him that," Victoria assured me. "It's the same every single time. He memorized it."

"You think?"

"I do. But what could it mean?"

Just as she finished speaking, Buster's throat made the warbling noise of a ringing telephone. He tipped his head over to one side and considered me with an inquiring gaze.

"Holy cow," Victoria said. "Is it a telephone number? Maybe it's for the ambassador. You know, in case Buster ever got lost."

I pouted. It was possible, I supposed. I pulled out the prepaid mobile Gert had provided me with and tapped in the numbers Buster had reeled off—638 427 736 29. But the phone didn't connect. The call didn't lead anywhere at all.

"Hmm. Then what could it mean?" Victoria pondered, as if to herself.

"Sixthreeeightfourtwosevenseventhreesixtwonine." Buster flapped his wings insistently. *"Sixthreeeightfourtwosevenseventhreesixtwonine."*

I could see the numbers in my head by now. They were scrolling through my mind as if they were appearing on an electronic display . . . *63842773629, 63842773629, 63842* . . . Surely they had to *mean* something. It couldn't just be a coincidence. Could it?

"Oh," I said, suddenly. "Oh, that could be brilliant."

"What? What's brilliant?"

I picked up a handful of sunflower seeds and scattered them from a great height into Buster's cage.

"Eat up, buddy," I said. "I think you've just given us the answer."

"The answer? The answer to what?" Victoria asked. "Charlie, tell me. Please."

And so I did. And the more I talked, the crazier and more speculative it sounded. But I was past caring. I was going with my instinct. With my gut. And I felt a sudden and overwhelming surge of confidence, the like of which I hadn't experienced in days.

THIRTY-NINE

We couldn't act straightaway. We needed to wait for daylight. So once I'd finished talking things through with Victoria, I told her we might as well try to get some sleep.

"Sleep?" she said, as if I was crazy. "Where are we going to do that, exactly?"

"Right here."

"You expect me to sleep on the floor?"

"Hey, I'd offer you a bed if there was one. Or I suppose we could snoop around and try to find an empty apartment with some furniture in it."

Victoria gave me the kind of look that could leave permanent scarring.

"I'll turn the lights off," I said. "That'll keep Buster quiet. I'll even sing you a lullaby, if you like."

"But this floor is too hard, Charlie. And it's cold in here."

"Humor me, why don't you? Give it a whirl."

I flipped off the lights and plunged the room into darkness.

Then I spread myself out behind the front door, lying on my back, with my hands laced together beneath my head.

To begin with, the darkness seemed very intense. But after a minute or so, the uniform blackness began to fracture and weaken. Tilting my head, I could see thin bars of light sneaking through the slats in the Venetian blind from the street lamps outside. The ghostly light rippled across the ceiling like moonlit water. Closer still, I could glimpse the outline of Buster's cage and Victoria's prone body. Buster was scrabbling along his perch, finding just the right spot to take a nap.

Victoria exhaled sharply and slapped her palms against the floor. "Exactly how long do you expect us to stay like this?"

I checked my wristwatch. It was fitted with a luminous display. "It's close to midnight," I said. "I think we should aim to leave here in five hours or so. Unless you want to snooze for a little longer."

She grumbled. She cursed. She curled herself into a ball on the floor, her face resting on her hands.

"I won't sleep," she said again. "Not in this apartment. Not now we know a woman really *was* killed here. And not with her body just across the hall."

I didn't reply. I knew just what she meant. Every time I closed my eyes, all I could see was a vision of poor Jane propped up in the bath, her skin as white as the bathroom tiles that surrounded her, her eyes glassy and flat, her throat a dark, swollen mess.

"Try," I told Victoria. "Rest your eyes, at least."

A couple of minutes passed. The ticking of my watch was loud in the room. The occasional ruffle of Buster's feathers was like a billowing sail.

"Charlie?" Victoria hissed. "Are you still awake?"

I waited a moment, trying to decide if I should respond. "Yes," I said.

"What will you do?" she asked. "When this is over, I mean. Where will you go?"

"I don't know, Vic." I adjusted my weight on the floor. I was already uncomfortable and her question only made it worse. "I haven't allowed myself to think that far ahead."

"You're beginning to run out of countries it's safe for you to be in."

"Tell me about it."

More silence. It lasted no longer than thirty seconds. But there was a tension in the air. I felt like I could almost hear Victoria's thoughts shifting around inside her head.

"Would you do me a favor?" she asked. "Would you consider London for once? I could keep an eye on you there. Make sure you hit your deadlines. And it would be good for your writing career."

Would it? I guessed she was probably right. And in some ways, it wasn't quite the unwelcome prospect I might have imagined.

But it was still mighty scary. Undeniably so. It was terrifying because I was tempted. And I felt that way because of her.

"I'll think about it," I said.

"Will you, though?"

"Sure," I said again.

"I'd like that."

A long, weighty silence followed her words. She lay still for a while, and I began to think about pushing up from the floor onto my hands and my knees and crawling over to stretch out beside her in the dark. I thought about resting a tentative hand on her hip. About nuzzling her neck.

Oh, I thought about a whole bunch of stuff besides. Of decisions and actions and risks. Of responses and consequences and repercussions. Of good outcomes and bad. Of those things that would never be the same again. Of the changes that could never be undone.

And truth be told, I was just rolling over and levering myself up with my elbow when I heard her first slow, nasal inhalation. It was light. It was a barely there sniff. But it was completely unmistakable.

She was snoring. She'd drifted away into sleep. And my sudden resolve drifted away with her.

I propped my head on my fist and watched over her for a long time. Watched her chest rise and fall. Watched her mouth open and close. Watched the hair across her face shift gently with her breathing.

And then, when I couldn't bear it anymore, I eased my shoes off my feet and padded across the room in just my socks toward the window, where I parted the slats in the blind and peeked out at the street below. I supposed this might be the last time I'd watch over Berlin at night for quite a while. I guessed it was possible that I might never see the city this way again. And when I lowered my eyes to the building across the way and fixed my gaze on the unlit window of Daniel Wood's apartment, I cursed myself for ever having been stupid enough to step inside it in the first place.

FORTY

Come the morning, it was raining. Again.

I stumbled out of the apartment building, followed by Victoria, and the rain instantly beaded on my hair and my clothes. It was drifting on the air in a fine mist and had settled into a glistening film across the exterior of the Trabbi.

The Trabbi was achingly cold inside. I sparked the exposed wires beneath the dash, just as Gert had shown me, and once the engine was turning over I discovered that the windscreen wipers didn't work. I clambered back out and smeared the screen with the sleeve of my coat, and then I drove across the city in a grim silence, crouched forward over the steering wheel, peering hard into the watery dawn light.

Victoria was huddled beside me in her tracksuit with Buster's cage on her lap. She didn't look altogether rested and refreshed. Her eyes were swollen and pouched, her skin was ashen, and her lips were pressed together into a thin, puckered line.

I wasn't in tiptop condition myself. My mind felt as gray and dreary as the weather. I hadn't slept at all. Not for one minute. Not for one second. My eyes were scratchy and sore, my neck was cricked, and my stomach was aching from where I'd been pummeled. My morning breath, when it wafted back from the windscreen, smelled like I'd been chewing on the sawdust in the bottom of Buster's cage.

"Do you really think they'll be gone?" Victoria asked, in a shaken voice. "All of them?"

I clenched the steering wheel and squinted out at the dissolving world on the other side of the glass. "I hope so. Though there might be people watching, I suppose."

"Boy, that's reassuring."

I glanced across at her. "If you're seeking a confident, sunny outlook, you've come to the wrong guy. The wrong city, for that matter."

It seemed foolish to pretend otherwise. As morning had arrived, and the rain had floated in, my optimism of the night before had failed me as surely as my search for a pack of gum in the pockets of my overcoat. I felt like I was relying on the slimmest of chances. And based on what? The haphazard chanting of a talking bird. Nothing more. Nothing less. I must have been mad.

Our prospects only looked bleaker when we parked at the base of the Devil's Mountain. The wind had picked up and the rain was falling hard, banging and drumming off the fragile shell of the Trabbi, lashing the windscreen.

Buster didn't like it. He was darting around his cage and flapping his wings in an agitated fashion. He squawked and squeaked and burbled and twittered.

"We can't leave him here alone," Victoria said.

I didn't reply.

"We *can't*," Victoria insisted. "Look at him. He's scared."

He wasn't the only one.

"Listen, if you want to bring him," I told her, "then you can carry him."

"Fine."

Except it wasn't fine. Halfway up the hill, with the wind rattling the tree limbs above us and the rain soaking down through the autumn leaves, Victoria held Buster's cage out to me with a pitiful expression on her face. She was thoroughly drenched and visibly shaking. Her dark blue tracksuit was soaked and clinging tightly to her body. I suppose I should have been a gentleman and offered her my raincoat, but I had a feeling she was about to exhaust my goodwill.

"Can you take Buster?" she whined.

"Already?"

"He's *heavy*."

I was tempted to tell her that Buster wasn't heavy in the slightest. That he was, in fact, about as light as it was possible for a living organism to be. It was just his huge, stupid cage that was the issue. But I wasn't about to get into an argument about it.

I snatched the cage and lugged it up the hill ahead of me, feeling bad about how soaked and bedraggled Buster was becoming, and not a lot better about how Victoria and I were faring.

Eventually, after a lot of muttering and griping, after slipping and sliding on greasy leaves and boggy mud, and after banging Buster's cage against my knees and shins more times than I really cared for, we made it to the top of the slope and approached the listening station.

I couldn't see anybody monitoring the area through the downpour, though I guessed it was possible a lookout might be sheltering inside. We advanced with caution, stepping over loose rubble and litter toward an opening in the concrete structure at the base of the complex.

The interior had the appearance of a multistory car park and the echoing, empty feel of a building half constructed or half demolished. Every surface was layered in graffiti. The walls. The ceilings. The support pillars. Even the floor, in places.

But it was a relief to be out of the rain, and I spent a few moments catching my breath and wiping the water from my face and hair, gazing back toward the squally deluge.

"This place gives me the willies," Victoria whispered.

Buster cooed softly, like he was in complete agreement.

"I don't picture anything being hidden out here," I said.

"Where, then?"

"Farther inside, I guess. Maybe in the listening domes themselves."

I paced toward a red metal door set into the wall some distance ahead of us. It was weighty and the hinges were rusty. I barged into it with my hip and stepped through onto a scattering of broken glass, decaying fast-food containers, empty beer cans, and used syringes.

Victoria covered her nose with her tracksuit sleeve. "Smells charming," she mumbled.

"Could be worse."

"Oh?"

"Whoever dumped this stuff could still be here."

I guess it wasn't the most sensitive of observations. Victoria's jaw gaped as she gazed at the rotting litter and the cement staircase that lay ahead. There was an elevator shaft to the side, containing nothing but a cavernous hole and some lengths of frayed steel cable.

"We should keep moving." Victoria swallowed thickly. "It can't all be as bad as this."

But some of it was, and some of it was worse. There were signs everywhere warning us of the perils of falling masonry, unguarded ledges, and electric shock. The complex was very large, and it was mazelike and confounding. It was hard to know where to start, and easy to get lost. It would have made sense for us to split up and tackle different zones individually, but neither of us suggested the idea. This wasn't a place you wanted to wander around by yourself, still less when there was a chance that a bunch of ruthless foreign agents might return at any moment.

As for what we were seeking, that was simple enough. We were looking for numbers. We were trying to locate the exact combination Buster had repeated over and over—63842773629. I still had the numbers entered into the phone Gert had given me so that we wouldn't forget.

It had seemed perfectly clear the previous night. It had appeared obvious to me that it was the very final piece of the puzzle. The last page of code had included the words "I leave you the sequence." It seemed logical to suppose that the "sequence" could have been printed on another scrap of paper, a code card, or something else entirely. But however it had been left by the author of the code, my betting was that the sequence in question was the eleven-digit number Buster had been trained to recall.

Problem was, now we were inside the listening post, prowling its derelict rooms and dank, unlit spaces, its canvas-covered spheres and featureless staircases, finding whatever the sequence related to seemed close to impossible.

Oh, we found numbers. Plenty, in fact. But none of them matched the combination Buster had reeled off.

There were random digits on doors and above doorways. On heavy concrete hatches located in floors and in ceilings. On signs, in graffiti murals, and branded on old wooden packing crates that had been left to rot.

We'd been searching for close to an hour when I started to fear it was hopeless. I could tell Victoria was feeling the same way. She was grouchy and irritable. She was murmuring an awful lot.

Finally, she stomped her foot and said, "Charlie, this is impossible."

"I'm inclined to agree with you."

"Then can we just go? We should get out of here while we still can."

"Out of this building? Or Berlin?"

"Either. Both." She threw up her hands. They were white with cold. "I honestly don't care anymore. I'm tired of solving improbable mysteries. I'm tired of putting our lives at risk. I just want to go home to London, and I want you to come with me and write a big chunk of your new book before your deadline is due and I have to explain to your publishers why we have nothing to show them."

"Gee," I said. "Why don't you just tell me how you really feel?"

Her shoulders slumped. "*Please*. Can we just quit? Just this once?"

"Okay."

She paused. She frowned. "Say again?"

"I said, *okay*. Just as soon as we've climbed up as far as the final dome."

The final dome was at the very top of the central tower. The tower was six stories tall.

"Oh, crap," Victoria said. "Are you serious?"

"Humor me."

"I've *been* humoring you. I spend my *life* humoring you."

"Another half hour. Thirty short minutes. That's all I'm asking."

She scrutinized me closely. "And then can we get out of here?"

I held up my arthritic fingers. "Scout's honor."

Victoria was far from convinced, but after rolling her eyes halfway inside her head, she trudged past me toward the cement stairwell and started to climb.

I followed her to level one, where we stepped out onto a circular floor space. Back in its prime, the tower had been enclosed by the same white tarp as the listening domes, but decades of howling winds had ripped the sheeting away, like skin being flayed from a body. The few torn strips that remained flapped loudly in the gusting breeze, snapping and popping in the air.

The smooth concrete floor had been drenched by the pounding rain and it was wet and slippery, puddled in places. The gusting wind scoured the surface of the pooled water and buffeted against me.

I carried Buster's cage in my left hand and crooked my free arm in front of my face, leaning into the soggy wind. Concentric wires were stretched taut between a series of metal pillars that were evenly spaced around the circumference of the floor. The wires didn't look very sturdy, and they were only waist high. I was beginning to understand why there'd been so many signs warning us of the dangers of falling.

I stayed clear of the edge and battled the wind and rain to the opposite side of the tower, where I sheltered behind the stairwell to catch my breath. I found myself looking out over the tops of countless blurred trees toward the brown concrete bowl of the Olympic stadium where Jesse Owens had won four gold medals in 1936.

Victoria leaned against the wall beside me. Her hair was soaked, hanging in matted rags and knotted tendrils. Water was dripping from her sodden tracksuit, the fabric sagging away from her lower arms. Her white trainers were shiny with damp. She turned and gazed up at me, her face as clammy as if she had the flu.

I was about to make some dumb crack about how immaculate she looked, when something caught her eye and she squinted hard at a spot on the wall above my shoulder. She looked perplexed. Then she looked astonished. She patted my cheek with icy fingers and tilted my chin until I could see exactly what had intrigued her.

There was a metal fuse box fitted to the wall above our heads. It was dull blue in color, a little corroded and a touch askew. A collection of heavy-duty electricity cables were snaking into and out of it. Some of the cables had been trimmed and tied off into loops. Others stretched away across the wall and over the ceiling.

There was a number stenciled in faded black paint on the front of the box. It wasn't the number we were looking for, but it was close.

638427–73621

"Tell me I'm not imagining things," Victoria said, panting.

"Not unless I'm imagining them, too."

"There have to be more boxes like this one, right?"

"It'd be nice to think so."

"Higher or lower?"

We went higher. We took it floor by floor, consulting the combination I'd input into the prepaid mobile to make sure we didn't make a mistake. It turned out there were two fuse boxes on each level, fixed to opposite sides of the stairwell. The boxes were numbered sequentially and we found box number 638427–73629 on the fifth floor, one level below the main listening dome.

By the time we tracked it down, I was breathless and sweating and feeling more than a touch faint. I can't pretend the height of the tower didn't play a part in that. I'm not crippled by vertigo, but I can appreciate the downsides of nose-diving from the fifth story of a building onto a flat concrete roof as much as the next man, and when the building in question is somewhat lacking in walls, not to mention slick with rain, it does tend to grab one's attention.

The wind felt a lot stronger up here, as if a rogue gust might be capable of shunting me toward the crumbling edge against my will.

The rain was pelting down ever faster. It was blasting in through the shredded tarpaulin, splattering against the concrete, and tumbling in thick rivulets from the level above.

"Open it," Victoria said.

I pocketed my mobile and set Buster's cage down on the floor, shielding him from the soggy gale with my legs, and then I snatched open the fuse box to reveal several rows of large plastic fuses. There was plenty of cabling, some brick dust and masonry debris, a couple of faded maintenance stickers, and not a lot else.

"Well, that's bloody typical," Victoria said.

I said something a lot ruder.

Then I backed away and rested my hands on my hips and glanced all around us.

"What are you doing?" Victoria asked.

"Maybe it points to something. Maybe it directs us somewhere else."

"Yes. To London." Victoria bent down and lifted Buster's cage. "If ever there *was* something here, it's been gone a long time. We're far too late."

"Patience, Vic."

"No, Charlie. I'm leaving. Are you coming?"

"Just a few minutes more."

Victoria shook her head and made for the stairs. I thought about following, but I turned back to the fuse box instead. I tipped my head and studied the thing closely. Then I reached inside my coat for my spectacles case and removed my penlight, shining the beam inside the metal box.

I saw just what I'd seen before. Plastic fuses. Thick black wires. Dust. Debris.

Wait a minute.

Brick dust. *Masonry* debris.

291

I pushed my face closer and raised myself up on my toes. I yanked cables to one side and angled the penlight in behind them.

There was a cavity in the wall. And there was something inside it. Something shiny that reflected the light of my torch back into my eyes.

I tried to reach it with my hand but the stiff cables were in the way. I returned to my spectacles case and removed a screwdriver. There were four screws holding the fuse box against the wall. They were old and mangled, and removing them took a good deal of effort. But I had the scent of success in my nostrils and I worked hard at the screws, grunting and grimacing, twisting and turning, until the final one fell out of the wall and tinkled on the ground by my feet.

I braced my foot against the wall and yanked on the fuse box and after a few determined tugs I managed to pry it away and tilt it to one side, shifting the cables with it.

The gap that had opened up wasn't big. I cupped my hand and fed it in very carefully between the cables. I gripped the object tightly and eased it out.

It was a petty-cash box. The metal exterior was a bluish-gray, though it was aged and patched with rust and corrosion. There was a dinky pin-and-tumbler lock on the front. The lock was engaged.

I shook my head. It was beginning to feel a bit like I was dealing with a set of Russian dolls. I'd opened up one metal box and found another metal box inside. Who was to say there wasn't another, even smaller box after that?

I returned once again to my trusty spectacles case. The pick and the torsion wrench I needed were the smallest ones I carried. It took me a moment to locate them, but once I had them, I went down on one knee, propped the cash box on my thigh, rubbed some warmth into my hands, and probed away at the lock. It was stiff and I could immediately tell that it hadn't been turned in a long time. But I tickled it. I tweaked it. I whispered sweet nothings to it. And when the final pin had tumbled and the lock was putty in my hands, I wedged my thumb under the lid and prepared to pry it open.

And that was when a voice from behind me shouted, "Oh, no, young man. I wouldn't do that if I were you."

FORTY-ONE

I listened and I obeyed. I didn't open the box. There were a couple of reasons why. One was that the man issuing the instructions had his arm coiled around Victoria's neck, squeezing her throat. The other was that he was holding a knife blade against the corner of her left eye.

Victoria was bent at the hip, her head clamped beneath the man's armpit. Her face was awful to see. It was scarlet, and her lips, cheeks, and eyes were bulging. Her skin was pinched and very white around the knife blade.

Her hand went limp and she dropped Buster's cage. It crashed to the floor and tipped onto its side and rolled away in an aimless half-circle, spilling wood shavings on the sodden ground. Buster squawked and beat his wings in panic, bouncing and thrashing off the metal bars.

Victoria stared at me wildly, imploring me to do something. The wind and the rain blasted against my back. Time stuttered and lagged.

I didn't move.

294

I didn't move because I knew exactly what this guy was capable of. He was the man I'd seen throttle Jane Parker in the apartment in the Tiergarten.

There was not a shred of doubt in my mind. He had the same tall stance. The same powerful build. The same dark woolen coat and black hair and prominent ears. And the same alarming tendency to squeeze the life from a woman with a relentless conviction.

"Put the box down," he said, with all the poise and command of a true English gent. "Cooperate, and the lady won't be hurt."

The lady was already hurt. But I didn't want it to get any worse.

I set the box down on the floor. Then I used my initiative and backed away from it. One step. Two.

I gazed up at him and was about to speak for the first time, but Buster beat me to it.

"Ooh, Ambassador," he squeaked, leaping around fitfully inside his cage. *"Buster says hello. Cooee. Buster says hello."*

I glanced between Buster and the tall man with the knife. I breathed for what felt like the first time in a long while.

"Mr. Ambassador," I said, and cleared my throat, "you can have the box, by all means, sir. You're very welcome to it. Just let my friend go."

"Damn bird," he spat, from the corner of his mouth. "Never will shut up."

"Cooee," Buster squawked.

"See?" he growled.

"With respect, sir, I had a feeling it was you," I said. "Not that I care. Not that I'm the least bit interested in you or the contents of this box. I just want you to release my friend. We're leaving Berlin today, sir. We won't trouble you in the slightest if you let her go."

Part of me really believed it. Problem was, I didn't get the impression the ambassador was quite so sure. He hadn't eased the pressure on Victoria's neck in the slightest. One slip of his knife would have the most terrible consequences.

"Sir," I said again, "it's time to let Victoria go."

He disagreed. He squeezed harder. Victoria tried to pry his arm away, but her movements were becoming weak and vague. She whined and she wheezed. He lifted her up by the throat. Her feet scrabbled against the concrete and she strained to balance on her toes. She teetered there, swaying at the knees, looking more stricken at every moment.

My thoughts turned to the aged pistol in my pocket. To the grenade I was still carrying. But I couldn't see what good they might do. Just reaching for either weapon would draw his attention. One sudden move and he might stab Victoria in the eye.

I flexed my hands at my sides, like a cowboy gunslinger. My mind was racing. Go for the pistol or not? Suppose he didn't react right away. What then? I wasn't a crack shot. I wasn't capable of picking him off. And I couldn't afford a drawn-out confrontation. Victoria wouldn't last that long.

He was still compressing her throat. Still tightening his hold.

"Come and take the box for yourself," I said. "Release Victoria and that can be the end of it. You really don't want any more deaths to contend with."

Mistake. The ambassador tensed instantly. He clenched Victoria even harder. She issued a choked, gargled squeak, and a thread of saliva slipped from her lips, stretching toward her knees.

The ambassador closed his eyes in a squint, peering down at me through the lashing rain.

"Jane Parker," I blurted out. "I watched you kill her. I watched you strangle her."

He frowned. How could I have seen? How did I know?

And in that moment of confusion, in that instant of self-doubt, he relaxed by a crucial half fraction and Victoria used the last of her strength to make her move.

First, she grabbed for the knife and yanked the ambassador's arm down and away from her face. Then she twisted at the hip and drove her right knee hard into the ambassador's groin. He howled and crumpled, and the knife slashed through the sleeve of Victoria's tracksuit, then continued on an inward arc toward the ambassador. He was bending low, covering his groin instinctively, and with a final desperate shove from Victoria, the knife plunged deep into his gut.

He uttered a pinched, fractured scream, and collapsed to the floor, clutching his belly.

Victoria scrambled away on her hands and knees. She bowed her head and drooled on the floor, croaking raggedly as she searched for a lungful of air. She gasped. She heaved. Then she collapsed sideways and rolled over onto her back, and her chest arched up as she finally managed a groaning breath.

The ambassador wasn't going to be recovering any time soon. He was sprawled limply on the ground, his long legs wide apart, the handle of the knife sticking out perversely from his midriff. His lean hands were clasping his stomach hopelessly. They were coated in blood. The blood was thick and inky and pooling freely between his fingers.

I drew the gun from my coat. I held it in a two-handed grip and edged toward him, aiming for the center mass of his chest.

He looked up at me distractedly, eyes roving in his head. "For God's sake, man," he spluttered. "Help me."

Oh, I was going to help him, all right.

I reached behind him and grabbed a knuckleful of collar, then dragged him hard across the ground. He yowled. He hollered and screamed. Buster had nothing on the racket he was making, but I didn't ease off at all. Moving him took a lot of effort. A lot of strength. But I was humming with adrenaline and rage and conviction.

I pressed the gun muzzle to the back of his skull and kept dragging until we were close to the edge. Then I tugged one last time and propped his upper body against the thin steel cables running around the circumference of the tower. I peered over the side. The drop ended in the flat concrete roof of a building sixty feet below.

I braced a foot on the bottom cable, the sole of my baseball shoe squeaking on the soaked wire. I added some weight. The cable was old and it had some flex in it. It began to sag. The ambassador slumped backward. He yelped, then grimaced. The wind and the rain whipped around us.

"I should let you fall," I shouted, into the gale. "For what you did to Jane. For what you've just done to my friend. What kind of man are you, anyway? You're supposed to be respectable."

No, he mouthed. He was too panicked to speak. Or maybe the blustering wind snared his words and stole them from me. *Please.*

"Please? You're asking for mercy? The kind of mercy you showed to that poor woman I watched you kill."

He glanced over his shoulder at the great depths of swirling nothingness behind him. The wind tore at his hair. Rain splattered his face. "You don't understand," he stammered. "You don't know what's at stake."

"So tell me. What's in the box?"

I could have looked for myself, I suppose. I could have taken my time over it, too. But I was done with searching for clues, with secrets and codes, with mysterious packages and concealed hiding places. I wanted answers and I wanted them now.

"Names," he breathed, closing his eyes against the fear and the pain.

"Just names?"

I pressed down harder on the wire. He slumped some more,

breathing sharply as the movement shifted the blade around in his gut.

"Names of informers," he managed, his jaw clenched tight. "British agents."

I laughed. "Spies?" I yelled. "Come on."

"Not spies. Just people with information." He panted. Caught his breath and glanced in horror at his bloodied hands. "People of influence."

"In Berlin?"

"Some."

"And the others?"

"Moscow. Paris." He looked at me with utter desperation.

"The States?"

"Yes," he said, insistent now.

"Really?"

I was having trouble with the concept. The cash box looked like it had been in the hole behind the fuse box for a very long time. The dated code that had revealed its rough location had been scrawled on yellowed paper in faded ink. I found it hard to believe that the information could be relevant today.

"Are you saying these people are still active? That they're still cheating on their countries?"

"Some. Why not?"

"And the rest?"

He spat blood from his lips and groaned in panic. "Please. I need help. A hospital."

"Yeah? Maybe you should have thought of that before you played my friend's throat like a bagpipe."

"An ambulance, then. Something."

I thought about his request. I guessed it was something I could do. But I didn't plan on being here when the emergency services turned up, and I wasn't crazy about the idea of leaving him all by himself. He'd killed a woman. I'd watched him do it. And he'd come close to choking the life from Victoria, too. Right at that moment, I didn't care who he was. I didn't give a damn about what might be at stake.

I glanced toward Victoria. She was sitting with her back against the wall of the stairwell, her elbows propped on her knees. Her face was flushed and she was breathing shallowly, her chest rising and falling like she was recovering from a long-distance run. She glared out through wet, tangled hair. She didn't appear to be in a forgiving mood.

The cash box was off to one side, not far from Buster's cage. I snatched my foot away from the cable and went and scooped it up in my hands, trying to decide if I should open it or not. I was still making up my mind when I heard footfalls approaching fast from below. I twirled and raised my pistol and aimed toward the stairs just as Freddy emerged, followed by a second man.

Freddy was ruddy-faced and sweating, and if I hadn't known otherwise, I could have believed that he was the victim of an attempted strangling himself. He braced a hand against the wall, panting and wheezing.

The second man was Andrew Stirling. I recognized him from the photo I'd seen clipped to his personnel file, though he looked many years older in the flesh. His dark hair was flecked with gray at the temples and the roots of his side parting, and his face was deeply lined and jowly.

He appeared a lot more composed than Freddy. He was strong and fit and determined enough for a man half his age. He paced into the middle of the floor, ignoring the gun in my hand entirely.

"Donald," he said, addressing the ambassador with measured concern, "we're going to get you some help. Freddy here is going to call for an ambulance. You have to hold on. Understand?"

"Better call the police, too," I told him. "They can arrest him for murder."

Stirling's body sagged. He half turned toward me. "Jane?" he murmured, eyes downcast.

I nodded. "He strangled her. And he nearly did the same thing to Victoria, here."

At my prompting, Victoria raised her head and unzipped the collar of her saturated tracksuit top, exposing her throat. Her skin was angry and enflamed. It was starting to bruise.

"Very well," Stirling said, and clenched his fists at his sides. "You can put the gun down now. And you can hand me the box."

"You're asking me to trust you?"

He straightened his shoulders and stared at me forcefully. "I am."

I'd barely opened my mouth to respond when I became aware of some scuffling and grunting off to my side.

"Donald, No!" Freddy shouted, breaking into a run.

But it was too late.

I saw the ambassador's lower legs and his shoes disappear over the edge. I heard the fractured note of his deathly wail. I didn't hear the squishy impact of his body striking the uncompromising concrete way below, and it's something I'll be forever grateful for.

Stirling and Freddy rushed toward the safety cables, skidding to a halt. They glanced over the side, then recoiled and covered their eyes with their hands.

I'd moved as well. I'd already determined what I would do. The contents of the box had been responsible for two deaths I knew of. My best friend had almost been victim number three. And I'd had all kinds of people pursuing me and threatening me, issuing ultimatums and manipulating me.

Who was to say giving the box to Freddy and Stirling was the right thing to do? Who was to say it wouldn't lead to more trouble down the line?

I freed the grenade from my pocket, and with shaking hands, I pulled the pin, flipped back the lid on the cash box, and dropped the grenade inside. I closed the lid. I drew back my arm. Then I flung the box out from the tower, as high and as far as I could manage, and just as it lost height and began to plummet, the thing exploded like a solitary, wretched firework at a rained-out display.

FORTY-TWO

We were driven away in another blacked-out town car after Stirling had summoned some embassy staff to control the scene and before the emergency services had been contacted. During our journey across Berlin, speeding toward the British embassy, I shared everything I knew about the ambassador's killing of Jane Parker with Freddy and Stirling. I told them where her body could be found. I assured them that seeing her strangled was something I would never forget. And I made it clear that the ambassador had deserved much worse than the cowardly dive he'd taken from the top of the listening tower.

They didn't say a lot in response. Maybe they thought I was just blowing off steam. Maybe they believed I was having a bad reaction to the shock of it all. Or maybe they were just so peeved about me blowing up the list of informers and British agents that they found it difficult to cool down and talk to me.

Victoria seemed to be suffering from a similar complaint. She barely spoke until we found ourselves inside Freddy's office, with only a damp and mercifully subdued Buster for company. Freddy was consulting with Stirling elsewhere in the building, but he'd arranged some blankets and brandy for us. I'd used my blanket to dry my hair and face, then dropped it to the floor. Victoria was wrapped tightly in hers, clutching it around her shoulders like she was about to start a campfire sing-along. I just hoped that Buster wouldn't come round from his daze and decide to join in.

"You shouldn't have destroyed that list," she said, pressing her face close to the still-wet bars of Buster's cage and offering him a concerned look. Her voice was hoarse and scratchy. She caressed her throat with her fingertips, like she was badly in need of a throat lozenge. Combine the gesture with the woolen blanket, and I could have believed that she was battling a dose of flu.

"You could be right," I told her. "But I was angry. I was fed up with being pushed around."

"This situation is bigger than just us, Charlie."

"Tell me about it. We know the British ambassador was a killer. We could create a big scandal."

"Oh, hush." Victoria nudged Buster's cage away from her, as if to shield him from our conversation. "You're forgetting that we don't have all the details. For all we know, he could have been trying to *protect* the list."

I turned and stared at her. We were sitting in a pair of visitor chairs facing Freddy's desk. His tin robot was close at hand and his silly Airfix planes were arranged on the shelving unit just across from us. I was tempted to wield the robot like a mallet and set about obliterating every last one of his models. Victoria's reasoned tone only made it worse.

"He . . . tried . . . to . . . kill . . . you," I said, as though I was hammering the words into her brain. "I had to watch him do it. I had to stand there, helpless, as he squeezed the air from your throat."

Victoria cast another protective look toward Buster. His dark plumage was oily and matted, kicked up into an incongruous quiff on the crown of his head. The streak of orange around his neck and the flashes of white on his wingtips seemed faded and dull.

"Do you know how hard that was?" I asked. "Do you get it?"

"I have a feeling it was worse for me," Victoria whispered, hunkering down into her blanket.

"I thought I'd lost you."

"I'm no victim," she said, and fixed her jaw like she meant it. "If you had to write a role for me, I'd be the kick-ass heroine. You should have known that I'd be okay."

"But I wasn't writing the scene, Vic."

"Oh, I know." She smiled faintly, her skin colorless and waxy. "It was way too graphic. And I didn't spot any typos."

For once, I couldn't engage in this old game of ours. I wasn't in the mood to make the real seem fictional. I was trying to tell her something important here. I was doing my best to explain my emotions. The worrying part was I suspected she knew that very well. And yet she'd diverted me regardless.

"Vic," I began again. "I went through hell up there. I didn't know what to do. And the reason it was so bad is because—"

But I didn't get to finish what I was saying. Right then, the door behind me swung open fast and Stirling marched inside, followed by Freddy.

"We found Jane," Stirling said, his words a rushed mumble. He advanced behind Freddy's desk and leaned his weight on his hands. His shirtsleeves were rolled up on his forearms. His tie was loosened and his collar unbuttoned. "She was dead, just like you said."

"We wouldn't have left her if there was any chance that she could have been revived," I told him.

"You shouldn't have left her at all. You should have contacted Freddy immediately."

"Oh?" I shot a look toward Freddy. He was standing with his back against the closed door to the ambassador's office. He didn't seem to know what to do with his hands. First, he tried clasping them behind his back. Then he took to wringing them together in front of his belly. He became even more agitated when he caught sight of Buster's cage. Clearly, he didn't appreciate the way it was dripping rainwater onto the lush varnish of his desk. "And why would I do that?" I asked. "I didn't know who I could trust."

"You were working for Freddy."

I shook my head. "I work for myself. Freddy hired me, yes. But my first priority was to protect myself and Victoria."

"Fine job you did of it."

"Hey," I complained. "I really don't know why you're so keen to defend Freddy. He had me break into your home, don't forget." I paused for a moment. Then I tapped my temple. "Come to mention it, you were the one who had Buster. Care to expand on that?"

"I don't have any reason to explain myself to you."

"Maybe not. But you owe it to Victoria, at least. Do you see what your boss did to her? Go on, take a good look. She's lucky to be alive. You were working for a killer. A guy who was cold enough to throttle a member of your staff and then show up here to drink champagne and scoff canapés with the mayor of Berlin a half hour later."

Stirling bunched his fists, and the muscles and tendons in his arms squirmed beneath his skin. "You think I don't know that?" he asked, in a low rumble. "You think we're not all horrified by what's happened?"

"Are you?"

His jaw was trembling. I got the impression he was having to fight the temptation to vault across the desk and show me how to *really* throttle someone. But he contained himself. He pushed off from the desk and waved his hand at Freddy, like he wanted him to step in.

"The fact is, there's actually been a bit of a mix-up," Freddy said, worrying his hands even faster.

"Talk about an understatement," Victoria muttered.

Freddy took a hesitant step toward us, as if he was afraid that the area of carpet in front of him might give way and collapse.

"It seems Andrew had been suspicious about the ambassador's conduct for quite some time. He'd noticed one or two examples of . . . unusual behavior."

"Such as?"

"Such as he was meeting with people. Representatives of foreign governments."

"Doesn't sound so unusual to me," I said. "Isn't that what an ambassador is supposed to do?"

"Not like this." Freddy tucked his hands beneath his armpits. He rocked on his heels. "The meetings weren't sanctioned. Or recorded."

"Oh."

"They were taking place late at night," Stirling cut in, growing impatient. "I know, because I followed him. He was using a number of unoccupied apartments that the embassy rents in the building where you found Jane's body. We're between postings at the moment, or else there'd be staff living in them."

"Why was he doing it?" Victoria croaked, then reached for the glass of brandy on the desk in front of her.

"Money," Freddy said. "It appears that he was trying to sell information."

"What kind of information?"

"The pages of code you found. The location of the list of informants who've assisted our government."

Victoria sipped her brandy and swallowed with some difficulty. "So he was betraying you," she said, her voice a dry rasp.

"It seems so."

"Where did the code originate from?"

Freddy took another anxious step forward. Any closer and I

feared he might break out in hives. "The ambassador's uncle," he said. "He worked in Berlin during the Cold War. In the listening station, as a matter of fact. We believe he compiled the list of names in the first place."

"Of course," Stirling added, tossing me a hostile look, "thanks to you, we're no longer in a position to verify if the list was accurate. But if just one name had been correct, it could have been disastrous for us. Embarrassing, certainly. Many of the people identified might be dead or inactive, but at least some of them could have been or may still be prominent individuals. Even now, this whole situation could still cause ructions. Suspicion. Accusations. Repercussions for certain influential families or organizations. A mess, in short."

Freddy waited until Stirling was done before picking up the thread. "Donald's uncle died a little over a year ago now. After he passed away, Donald was posted to Berlin as the British ambassador and his aunt had some of his uncle's old papers shipped over to him. We believe Donald found the handwritten pages of code among them."

And the numbered sequence, I supposed.

"And his first thought was to make some fast cash?"

Freddy blew air through his lips. "He was under a lot of stress. A lot of strain."

"Nonsense," Stirling said. "He was a greedy sod. Always had been. Spineless, too. That's why he didn't fetch the hidden package for himself in the first place. Scared of being followed, I imagine. So he thought he'd sell its location to the highest bidder. Hence his meetings with the Russians, the Yanks, the French—"

"And that's how they were on to you so quickly," Freddy cut in. "Once you started working for me, and once they heard that you were searching for a missing package, they must have realized that it could be connected somehow. They must have guessed they had an opportunity to grab the list without paying the fee

Donald was demanding, and before anyone else might get their hands on it."

I decided now really wasn't the time to blab about how Freddy had let most of the information slip out in his telephone conversations with his brother.

"But that still doesn't explain *why* I was hired." I looked at Stirling. "Or why you stole Buster's cage in the first place."

"My name is Buster. Buster says hello."

"Hey," Victoria said, smiling wanly at Buster. "You're talking again."

"Buster says hello." He ruffled his bedraggled wings, showering himself in a watery haze.

"What a relief," I mumbled.

"Wanna sing a song?" Buster asked, bobbing his head up and down.

"NO! No bloody song. And no bloody counting!"

Buster uttered a fractured chirp and fell silent again.

The silence was really quite noticeable.

And for some reason, everyone appeared to be staring at me.

I coughed. I shifted my weight in my seat. I motioned for Stirling to continue. "You were going to tell us about the cage, I believe?"

Stirling looked quizzically between myself and Buster, as if he couldn't quite understand my outburst. Then he finally picked up the thread again.

"I stole the cage because I was listening outside Donald's office last week and I noticed that he was repeating a sequence of numbers over and over until the bird began to recite it. I'd already contacted a trusted colleague in London by then. Jane had been assigned to discreetly investigate my suspicions about the ambassador's conduct and she'd been able to obtain the first pages of code from a locked drawer in Donald's desk. But once she deciphered the code, she discovered that the pages were incomplete. She'd

309

been unable to find the rest, even though she'd searched his office, his car, his home."

Stirling paused, as if only just remembering that the woman he was talking about was now dead. He cleared his throat.

"After I heard him repeating the sequence, it aroused my suspicions," he went on. "Jane had told me that she was thinking of confronting Donald, but I decided it was best to take matters into my own hands and claim Buster for myself until the picture became clearer."

"Wait," Victoria said. "Are you saying Jane was killed by the ambassador because she challenged him about the code?"

"In a word."

"And you didn't know any of this?" she asked Freddy.

"Well, you'll remember I was suspicious of Andrew, here," Freddy said, hurriedly. "That I'd seen him loitering around the ambassador's office and that he'd been querying my role for the ambassador in a way that I felt was . . . troubling."

"Truth was," Stirling told him, "I feared you might be in on it, too."

"Understandable," Freddy replied, in something of a rush. "And so it's no surprise that Andrew and Jane were keeping their suspicions to themselves. They couldn't risk alerting the ambassador or any of his staff."

"But I imagine he knew something was up," I put in.

Freddy nodded. "He would have known the moment the first four pages of code went missing. As soon as Jane took them, he would have been alert to the idea that *someone* was on to him. But he'd been cautious enough to remove the final, crucial page of information, so it wasn't altogether fatal for him. Plus, he'd made Buster memorize the numerical sequence that pinpointed the data drop. I'm not entirely sure that was intentional, by the way. Perhaps he was just reciting it to himself, so that he could remember it without a written prompt, and Buster happened to pick up on it. But either way, it became a problem for him when Buster went missing, too. Suddenly, someone might have free access to the data Donald had been trying to sell. And in hindsight, one can see why he was so keen on having me arrange quite such an unconventional solution by hiring you, Charlie."

"Because he was the guy in the wrong. Not any of the supposed thieves you wanted me to finger."

"Quite."

"Huh." I drummed my fingers on my chin. "So what brought you both to the listening station this morning? How did you know we were there?"

"We didn't," Stirling said. "We were following Donald. Once I got home last night to find that Buster had been stolen—along, I might add, with a broken lamp, a ruined bathroom door, and a bullet-riddled elevator carriage—I decided it was finally time for me to inform somebody else about what had been happening. I'd been unable to hail Jane—for obvious reasons, as we now know—so I took a chance on Freddy and we pooled information. We were both concerned by Jane's disappearance and we determined to keep an eye on Donald together. This morning we watched him leave his home early and make his way to the listening station. He must have decided it was finally time to take a risk and retrieve the list before somebody beat him to it. We tracked him there."

"Oh, you did, huh?"

"That's right."

"And now the list is gone," I said. "And the ambassador is dead, along with Jane. And you have a nasty scandal on your hands."

Stirling did his best to maintain an even tone. "Only if you wish to make it so."

"You can't excuse him from murder," I said. "He killed in cold blood. He was a traitor to his country."

"Technically, no." Stirling shook his head. "He never passed on the list. It *might* even be argued that he arrived at the listening post to safeguard it. To deliver it into British hands."

"And is that what's going to be argued?"

"Well," Freddy said, a little shamefaced, "that rather depends on you."

I turned to Victoria. She was studying me intensely. I glanced away toward one of the silly airplane models on Freddy's shelves. It was a Spitfire. A symbol of a different time. An age of honor and moral fortitude and courage. Not the world I was living in today.

"How would you deal with Jane's murder?" I heard myself ask.

"Charlie, no," Victoria hissed. She reached out and clenched my thigh, digging her nails into my flesh. "We mustn't."

I held up my hand. Fixed my gaze on Stirling.

"How?" I asked him.

"So far as the German police are concerned, it would be unexplained. An unsolved murder."

"Did she have family?"

"Her parents. A sister."

"What would they be told?"

"They'd know she died in the service of her country. I'd make sure of that personally."

I let go of a long breath. I could feel myself shaking. Victoria's nails were clamped to my thigh like talons.

"Don't forget," Stirling said, "you've drawn a great deal of attention to yourselves. You've aggravated powerful people. The Russians and the Americans, Freddy tells me."

"The French, too," Freddy said.

"These are not the type of people you want as enemies, young man. Least of all if you're on your own."

"Oh, I get it. Like that, is it?" I felt Victoria's grip tighten one last fraction. I reached across and took her hand. I squeezed it, then returned it to her, abandoning myself to what I was about to do. "So I guess we can trade," I said. "We'd need safe passage out of Berlin. We'd need assurances that we'd be protected from anyone with an interest in this list, and from anyone who might try to compel us to give evidence against the ambassador. And it goes without saying that I expect to be paid. The remainder of the fee I agreed with Freddy. Plus the bonus."

"I won't stand for this," Victoria muttered.

I fixed on Stirling. "Fulfill your side of the bargain and you can rely on us."

"Not me," Victoria said, shaking her head.

But I knew otherwise. I knew that she would endure it if I asked her to. I knew I could convince her that our safety depended on it, that sometimes imperfect solutions were the best we could hope for.

But I also knew that it would cost me. Maybe more than I could stand.

FORTY-THREE

"I don't know how you intend to live with yourself," Victoria snapped, as we were driven away from the embassy gates. "I'm really not sure that I can."

She was wearing a fresh set of clothes that one of Freddy's assistants had run out to buy her—dark jeans, a fawn sweater, and a pair of flat shoes—and she was sitting about as far away from me as it was possible to get in the rear of an unwashed Volkswagen Golf. The Golf had been my request. I wanted something ordinary that would draw as little attention as possible. Plus, I'd just about had my fill of blacked-out town cars.

The man who was driving us didn't appear to be interested in our conversation. I was pretty sure that was an act. He looked squared away and professional. He was wearing a cheap gray suit that bulged menacingly at the hip, and a flesh-colored wire that coiled out from beneath the collar of his shirt to connect with a radio earpiece. I only hoped he was a lot more competent than the men I'd managed to fool at the embassy entrance the previous morning.

"We didn't have a choice," I told Victoria. "Remember that."

"Oh, we had a choice. It was a difficult one. No question. But we could have made it."

"And what if we had? We'd have been on our own right now. I wasn't prepared to risk anything happening to you."

"It wasn't *your* risk to take. We should have discussed it, at least. Think of that poor woman, Charlie. What does her death mean now?"

"I did it for you, Vic."

She closed her eyes. Shook her head. "Don't," she said, in a hoarse whisper. "I can't bear it."

"And London? Do you still want me to come?"

"Do as you like," she whispered. "Face it. You always have."

I propped my head against the window glass and watched the wet, gray streets of Mitte glide by outside. This wasn't how I'd imagined my time in Berlin would come to a close. This wasn't how I wanted things to be with Victoria. In the past, I'd always escaped from my scrapes a winner. I'd emerged with a flourish and a joke. But sometimes, I guessed, things just weren't destined to conclude that way, and perhaps this was the fate I'd always been doomed to accept.

Victoria had been sucked into my world, and now it had chewed her up and spit her back out again. Perhaps I'd been kidding myself all these years. Maybe it just wasn't possible to be a friendly, harmless criminal. Maybe there was no such thing as a good thief. It could just be that I was as morally corrupt as the next crook, and chances were I was losing Victoria because of it.

My toe nudged Buster's cage down in the foot well, but Buster didn't stir. I'd covered his cage with the blanket Freddy had given me, and I guessed he was catching up on some sleep.

Our driver cleared his throat. "Approaching your first stop," he said. "You sure your man will be here?"

315

I clutched tightly to the phone Gert had equipped me with. "No reason to think otherwise."

"I'll allow you five minutes. Then I expect you back inside this car. Or I'm coming to get you. Understand?"

I didn't bother with a response. The driver pulled over to the curb, just along from a fancy hotel and a gaudy cocktail bar, and I lifted Buster's cage onto my lap, blanket still in place.

"Say good-bye to him for me," Victoria said, in a hollow voice.

I nodded. I wasn't sure if she meant Buster or Gert, but I didn't hang around to find out. I waited for a gap in the traffic, then turned up my collar against the steadily falling rain, cradled the cage against my chest, and hurried across the street toward the grand open space of the Gendarmenmarkt.

The vast grid of gray cobbles and flagstones were slick and greasy from the rain. Ahead of me was Schinkel's grand Konzerthaus, flanked on either side by the domed churches of the Deutscher Dom and the Französischer Dom, both so similar in scale and design that I could have believed that a giant mirror was all that separated them.

I dodged pedestrians and tourists, heading for a lone tree that was half stripped of autumn leaves, its blackened limbs stiff as iron against the ashen sky. Like most trees in the city, it was branded with a numbered plaque. Bureaucracy gone mad, you might think. But this particular tree just happened to be number one, and it made for a meeting point that avoided confusion.

Gert was standing close by, sheltering beneath a large blue umbrella that featured the slogan of a major German bank. I ducked down and joined him, listening to the spit of rain on canvas, standing on a soft mulch of fallen leaves.

"You came," I said, and clasped his spindly hand.

"*Ja*. You told me it was urgent."

I slapped him on the back. I felt a great swell of affection for the

316

guy. Sure, he was a kook. Yes, he would benefit from a decent hair-cut and a set of clothes that fit him properly. But staring up at his gaunt, bearded face and into his guileless eyes, I couldn't help but grin.

"Gert, I'm leaving Berlin," I told him. "Right away. But I wanted to thank you for all your help. And I need to ask you one last favor."

I whipped the blanket away from Buster's cage. Buster was still a little docile, but the moment he saw Gert, he got excited very fast. He spread his wings wide. He elongated his neck and hopped from one foot to the other, shuffling along his perch in a nifty little jig.

"Buster says hello. HeLLO! Buster says hello."

Gert beamed with amusement and wiggled a finger through the bars of Buster's cage.

"Hello, my friend."

"Will you care for him?" I asked. "Permanently?"

Gert stared up at me. He blinked his fair lashes.

"The ambassador is dead," I said. "He killed himself. And I'd rather Buster stayed with someone he likes. Someone who could maybe use a little company."

Gert blinked some more. He lowered his face to the cage. He didn't speak for a few moments. But then, he didn't need to. Buster did it for him.

"Buster says hello. Wanna sing a song? Buster says hello."

"For sure," Gert said, nodding abruptly and taking the cage from me. "I can do this."

"Great." I reached a hand inside my coat and removed the pad-ded white envelope stuffed with cash that Freddy had given me back in his office. It was the remainder of my fee. Every last euro of it. "He'll need some things," I said. "Toys. Treats. This should keep him in bird seed for quite a while."

I tried to slip the envelope inside the heavy woolen jacket Gert had on, but he backed away from me, as if offended.

"Take it," I told him. "You might not have noticed just yet, but I'm not in a position to return your car. I could tell you where it is, but I'd advise you not to try and reclaim it. There are a bunch of people who might be watching. And this will help you and Buster to find some new wheels."

"But I did not buy this car, Charlie."

"Oh, I know," I said. "You collected it. But I can't keep this money. It wouldn't be right, for reasons I don't have time to go into just now. And I'd very much like you to have it. Please."

I turned the envelope on its side and fed it in through the bars in Buster's cage, like I was posting a note through a letterbox. Then I slapped Gert on the arm and backed away from the cover of his umbrella, saluting him as I left.

"Good luck," he called after me. "And please tell Victoria, *auf Wiedersehen.*"

"Buster says goodbye! Buster says goodbye!"

I laughed. "So long, Buster," I yelled. "It was good meeting you both."

My five minutes were almost up, but I wasn't surprised to see that our chauffeur hadn't left the warmth of the Volkswagen to come and fetch me. I dropped inside and was still closing my door as he shifted gears and accelerated away along the street.

"Gert sends his regards," I told Victoria, as I settled into my seat. "Buster, too."

She nodded and stared out her window, turning her back on me. We didn't talk during the rest of the journey. I opened my mouth to start a new conversation a bunch of times, but nothing I could think to say seemed capable of healing the rift that had developed between us. We were so far apart in the back of that car we might as well have been sitting on opposite sides of the Berlin Wall.

Ten minutes later, our driver cleared his throat again. "We're getting close," he announced, and I gazed out through the windscreen to see that we were approaching the Kollwitzplatz. "It doesn't look good. We have company. I see one guy already."

I saw him, too. It was Henri. He was sitting on a bench behind the park railings, sheltering beneath a drooping tree, close to the table-tennis tables. He held a folded newspaper in one hand and a steaming takeaway cup in the other. A large wadded bandage covered his nose.

"Looks like the Americans are here, too," Victoria said, her voice quickening. "Do you see their car?"

I saw it. It was parked off to the left, close to a sidewalk café and within sight of the front door of my building. There was no way to see inside through the tinted windows, but I was pretty confident the car was occupied.

"Then I think it's safe to assume the Russians are also here."

"We should abort," the driver said, eyeing me in the rearview mirror.

But there was no way I was going to give up. I had some things I needed to collect. Belongings I couldn't possibly leave behind.

"Turn here," I said, pointing to a side road that headed off to the right. "Keep going." He did as I instructed. Once we were a half mile or so away, I had him turn left and park. "Wait here for me," I said, and cracked my door.

"This is a bad idea," he told me. "I should take you to the airport."

"Relax. Sneaking in places is what I do best. And breaking into my own home is about as easy as it gets."

I stepped out onto the street. I had the car door in my hand and I was poised to swing it closed when I heard Victoria call my name. I ducked my head and looked in at her.

Her face was drawn, skin pinched. Her eyes were damp and fidgety. We'd known each other for years, but right now I didn't have the faintest idea what she was thinking.

319

"Be careful," she said, finally.

"Always."

And then I did something that surprised us both. I dived inside and kissed her softly on the lips. I pulled away, raising my hand to her hair and cupping her neck. Then I backed out of the car, closed the door behind me, dug my hands in my coat pockets, and slinked off down the street, not daring to glance over my shoulder.

I didn't think I was being followed. I didn't think any of the people who were waiting for me to show up could be that fast to react. But I threw in a couple of wrong turns and loitered behind a few obstacles until I was certain I didn't have anyone on my heels. Then I headed around to the narrow, abandoned alley that ran along the back of my building.

The ladder was still there, lying on the ground amid wet foliage and puddles and litter. I lifted it up and swung it around and propped it very gently below the ledge of my broken window. Then I started to climb, my movements slow and deliberate, the metal rungs slippery with muck and rain.

The ladder was unsteady. It was braced precariously on the slimy tarmac below. I could have done with somebody holding it for me, but I wasn't about to return to the car and ask Victoria to volunteer.

I clung tight and climbed on, and eventually made it to my window. It was locked. I'd left it that way. I reached in through the broken pane and undid the catch and heaved up the bottom sash. Then I grabbed a handful of window ledge and squirmed my way inside, tumbling onto my bedroom floor headfirst.

My bedroom was in much more of a mess than I remembered. My bed had been stripped and pulled away from the wall. My drawers had been yanked out and their contents upended on the floor. My wardrobe had spewed clothes and shoes and suitcases onto the carpet.

It was the same in the hallway. The same in Victoria's bedroom. The same in the bathroom.

Oh, and it was even worse in the kitchen. All my cupboards and drawers had been checked. All my food and household goods had been scooped out and opened up and emptied. The counters and the floor were a chaos of liquids and powders, packaging and stinking organic mush.

The entire apartment had been ransacked. The perpetrators had been in a frenzy and they hadn't cared about being subtle or delicate. It seemed to me they had some rules of their own, and they were a lot more crass than the rules I tended to abide by.

I asked myself who the likeliest culprits were and I honestly couldn't decide. It could have been any one of the people who'd been following me and searching for the final clue to the cash box full of data. It could have been other foreign agents who'd joined the hunt for the same thing. Hell, maybe they'd all trooped in one after the other, taking turns to wreak more havoc. It really didn't matter. The oafish, stinking outcome wouldn't change in the slightest.

I made my way toward my front door. It was listing badly to one side, hanging loosely from a single hinge. A splintered hole had been smashed right into the center of it. My three locks had been torn from the frame. It looked like the work of a battering ram or just possibly a badly scarred Russian.

The living room was just as sorry as everywhere else. The sofa had been toppled over. The cushions had been sliced and the stuffing removed. My desk had been ripped apart and left in broken pieces. My laptop appeared to have been swiped, along with my stalled novel. My writing notes had been flung across the room. My books had been riffled through and dropped haphazardly here and there.

I waded inside, keeping my distance from the windows, and it took me a good twenty minutes to find the first item I was looking for. It was sheltering beneath the upended sofa like a frightened animal. I went down on my hands and knees and scooped it out carefully.

It was my precious copy of *The Maltese Falcon*. The singed jacket had been bent backward along the middle, imprinting a crease that would be impossible to flatten out. The bottom corners of a number of pages had curled in on themselves and the spine was starting to split. A few flakes of burned paper adhered themselves to my greasy hands, like the book was slowly disintegrating.

It pained me to see it suffer even more damage, but the important thing was that I still had it. I flipped to the first full page and traced my fingertips over the scrawl of Dashiell Hammett's signature. I clutched the book to my chest. I pushed up from my knees.

Then I went hunting for item number two. I kicked over books and sofa cushions with my feet. I rooted through the remains of my desk. I stood on a chair and turned in a circle, scanning the mess surrounding me. Finally, I spotted it, nestled in a far corner, glinting in the dreary gloom.

Victoria's watch. The gift from her father. I climbed down and gripped it tight, checking that the face was still intact. It was unblemished. Not even a scratch. I flipped it over and read the inscription on the back. *To Sugar Plum, Love, Daddy.*

Perfect.

I slipped the watch into my pocket. There was nothing else I required. Nothing urgent, in any case. So I turned on my heel, intending to return to my bedroom and the handily located ladder, only to find that my exit was blocked.

It wasn't the Russians or the Americans or the French guy.

It was the German police. There were two of them, a man and a woman, stepping in through my busted front door and looking about them in surprise and bemusement. They were wearing blue uniforms with nametags on their chests and peaked caps on their heads.

I'd never seen the man before, but this wasn't the first time I'd seen his companion. Officer Fuchs was the policewoman who'd stayed behind to follow up on my emergency call in the Tiergarten.

She started when she saw me, then reached instinctively for her belt. There were a lot of pouches and a bunch of equipment at her disposal. She looked to have a gun or a spray of some description. She also had a pair of handcuffs.

"Herr Howard?" she asked.

I thought about sprinting for my bedroom. I pictured myself barging my way past them and trying to escape. But the hallway was too confined. And there were two of them, and the guy was very large.

"Herr Howard?" she asked again. "Herr Charles Howard?"

I nodded. My mouth had gone dry. I was finding it tough to speak.

"We would like to talk with you, please."

"About my break-in?" I asked, and gestured fitfully at the destruction that surrounded me.

"No," she said, unclipping the buckle that held her handcuffs in place. "We wish to talk with you about some burglaries here in Berlin. You are a writer, yes? The people who were robbed work with books, too. They are publishers."

Editors, she meant. And I knew just who she was talking about. Victoria had been right from the very start. I really had been an idiot.

I could hear a whistling in my ears. A buzz and a click when I swallowed.

"This is not a good time," I said. "You can see that, right?"

Fuchs freed her handcuffs from her belt. She edged toward me, her burly colleague monitoring me closely from over her shoulder.

"We can arrange for somebody to come," she said. "They will secure your home."

"Look, I really don't know what this has to do with me. You've made a mistake. Maybe the person who broke in here is also responsible for these burglaries you mention."

She took another step forward. "It is no mistake. We are here to arrest you. There was a witness. We have a description. And footage from a security camera. One of the publishers recognized you."

I took a step back. My heels became entangled in something. I was in danger of falling, but she grabbed my hand by the wrist and slipped a cuff onto me. Then she twirled me around, yanked both arms behind me, and secured my second wrist.

She freed Hammett's book from my grip. Went to toss it onto the floor.

"Wait," I said. "Not that. I need it. It's important to me."

She shrugged and dropped it onto the floor regardless, grabbing a fistful of my collar and jolting me toward her colleague.

Her partner seized me by the elbow and manhandled me out through my broken door and down the stairs. The Russians were lurking in the entrance to my building. Vladislav was sitting on a radiator, smoothing his fingers over his scarred face and stubbled cheek. Pavel was leaning against the tiled wall, his hands behind his back, as if mimicking my predicament. Vladislav smirked as I passed him. His boss offered no reaction at all.

The marked police car was parked right outside the front steps. Officer Fuchs opened the rear door and her colleague placed his hand on my head and forced me inside. They climbed in the front and engaged all the locks.

Henri tossed his coffee cup into a litter bin. He stared hard at me over the park railings and his battered nose as we sped away from the curb. We accelerated past the town car belonging to the Americans. I turned and glanced back through the rear window at them. Nancy Symons and Duane had stepped out onto the street and were watching after me, their hands shielding their eyes from the falling rain.

There was a scuffed plastic screen in front of me. No visible handles or locks on the rear doors. My cuffed hands were crossed behind my back.

I considered my reflection in the driver's rearview mirror and I smiled a silly, dazed smile at myself.

I was thinking of Victoria. I was thinking of her waiting for me in the back of the Golf, growing impatient and frustrated and wondering where I was, asking herself what my kiss might mean, where we might go from here. I didn't imagine she'd be altogether surprised when she eventually heard the news. Would she come and visit me? I didn't know. I honestly couldn't tell. But I sincerely hoped that she would. I needed to return her watch, after all. I could feel its weight in my pocket.

But meantime, I had a choice to make. A decision about the type of person I really was. Because resting inside another pocket in my damp raincoat was a crumpled bundle of paper. It was the collection of handwritten pages that had been inside the cash box up at the Devil's Mountain listening post. I'd taken the pages out, you see. I'd swiped them from under Freddy's and Stirling's noses before shoving the grenade in the box and creating the most explosive of all diversions. And right now, I needed to decide what to do with the information I'd acquired.

It sounded as if the German police had some pretty solid evidence against me. It seemed more than likely that they'd prosecute me for my thefts, and if they built their case halfway competently (which I had no doubt they would), then in all likelihood I'd be found guilty and I'd be imprisoned for a period of time ranging from somewhere between inconvenient and uncomfortable.

But the list of names I'd stolen was valuable. Plenty of people had been keen to get their hands on it. And, I imagined, the German authorities might find the information of interest, too. But was I that guy? Was I prepared to trade the list for my freedom, with no concern for the sacrifice Jane Parker had made in protecting it? Was I the weasel Victoria feared I might be? Or was I better than that? More noble? More good? The type of man who might opt to destroy those pages the first opportunity that came my way?

I stared long and hard at my reflection in the rearview mirror of that police car, and I did my very best to decide for myself.

ACKNOWLEDGMENTS

Heartfelt thanks for their help and support in the writing of this book to Vivien Green, Valerie Borchardt, and the teams at Sheil Land Associates and the Georges Borchardt Literary Agency, to Hope Dellon, Silissa Kenney, and all at St. Martin's Press, to Sabine Lemmer-Brust, Katrina Hands, Olesya Skirtach, Luca Veste, Mum, Dad, Allie, and, as always, to my wife, Jo, and our daughter, Jessica.